About the Authors

Previously a teacher, pig farmer, and builder (amongst other things), **Meredith Webber** turned to writing medical romances when she decided she needed a new challenge. Once committed to giving it a 'real' go she joined writers' groups, attended conferences, and read every book on writing she could find. Teaching a romance writing course helped her to analyse what she does, and she believes it has made her a better writer. Readers can email Meredith at: mem@onthenet.com.au

Susan Carlisle's love affair with books began when she made a bad grade in math. Not allowed to watch TV until the grade had improved, she filled her time with books. Turning her love of reading into a love for writing romance, she pens hot medicals. She loves castles, travelling, afternoon tea, and hearing from her readers. Join her newsletter at: SusanCarlisle.com

Karin Baine lives in Northern Ireland with her husband, two sons, and her out-of-control notebook collection. Her mother and grandmother's vast collection of books inspired her love of reading and her dream of becoming a Mills & Boon author. Now she can tell people she has a proper job! You can follow Karin on Twitter, @karinbaine1 or visit her website for the latest news – karinbaine.com

The Surgeon Collection

The Surgeon's Crown

MEREDITH WEBBER

SUSAN CARLISLE

KARIN BAINE

MILLS & BOON

First Published in Great Britain 2023
by Mills & Boon, an imprint of HarperCollins*Publishers* Ltd,
1 London Bridge Street, London, SE1 9GF

www.harpercollins.co.uk

HarperCollins*Publishers*
Macken House, 39/40 Mayor Street Upper,
Dublin 1, D01 C9W8, Ireland

The Surgeon's Crown © 2023 Harlequin Enterprises ULC.

Date with a Surgeon Prince © 2013 Meredith Webber
The Surgeon's Cinderella © 2017 Susan Carlisle
Reunion with His Surgeon Princess © 2020 Karin Baine

ISBN: 978-0-263-31952-1

	MIX
	Paper | Supporting responsible forestry
FSC www.fsc.org	**FSC™ C007454**

This book is produced from independently certified FSC™ paper
to ensure responsible forest management.

For more information visit: www.harpercollins.co.uk/green

Printed and Bound in the UK using 100% Renewable Electricity
at CPI Group (UK) Ltd, Croydon, CR0 4YY

DATE WITH A
SURGEON PRINCE

MEREDITH WEBBER

PROLOGUE

'*ARE YOU COMPLETELY mad? Bonkers? Round the twist?*'

It wasn't often Marni yelled at her grandfather. In fact, if she'd been in any fit state to think about it, she'd have realised it was probably the first time. But this was just too much.

'*It says here the man's a prince. Just because he hasn't married doesn't mean he'll be interested in some cocka-mamie story about being betrothed to me when he was three!*'

She was still yelling, and brandishing the newspaper Pop had been reading at the same time, while the voice that lived in *her* head told her it would be a bad idea to bash an ailing eighty-four-year-old man to death, es-pecially as she loved him to bits and couldn't bear the thought of life without him.

Except that she had to start—start imagining it, that was. Eighty-four, with a blocked valve in his heart and blocked stents in the vital arteries that fed the heart mus-cle.

The specialist wanted to do open-heart surgery to re-place the valve and, at the same time, the surgery nec-essary to bypass the stents. Pop was vacillating, another cause for anger because as a nurse she thought he should have the operation. Of course he should, he was a man who enjoyed life, and, selfishly perhaps, she really, really didn't want him dying of heart failure.

'You finished?' Pop retrieved the flapping paper from her now limp grasp, and opened it up to fold it at a different page. 'For your information, he was six, *you* were three. Now, look at this page near the back.'

Ignoring a momentary pang that she could no longer see the photo of the strong-featured face, framed by a white headdress, that had started the conversation, she peered over Pop's shoulder to read what he was showing her.

Not that her mind would take in much—she was still struggling with the little gem the old man had delivered earlier, finger pointing at the picture, voice full of wonder as he'd said, 'That's Ghazi. His father and I pledged the two of you would marry. Says here he's still single. You should get in touch.'

Forget this prince business and get with it, the inner voice in her head said firmly. Pop's made it clear he doesn't want you hanging around here while he's getting over the op, no matter how much you might want to be with him. Perhaps a short contract job somewhere else?

'See,' Pop was saying, and for a moment Marni wondered if he could hear her thoughts because he was pointing at a job advertisement. 'Theatre nurses wanted for new children's hospital in Ablezia. That might be why Ghazi's out here. He's looking for nurses.'

Yeah, right, she thought. Of course the crown prince of any country would have to check out hospital staff!

But Marni ignored the voice in her head this time, intent on reading exactly what was on offer in this place she'd never heard of, which, presumably, was far enough away from the Gold Coast, Queensland, Australia for her not to be tempted to ignore Pop's plea to keep away while he went through his operation.

If he went through with the operation!

Six months' contract' extendable, the advertisement read, air fares and accommodation provided. Six months would bring her up to Christmas and if Pop had the operation as soon as possible, then he'd be well on the way to recovery by the time she got home.

Six months! It was the answer to the other problem plaguing her too—her virginity! Given six months, thousands of miles from home—*surely* in six months she'd meet *someone*...

She sighed as she looked blankly at the paper, sighing because the virginity thing, as she thought of it, shouldn't really be a problem. It wasn't as if she'd held onto it deliberately, she'd just put things off for various reasons—Pop, Nelson, her mother's behaviour—then the cruel words of the last man she'd become involved with had made her realise it was a burden as well as an embarrassment.

Read the ad!

The pay scale seemed staggeringly generous, but it was the thumbnail description of the country that made her heart flutter. Set by the warm waters of the Ablezian Sea, the country was well known for its underwater wonders—coral reefs, abundant marine life, nesting turtles on the beaches...

This idea could actually solve some problems. She could make Pop happy by taking the job and getting out of the way while he recovered, make him even happier by at least meeting this prince guy—she owed Pop that much—and maybe, as a bonus, find someone with whom to have a holiday romance, or a work romance, or even just a little fling...

'I'll get the picture,' Pop said.

Marni lost herself in thoughts of diving into warm gulf waters and playing with the fish and turtles. She barely heard Pop as he left the paper in front of her at the breakfast table and disappeared into his study.

Nelson, who'd been with her grandfather as long as Marni could remember, as valet, butler, cook and probably secretary, appeared in his usual silent way.

'I don't know, Nelson,' she said quietly. 'It seems wrong to even think of going away. Pop's taken care of me and been there for me all these years, surely now I can be there for him?'

Nelson shook his head.

'You know he probably won't have the op if you're around, because he doesn't want you to see him weak and sick. He wants you to remember him as the strong, active man he's always been, and can be again. He's far more likely to agree to the procedure if he knows you're not fretting over him.'

Nelson paused then, with only the slightest quaver in his voice, continued, 'You know I'll take good care of him.'

Blinking back the tears that had filled her eyes, Marni got to her feet and hugged the man she'd known since the age of two, when she'd been dumped on her grandfather because her mother's third husband hadn't wanted a kid around the place.

'I know you will, Nelson, and I know you're right about him recovering more quickly if I'm out of the way. If he's so set on me leaving, I'll do it. I'll take this job and check out this prince bloke, say hi to him from Pop, and report back. Can't you just imagine it—me rocking up to a palace in the desert to tell the local ruler he's betrothed to me! I'd be arrested and thrown into the deepest, darkest dungeon, or fitted with a straitjacket, or at the very least deported on the first plane out.'

Nelson's serious brown eyes studied her for a moment.

'It would make your grandfather very happy if you did meet the guy,' he said, so seriously that Marni groaned.

'Not you too!' she protested.

'Well, he was a really nice little kid and he was very good to you, although in those days you were a right little tantrum-throwing madam.'

'I met him? I knew him? When was all this?'

Marni frowned, trying to remember, to place a time she might have played with a prince.

Not something everyone would forget!

'It was shortly after you first arrived to live with us,' Nelson explained. 'Your grandfather had only recently moved into this apartment and Ghazi's father booked out the entire hotel section for himself, his family and his staff.'

'The whole hotel?'

'He had a lot of wives and daughters,' Nelson said, as if that explained everything.

The Palazzo Versace was the first six-star hotel built on the Gold Coast, her grandfather's apartment one of a few privately owned condominiums included in the ritzy complex. As residents, they were free to make use of all the hotel facilities, the beautiful pools, the restaurants and the day spa, so she'd often played with the children of hotel guests as she had been growing up.

But one called Ghazi?

She had no memory of it at all, even when Pop returned with a box of photos showing her as a very small child with a boy who stood much taller. The photos told her they'd had fun together, two children at play while slender, black-robed figures sat in the shade by the pool.

'This is the one,' Pop, who'd been sifting through the photos, declared.

He handed it to her.

It was a more formal shot showing a tidily dressed little girl, blonde hair in pigtails, pale blue eyes looking up at the boy sitting on the arm of one of the big lounge chairs in the hotel's foyer—a white-robed boy, who was holding her hand and smiling down at her.

Even then you could tell he was going to be good looking, although the miniature white headdress he was wearing in the photo concealed all but his profile. Strong nose and jaw, a high forehead, shapely lips widened in a slight smile—

'Hey, I was looking at that,' Marni protested as Pop turned the photo over.

He ignored her, pointing at the writing on the back. The top line was in his handwriting and, sure enough, there was this nonsense about the two of them being betrothed, Pop's signature at the end of the statement.

Beneath that was a line of beautiful, flowing, Arabic script, and presumably another signature.

'Honestly, Pop, you can't read Arabic so for all you know the man's written something like, "This nonsense should make the man happy!"'

Marni regretted her words the moment they'd popped out of her mouth and she caught the hurt in her grandfather's eyes, hurt that prompted a quick hug and a totally impulsive promise to go right now and apply for the job in a country called Ablezia.

'*And* I'll do my best to see this guy but only if you agree to have the operation,' Marni added. 'Deal?'

'Deal!' Pop agreed, and they shook on it, the slight tremble in her grandfather's hand reminding her just how frail he had become.

CHAPTER ONE

WAS IT THE subtle scent that perfumed the warm air—salt, spices, a fruit she couldn't identify—or the air itself that wrapped around her like the finest, softest, mohair blanket? Or was it the mind-boggling beauty of a landscape of red desert dunes alongside brilliant cobalt seas, the dense green of a palm grove in an oasis at the edge of the desert, or the tall skyscrapers that rose from the sand like sculpted, alien life forms?

Or perhaps the people themselves, the shy but welcoming smile of a headscarfed woman, the cheeky grin of tousle-haired boy, pointing at her fair skin and hair?

Marni had no idea. She couldn't give an answer to the question of why she'd fallen in love with this strange, exotic land within hours of stepping off the plane, but in love she was—flushed with excitement as she explored the narrow market lanes that sneaked off the city highways, trembling with delight the first time she dived into the crystal-clear waters, and shyly happy when a group of local women, fellow nurses, asked her to join them for lunch in the hospital canteen.

This was her first day at the hospital, her schedule having allowed her four free days to explore her new home before starting work, and today was more an orientation day, finding her way around the corridors, feeling at home with the unfamiliar layout and the more familiar hospital buzz. Now her new friends were telling her about the theatres where they all worked, which surgeons were quick to anger, which ones talked a lot, which ones liked music as they worked, and which ones flirted.

Hmm! So there *were* some flirts!

Would they flirt with her?

Seriously?

The young women giggled and tittered behind their hands as they discussed this last category and Marni wanted to ask if they flirted back, but felt she was too new to the country and understood too little of the local ways. So she listened to the chat, enjoying it, feeling more and more at home as she realised the women's words could be talk among theatre nurses anywhere in the world, except that it was never personal—no mention of family or relationships—usually the main topics of conversation among nurses back home.

But for all the ease she felt with her fellow nurses, nerves tightened her sinews, and butterflies danced polkas in her stomach when she reported for duty the next day.

'Welcome,' Jawa, one of the nurses she'd met the previous day, said as Marni pushed through the door into the theatre dressing room. 'This morning you will enjoy for Gaz is operating. He's not only a good surgeon, but he takes time to tell us what he is doing so we can learn.'

Aware that many of the staff at the hospital were imports like herself, she wondered if Gaz might be an Australian, the name a shortened Aussie version of Gary or Gareth. Not that she had time to dwell on the thought, for Jawa was handing her pale lavender—lavender?—theatre pyjamas, a cap and mask, talking all the time in her liltingly accented English.

'So we must hurry for he is not one of those surgeons who keep patients or staff waiting. He is always on time.'

Jawa led the way through to the theatre where they scrubbed and gloved up, ready for what lay ahead. The bundle of instruments on the tray at Marni's station—she would be replenishing Jawa's tray as Jawa passed instruments to the surgeon—looked exactly the same as the bundles at home, and relieved by the familiarity of that and her surroundings she relaxed.

Until the gowned, capped, gloved and half-masked figure of the surgeon strode into the room, when every nerve in her body tightened and the hairs on her arms and back of her neck stood to attention.

He's just a man! she told herself, but that didn't stop a tremble in the pit of her stomach as he looked around the room, dark eyes taking in the newcomer, his head nodding in acknowledgement, the eyes holding hers—a second or two, no more—yet causing heat to sear downwards through her body.

'So, we have a stranger in our midst,' the man who was causing the problems said, his voice reverberating through her like the echoes of carillon bells. 'And you are?'

'Marni Graham, sir,' she said, hoping she sounded more in control than she felt.

'In here I'm Gaz, just Gaz, Marni Graham,' he said. 'Welcome to the team.'

She really should say something—respond in some way—but her voice was lost somewhere in the general muddle of the new and unbelievably vital sensations she was experiencing right now.

Lust at first sight?

It can't be, Marni argued with herself, but silently and very weakly.

The man in question had pulled his mask up to cover

his nose and mouth, and seemed about to turn away, but before he did so he smiled at her.

Of course, she couldn't see the smile, not on his lips, but she was certain it was there, shining in his eyes and making her feel warm and very, very unsettled.

What she had to do was to appear totally unaffected by the man, which, of course she was, she told herself. The reaction had been nerves, first day on the job and all that. Yet she was aware of this man in a way she'd never been aware of anyone before, her skin reacting as if tiny invisible wires ran between them so every time he moved they tugged at her.

Was this what had been missing in her other relationships—the ones that had fizzled out, mainly, she had to admit, because she'd backed away from committing physically?

She shook the thought out of her head and concentrated on the task at hand, on the operation, the patient, a child of eight having a second surgery to repair a cleft palate.

'This little boy, Safi, had had his first repair when he'd been six months old,' Gaz was explaining, his voice like thick treacle sliding down Marni's spine. 'That was to repair the palate to help him feed and also to aid the development of his teeth and facial bones.'

He worked as he talked, slender gloved fingers moving skilfully, probing and cutting, everything done with meticulous care, but Marni gave him more points for knowing the child's name and using it, humanising the patient, rather than calling him 'the child'.

'Now we need to use a bone graft to further repair the upper jaw where the cleft is, in the alveolar.'

Marni recited the bones forming part of the maxilla, or upper jaw bone—zygomatic, frontal, alveoal and palatine—inside her head, amazed at what the brain could retain from studies years ago.

'If we had done this earlier,' Gaz was explaining, 'it would have inhibited the growth of the maxilla, so we wait until just before the permanent cuspid teeth are ready to erupt before grafting in new bone.'

He continued speaking, so Marni could picture not only what he was doing but how his work would help the child who'd had the misfortune to have been born with this problem.

It had to be the slight hint of an accent in his words that made his voice so treacly, she decided as he spoke quietly to the anaesthetist. So he probably wasn't an Australian. Not that it mattered, although some contrary part of her had already wound a little dream of two compatriots meeting up to talk of home.

Talk?

Ha!

Her mind had already run ahead to the possibility that this man might just be the one with whom she could have that fling.

You're supposed to be concentrating on the job, not thinking about sex!

She hadn't needed the reminder, already shocked by how far her mind had travelled while she'd worked.

And *where* it had travelled!

The man was a complete stranger...

A complete stranger with mesmerising eyes and a sexy, chocolate-syrup voice!

The operation, which seemed to have gone on for ever, wound up swiftly. The surgeon and his assistant left, although Gaz did turn at the door and look around, frowning slightly as he pulled his mask down to dangle beneath his chin, revealing a sculpted line of barely-there beard outlining a jaw that needed nothing to draw attention to its strength.

He nodded in the general direction of the clump of nurses where Marni stood, before disappearing from view.

There was no rush of conversation, which seemed weird as either the surgeons or their skills usually came in for comment during the post-op clean-up. But here the women worked competently and silently, Jawa finally telling Marni that was all they had to do.

'We have time for lunch and you're back in Theatre again this afternoon—you and me both, they have paired us for a while.'

'I'm glad of that,' Marni told her. 'I still need someone to lead me around.'

She opened her mouth to ask if the surgeon called Gaz would be operating again, then closed it, not wanting to draw Jawa's attention to the fact the man had affected her in some strange way.

A *very* strange way!

The afternoon operation was very different, removal of a benign cancer from the ankle of a little girl. The surgeon was French and seemed to think his nationality demanded he flirt with all the nurses, but his work was more than proficient and Marni decided she'd enjoy working here if all the surgeons were as skilled as the first two she'd seen.

A minor operation on a child sent up from ER, repair of a facial tear, finished off her shift, but as she changed into her outdoor clothes she wondered about their first patient, the little boy who'd been born with a deformity that would have been affecting his life. No child liked to look different from his mates...

Uncertain of protocol but needing to know how he'd

come out of the operation, Marni asked Jawa if she'd be allowed to see him.

'Just a brief visit to see he's okay,' she added.

Jawa consulted her watch and decided that, yes, he should be well and truly out of Recovery and back on the children's post-op ward.

'Of course you can visit him,' she assured Marni. 'I would come with you but I have an appointment.'

The faint blush that rose in her cheeks as she said this suggested the appointment was special, but Marni forbore to tease, not knowing Jawa or the local customs well enough.

The post-op ward was easy to find. The hospital was set up rather like an octopus with all its tentacles spread flat on the ground. The operating theatres, recovery rooms, the ICU and the administration rooms were all in the tall body of the beast, while the arms supplied different wards.

In the post-op ward, bright with murals of colourful forests and wild animals, Marni found most rooms occupied not only by the patient but by a clutch of family members as well—black-robed women, white-robed men.

'Can I help you?' a passing nurse inquired.

'A little boy who had a cleft palate operation this morning. I was one of the theatre staff and wondered how he was doing.'

'Ah, you mean Safi. Do you wish to visit him?'

'I wouldn't want to intrude on his family,' Marni said.

'You won't,' the nurse told her. 'In fact, it would be good if you could visit him. He's not local but has come here for all his surgery. The hospital takes many children from neighbouring countries because we have the doctors with the skills to help them, and this wonderful facility where they can recover, but often the parents cannot afford to accompany the child. The nurses will do their best to see these children are not too lonely, but most of the time—'

'You're too busy,' Marni finished for her. 'I understand, but I'm far away from home myself so I'll be happy to visit Safi when I can.'

Following the nurse's directions, she found Safi's room, knocked quietly then went in. The little boy turned wide, troubled eyes towards her.

'Hello,' she said, aware he probably had no idea of English but not knowing what language he might speak. 'I've come to visit you.'

She sat beside him and held his hand, wishing she'd brought a toy or a book. Although this boy was eight and she'd been only two when she'd first gone to live with her grandfather, she remembered how Pop had helped her feel at home—he'd sung to her.

Dredging back through her memory, she sang the nursery rhymes of her childhood, using her hands as she had back then, making a star that twinkled in the sky and an itsy-bitsy spider climbing up a water spout.

Safi regarded her quite seriously but when she sang 'Twinkle Twinkle Little Star' for the fourth time, he joined in with his hands then smiled at her.

The smile made her want to cry for his aloneness, but apparently the music had soothed him and he fell asleep.

Not wanting to disturb him too soon, she sat by the bed, holding his hand, her mind drifting through the memories of the tumultuous few weeks since she'd made the decision to come to Ablezia, stumbling out of the drift when she thought of her goal—*her* goal, not Pop's.

Could she do it? Go cold-bloodedly into a relationship with a man simply to rid herself of her virginity?

Hot-bloodedly if it was Gaz! The thought popped into her head and Marni knew heat was colouring her cheeks.

Think sensibly!

It wasn't that she'd thought it precious, the virginity thing. It had just happened, partly, she knew, as the result of having a wayward mother who flitted like a butterfly from man to man. But the biggest hurdle had been growing up with two elderly men who thought the world of her, and not wanting to ever do anything that would make them think less of her.

So she'd pulled back through her late teens when her friends had been happily, and often unhappily, experimenting with sex, although, to be honest, there'd never been a boy with whom she'd desperately wanted to go to bed.

At university, her lack of experience had embarrassed her enough for her to be cautious, then, probably because of the virginity thing, she'd virtually stopped dating, somehow ashamed to admit, if a relationship *had* developed, her intact state. Until Jack—

Enough brooding!

But Marni still sighed as she lifted the little fingers that had been clasped in hers and kissed the back of Safi's hand.

Who would have thought it could be so hard?

She stole silently out of the room, turning her thoughts back to the child, knowing she'd return and wondering just where she could buy toys and books to cheer the little boy's recovery.

Nelson would send whatever she wanted but he was busy with Pop—she'd check out the internet when she went back to her room.

As she passed the nurses' station, nerves prickled along her spine and glancing over her shoulder she saw the back of a tall, dark-haired man bent slightly to listen to what the nurse at the desk was saying.

Of course it's not him, she told herself, though why had her nerves reacted?

Surely she wasn't going to tingle when she saw every tall, dark and handsome stranger!

CHAPTER TWO

No Gaz in Theatre the next day or the next, and Marni decided, as she made her way down the children's ward to visit Safi, that she was pleased, she just had to convince herself of the fact. But the sadness in the little boy's eyes as she entered his room banished all other thoughts. She sat beside him, took his hand, said 'Hello' then '*Salaam*', one of the few words she'd managed to remember from Jawa's language lessons.

Safi smiled and repeated the word, then rattled off what might have been questions, although Marni didn't have a clue. Instead she opened up the folder of pictures she'd printed off the internet, showing Safi a map of Australia and pointing to herself, then one of Ablezia. Using a cut-out plane, she showed how she'd flown from Australia to Ablezia.

The little boy took the plane and pointed from it to her. She nodded. 'Aeroplane,' she said. 'A big jet plane, from here...' she pointed again '...to here.'

Safi nodded but kept hold of the plane, zooming it around in the air.

Marni flipped through her folder, bringing out pictures of a koala, a wombat and a kangaroo. She put them all on the map of Australia and when Safi picked up the picture of the kangaroo, she hopped around the room, delighting the little boy, who giggled at her antics.

'Kangaroo,' she said, hoping the books and toys she'd ordered would arrive shortly—she'd paid for express mail. She'd actually found a female kangaroo with a joey in its pouch among the soft toys for sale, and had made it her number-one priority.

Safi was jumping the picture of the kangaroo on the bed now and pointing towards her, so Marni obligingly jumped again, her hands held up in front of her like the kangaroo's small front paws. Unfortunately, as she spun around to jump back past the end of the bed, she slammed into an obstacle.

A very solid obstacle!

Stumbling to recover her balance, she trod on the obstacle's feet and mashed herself against his chest, burning with mortification as she realised it was the surgeon— Safi's surgeon—the man called Gaz.

'S-s-ir!' She stammered out the word. 'Sorry! Being a kangaroo, you see!'

Marni attempted to disentangle herself from the man.

He grasped her forearms to steady her and she looked up into eyes as dark as night—dark enough to drown in—felt herself drowning...

Fortunately he had enough presence of mind to guide her back to the chair where she'd been sitting earlier and she slumped gratefully into it, boneless knees no longer able to support her weight.

He spoke to Safi, the treacly voice light with humour, making the little boy smile and bounce the picture of the kangaroo around the bed.

'I am explaining to him you come from Australia where these animals are,' Gaz said, turning to smile at her.

The smile finished her demolition. It lit fires she'd

never felt before, warming her entire body, melting bits of it in a way she didn't want to consider.

'Well, well, well,' he said, so suggestively she had to wonder if he'd read her reaction to him. Surely not, although the smile playing around his lips—gorgeous lips—and the twinkle in his eyes suggested he might have a fair idea of it.

'You're the new surgical nurse.'

A statement, not a question.

'Marni Graham,' she said, holding out her hand then regretting the automatic gesture as touching him, even in a handshake, was sure to cause more problems.

You've fallen in lust! Twenty-nine years old and you've finally been hit by an emotion as old as time.

'It's not lust,' Marni mumbled, then realised she'd spoken the words, although under her breath so hopefully they hadn't been audible to the surgeon, who was bent over Safi, examining the site of the operation and speaking quietly himself in the soft, musical notes of the local language.

The little boy appeared to know the man quite well, for he was chatting easily, now pointing to Marni and smiling.

'You have visited him before?' Gaz asked as he straightened. 'For any reason?'

'Should I not have come? Is it not allowed?' The man, the questions, her silly reactions all contributed to her blurting out her response. 'Jawa said it would be all right, and the nurses here don't have a lot of time to spend with him.'

The tall man settled himself on the bed, his knees now only inches from Marni's, although she could hardly push her chair back to escape the proximity, tantalising though it was.

They're knees, for heaven's sake!

Marni forced herself to relax.

'Of course you are welcome to visit. Safi appreciates it and looks forward to your visits, but I wondered why you come. You are a stranger here, are you not being looked after? Have you not made friends that you spend your spare time with a child?'

The man had obviously painted her as pathetic.

'Of course I've made friends, and everyone has been very welcoming, and I've done a lot of exploring, both on my own and with others, but...'

She hesitated.

How to explain that while she loved theatre nursing, the drama of it, the intensity, she missed patient contact?

He was obviously still waiting for an answer, the dark eyes studying her, his head tilted slightly to one side.

'Like most nurses,' she began, still hesitant, 'I took it up because I felt I could offer something in such a career. I enjoyed all the facets of it, but especially nursing children. Early on, I thought I'd specialise in paediatric nursing, but then I did my first stint in Theatre and I knew immediately that's where I really wanted to work. But in Theatre a patient is wheeled in and then wheeled out and somehow, even with the good surgeons who use the patient's name, they don't become real people—there's no follow-up to find out if the operation was a success, there's no person to person contact at all—'

Aware she'd been babbling on for far too long, she stopped, but when her companion didn't break the silence, she stumbled into an apology.

'Sorry, that sounded like a lecture, sorry.'

He reached out and touched her lightly on the knee, burning her skin through the long, loose trousers she was wearing.

'Do not apologise for showing humanity. It is all too rare a trait in modern medicine where everyone is under pressure to perform and seek perfection in all they do, so much so we have little time to think about those under our care as people rather than patients. In this hospital we allow the families to stay, so our patients have them to turn to, but children like Safi, who have come from a neighbouring country, often have no one.'

'Except you,' Marni pointed out. 'The nurse told me you'd been in earlier and that you stayed with him that first night.'

'I was worried he'd be afraid, alone in a strange place, and I've learned to sleep anywhere so it was no hardship.'

Not only gorgeous but nice, Marni thought, and she smiled at him and told him so—well, not the gorgeous bit.

'That was very kind of you,' she said, 'but have you done it every night? Surely that would be too much if you're operating every day?'

Gaz returned her smile, but it was absent-minded, as if it had slipped onto his lips while he was thinking of something else.

'Not every night, no, but an old friend of mine comes in now and stays with him. It was she who heard the story of a foreign woman visiting.'

'So you came to check?' Marni asked, not sure whether to be pleased or put out. Pleased to have seen him again, that was for sure...

'Of course,' he said. 'Not because I doubted your good intentions, but to see who it was willing to put herself out for a child she did not know.'

The smile this time was the full effort, its effect so electrifying in Marni's body she hoped he'd go away—disappear in a puff of smoke if necessary—so she could sort herself out before she tried standing up.

'And now that I do know,' he continued, oblivious of the effect he was having on her, 'I wondered if you'd like to have dinner with me, a kind of welcome to Ablezia and thank you for being kind to Safi combined. There is a very good restaurant on the top floor of the administration building right here in the hospital. We could eat there.'

So it would seem like colleagues eating together if your wife or girlfriend found about it? Marni wondered. Or because you have rooms here and it would be convenient for seduction? Well, the seduction part would be all right— after all, wasn't that one of the reasons she was here?

Although annoyed by her totally absurd thoughts, Marni realised her first question had been plausible enough—a man this gorgeous was sure to be taken!

Taking a deep breath, she put the whole ridiculous seduction scenario firmly out of her head.

'I'd like that,' she said, and was surprised to find her voice sounded remarkably calm. 'That must be a part of the building I haven't explored yet. My friend Jawa and I usually go to the staff canteen on the ground floor.'

Shouldn't you check whether he's married before you get too involved? Marni thought.

Having dinner with a colleague was hardly getting involved!

Or so she told herself!

Until he took her elbow to guide her out of the room.

She knew immediately there was a whole lot wrong with it. She'd made a serious mistake. It was utter madness. That, oh, so casual touch made her flesh heat, her skin tingle and her heart race.

Although wasn't that all good if—

She *had* to stop thinking about seduction!

He dropped her elbow—thankfully—as they walked back up the corridor to the big foyer in the middle of the building, which, again thankfully, gave Marni something to use as conversation.

'It's been beautifully designed, this building,' she said—well, prattled really. 'I love the way this atrium goes all the way up, seemingly right to the roof.

'You'll see the top of some of the taller palms from the restaurant,' Gaz said. 'In arid countries we long for greenery so when there's an opportunity to provide some, either indoors or out, we make the most of it.'

The pride in his voice was unmistakeable and although Marni knew from Jawa that the locals didn't encourage personal conversation, she couldn't help but say, 'So, you're a local, are you?'

The lift arrived and as he ushered her in he smiled at her.

'Very much so.'

The slightly strained smile that accompanied the words told Marni not to pursue the matter, so she talked instead of her delight in the markets, the colours, the people, the aromas.

Still prattling, she knew, but the man made her nervous in ways she'd never been before.

The lift doors slid open, and they stepped out into a glass-sheathed corridor, the inner wall displaying, as Gaz had said, the tops of the palm trees in the atrium.

Drawn to the glass, Marni peered down.

'It's beautiful,' she said, turning to him to share her delight.

He was staring at her, a small frown on his face, as if something about the sight of her bothered him.

'What?' she asked, and he shook his head, before again, with another light touch on her elbow, guiding her forward, around the atrium to the far side, where a restaurant spread across the corridor so the atrium was indeed visible from the tables.

The place was dimly lit and quiet, only a few tables occupied.

'Are we too early or too late for the usual dinner hour?' Marni asked, desperate to talk about something—anything—to distract herself from the effect this man was having on her, especially with his casual touches and watchful dark eyes.

'Early for the diners coming off late shift, late for those going on night duty,' Gaz told her as the young man on the reception desk greeted Gaz in his own language then bowed them towards a table close to the atrium.

Gaz held up a hand and said something, and the young man bowed again and led them in a new direction so they crossed the room.

'You have seen the tops of the palms in the atrium,' Gaz explained, 'but possibly not the desert in the moonlight.'

The table was beside a wall of glass, so Marni felt she was seated in space above the long waves of dunes. The moon silvered the slopes it touched, and threw black shadows in between, so the desert seemingly stretched away for ever with a patterned beauty that took her breath away.

'I hadn't known—hadn't realised...'

'That it could be so beautiful?' Gaz asked as her words stumbled to a halt.

She smiled at him, but the smile was an effort because something in the way he said the word 'beautiful' made it seem personal—although that could hardly be true. The women she'd met here were so stunningly attractive she felt like a pale shadow among them, a small daisy among vibrant dark roses.

Answer the man, her head suggested, and she struggled

to get back into the conversation—to at least *act* normal in spite of the chaos going on in her body.

'Yes, that,' she said, 'definitely that, but I hadn't realised the hospital was so close to the desert. I've always come to it from the direction of the city, from the sea side, but the desert's right there—so close you could touch it—and so immense.'

'And dangerous, remember that,' Gaz said.

'Dangerous?' Marni repeated, because once again there seemed to be an underlying message in his words.

It's the accent, you idiot, she told herself. Why should there be some sensual sub-text when the man barely knows you?

'You have deserts in Australia—inhospitable places where a man without water or transport could perish in a few days.'

'Of course. I hadn't thought about it but it would be the same in any desert, I imagine.'

She'd caught up with the conversation, but it hadn't mattered for Gaz was now conferring with a waiter, apparently discussing the menu. He turned to her to ask if she'd like to try some local dishes, and if so, would she prefer meat, fish or vegetarian.

'Meat, please, and yes to local dishes. I've tried some samples of the local cooking in the souks. There's a delicious dish that seems to be meat, with dates and apricots.'

'And to drink? You would like a glass of wine?'

And have it go straight to my head and confuse me even further?

'No, thank you, just a fruit juice.'

Her voice was strained with the effort of making polite conversation. Her nerves were strung more tightly than the strings of a violin, while questions she couldn't answer tumbled in her head.

Was the attraction she felt mutual?

Could this be the man—not for a lifetime, it was far too early to be considering that—for a fling, an affair?

Worse, could she go through with it if by some remote chance he was interested?

The waiter disappeared and Marni took a deep breath, knowing she somehow had to keep pretending a composure she was far from feeling. But how to start a conversation in a place where personal conversations just didn't seem to happen?

Gaz saved her.

'You mentioned the souks. You have had time to see something of my country?'

She rushed into speech, describing her delight in all she'd seen and done, the beauty she'd discovered all around her, the smiling, helpful people she'd encountered.

Gaz watched her face light up as she spoke, and her hands move through the air as she described a decorated earthen urn she'd seen, or the tiny, multicoloured fish swimming through the coral forests. He saw the sparkle in her pale, grey-blue eyes and the gleam where the lights caught her silvery-blonde hair, and knew this woman could ensnare him.

Actually, he'd known it from the moment he'd seen her—well, seen her pale eyes framed by the white mask and lavender cap on her first day in Theatre.

There'd been something in those eyes—something that had caught at, not his attention but his inner self—a subliminal connection he couldn't put into words.

At the time he'd dismissed the idea as fanciful—the product of a mind overburdened by the changes in his life, but now?

Impossible, of course! He had so much on his plate

at the moment he sometimes doubted he'd ever get his head above water.

He groaned inwardly at the mess of clichés and mixed metaphors, but that's how his life seemed right now. He'd stolen tonight from the schedule from hell, and by the time he had his new life sorted, this woman would be gone.

There'll be other women, he reminded himself, then groaned again.

'Are you all right?'

The pale eyes showed genuine concern, and a tiny line of worry creased the creamy skin between her dark eyebrows.

'I will be,' he answered. 'There are some massive changes happening in my life right now, which, as far as I'm concerned, is really bad timing.'

He reached across the table and touched her hand, which was wrapped around the glass of pomegranate and apple juice the waiter had set in front of her.

'Bad timing?' she repeated.

'*Very* bad timing,' he confirmed, and said no more, because he knew that although an attraction as strong as the one he was feeling couldn't possibly be one-sided, there was nothing to be gained from bringing it out into the open. He simply had no time! No time for them to get to know each other properly.

No time to woo her.

Instead, he asked how much diving she'd done, and listened as her quiet, slightly husky voice talked about the Great Barrier Reef, a holiday she'd had in the Seychelles, and compared other dives she'd done with the Ablezian Sea.

Was he listening? Marni had no idea, but she was happy to have something to talk about and as she spoke she relived some of her underwater adventures, and remembering the joy and fun she'd experienced eased the tension in her body so talking now was easy, her companion prompting her to keep going if she lagged.

The meal arrived—a covered earthenware dish set in the middle of the table, another dish of rice set beside it. The waiter added small plates of cut-up salad vegetables and a platter of the flat bread that she was beginning to realise was part of every meal in this country.

'Traditionally, I would serve you, but perhaps you would prefer to help yourself,' Gaz said, lifting the lid of the earthenware pot and releasing the mouth-watering aroma of the dish. 'I would not like to give you too much or too little.'

Ordinary words—common-sense words—so why was she all atingle again?

It was his voice, she decided as she helped herself to rice then added a scoop of the meat dish, before putting a little tomato salad on her plate and taking a piece of bread. His voice sneaked inside her skin and played havoc with her nerves, but when she'd finished her selection and looked across at him, his eyes, intent on her again, caused even more havoc.

Totally distracted now, she picked up her glass of juice and took too big a gulp.

At least half choking to death brought her back to her senses. Marni finished coughing and, flushed with embarrassment, bent her head to tackle her meal.

Fortunately, Gaz seemed to sense her total disarray and took over the conversation, talking about the hospital, built within the last two years, and with the charge of looking after not only local children but those from nearby countries that did not have the facilities this hospital had.

'We have a big oncology department, keeping children

here during their treatment so they don't have to travel to and fro. With those children, we try to make sure they have someone from their family travel with them—sometimes, it seems, the entire family.'

His rueful smile at this confession undid all the good concentrating on her food had done for Marni, mainly because it softened his face and somehow turned him from the sexiest man she'd ever laid eyes on to a real, caring human being.

All you're wanting is an affair, not to fall in love, she reminded herself.

But at least hospital talk got them through the meal and when they'd finished, Marni sat back in her chair.

'Thank you, that was utterly delicious. Wonderful. Perhaps I could pay the bill as thanks to you for introducing me to this place? Is that allowed in Ablezia?'

She offered what she knew must be a pathetic smile, but now they'd finished eating she had no idea how to get away—which she needed to do—or what was the polite thing to do next.

Say goodbye and leave?

Wait for him to see her back down to the ground floor?

And if he offered to walk her back to the quarters—through the gardens and lemon orchard, the scented air, the moonlight…

It was too soon even to think about what might happen and the man had already said he had no time.

'You definitely will not pay when I invited you to dinner,' Gaz was saying as she ran these increasingly panicked thoughts through her head. 'It is taken care of but, come, you must see the desert from outside, where you can really appreciate its beauty.'

He rose and came to stand beside her, drawing out her

chair, which meant his entire body was far too close to hers when she stood up.

Turning to face him, this time with thanks for the courtesy of the chair thing, brought her even closer—to lips that twitched just slightly with a smile, and eyes that not only reflected the smile but held a glint of laughter.

The wretch knows the effect he's having on me, Marni realised, and found a little anger stirring in the mess of emotions flooding through her body.

Good!

Anger was good—not argumentative anger but something to hold onto. The man was a born flirt and though he obviously couldn't help being the sexiest man alive, he didn't need to use it to snare unwary females.

Wasn't wanting to be snared one of the reasons she'd come here?

Marni ignored the query and allowed Gaz to lead her out of the restaurant and along another corridor that led to a balcony overlooking the desert—the magic sea of black and silver.

She sniffed the air, then breathed it in more deeply.

'It's strange,' she said, turning to her companion, her reaction to him almost forgotten as she considered the puzzle the desert air presented. 'I know the sea is just over there, but there's no smell of salt in the air, no smell of the spices escaping from the restaurant or the lemon blossom that I know is out in the gardens down below us. No smell at all, really.'

He smiled again—a genuine smile this time, not a teasing one—but this one made Marni's heart flutter.

'The desert is a great cleanser. Over the centuries much blood has been spilled on the sands, and civilisations have risen and collapsed, their ruins buried by the sand. For people like me, with Bedouin blood, the desert is as necessary as water, for it is where we replenish our souls.'

He was serious, the words so graphically beautiful Marni could only shake her head.

And smile.

A small smile but a genuine one.

A smile that for some reason prompted him to inch a little closer and bend his head, dropping the lightest of kisses on her parted lips.

Had she started, so that he put his hands on her shoulders to steady her?

Marni had no idea, too lost in the feel of his lips on hers to think straight.

So when he started talking again, she missed the first bit, catching up as he said, 'You are like a wraith from the stories of my childhood, a beautiful silver-haired, blue-eyed, pale-limbed being sent to tempt men away from their duties.'

She was still catching up when he kissed her again.

Properly this time so she melted against him, parted her lips to his demanding tongue, and kissed him back, setting free all the frustration of the lust infection in that one kiss.

It burned through her body in such unfamiliar ways she knew she'd never been properly kissed before—or maybe had never responded properly—which might explain—

It sent heat spearing downwards, more heat shimmering along her nerves, tightening her stomach but melting her bones.

Her head spun and her senses came alive to the smoothness of his lips, the taste of spice on his tongue, the faint perfume that might be aftershave—even the texture of his shirt, a nubby cotton, pressed against the light cotton tunic top she wore, was sending flaring awareness through her nipples.

A kiss could do all this…

Gaz eased away, shaken that he'd been so lost to propriety as to be kissing this woman, even more shaken by the way she'd reacted to the kiss and the effect it had had on him. Heat, desire, a hardening, thickening, burning need….

For one crazy moment he considered taking things further, dallying with the nurse called Marni, seeing where it went.

Certainly beyond dallying, he knew that much.

Al'ana! Where is your brain? his head demanded. Yes, I thought so! it added as if he'd answered.

He looked at the flushed face in front of him, glimpsed the nipples peaked beneath the fine cotton tunic, the glow of desire in her eyes.

Yes, it would definitely have gone further than dalliance…

'I had no right to do that. I have no time. None! No time at all!' He spoke abruptly—too abruptly—the words harshly urgent because he was denying his desires and angry with himself for—

For kissing her?

No, he couldn't regret that.

Angry at the impossible situation.

This time when he turned to lead her back inside, he didn't touch her elbow and guide her steps but stayed resolutely apart from the seductive siren who'd appeared, not from the sky but in full theatre garb, then jumped like a kangaroo right inside his skin…

Obviously married, Marni told herself. Serves you right, kissing on what wasn't even a first date.

But she was too shaken by the kiss to care what the

sensible part of her brain was telling her. Too shaken to think, let alone speak.

Standing silently beside Gaz in the lift, the foot of space between them was more like a million miles.

Back in the foyer, he spoke to one of the young porters who seemed to abound in the place.

'Aziz will see you back to the residence,' Gaz told her, then he nodded once and was gone, seeming to disappear like the wraith he'd called her.

Aziz was beckoning her towards the door so she followed, deciding she must be right about his marital status if the man she'd kissed didn't want to be seen walking her through the gardens.

So she was well rid of him.

Wasn't she?

Of *course* she was!

The gardens were as beautiful as ever, the scent of lemon blossom heavy in the air, but the magic was dimmed by her memory of the kiss, and now that embarrassment over her reaction was creeping in, she was beginning to worry about the future.

She was a professional. Of course she could work in Theatre with Gaz without revealing how he affected her. Not that he didn't know, given her response, but at least she didn't have to be revealing just how hard and fast she'd fallen for the man.

Lust, her head reminded her, and sadly she agreed.

For all the good it was going to do her when he'd made it obvious he wasn't available!

She sighed into the night air. It was all too complicated!

CHAPTER THREE

HIDING HER REACTIONS to Gaz in Theatre proved unnecessary, because although she worked for five straight days, he was never rostered on in the same theatre as her.

She didn't kid herself that he'd had his schedule changed to avoid her, doubting she was important enough to cause such a change, and caution told her not to mention him to Jawa, not to ask where he was operating or seek answers to any personal questions about the man, in case she unwittingly revealed how she felt.

Besides, they just didn't do personal conversations, these Ablezians.

But her reaction to Gaz had certainly put a damper on her virginity quest, other male colleagues seeming pale and uninteresting by comparison, although she did accept an invitation to the movies from a young doctor on Safi's ward.

She'd even accepted a goodnight kiss but she had felt nothing, not a tingle, not a sign of a spark—and the poor man had known it and had avoided her ever since.

So she worked, visited Safi, and worked again until finally she had time off—three days.

Nelson had emailed to say Pop was talking to the surgeon but was still undecided about the operation, although now he could walk barely a hundred metres without tiring.

She had to forget about Gaz and find a way to see this prince! Once she'd kept her part of the bargain, Pop would *have* to have the operation. He wasn't one to renege on a deal.

And at least sorting out how you're going to approach *him* should get your mind off Gaz, she told herself.

And it did, the whole matter seeming impossible until she read in the English-language newspaper that the new prince had reintroduced his father's custom of meeting with the people once a week. Each Thursday he held court in a courtyard—was that where courtyards got their name?—at the palace, hearing grievances or problems, any subject allowed to approach and speak to him privately for a few minutes.

Reading further, Marni discovered the custom had stopped while his uncle had been the ruler but had been reinstated some weeks previously and was a great success.

She wasn't actually a subject, but that couldn't be helped. If she tied a black headscarf tightly over her hair and borrowed an all-concealing black abaya from Jawa *and* kept her head down—maybe with part of the scarf tied across the lower part of her face—she could slip in with the locals, have a minute to introduce herself and show the photo, perhaps even have a laugh with the man who'd been kind to her as a child.

The planets must have been aligned in her favour—though they'd definitely been against her last week—for the next meeting was the following day.

She emailed Nelson to tell him she was keeping her part of the bargain and to warn Pop she expected him to keep his, then went to collect the clothing she'd need.

Which was all very well in theory!

In practice, once dressed and sitting in the back of a cab on her way to the palace, a building she'd glimpsed from afar in her explorations, she realised just how stupid this was, how ridiculous the whole thing—making a deal with Pop so he'd have a lifesaving operation—fronting up to the prince of a foreign land to show him a photo of himself as a child.

The enormity of it made her shake her head in disbelief.

Yet here she was!

Huge arched gates in a high, sand-coloured wall opened into a courtyard big enough to hold a thousand people. It was an oasis of green—she remembered Gaz telling her how important green was—with beds of flowering roses, tinkling fountains, fruit trees and date palms. The garden had been designed and planted to provide shade but also to form little spaces like outdoor rooms where one could sit and read, or think, or just do nothing.

In the centre, facing the immense, low-set building, was an open grassed area and here the supplicants were gathering, seating themselves cross-legged on the ground in neat rows. Thankfully, there were not as many as Marni had expected, although, contrarily, part of her had hoped there *would* be too many and she could put off her ridiculous venture for another day.

She seated herself beside the last man in the back row, pleased it was a man as she knew he wouldn't attempt to make conversation with a woman he did not know.

An exchange of *salaam*s was enough, Marni with her head bent, not wanting to reveal pale eyes surrounded by even paler skin.

Intent on remaining unseen, she barely heard the words from the wide veranda that ran along the front of the palace. Not that hearing them more clearly would have helped.

Really smart idea, this, she thought despairingly. Just pop along to a meet and greet without a word of the language to tell you when it's your turn to front up to His Maj!

A long line was already forming and as it snaked towards the veranda the man beside her said something then stood and joined the line. Checking that it already held some women, Marni slid into place behind him, her heart beating such a crazy rhythm she was surprised she could stay upright.

The line inched forward until she could see, on a low couch on the veranda, a white-robed figure, bowing his head as a supplicant approached him, apparently listening to the request or complaint before assigning the person to one of the men who stood behind the couch.

Some people were led to the edge of the veranda and returned to the courtyard, while others were taken in through a door behind the couch, perhaps to sort out business matters or to leave more details. Whatever reason people had to be here, the line moved without a hitch, the meet and greet, as Marni thought of it, a smoothly organised process.

The man in front of her reached the steps, and although instinct told her to flee, the memory of the greyness in Pop's face held her steadfast in the grassy courtyard.

He *had* to have the operation!

The man moved on and one of the flunkeys supporting the main act waved Marni forward. Following the actions of those she'd seen, she approached swiftly, knelt on the pillow set before the robed figure and bowed her head, then lifted it to look at the face she'd seen in the newspaper back home and on billboards around the city.

The face she'd seen in Theatre, only in his snowy headdress he looked so different...

'But—you're—you're *you*,' she managed to get out before words evaporated from her head.

Gaz was staring at her, as bemused as she was apparently, although once again she suspected there was a smile hovering somewhere in his eyes.

'I am,' he finally said. 'Definitely me. How may I help you?'

The voice had its usual effect, and Marni dissolved completely into a morass of words and half-sentences that she knew were making no sense at all.

'Stupid, I knew that—but Pop needs the op—and then the photo—photos really—you were in the paper—and the job there—here—and I know it's silly but he really wanted—so I came—'

'You came?' Gaz repeated.

Marni took a deep breath, looked into the face of the man she lusted after and smiled at the absurdity of it all.

'Actually,' she said, almost totally together now, 'I came to—well, to say hello and show you a photo. Apparently we were betrothed, you see, a long time ago, and I know it's stupid but I promised Pop I'd try to meet you and—'

She was rattling on again so she stopped the babble and reached into the pocket of her borrowed abaya, but before she could pull out the photo the man she'd written off as a flunkey had grabbed her wrist in a grip of steel.

'I think she wants to marry me, not shoot me,' Gaz said, adding something in his own language so the man withdrew his hand and stepped away, leaving Marni burning with embarrassment.

Gaz took the photo, frowning at it, thinking back perhaps, looking from it to Marni, shaking his head, serious now, although a gleam of amusement shone deep in his eyes.

'Oh, but this is wonderful!' he finally declared, a delighted smile flashing across his face. 'We cannot talk now, but you have no idea how fortuitous this is. Mazur will take you to a side room, get you tea or a cold drink. I will join you shortly.'

Marni was still trying to work out the wonderful and fortuitous bits when Gaz reached out to help her back to her feet, indicating she should follow the man who'd stepped forward on his other side.

Totally bewildered by the whole charade—Gaz was Prince Ghazi? How could that be?—she followed Mazur, stumbling slightly as she was about to enter the room and realising she hadn't removed her sandals.

They entered a huge, open room, with high, arched doorways curtained in what looked like gold-coloured silk, the drapes pulled back and held with golden, heavily tasselled cords. The floor was of white marble, inlaid with coloured stones that made twining patterns of leaves and flowers, so brilliantly beautiful she had to pause to take them in.

Scattered here and there were immense carpets, woven in patterns of red, blue and green. Low settees were placed at intervals along the walls, cushions piled on them. Here and there, groups of people sat or stood, obviously waiting for further conversation with Gaz—Prince Ghazi!

'This is the *majlis*, the public meeting room,' Mazur explained. 'but you will be more comfortable in a side room.' He led her towards an arched opening to one side of the big area and into a smaller version of it—patterned marble floor, a bright rug and a pale yellow sofa with bright cushions scattered over it.

Mazur waited until she was seated on the softly sprung sofa before asking, 'You would like tea perhaps? We have

English tea or mint tea, cardamom, of course, and other flavours if you wish.'

His English was so impeccable, his courtesy so effortless he could have worked for English royalty.

Though apparently Gaz *was* royalty...

And she'd *kissed* him? Considered—well, more than considered—him a potential lover!

'Mint tea would be lovely,' Marni managed to reply, and waited until he'd departed before burying her head in her hands, desperate to make sense of what had happened.

She was finishing her tea and nibbling on one of the little cakes Mazur had produced when Gaz appeared, looking so utterly regal in his pristine white robe and starched headdress, a coronet of black silk cord holding it in place, that her heart fluttered again but this time with a degree of not fear but definitely trepidation.

'So, we are betrothed?' he teased, not bothering to hide his smile.

'Well, that's what Pop wrote, but who knows what your father put underneath—probably something about pleasing a daft old man—but it was all just a kind of a joke, me coming here. I didn't come here to hold you to a ridiculous betrothal, but with Pop so sick I made a deal with him. It's hard to explain...'

Marni was doing her best to sort things out, but she was becoming increasingly annoyed because the wretched man was so obviously amused by the whole thing while she was squirming with embarrassment.

Gaz came closer and the white gown did nothing to stop all the physical manifestations of lust that had struck Marni when she'd first set eyes on him.

Lust, she had discovered very quickly, was stronger than embarrassment, for all the good it was going to do her. This man was way out of her league in every way, so a casual affair was out of the question.

She watched him, nervous, apprehensive, wondering just what he might be thinking.

'Actually,' he said, coming to sit beside her on the couch, 'the betrothal is a splendid idea. You may not know it but I have seven sisters, six of whom are bent on finding me a wife.'

'Only six?'

Marni was interested in spite of herself, although she had to admit to a little twinge of dread as to where this betrothal idea might be leading.

'The seventh's heavily pregnant at the moment and fortunately has other things on her mind. But having six sisters producing eligible women for you almost daily is very difficult, especially when I'm trying to come to terms with this job. So your arrival has come at just the right time, and with the photo as proof that my father arranged it, my sisters can do nothing but accept it. It's perfect!'

Marni stared at him in disbelief.

'Perfect?'

'Absolutely perfect!' The dark eyes were definitely smiling.

'Are you saying you'll tell your sisters we're betrothed?'

'Of course.'

She shook her head then pulled herself together enough to demand, 'But that's all? Just betrothed? A temporary arrangement to stop them dangling women in front of you? That's all you want?'

'For the moment,' the white-robed figure replied, while Marni quelled an urge to run a fingertip along the fine dark line of his beard. 'I wouldn't rush you into marriage.'

'Marriage!'

The word came out as a startled squeak, and it was the squeak that brought her to her senses.

Mature, professional women did not squeak!

'Let's just back up here,' she said firmly, trying hard not to notice how exotically handsome he looked in his prince outfit. 'I know it was a ridiculous thing for me to do, coming here and rattling on about a betrothal, but you were meant—no, you weren't meant to be you to start off with—you were meant to be this kindly prince and I'd burble out my stuff, you'd laugh, I'd let Pop know I'd done it, he'd have the op to keep his part of the bargain, and everything would be fine.'

She hesitated then added, 'To be honest, it did cross my mind you might not be so kindly and I just might end up in a dungeon or deported at the very least, but Pop needed—'

Gaz held up his hand, the white robe falling back from his lower arm so Marni could see his wrist, fine dark hairs on his forearm, smooth olive skin...

'This Pop you talk of—he's the one who wrote on the photo?'

Marni swallowed hard, unable to believe a little bit of a man's arm could have excited her so much.

She managed a nod.

'What operation?'

Whether it was the tension of the day or her concern over Pop or simply relief to be talking about something other than her reason for being here, suddenly words flowed freely.

How Pop had always been an active man, involved in so many things, running different charities, on the boards of hospitals and refuges, years ago two stents had been put in and he'd continued on without missing a beat then suddenly this tiredness, exhaustion and a diagnosis of a faulty heart valve and blocked stents, two bypasses and open-heart surgery the only answer.

'We're sure he'll get through it, Nelson and I, but Pop feels at his age maybe it isn't worth it—'

Again Gaz lifted his hand and this time Marni refused to look at that erotic bit of forearm.

'Nelson?' Gaz asked, frowning now.

'The man who looks after Pop—he's been there for ever, looked after me as well. A kind of general factotum.'

But Gaz wasn't listening. He'd pulled out the photo and was staring at it.

'Where was this taken?' he demanded, and Marni explained.

'Apparently your father took over the whole hotel,' she added, and Gaz smiled.

'He was never one to do things by halves and I suppose if I was as young as I look then some of my sisters would already have been married, then there were the wives and the aunts and all the women the women needed to look after them whenever they travelled. But if he took over the whole hotel, where did you come into it?'

So Marni explained about the apartments.

'Pop bought one when the hotel was built and still lives there with Nelson, so when I was dumped on him by my mother, I lived there too. We were allowed to use all the hotel facilities so I probably met you in the pool or garden.'

'Nelson!' Gaz said. 'That's what brought it back to me. I kept calling him Mr Nelson and he'd tell me, no, his name was Nelson.'

He looked from the picture to Marni then back to the picture, tracing his finger across the images of the two children.

'I asked you to marry me,' he said quietly.

Being flabbergasted took a moment, then Marni laughed. And laughed!

'Oh,' she said, finally controlling her mirth, 'that's what it must be about. A child's proposal—the sort of thing that would happen at kindergarten—then your father and Pop humouring you by having the photo taken and writing on the back.'

It took her a moment to realise her amusement wasn't shared. In fact, Gaz was looking particularly serious.

'But don't you see?' she said. 'It was a joke between the two men. It's not as if it meant anything.'

Gaz continued to study her.

'Would you mind very much?' he asked after the silence had stretched for ever.

'Mind what?'

'Being betrothed to me?'

Mind? Marni's heart yelled, apparently very excited by the prospect.

Marni ignored it and tried to think, not easy when Gaz was sitting so close to her and her body was alive with its lustful reactions.

'To help you out?' she asked, hoping words might make things clearer. 'With your sisters?'

Gaz smiled, which didn't help the lustful business and all but destroyed the bit of composure she'd managed to dredge up.

'That, of course, but it's more than the sisters. I have to explain, but perhaps not here, and definitely not now. There are people I need to see, supplicants from this morning. Are you free for the rest of the day? Would you mind very much waiting until I finish my business? Mazur will see you are looked after, get you anything you want. You could explore the garden or even wander around the palace. It's exceptionally empty now without the harem, so you needn't worry about disturbing anyone.'

He touched her hand and stood up, apparently taking her compliance for granted, although, in fact, her mind had stopped following the conversation back when he'd said the word 'harem', immediately conjuring up visions of dancing girls in see-through trousers and sequinned tops, lounging by a pool or practising their belly dancing. Was it because he'd said the word with a long 'e' in the last syllable, making 'hareem' sound incredibly erotic, that the images danced in her head?

She watched the white-clad back disappear through a side door.

He *had* made it sound as if the lack of a harem was a temporary thing, a slight glitch, she reminded herself. Which meant what?

And wasn't having no harem a positive thing?

What was she thinking?

A harem or lack of one would only affect her if she was *really* betrothed to him, and as far as she could re-member—it had been a very confusing conversation—she hadn't actually agreed to even a pretend betrothal.

Had she?

And surely harems no longer existed?

Not dancing-girl harems anyway...

She pushed herself off the sofa and, too afraid to wan-der through the palace, even one without a 'hareem', she retreated to the gardens, thinking of pronunciations. Gaz with its short 'a' sound, suggested a friendly kind of bloke, sexy as all hell but still the kind of man with whom one might have had an affair, while Ghazi—which she'd heard pronounced everywhere with a long 'a', like the one in 'bath', sounded *very* regal.

Frighteningly regal!

And it totally knocked any thought of using the man to overcome her other problem right on the head! Ordinary women like Marni Graham of Australia didn't go around having affairs with kings or princes.

Even a pretend betrothal was mind-boggling!

A wide path led to a central fountain and, after playing with the water for a while, she turned onto another path, this one running parallel to the main building, leading to what appeared to be another very large building. In front of it, on a wide lawn, four boys were kicking a soccer ball. A wayward kick sent the ball hurtling in her direction and, mindful of Nelson's coaching tips, she kicked it back, high and hard, aiming it at the tallest of the boys, who raced to meet it and headed it expertly towards the makeshift goal—two small topiary trees spaced conveniently apart.

The lad high-fived all round then turned towards her, speaking quickly.

Marni held up her hand and shook her head.

'I'm sorry, I don't understand your language.'

The older boy came closer, looking her up and down, waving his hands towards her clothing as if to ask why she was dressed like she was.

She lifted up the black abaya to show her jeans and the boys laughed, the tall one inviting her to join the game.

'That's if you can run in a skirt?' His easy command of English made her wonder if he went to school overseas, or perhaps to an English language school here.

'I'm sure I can,' she assured him, and joined the boys, kicking the ball from one end of the grassed area to the other. She'd just sent it flying over the top of the topiary goal posts when a tall figure appeared, not in scrubs, or in the intimidating white gown, but in jeans as faded as hers, and a dark blue polo shirt that had also seen better days.

'Ghazi!' the boys chorused in delight. 'Come and play. This is Marni, she's nearly as good as you.'

Although he'd been looking for her, he'd hardly expected to find her playing soccer with his young nephews. The hood of her cloak had slipped off her head and her headscarf was dangling down the back of her neck, hiding the thick plait of fair hair. Her face was flushed, but whether from exertion or embarrassment he had no idea, and she was the most beautiful thing he'd ever seen.

Best not to get further entangled, his common sense warned, for all the betrothal idea was so appealing. But against all common sense he joined the game for a few minutes then told the boys he had to take their playmate away.

He was pleased to see they all went up to her and held out their hands to say goodbye, only Karim, the eldest, bold enough to invite her to play with them again.

How old was Karim? Surely not yet a teenager, although these days who knew when hormonal changes would rear their heads.

Marni had fixed her scarf and pulled the hood back over her head as she approached him.

'I do hope I wasn't doing the wrong thing,' she said, the flush still visible in her cheeks. 'The ball came towards me, I kicked it, and next thing I knew I was part of the game. They're good, the boys. I played for years myself, never good enough to make a rep team but enough to know skill when I see it.'

'They're soccer mad, just as their father is. His dream is to get Ablezia into the World Cup. For a country that doesn't yet have its own international team, it's a huge task. I'm pretty sure that's why I landed this job.'

'This job?'

The pale grey-blue eyes looked into his, the question mirrored in them.

'Ruler—supreme commander—there are about a dozen titles that my major-domo reads out on formal occasions. My uncle succeeded my father, who was an old man when I was born—the first son after seven daughters. Here, our successors are chosen from within the family but not necessarily in any particular order, but I had assumed Nimr, my cousin, would succeed *his* father and I could continue my surgical work, but Nimr the Tiger didn't want the job—his focus is on sport—and so here I am.'

Had he sounded gloomy that he felt soft fingers touch his arm?

'Is it such a trial?' the abaya-clad blonde asked.

'Right at this very moment?' he asked, covering her hand with his. 'Not really!'

The boys started whistling as boys anywhere in the world would do at the tiniest hint of romance, and he stepped back, gave them what he hoped was a very princely glare and put his hand on Marni's back to guide her away from them.

He'd have liked to tell them to keep quiet about her, but that would only pique their curiosity further, and he knew that before they'd even eaten lunch the boys would have relayed the story of the soccer-playing visitor to Alima, his eldest sister, wife of Nimr and mother of the precious boys they'd waited so long for.

'And the prime mover in the "find a wife" campaign,' he added, the words spoken aloud before he realised it.

'Who's the prime mover?' Marni asked, stopping by a pomegranate tree and fiddling with her scarf.

Gaz explained the relationship.

'Is that why they live so close? Not in the main building but within the walls?'

He looked at her, wondering if the question was nothing more than idle curiosity, although he was coming to believe that was unlikely. He was coming to see her as a woman who was interested in the world around her, eager to learn about it and discover new things.

Could this crazy idea work beyond a pretend betrothal?

'My uncle was living in the palace when they married, so naturally he built them the house nearby. This palace is new, or newish. My father built it when he tired of travelling from our home in the old city to here. Ablezia came late into the modern world, and we are a people who are slow to change. Obviously when the world changed so dramatically in these parts, we *had* to change—to learn new ways, to understand the intricacies of new business structures and international relations. My father was the right man for the job, because he understood it had to happen.'

'And you?' his perhaps betrothed asked softly. 'Are you the right man for the job?'

CHAPTER FOUR

GAZ—SHE COULDN'T think of him as anything else—didn't reply, simply putting one hand in the small of her back to guide her along a path between the huge houses towards what looked like stables beyond more garden.

Not stables but garages.

'There *are* horses,' he said, 'at the old palace, but I think my father realised we'd have no use for them here, so where, traditionally, the stables would be, he built "stalls" for cars.'

'So many cars?' Marni queried, seeing the long line of garages.

Gaz shrugged.

'Oh, you never know when someone might need to go somewhere,' he said, nodding to an elderly man who came forward to meet them. The man wore the loose trousers and long tunic top common among the locals, with a snug-fitting, embroidered cap on his head.

Listening to the fluid sounds of the words as Gaz spoke, Marni felt a longing to learn the language—to learn all she could about this fascinating country, although, she realised rather glumly, once the pretend betrothal ended she'd certainly have to leave.

If there *was* a pretend betrothal…

'I was explaining we won't need a big car and driver,

but Fayyad is horrified. He feels I'm not respecting my position enough.'

Again a touch on the small of her back, and her body's inevitable response.

Gaz steered her to where a battered four-wheel drive was relegated to a car port rather than a garage, and held the passenger door open for her.

Still totally bemused by the outcome of this visit to the palace, Marni climbed in. The day had taken on a dream-like quality, and she was moving through the dream without conscious thought. Gaz slid in behind the wheel and drove out through a rear gate, waving to the two men who squatted on the ground beside the big open doors.

'To answer your question,' Gaz said, taking what seemed like a little-used track that appeared to lead directly into the desert, 'I am reluctantly coming to the conclusion that I *am* the right man for the job, although I would far rather have continued my surgical career. All I can hope is that once I've got the job sorted—I've only been in it a couple of months—I can continue operating, at least on a part-time basis.'

Intrigued by his answer, Marni turned to look at him—not a good idea, for he flashed her a smile and the reactions the light touch on her back had stirred came fully to life.

'So, what's the job, as we seem to be calling it, entail?'

Another flashing smile, though this one was slightly rueful.

'I'm still coming to grips with it, but it's mostly formal stuff—meeting representatives from foreign countries, listening to delegations from various committees, making rulings on things that are more to do with our cultural heritage than politics—we have an elected congress that takes care of politics. And then there's the entertaining—endless entertaining.'

The road had petered out and he drove swiftly and skilfully across the sand, taking a slanting line across a dune and pulling up on the top of it. Beneath them the sand fell away to rise again, and again, and again, rolling waves of red-gold, brilliant in the sunshine. Breathtaking in its beauty. Marni remembered what he'd said about the desert being as necessary as water to his people. Did he need its power now? Need to refresh himself in the same way as she looked to the ocean for the replenishment of her spirit?

She was staring at the dunes, her mind asking questions she couldn't answer, so didn't realise he'd climbed out of the car and walked around to open her door. Beyond him, she could see a low-slung shelter, dark cloth of some kind, held up in front by sturdy poles, high enough to sit under to escape the sun. In front of it a low fire burned, beside the fire were two ornate silver coffee-pots, like others she'd seen in the souk.

'Come,' he said. 'We have to eat so why not here?'

He took her hand to help her down, his words perhaps answering her question about his need for the power of the desert.

Leading her to the shelter, he motioned to a faded rug, spread on the sand and heaped with cushions. A large woven basket was set in the shade beside the rug, its lid open to reveal an array of goodies.

Marni sank onto the rug, tucking her legs sideways so the abaya fell around her. The desert was framed now by the dark material of the tent and she could only shake her head in the wonder of its beauty.

Shake her head about the fact that she was actually

here, not to mention seeing it with the man who ruled the country.

Impossible!

Gaz settled beside her, closer to the fire.

'We must have coffee first,' he said, lifting one of the ornate pots and taking two tiny handle-less cups from the top of the basket. He poured the strong, thick brew easily into the tiny cups, passing her one before setting the pot back by the fire.

'Traditionally you should drink three cups, but it's definitely an acquired taste so you may stop at one.'

His smile teased at her senses and in an attempt to settle herself she gulped the drink, tasting the gritty lees but not finding them distasteful.

'And now we eat,' he said, and she wanted to protest— to ask what they were doing there, apart from picnicking, of course. To question the betrothal stuff and try to sort out what was happening. But he was producing bread, and cold meats, salad vegetables and fruit, serving her this time, piling goodies on a silver platter, handing it to her and urging her to eat.

Looking at the food, varied and enticing, she realised how hungry she was, and, not having much option now he'd handed her the plate, she ate.

Gaz watched her while he ate, wondering about this woman fate had thrust into his life. She was using her bread as cutlery, in the local way, and managing to do it without too much spillage. And as she ate she smiled, or muttered little sounds of appreciation, looking up from time to time to ask what a particular morsel might be.

She fascinated him, and not just in a physical way, although the physical attraction was extremely strong. Could this extraordinary idea work?

It was certainly worth a try.

He thought back to the night he'd first kissed her on the balcony outside the restaurant and remembered the surge of desire he'd felt—a surge that had almost led to his suggesting they take it further...

A betrothal would put that off limits. He could hardly be seen sneaking in and out of her room, or sneaking her in and out of the palace, although...

There was no although, but what if the betrothal led to marriage?

It needn't be a long betrothal, and if the marriage didn't work he would make sure she was amply compensated—these things were understood in his country...

Marriage was the logical answer. His body tightened at the thought, but she hadn't actually said yes to the betrothal, had she? He'd have to start there, he realised as she set aside her plate, all but empty, and wiped the damp, scented towel he handed her, across her lips.

'That was amazing,' Marni told him as she put her plate down on another mat. 'Just amazing!'

He turned to her, and reached out to touch her chin, tilting her head so he could look into her face.

'I'm glad,' he said, 'and now we're both fed, perhaps we can get back to the conversation.'

'The job?'

'The job!' he confirmed. 'Actually, endless entertaining is more time-consuming than difficult. I'm concerned that it might bore you to death.'

He had moved towards her as he spoke and now he leant forward and kissed her on the lips.

Thankfully, the shock of what he'd said lingered long enough to prevent Marni from responding to the kiss.

'Won't bore *me* to death?' she shrieked. 'Why on earth would it bore *me* to death?'

Now he frowned, and his eyes seemed darker than ever, though could black be any blacker?

'You think you'd enjoy it?' he asked. and it was her turn to frown.

'Why should I enjoy it, or be bored by it?' she demanded.

His answer was a smile, and if she'd managed to squelch her reaction to the kiss, she failed with the smile.

'Because, as my betrothed, you'll be by my side a lot of the time. I know that's an imposition, but I have women who'll help you all the way. The harem will be back in the palace next week, and I've sisters and nieces and cousins, even aunts, who'll be only too happy to shop with you for suitable clothes, to set you up with anything you need, and make sure you know the protocols.'

It would have been confusing if once again Marni's mind hadn't balked at the 'harem' word. Although if it was only a pretend betrothal, did the harem really matter?

Yes!

'This harem?' she asked, then stopped as she really didn't think she could mention belly-dancing females in see-through trousers.

'The harem?' Gaz repeated, making it exotic again with his pronunciation.

He looked puzzled then suddenly began to chuckle.

'You weren't imagining a seraglio, where you?'

'I've no idea what a seraglio is,' Marni said crossly, 'but if it's scantily clad women, lounging around limpid pools eating grapes and belly dancing then, yes—that's how everyone *I* know imagines a harem.'

The chuckle became a laugh and looking at him, with the tension she'd seen earlier washed from his face, she was once again tugged into the extraordinary sensual power of this man.

'The harem is simply a group name for the women of the family—women and children, in fact. My mother is part of it, my father's other wives, aunts and cousins and even more distant relations, also friends of all the women. Some come and go but the core of them moves together.

'Right now they are all at the old palace where one of my nieces is preparing her wedding chest. Years ago it would have meant a trip to London and Paris and taking over hotels, having stores like Harrods opening at night especially for them, but now they've discovered the internet, shopping has taken on a whole new dimension.'

There was more than a touch of cynicism in his voice so it took a moment for Marni to absorb what he'd said—taking over an entire store?—and then she wondered about the wedding chest. Should she ask? No, another diversion would take her further from where she needed to be.

'Okay,' she began then found she didn't know how to continue. She gazed out at the desert sands but there was no help to be had there. *What* had he been saying before she was thrown off track?

Shopping, suitable clothes, protocol—

'Okay?' Gaz prompted gently, and she turned to face him once again, his gentle smile causing so much confusion she stuttered into speech.

'B-b-but if it's just pretend—just for your sisters—do I have to do all that formal stuff? The "by your side" stuff? I've got my job, you know—well, of course you do—so surely...'

The words fell off her lips as something in his eyes—intensity, or was it intent?—caused such severe palpitations in her chest she couldn't breathe.

It had been intent she'd read. She realised that the moment his lips, once again, closed on hers.

Her mind shut down completely.

Was it a minute or an hour later that he released her? She had no idea, only knew she felt so weak and shaken she had to lean against him, her breath coming in little gasps, her brain slowly returning to work, though not offering much by way of explanation as to why this man, of all the men she'd met in her life, should have such a disastrous effect on her.

Nothing to do with the fact he's the most gorgeous guy in the known universe, the voice in her head suggested.

There was that, of course, but why her?

He eased away, smiling at her, a teasing smile, as if he knew exactly how much damage his kisses did to her.

'I don't think we have to pretend about the attraction between us,' he murmured, and the shiver that ran down Marni's spine told her just how dangerous this situation was.

'But that's different. It's the betrothal thing—*that's* the pretence.'

She was babbling again!

'So you're not denying the attraction?'

The words may have been innocent but she heard the challenge behind them and glared at him.

Pulling herself together with a mammoth effort, she tried again.

'I'm not talking about the attraction, Gaz,' she began, then hoped she wasn't breaking some unknown protocol by continuing to call him that. 'I know I started this nonsense about the betrothal by showing you the picture and, yes, when you said it would help you out, I kind of went along with it. But appearing in public, wearing clothes, meeting people, deceiving them really, well, I don't think that's quite me.'

'You'd rather meet people naked?'

It was the glint in his eyes as much as the words that made her want to belt him one. Except she probably *would* be thrown into a dungeon if she hit the ruling prince.

Would that be such a bad idea? A nice cool jail cell with no diversions?

'You know what I mean,' she retorted. 'It's not so much the fuss and public stuff, though that's mind-boggling enough, but the—the deception. I mean, your family, your mother, people who care about you, what are they going to think when the pretence ends and I go back home?'

He smiled and took her hand, rubbing his thumb across the backs of her fingers, sending tingling messages along her nerves and searing heat through her body.

'Don't worry about that for an instant—they'll all blame me. I've been a lost cause to the family ever since I insisted on studying medicine instead of business or commerce. It's one of the reasons I thought I was safe from the ruler's job, but as it turned out, there are so many people in our parliament and public service with all the right degrees, the fact that I don't have a huge amount of knowledge about international business isn't a disadvantage.'

Somehow his mood had changed and Marni sensed hidden depths in this man, for all he joked about the 'job'.

'But you *do* know people, surely that's more important than a business degree,' she said softly, and his hand tightened on her fingers.

'Ah!' he said softly. 'So someone understands.' Uncertain what he meant, Marni was about to ask, but he'd turned to look out at the desert again, and she sensed a remoteness in him, as if he was disconnected by his thoughts.

Disconnected from her as well.

Did someone not want him to be the ruler?

Someone in his family?

Or did he feel detached from his family?

Had it been a real problem for him, going against their wishes to follow his own path? He had certainly seized on her silly betrothal photo, grabbing it like a drowning man would grab a tiny stick, so his sisters' representations must have been bothering him.

And now you're back at the betrothal!

Had he guessed that her thoughts had returned to it that he turned back to her and lifted his hand to tuck a stray lock of hair behind her ear?

'Maybe our betrothal could turn out to be more than a pretence, Marni,' he suggested, his voice deep and husky.

With desire?

She was still wondering when he continued, 'We may not know each other very well, but there's time enough to remedy that, and you can't deny the attraction between us.'

His eyes held hers.

No, she couldn't deny the attraction, but…

She shook her head.

'I'm sorry, but I simply cannot imagine what would lie ahead, so how could I possibly agree to anything?'

'I would be there with you all the way. I would give you every support, give you anything you needed or wanted,' he said, his voice so serious she found herself shivering, although the air was warm.

The tension in the shade of the tent was palpable now, so thick Marni imagined she could feel it pressing against her skin and taste it on her lips.

But how to break it?

'Let's just go with the betrothal for now,' she said. 'And maybe keep it quiet—just letting your sisters—your family—know. You can use the excuse of Pop's operation—blame me for not wanting a fuss at this stage. Then if you need me to accompany you to official functions, I can start slowly, so it isn't some big deal but something people gradually get used to. Would that be possible?'

He rested his palm against her cheek.

'Anything is possible,' he said, as he slid the hand behind her head to draw her close.

The kiss was so gentle she responded in spite of herself.

Responded and was lost.

Admittedly, with Pop and Nelson's opinion of her always in her mind, she'd come late to the kissing scene, although she'd eventually made up for lost time, exchanging kisses with any number of young and not so young men over the years.

But had she ever experienced a kiss that made her toes tingle?

A kiss that sent shivers spiralling along her nerves, sensitising the skin at the back of her neck, along her arms, across her breasts, not to mention other places previously immune to spiralling shivers?

Not that she could recall.

And surely if she had, she wouldn't have the other problem.

Dear heaven, she was melting, disintegrating, a helpless mass of quivering flesh.

His hand was moving on her arm, leaving lines of heat where it had touched yet still his lips held her in thrall, held her and seduced her, his searching tongue making promises she barely understood.

Eventually he lifted his head, looking down into what was undoubtedly a face flushed scarlet by her reactions.

'I'll need to find you somewhere to live,' he said as calmly as if he hadn't just destroyed any common sense and will-power she might once have had. 'The harem would swamp you, drive you mad with all their so-called help. My sister, Tasnim, the pregnant one, would be best. Her husband is away so she'll enjoy the company. She's banished all the women in her family to the main harem because they were fussing over her too much, but she'll love to have you visit.'

Still trying to collect herself post-kiss, Marni could only stare at him. Then, as the words took on a slightly suggestive air, she pulled herself together.

'I have a perfectly good little flat at the hospital,' she reminded him.

He smiled in such a way the shivers started all over again, but rather than pointing out that he couldn't be seen visiting her at the nurses' quarters, he merely said, 'Security!' and helped her up off the mat, leading her back to the car, seeing she was buckled in.

Was he really intending to go through with this absurd betrothal? Gaz asked himself as he eased the vehicle back down the dune.

He thought of the kiss and the fires it had lit within him, then shook his head at the absurdity of the situation.

Was it lust or simply one-upmanship against his sisters that was making him push it?

And if it was lust, wasn't becoming betrothed to her the one certain way of ensuring he couldn't act on the lust—well, not beyond a few very heated kisses?

Very, *very* heated kisses, he amended, thinking of the taste of her, the softness of her lower lip as he'd sucked it gently into his mouth...

He glanced at the woman who sat so quietly beside him, the colour subsiding from her cheeks. If he could only get past his visions of how good they'd be in bed, maybe he could think clearly about the future—the immediate future anyway.

Men in his family didn't marry for sex. Such appetites could be satisfied in other ways with willing partners who were well looked after financially when the arrangement ended.

Not that he'd had any such arrangements, though there'd been affairs, some almost serious, during his student and university days.

But marriage?

Essentially, one married to produce children, but also, more often than not, for political reasons—uniting warring tribes, gaining power against a neighbour, improving the bloodlines of their breeding horses or camels.

He found himself chuckling at the thought and when the blonde who'd exploded into his life turned towards him, he shared his thoughts—not the children part, but the rest.

She grinned at him.

'Well, if your camels need some improvement in their genetic make-up then even being betrothed to me might ruin your chances with someone whose father has vastly superior camels.'

He reached out to touch the silvery fair hair.

'My camels will just have to take their chances, although you have no idea what a sacrifice I'll be making. My family have bred beautiful camels for generations. And we expect to win most of the prizes at the annual camel show.'

'A camel show? The camels all on show? How are they judged?'

Her interest was so apparent he felt warmth stirring inside him—something quite different from the heat he'd experienced earlier. This was pleasure, pure and simple—pleasure at how this woman took such an interest in everything about his country, a genuine interest that went beyond politeness. He wanted to stop and talk to her again, this time about the camels—*his* camels—but the palace was in sight and he'd already stolen too much time out of his schedule.

He slowed the car then stopped so he could explain.

'I must go back to my office before someone sends out a search party, but Fayyad will drive you to the hospital and wait while you pack, then take you to Tasnim's house. Fayyad will let me know when you are on your way and I will meet you there. In the meantime, I will phone her and explain and organise a permanent driver for you if you want to continue to work while we make the necessary arrangements for our betrothal.'

He saw the objections rising in her mind but before she could launch them he claimed her lips once again, thankful for the darkly tinted windows in the vehicle for they were right outside the palace gates.

He felt her resistance, but only momentarily...

CHAPTER FIVE

MARNI SANK DEEP into the softly cushioned seats in the black limousine and battled to make sense of the day. Not even a full day, for it was still early afternoon. Yet here she was being driven to her flat under orders to pack and go off to stay with a total stranger—a pregnant stranger—who would help her deal with being betrothed to the country's ruler.

How had this happened to her?

She certainly hadn't set out to become betrothed to the man—all she'd wanted was for Pop to have his operation.

Pop!

What on earth could she tell Pop?

She heard the groan that escaped her lips then realised she needn't tell him anything—not yet. All she had to do was email to say she'd kept her part of the bargain and met Ghazi, and she expected Pop to let her know the date of his operation.

Ghazi!

The Gaz-Ghazi thing was a whole different problem. Yes, she'd been attracted to Gaz right from the beginning, but the man she'd been kissing wasn't Gaz, he was Prince Ghazi and given that the betrothal was a pretence, she really should stop responding to his—Gaz's? Ghazi's?—kisses.

Shouldn't she?

Nothing was going to come of it—of the kissing business. Given her private reason for coming to Ablezia, she might well have had an affair with Gaz if things had turned out differently, like if he'd been Gary from Australia, but she had a nasty suspicion that rulers of places like this didn't have affairs with women to whom they were publicly betrothed. With other women probably, but not their betrotheds.

And as for the other nonsense he'd been talking—about how maybe the betrothal would not be a pretence—well, that was just ridiculous. He was the ruler of his country. He might have joked about a suitable marriage for the good of his camels, but surely, in all seriousness, there would be certain expectations of him in regard to marriage—either political or familial—and she doubted she'd be considered suitable by any of his advisors or power-brokers.

She buried her face in her hands. 'Oh, Pop, what have you got me into?' she whispered, but Pop was a million miles away and hopefully in hospital so he was no help. She'd just have to sort this out on her own.

Why in the name of fortune was he doing this? The question lurked in the back of Ghazi's brain as he talked with supplicants who had been given lunch while waiting for his final decisions on their claims. His officials looked into all the claims then gave him their opinions so he could make a judgment. He discussed land rights, and the sale of camels, and fixed a bride price for the father of a young woman keen to marry out of her family—marry a foreigner, in fact.

Ironic, that! Should he be offering a bride price to Marni's grandfather?

Marni!

Her name sang its way into his conscious mind and he needed Mazur's discreet cough to bring him back to the subject at hand—an altercation over the placement of two stalls in the souk.

'Your families have worked stalls side by side for generations,' he told the two men sitting cross-legged in front of him. 'Why the trouble now?'

'It's his daughter,' one said.

In chorus with, 'It's his son,' from the second man.

'They like each other?' Ghazi guessed.

'Too much,' the father of the daughter spat. 'But she is already betrothed to a distant cousin—from when she was four—but young people these days!'

The situation was far too close to this morning's astonishing revelations, and he was feeling more and more uncomfortable as the two men explained all the reasons why their children should not marry, and therefore why their stalls should be moved so the young people were not in constant contact.

'A betrothal at such a young age need not stand,' Ghazi said cautiously, ignoring the fact that he was pushing for just such a betrothal to stand in his own situation. 'Times have changed, my friends, and if these two love each other, instead of fighting, can you not put your heads together and work out a way for them to marry and be happy? After all, you could then combine your stalls and have twice the space and twice the customers, surely. I could possibly arrange extra space for the expanded stall, by way of a marriage gift for the couple.'

Behind him, he heard Mazur's sharp intake of breath, and knew he'd overstepped some invisible barrier, but if the two young people were genuinely in love…

He heard the phrase—genuinely in love—echo in his head and wondered if he'd lost his mind.

'I want to see both of them,' he said, 'to hear from them how they feel. Make sure they are at the next citizens' meeting.'

Thus dismissed, the two men departed, united now, he had no doubt, in horror over what he had suggested.

'Genuinely in love!' Mazur mocked. 'What on earth has got into you, Ghazi? Since when was love a factor in the settlement of disputes? Or in marriage, for that matter?'

Ghazi turned to the man who was not only his first advisor but also his best friend, aware he had to be careful.

'We must move with the times, Mazur,' he said. 'You know full well that the system of arranged marriages is not infallible—many such marriages fail and many of our people seek and are granted divorces. Maybe marrying for love will be more successful—and don't start quoting me figures from the West where people do it all the time. I know about their divorce rates. But young people have always longed for love, so surely if they find it, can we deny it to them? Can we break up two families by standing in the way of these young people?'

He was obviously losing his mind, Ghazi decided as Mazur gave a disbelieving snort and walked away.

Surely it couldn't have been the couple of kisses he'd shared with Marni that had him turning an age-old tradition on its head.

Marrying for love?

No wonder Mazur was snorting.

Marni packed her things then sat on the bed in the small bedroom and tried to work out exactly what she was doing.

And why.

If you're finding it hard to make a decision, write a list, Pop had always said. That was how she'd decided which university to attend, which course to take, even, one slightly embarrassing time, which of two young men would take her to the hospital ball.

So, mentally, she made her list.

For going along with Gaz—Ghazi—on this betrothal thing was that she would be doing him a favour, and it was never a bad thing to have a favour owed.

Besides, Nelson had said he'd been a nice little boy who'd been very kind to her at a time when she'd been desperately alone and confused, so maybe *she* owed *him* one.

Then there was Pop, who'd be delighted, and by the time the betrothal ended, however they were to manage that, he'd be over the operation so could handle the news without too much of a problem.

And...

She couldn't think of an and!

Well, she could, but she'd already decided he probably wouldn't seduce her while they were betrothed.

Against—well, that was easy. The disruption in her life for a start, the hassle of whatever the betrothal would entail in the way of public appearances, the interruption to her work, having to get new clothes—

She smiled to herself and wondered if that should go on the 'for' list...

Then there was Gaz.

Was he a for or against?

A bit of both really, because as Gaz she liked him and more than liked his kisses, but as Ghazi, wasn't there something wrong with kissing him if their betrothal was only pretend?

Fayyad would be wondering what had become of her, but still she sat, looking down at her watch as she tried to work out what time it would be at home.

If she phoned Nelson, she could ask him what he thought, ask him what she should do, as she'd always asked him what to do, relying on his common sense and good judgement.

But Nelson had enough on his plate right now, looking after Pop, so she was on her own.

She stood up, grabbed her suitcase and made her way down to the foyer and out to the door, where Fayyad waited patiently in the car, climbing out when he saw her to open the back door for her.

'I need to stop at the hospital to see a patient,' she told him, feeling guilty because with all the 'will I, won't I' that had gone on in her head about attending the citizens' meeting she hadn't seen Safi for two days. 'I'll be half an hour, maybe a little more. Do you have to wait in the car, or can you go into the canteen and have a cool drink or a coffee?'

Fayyad smiled at her then lifted a Thermos and a book to show her.

'I am never bored while waiting,' he said, 'but thank you for your consideration.'

His English was so good she wanted to ask where he'd learned it but remembered that personal conversations seemed not actually forbidden but perhaps impolite. She must ask Gaz.

Ask Gaz?

Just because he'd kissed her it didn't mean…

Didn't mean what?

And surely the kisses hadn't made her feel more at ease with him than she did with Jawa, for instance?

Totally muddled, she watched as Fayyad pulled up in front of the hospital.

'I will be watching for you,' he said, as he opened the door for her, making her feel a total fool. She thanked him and hurried inside, hoping none of the nurses she knew had seen her stately arrival. But the staff entrance was around the back so she should be safe.

These niggling worries hung around her like a cloud of summer midges as she walked towards Safi's room, but vanished as soon as she entered. She'd vaguely been aware of intense activity in one of the rooms she'd passed, and a lot of scurrying further down the passageway, but surely whatever was going on, someone would have checked on Safi recently.

His face was pale but red spots of fever burned in his cheeks and his thin fingers plucked at the dressing on his lip while his body turned and twisted on the bed.

'Safi!' she said, coming to take the hand that worried at his dressing, feeling the heat of it.

She found the bell and pressed it, then grabbed a towel and ran water over it in the little attached bathroom, wringing it out then bringing it back to sponge his face and chest, his arms and legs, desperate to cool him down before the spike in his temperature could cause a seizure.

No one had answered the bell.

She pressed it again, talking soothingly to the little boy, careful not to touch the dressing as his wound was obviously causing him discomfort, or more likely, pain.

He was staring up at her, wide-eyed, panic and pain in equal measure in his face.

'It will be all right,' she said, and although she knew he wouldn't understand her words she hoped her voice would soothe him. Her voice and the cool, wet towel…

Wrapping the towel around his head like a turban so it

pressed on his temples and the back of his neck and could cool surface blood vessels in both places, she grabbed his chart. Thankfully all charts were written in English because of the imported staff, and although she couldn't read exactly what he'd been given at the last check, she could tell that it had been at ten in the morning.

Had no one seen the child since then, apart from ward cleaners and the maid who'd carried in the meal that was uneaten on his table?

Giving up on the bell, she carried the chart out into the corridor, heading for the nurses' station, needing urgent attention for Safi and ready to demand answers.

The place was deserted, although she could tell there was still a major commotion in one of the rooms she'd passed earlier and a fair level of noise coming from a room further up the corridor.

There had to be a nurse in one of those rooms.

Three nurses and two doctors, in fact, and a crash cart pushed to one side.

'She just went flat,' the nurse Marni hauled into the corridor explained, 'about two hours ago. The doctors thought we'd lost her but she's coming round now.'

Marni accepted it had been an emergency but that only accounted for three of the nursing staff.

Not that she had time to complain! She hurried the nurse towards Safi's room.

'I came to visit, and there he was, burning with fever.'

'Oh, not Safi!' the nurse wailed. 'I'll have to page Gaz—he insists on knowing any change in Safi's condition—and get a ward doctor in as well. Can you go back and sit with Safi for a few minutes?'

She looked about her and frowned as if she'd just become aware of the emptiness of the corridor and nurses' station.

'I've no idea where the others are,' she added, peering vaguely around.

'I don't care where they are,' Marni snapped. 'I just need someone to see Safi and see him now.'

She might have raised her voice just slightly, but she was pretty sure she'd kept it below a shout, which was what she'd really wanted to do.

Hurrying back to Safi's room, she wet the now warm towel and bathed him again, pressing the cold cloth on his wrists and in his elbow joints, below his knees and against his neck and head, talking all the time, wishing she knew his language, wishing she would somehow conjure up his mother for him, for his little body was now slack, his eyes closed—the fight gone out of him.

The nurse came in and Marni stepped back while the woman checked his pulse, temperature and blood pressure, then a young doctor appeared, looked at the figures and fiddled with the drip, checking the catheter in the back of Sufi's thin hand, making sure the tape was in place.

'I've been off duty for a few days but I know that since the wound in his hip where they took the bone from has healed quite well, he's been walking around the hospital, even going outside at times. He must have picked up an infection,' the nurse suggested as the doctor drew blood for testing.

An infection that could cause such a rapid response?

Marni wondered about it but said nothing—in this room she was a visitor.

And she was still angry that the rise in his temperature hadn't been picked up earlier, before he'd become so distressed.

Gaz's arrival provided answers. He must have been on the phone during his journey from the palace to the hospital, telling her, as he examined Safi, that apart from the child who'd needed resuscitation, an accident to a school bus had brought a rush of, thankfully, minor injuries to the hospital, diverting staff to the ER, then to top it off the mother of another patient in the post-op ward had gone into labour and actually given birth in her daughter's hospital room.

'Still no excuse,' Marni thought she heard him mutter, but the barely heard words were followed by a rush of orders, arranging for Safi to go straight to Theatre.

'But with his fever—with the infection still so active?' Marni protested.

Gaz shrugged.

'Unfortunately yes. His temperature rose the day before yesterday and we've had him on vancomycin, which is usually the most effective drug for multi-resistant bacteria, but it obviously isn't working. I need to remove the grafted bone before the infection spreads into good bone.'

He paused for a moment, then said, 'There are still staff problems. Will you scrub?'

'Of course!'

An orderly appeared to wheel Safi to Theatre and Marni backed out of his room so he could be moved, waiting until he was wheeled out then falling in behind the little procession.

Gaz was walking beside the gurney and turned to glance back at the woman who'd erupted into his life, spinning it in a direction he'd never expected it to take— well, not right now.

She'd come from what must have been a fairly momentous day, given the job he was thrusting her into, to see a child she barely knew, and now was quite happy to spend however many hours it would take in Theatre for

Gaz to remove the bone graft because there was no way the infection could be anywhere else.

She'd stripped off the abaya and was wearing jeans and a loose shirt, and just the sight of her stirred thoughts he shouldn't be having right now.

'I suppose the infection can't be anywhere but in the graft?'

Marni had caught up and was walking beside him, but apparently her mind was still firmly fixed on Safi. Gaz swung his mind back that way, determined to concentrate no matter how distracting he found his colleague.

'The site's red and swollen and obviously painful. The nurse who changed his dressing this morning should have noticed and alerted someone.'

'I wondered,' Marni said, 'but I didn't like to touch it.'

'You did enough, cooling him down and alerting the staff. Without you—'

He stopped, so angry, so upset for the little boy he needed his own language—and bad words from it—to release his rage.

But not at Marni!

'Thank you for being there—for caring enough to call in to see him,' he said, and lifted his hand to touch her on the shoulder. 'From me and from Safi!'

She didn't move away from his touch but turned towards him, the slight frown he'd seen before creasing the smooth creamy skin of her brow—and even a frown caused inappropriate reactions.

'But he's been on antibiotics since the operation—I saw that on his chart—and you've started stronger antibiotics—would they not work in time?'

Gaz shrugged.

'I daren't take the risk. Yes, there's risk involved operating when he's harbouring something bad, but...'

He sighed, before adding, 'I thought because our hospital is so new we'd avoid things like this for a few more years. The problem is that so many of the bad ones target bone, and the grafted bone is likely to be badly compromised.'

The crease in his companion's forehead deepened.

'So you'll take the graft out, then how long before you could do another one? You'd have to clear the infection first, and where could you harvest the bone? His other hip?'

Her mind was obviously more focussed than his had been—no inappropriate reactions for Marni!

'I'll take it out, that's enough for Safi today. Later, when we know he's clear of infection, yes, I'll have to harvest some new bone and, yes, probably from his other hip. Poor lad. He's been through so much and bears it all so bravely. I'd have done anything to have saved him from this.'

They'd stopped in the corridor outside the theatre changing rooms; the orderly and nurse pushing Sufi's gurney moved on and through the theatre's swing doors.

'Will he be able to go home to his family before the next op?'

Gaz studied her for a moment, so aware of her as a woman it was hard to concentrate on the question she was asking.

'And why do you wish to know?'

A faint colour rose in her cheeks.

'Well, if you must know, although I genuinely care about Safi and want what's best for him, I'm so darned confused about all that's happened today, and then walking along beside you as if *nothing* had happened, well, it seemed best just to keep talking about practical things rather than have a fit of hysterics in the hospital corridor.'

Her cheeks grew pinker and her eyes dropped to study the floor between their feet, and he felt an overwhelming urge to give her a hug—a big hug, a warm hug, a non-sexy hug, although how long the non-sexy part would last was a moot point.

'Me too,' he said, ignoring the urge. He touched her lightly on the elbow and waved her through the door into the changing rooms.

He'd obviously made good use of his time during his trip from the palace to the hospital, for an anaesthetist Marni had worked with before was already attending to Sufi, talking quietly to him as he set his drip on a stand and prepared to give him a pre-op sedative.

Jawa was also there and greeted Marni warmly, although she did raise her eyebrows.

'But you're off duty,' she murmured.

'And doing me a favour.'

It was Gaz who answered for her, coming into the theatre behind her.

'It is Marni who found Safi so ill,' Gaz added, causing Jawa to look from him to Marni, so many questions in her beautiful dark eyes Marni knew she'd have some explaining to do later.

Personal explaining, for all it might go against the local custom!

Three hours later, Safi was wheeled away to Recovery, the open wound where the graft having been cleaned out and left with a drain in it to leach out any more of the poison. Marni felt tears prick at her eyelids and knew it was tiredness—well, tiredness and the stress of the totally bizarre day, *and* her heartache for little Safi, who had already suffered so much, and underlying it all her worry over Pop...

Gaz caught her arm as she was about to follow Jawa

out of Theatre. He'd pulled his mask down so it hung loosely below his chin, and the fine line of beard was a little ragged. His eyes, however, still held her gaze, drawing her into the darkness...

'You are exhausted,' he said gently. 'I would suggest you go back to your flat here at the hospital but Fayyad tells me all your things are in the car. Let me drive you to Tasnim's. She is expecting you and will have waited up for you.'

Marni dragged her attention back from his eyes and nodded, too tired to argue, and anyway he was right, all her belongings were in the car. She slipped into the changing room, and again saw the questions in Jawa's eyes.

'Tomorrow,' she said to her friend. 'I'll return your abaya and explain tomorrow. I'll meet you at the canteen at ten.'

But could she explain?

Explain it all?

And how would a local woman feel about her ruler's betrothal to a foreigner?

Not to mention if she said it was a pretence.

So many questions to which she had no answers...

The ruler in question was waiting for her in the corridor.

'Is it going to cause you problems with your people, this betrothal?' she asked as soon as she was close to him. 'I know it seemed like a good idea at the time to get your sisters off your back, but what about the local population? Might they not be offended in some way? Feel I've cheated you, or you them?'

Gaz—he was definitely Gaz at the hospital—stared at her for a moment then shook his head.

'Do you worry over everybody?' he asked, the smile

in his eyes, and somehow in his voice as well, making her stomach curl.

'Of course not, but Jawa must be wondering what's going on and I wouldn't like—well, she's been so kind to me, I really have to try to explain to her before you do this breaking me to the public gradually business, and then I thought—'

He brushed his knuckles across her cheek and her mind went blank.

'That I might be lynched, or deposed, for getting betrothed to a foreigner?'

Marni managed to nod, but with Gaz so close and the sensation of that touch lingering on her cheek, she found it impossible to speak.

Or think.

And only just possible to breathe.

'Stop fretting,' he told her, 'and that's an order!'

He then put his hand gently on the small of her back—again—and propelled her down the corridor, into the car and out again only minutes later, in front of the low open patio of a house the size of a hotel.

Tasnim was a short, glowing, heavily pregnant woman wearing designer jeans—who knew designers made pregnancy jeans?—and a tight purple top stretched across her swollen abdomen.

She greeted Marni with a warm hug and made no secret of her delight.

'This will be such fun!' she said. 'I was bored out of my brain. I did keep working but got so fat I couldn't sit behind the desk any more and Yusef—Ghazi's told you he's my husband, hasn't he?—said to stop, then the wretched man took off to Europe for some round of international monetary fund talks and just left me stranded here.'

Marni could only stare at the beautiful, bubbly, excited woman.

'She *can* talk,' Gaz said, giving his sister a kiss on the cheek and asking where Fayyad should put Marni's luggage.

'Oh, Ahmed will take it.'

Tasnim waved her hand towards a white-clad figure and the luggage disappeared.

'But are you sure this is okay?' Marni finally managed to ask. 'Me being here, I mean?'

'Of course,' Tasnim told her, giving her another awkward hug. 'Not only will I have the fun of getting clothes for you—and spending lots and lots of Ghazi's money—but every one of my sisters will be green with jealousy that you're here and not with them.'

She clapped her hands.

'Oh, it will be delicious!'

'But I wouldn't want your sisters—' Marni began.

'Don't worry,' Gaz told her, resting his hand on her shoulder. 'They play these games of one-upmanship all the time, my sisters, but they still all love each other. Just wait, they'll be vying with each other to give you the best gifts, take you to the best silk shops, the best seamstresses.'

Marni closed her eyes as she realised this whole betrothal thing had spun right out of control and taken on a life of its own. She turned to Gaz so his hand fell off her shoulder, which did make it slightly easier to think.

'I can't take gifts,' she said, which was as close as she could get to protesting in front of Tasnim. 'It wouldn't be right!'

'Of course it's right,' Tasnim argued. 'You're his betrothed.'

But it's pretend! Marni wanted to yell, and as she couldn't, she made do with a glare at the man who'd got her into this situation.

Well, it had been partly her fault...

Perhaps mostly her fault...

'She's exhausted,' she heard Gaz say. 'What she needs is food, a bath and bed, and no teasing her for explanations or gossip or any chat at all!'

'Yes, Master,' Tasnim teased, 'but don't think I'm going to turn round while you kiss her goodbye. We've all been waiting far too long for you to fall for someone.'

He hasn't fallen for me, it's all pretence, Marni wanted to say, but didn't because even thinking about it made her feel a little sad and, anyway, Gaz was obviously giving his sister a piece of his mind, so stern did his words sound. Then, with one last touch on Marni's shoulder, he stalked away.

'Come,' Tasnim said. 'I won't tease you.'

She took Marni's hand and led her through a bewildering maze of corridors, across carpets with glowing jewel colours, through arches with decorative plaster picked out in gold and set with precious stones. The rooms she'd seen in the palace had been plain, though there, too, the carpets had been beautiful, but this was like some fantasy out of an old-fashioned book and, tired as she was, it took on a dream-like quality.

'Here!' Tasnim finally said, going ahead of Marni into a room the size of her entire hospital flat. A huge four-poster bed, hung with dark blue silk curtains, dominated one end of the room while the inner walls were lined with a paler blue silk, padded somehow and indented with buttons of the same colour.

'The bathroom is through that door and a dressing room through the one next to it. You'll find plenty of clothes in the dressing room because we like our guests to feel comfortable and sometimes they may not have brought clothing that will fit special occasions.'

She flung open a door into what looked like a very expensive boutique. A long rack down one side held clothes ranging from ballgowns to tailored shirts and skirts, while further down were jeans and slacks and even, she rather thought, some long shorts.

The other side of the room had shelves of shoeboxes and drawers containing exotic-looking underwear, still in its original packaging, and beyond the drawers long, filmy nightdresses.

For the harem—no, seraglio—belly dancers? was Marni's immediate thought. Wasn't this proof they still existed?

'Not that you need any fancy clothes here,' Tasnim was saying. 'Wear whatever you like. Now I'm pregnant, I do cover up with an abaya if I go into the city, but I always worked in Western clothes.'

Marni wanted to ask what work she did, to find out more about this lively, fascinating young woman, but tiredness had fallen on her like a great weight.

'Have a bath and go to bed, Tasnim ordered. 'I'll have a light meal sent up to you—just eat what you want. Tomorrow we'll talk.

'Thank you,' Marni said. 'I *am* tired.'

CHAPTER SIX

SHE'D ENTERED A world of fantasy, Marni realised when she woke in the luxuriously soft four-poster bed to find a young woman sitting cross-legged by the door, obviously waiting for the visitor to open her eyes.

'Good morning, I hope you slept well,' the young woman said, rising to her feet with elegant smoothness. 'I am Shara and I am to look after you. I shall bring you whatever you wish—some tea or coffee to begin with perhaps, then you must tell me what you wish for breakfast. Ms Tasnim sleeps late and has her breakfast in bed.'

'A cup of tea would be wonderful,' Marni told her. 'English tea if you have it. I can drink mint tea later in the day but need the tea I'm used to to wake me up.'

The girl smiled and disappeared, her bare feet making no sound on the marble floor, although Marni fancied she could hear the swish of the soft material of the girl's long trousers and the long tunic she wore over them.

Marni had a quick shower and, aware of her appointment with Jawa at the hospital, dressed in one of the pairs of loose trousers she'd brought from home, adding a tunic in her favourite deep blue-green colour.

'You dress like us?' Shara commented when she returned with the tea.

'I decided before I left home that if I was going out

in public it would be polite to follow the local customs,' Marni told her. 'In my flat, and possibly while I'm staying here, inside the house, I might pull on my jeans.'

'I am the opposite, I wear jeans outside,' Shara said. 'This is just a uniform for work.'

Marni sipped at her tea, wanting to know more—about Shara, about Ablezia, about—

'You speak such good English,' she said. 'Did you learn it at school?'

'At school and at college too, and I listen to recordings at home as well. I am training to work in hotels, you see. We are building many hotels now in our country and they will all need staff. One day, I would like to manage one, but first I must learn the basics of housekeeping, then I must learn how to run a kitchen, not to cook but to understand what goes on, then—oh, there is so much to learn.'

She flashed a bright smile at Marni, who smiled back as she said, 'You'll go far, I'm sure.'

'Not if I don't get a breakfast order from you,' Shara said, still smiling. 'The chef will have my head. What would you like?'

What would she like?

'What do you have for breakfast?' she asked.

'You would like to try a local breakfast?' Shara asked, obviously delighted.

'As long as it doesn't take too long to prepare. I have to be at the hospital at ten.'

Shara disappeared, returning with a round brass tray on which nestled six small bowls. In the middle of the tray round flatbread was folded into cones, the whole thing like some wonderful display made for a picture in a food magazine.

'Here,' Shara said, as she set it on the small table by an arched window. She pulled a plate out from under the bread and a napkin from beneath that again, and waited for Marni to sit. She then pointed to each dish in turn.

'This is labneh, our cheese, a bit tangy but soft, and dahl, you know dahl from lentils, and these are eggs mixed up and cooked with spices, some olives, some hummus, and here is honey, and jam, apricot, I think, and halwa—you know the sweet halwa?'

'It looks fantastic but I can't possibly eat it all,' Marni protested, and Shara laughed.

'You just eat a little of whatever you want. You use the bread to scoop it up or there is cutlery on the plate if you prefer to use that. Now, we would drink tea but tea you have had, so perhaps coffee?'

Marni agreed that she'd like coffee and as Shara disappeared once more, Marni began to eat, scooping bits of one dish, then another, trying them alone, then together, settling on the spicy eggs and labneh as her main choices and eating far more than she normally would for breakfast.

Coffee and dates finished the meal, and as she was thanking Shara, Tasnim burst into the room.

'I've come to make plans,' she announced, but before she could continue Marni explained she was meeting Jawa—and soon.

'Oh!' Tasnim was deflated but not for long. 'That is good. I send you with a driver in the car to the hospital and when you are finished with your friend he will bring you to the Plaza Hotel. The shops there are discreet and we can enjoy shopping without a crowd.'

'The Plaza?' Marni echoed faintly, thinking of the enormous, palace-like hotel she'd seen but had never visited.

'Definitely the Plaza, it is the only place,' Tasnim insisted, before whirling out of the room to make arrangements for a driver.

'You will like the Plaza,' Shara said, her voice so full of awe Marni felt even more uncertain.

'Have you been there?' she asked the girl.

'Oh, no, but I hear it is very beautiful and the boutiques there—well, they are for the very rich.'

Which you obviously are not. Marni felt she could hear Shara's thoughts. She'd know that from unpacking her suitcase.

Marni ignored the questions she'd heard in Shara's voice. She grabbed a scarf to wrap around her hair, found her handbag, then asked Shara to take her to wherever the driver would be waiting with the car.

'I daren't walk out of the room for fear of getting lost,' she told the girl, who smiled but was still treating her with more reserve than she had originally.

Treating her like someone who shopped at the Plaza!

Hell's teeth, Marni thought. Does money really change things so much?

She was early when she arrived at the hospital, so her feet took her automatically to Safi's room. The little boy was sleeping, but she'd barely registered that when her body told her who else was visiting him, although the second person had been in the bathroom, washing his hands, as she'd come in.

He was in full prince gear, so—pathetically—her breath caught in her lungs and her heart stopped beating.

'You look beautiful,' Gaz—no, he was definitely Ghazi—said, crossing the room towards her and taking her hands. 'You slept well? Tasnim is looking after you?'

He raised her hands to his lips and kissed each knuckle in turn, making it impossible for her to answer him.

Soft footsteps in the corridor made him release her

hands and step back, but the look in his eyes was enough to bring all the embers of desire back to ferocious life.

Why *wasn't* he just Gaz?

'How is Safi?' Marni asked, in an attempt to dampen the heat.

'He is well, his temperature is down and his sleep is peaceful,' he replied, then he lifted one of her hands, dropped a kiss on the palm and left the room, muttering to himself.

It had to be the stupidest idea he'd ever had, he decided as he marched away from Safi's room. Here was a woman he desired more than he'd ever desired a woman before and he'd put her off limits by becoming betrothed to her.

And all to avoid the women his sisters were throwing at him!

But could he have accepted any of them, feeling as he did about Marni?

And how *did* he feel about Marni?

He desired her but was that it? Would an affair have satisfied that desire? Could they have shared some mutual pleasure and enjoyment then parted?

He wasn't too sure about that.

There was something about the woman. She was different, and not only in race but in…

Personality?

Guts?

It had taken guts to approach him yesterday, not knowing who he was or what might occur, but she'd done it for her grandfather…

He needed to know her better. He'd go back to Safi's room now.

'Sir!'

One of the junior doctors had caught up with him and

tapped him lightly on the shoulder. Had he called to him more than once?

'Your driver, sir, he has a message for you.'

Back to reality! Gaz strode towards the front entrance, aware his driver would only have sent for him if he was already late for the next thing on his interminable schedule.

Marni held the kiss in her hand as she made her way to the canteen. She felt slightly foolish. The kiss meant nothing so why hold onto it?

Did she want it to mean something?

Want it to mean love?

She shook her head at her thoughts and smiled sadly. Six times so far her mother had married for 'love' so, not unnaturally, Marni had a slightly skewed view of it.

The advent of lust into her life had really confused things, she decided as she dawdled down the corridor. Caught up in its snare, couldn't one mistake it for love?

Want it to be love?

Was that what had happened with her mother?

Again and again and…

She sighed, and put the problem out of her mind. Right now she had to get her head straight and work out exactly what she was going to say to Jawa.

Jawa!

Jawa meant passion or love—Marni had looked it up when she'd learned that most names had meanings. Ghazi—of course she'd looked it up as well—meant conqueror.

Hmmm!

Jawa was waiting in the canteen, two cups of coffee and a plate of sweet pastries on the table in front of her. Marni slipped into a chair opposite so she could look into her friend's face as she spoke.

The politeness of morning greetings and thanks for the coffee held off the revelations for a few minutes but finally she had to tackle the subject she'd come to discuss.

'You know I've mentioned Pop, my grandfather,' she began, then stalled.

'Your grandfather?' Jawa prompted.

'It's complicated, but I didn't know when I met him in Theatre that Gaz was Ghazi, your prince. The thing is, Pop had known him and his father when he was a boy—when Ghazi was a boy—and Pop wanted me to say hello to him while I was here, which was why I borrowed your abaya and went to the palace yesterday, and now we're kind of engaged to help him out with his sisters who keep finding women for him to marry.'

Jawa's eyes had grown rounder and rounder as Marni's disjointed explanation had stumbled from her lips.

'You're engaged to Prince Ghazi?' Jawa whispered, her voice ripe with disbelief.

'Only pretend—for his sisters,' Marni said desperately, but she rather thought that message wasn't getting through. 'And we're keeping it quiet but I've moved in to live with his pregnant sister, for security he says.'

It wasn't making much sense to Marni so she had no idea what Jawa might be making of it.

'The thing is, I don't know what his people—people like you—will think about it, because he should probably be marrying with better breeding stock for his camels.'

Drained now of words, Marni stared hopefully at Jawa, who seemed to have gone into some kind of fugue, although she did manage a faint echo.

'Camels?'

'So what do you think?' Marni eventually demanded, the silence adding to the tension already built up inside her.

'About the camels?' Jawa said faintly.

'No, not the camels, although apparently his camels are very important to him, but about me being engaged to him—betrothed?'

Jawa shook her head.

'I don't know what to think but if it's been arranged—your grandfather and his father—then that's how things should be. I know more of our people are marrying for love these days but arranged marriages have worked for centuries.'

'I'm not *marrying* him,' Marni told her. 'It's a pretend betrothal—because of his sisters—just while he sorts out his job—and then…'

'And then?' Jawa probed.

Marni shrugged.

'I have no idea,' she said. 'It's really all just too stupid for words, but I felt I should tell you because you've been so good to me. I'd like to keep working but we don't seem to have talked too much about that. Tasnim—that's his sister—seems to think clothes are more important.'

'Oh, clothes will be very important,' Jawa said, then she smiled and took Marni's hand.

'I only know him when he's Gaz, of course, as a colleague. He is much respected and admired. From the time he started work here, he has never made anything of his links with the ruling family and no one ever treated him any differently because of who he is. I don't think he expected to take over from his uncle, but he will do his duty well.'

Of course he will, Marni thought, feeling slightly let down, although she wasn't sure what she'd expected of this conversation.

Congratulations?

Certainly not!

Reassurance?

Of course!

'It's the pretence that bothers me,' she said. 'Will people—the local people—be upset when it ends?'

Jawa thought for a moment then turned Marni's hand in hers.

'I do not think so. They will accept his decision, whatever it is. Those who thought it was a bad idea to marry a foreigner will say at last he's come to his senses, and those who liked the idea will think, ah, that's the trouble with love because they will have been sure it was a love match.'

A love match?

For some reason, far from reassuring her, the words sent a wave of melancholy washing over Marni and she took back her hand—it wasn't the one with the kiss in it—and sighed.

Love, of course, was the other reason she had the virginity problem—her mother's version of love...

The Plaza Hotel was surely bigger than the palace!

That was Marni's first thought on seeing it as they drove up a long drive to an immense building spread across the top of a slight rise.

And far more opulent, she realised as she entered the enormous lobby so gilded and arched and carpeted it looked more like a posh showroom of some kind than a hotel.

Tasnim was waiting, perched on a chair beside a lounge setting.

'Would you believe they don't have ordinary chairs like this in the lobby?' she demanded, when she'd greeted Marni with a kiss on the cheek. 'I had to ask someone to find one for me. There's no way I could have stood up from one of those low, soft sofas without making a total fool of myself.'

Marni smiled, doubting the formidable Tasnim could ever make a fool of herself anywhere.

'Come,' Tasnim continued. 'We'll be given refreshments in the boutique. I phoned ahead and asked for my favourite one to be closed for us. The women from the other boutiques will come there with whatever else we need.'

A shop closed so she could shop? Once again Marni found herself in fantasy land.

'I've made a list,' Tasnim told her. 'I thought half a dozen everyday things for a start. Just things like you're wearing today so your way of dressing doesn't offend anyone. Then half a dozen formal outfits—two kinds—Western for entertaining diplomats and other foreigners, and Eastern for entertaining locals. And some casual clothes for at home and for when Ghazi visits.'

'I have my own clothes for at home,' Marni protested as they entered the boutique, a woman bowing them through the door.

'Nonsense! You can't be wearing the same thing every time you see Ghazi, now, can you?'

Couldn't she?

Marni felt a little lump of sadness lodged beneath her breast.

Because she knew Ghazi didn't really care *what* she was wearing?

Probably!

Although he *had* said she looked beautiful this morning...

The lump remained.

Tasnim was talking to the saleswoman, the words rattling around the beautifully set-up salon.

Marni was checked out, looked up and down, ordered

to turn around, then told to sit on a low love seat and offered tea.

She shook her head and looked about her. There was only one gown on display—a Western evening gown made of some silvery material, and sewn with beads and crystals so it shimmered under a discreetly placed light.

It appeared perfectly simple in style and cut and yet was breathtakingly beautiful.

'Local things first,' Tasnim declared, returning with the saleswoman and a young woman who was pushing a trolley hung with clothes, spectacular clothes in rich greens and blues, long loose trousers, patterned and beaded tunics that would go over them and at the end of the rack a selection of black abayas.

An hour later, Marni was the rather hesitant possessor of four new pairs of trousers and five new tunics. She'd put her foot down over Tasnim's suggestion she'd need half a dozen, listened in disbelief as Tasnim and the saleswoman claimed to have hundreds of such outfits, and had been talked into the fifth tunic because it was so beautiful.

It was the simplest of them all, not bright but a pale blue-grey with a pearl-coloured thread woven through it and the patterning around the bottom in the pointy-topped shape of the local arches, picked out in darker blue.

As for the abayas! Far from the plain cotton garment she'd borrowed from Jawa, these were woven from the finest silk, with delicate ebony bead embroidery around the hem, sleeves and neckline. Beautiful garments to cover other beautiful garments.

The fantasy deepened!

'If you choose a couple with hoods, it will save you tying a tight scarf over your hair when you go out,' Tasnim advised. 'Abayas used not to have hoods as we wore a hijab—a specially tied scarf—over our heads. But with the hoods, any of your scarves would go under the hood.'

The saleswoman hung the abaya Marni had tried for size back on the rack—on the buying side, not the reject side—and studied Marni yet again.

'Surely that's enough for one day,' she begged Tasnim, but her new friend wouldn't be distracted.

'We haven't done the scarves,' she scolded. 'If you're insisting on only having four outfits, at least you can vary them with scarves.'

Long scarves, as fine as gossamer, were produced, most in tantalising colours, all embroidered in different ways.

She was wearing the tunic she'd been unable to resist, and the woman found a scarf in the darker blue of the embroidery and draped it around Marni's head and shoulders.

'Perfect. It makes your skin gleam like alabaster and turns your eyes as blue as cornflowers,' Tasnim said, clapping her hands in delight. 'But you will need more. Darker ones are good for evening, and if you have a darker one over your hair, you can still tie it hijab style and need not pull the hood of the abaya over your head.'

Marni assumed Tasnim was talking sense but she was lost. She found herself drifting, doing whatever Tasnim or the saleslady told her, lost in the mad dream that had become her life.

The evening gowns were unbelievable—like things she'd seen actresses wearing on the red carpet when the Oscars were televised. And the names of the designers— names she'd heard with awe and had never in her wildest dreams imagined wearing clothes they'd designed.

But she was also tiring fast and after trying on and removing the sixth evening gown she found the energy to protest.

'Tasnim, we've settled on three, that's enough,' she said, although her eyes strayed to the silver creation on the shop model.

Tasnim saw her look that way then she said, 'Just one more,' and spoke to the saleswoman, who immediately began disrobing the mannequin.

'It's made for you with your fair skin and hair,' Tasnim insisted, and when Marni put it on she knew she had to have it. She'd never considered herself beautiful, but in this dress?

She remembered Gaz saying after dinner at the hospital that she was like a silver wraith—well, in this dress she almost was.

So why was that lump back in her chest and her heart hurting, just a little bit?

'Sandals next,' Tasnim decreed, and another saleswoman appeared pushing a trolley laden with shoeboxes. Marni gave up. She pushed her feet in and out of sandals, stood in them, walked around, and finally settled on a few pairs, although it seemed Tasnim was making her own decisions as at least ten boxes were piled together while the rest were wheeled away.

But when make-up and perfume were suggested, Marni stood her ground.

'I can handle that myself,' she said firmly. 'I have my own make-up and have always used the same perfume, a particular scent my grandfather first bought me when I was eighteen. I'm not changing that!'

Tasnim argued she needed more than one so she could choose according to the time of day and the occasion and the outfit, but Marni was adamant—she'd wear her own, any time, any day, anywhere!

Exhausted by the decision-making, all she wanted to do was go home—well, back to Tasnim's place, and lie on the bed, and try to make sense of all that had happened to her.

Although wasn't that bed part of the fantasy?

But Tasnim was ruthless.

'Of course we can't go home,' she said. 'We need to go over to the palace and get you some jewellery. Ghazi won't want people thinking he's too mean to give you jewellery and until he's got time to buy you some, there's a ton of stuff over there. Some of it's a bit old-fashioned, which is why we sisters all insisted our husbands bought us more—but we all got plenty of the family stuff in our bridal chests.'

Marni stopped outside the boutique to study the woman who'd taken over her life.

'Aren't pregnant women supposed to get tired and to need a lot of rest?' she demanded.

'Oh, phooey,' Tasnim replied. 'You sound like my mother. I'll rest later!'

So, to the palace they went, Marni regretting she hadn't stayed in one of her new outfits in case they ran into Ghazi, but that was stupid, wasn't it?

Once at the palace, Tasnim summoned Mazur and must have explained what they wanted for he led them through more tortuous passages, finally unlocking what looked like, but couldn't possibly have been, a solid gold door. Pulling a huge, old-fashioned key from beneath his kandora, he unlocked the door, pressed numbers on a very modern-looking security system pad, then turned on a light to reveal an Aladdin's cave of riches.

'Oh!'

Marni breathed the word, unable to believe that a picture from a childhood book could be springing to life in front of her. Yes, there were neat chests with little drawers in them, and glass cabinets with displays of stunning jewellery, but there were also open chests and large jars from which spilled what looked like all the treasures of the world.

'The children like to play with the chests and jars,' Mazur explained in a very disapproving voice. He was retrieving a long string of pearls from the floor as he spoke, and examining them for damage.

'But I couldn't possibly wear any of this kind of jewellery,' Marni protested. 'I'd look ridiculous!'

'So start simple,' the indomitable Tasnim told her. 'Take those pearls, for instance. They will go beautifully with that tunic you really like. Mazur, a bracelet or bangle to go with them and a ring, of course.'

Mazur poked through drawers, finally emerging with a bracelet that had six rows of pearls on gold wire and fastened with a gold catch.

'Perfect!' Tasnim declared. 'And now a ring.'

The ring he produced had a pearl the size of Tasmania, and Marni refused to even consider it, although a smaller ring, set with rows of seed pearls that went well with the bracelet, won her heart.

'Now that's enough,' she told Tasnim, but the woman was unstoppable. Ignoring Marni completely, she pulled out necklaces, bracelets and rings with stones that looked like emeralds and rubies. Studied them, then declared, 'No, we'll stick to sapphires because of your eyes, but now I am tired. Mazur, could you put together some sapphire sets and send them to my house?'

Mazur nodded, and followed the two of them out of the treasure trove, locking the door behind him before walking them out to the car. The driver held the door for Tasnim, while Mazur did the same for Marni, murmuring, as she slid past him, 'I am very happy for you and Prince

Ghazi.' Marni sensed the kindly man actually meant it and immediately felt depressed.

She hadn't realised just how much she would hate deceiving people—maybe not people generally, but nice people like Mazur.

Fortunately Tasnim seemed to have finally run out of steam so the drive back to her home was quiet.

'I *will* rest now,' she said, 'but the driver will take you wherever you wish to go, or you can ask Shara for anything you need if you decide to stay in your room. The boutique will package up all we've bought and send it here, probably by later today, so you can choose what you want to wear to dinner tonight.'

'Dinner tonight?' Marni queried.

Tasnim smiled.

'Did I not tell you? Ghazi phoned to say he would pick you up at seven to take you out to dinner. It will be to somewhere special so—no, I won't let you decide. I'll come to your room later and we'll decide together what you will wear. Remember, this will be your first public appearance and although as yet your betrothal is not known, people will notice you and begin to talk.'

Marni's stomach knotted at the thought, but she *had* agreed and she'd gone along with the purchase of all the new clothes so she couldn't deny being aware that they would be needed.

'Okay,' she said, letting the word escape in a sigh.

But underneath her trepidation a bud of excitement began to unfurl.

She would be seeing Ghazi—how easy it was to think of him that way after being with Tasnim most of the day—tonight!

Which was really pathetic if she thought about it. This was all pretence!

CHAPTER SEVEN

THE EXCITEMENT HAD waned by the time she was dressed, waiting with Tasnim in the big room at the front of the house. Her own reflection, as well as Tasnim's cries of delight, had told her she looked good, but uneasiness boiled inside her.

This dressing up in clothes paid for by someone else seemed to underline the fact that it was all pretence, and the subterfuge made Marni feel queasy. It was one thing to pretend for the sake of his sisters but for other people that she would surely meet, people who looked up to him as their ruler—was it right to be deceiving them?

'Ghazi will not be able to take his eyes off you,' Tasnim was saying, 'and how he'll keep his hands off you— whoo-hoo, it will be near impossible. Such fun!'

Considering her more personal reason for being in Ablezia, Marni would have liked to ask if Ghazi would *have* to keep his hands off her, as Tasnim seemed to be intimating. But that question was far too personal—too fraught with hidden mines and traps to even consider asking.

Beside which, she was reasonably certain formal betrothals didn't include the couple going to bed together, while actually making love with the ruler of a country—

any country—was so far beyond Marni's imagining it had to be impossible!

'The car is here!'

Tasnim's—was he a butler?—appeared, and made the announcement, then vanished in his usual silent way.

'Oh, bother Ghazi,' Tasnim muttered. 'He's sent a car, not come himself, and I did want to see his face when he saw you looking so beautiful.'

'It's just the clothes,' Marni told her, using words to hide the little stirring of disappointment at Gaz's non-arrival, and her embarrassment over Tasnim's praise.

'No, it is you,' Tasnim argued. 'Of course the clothes help, but you have a serenity about you that enhances whatever you are wearing, and that's part of true beauty.'

As if! her head mocked, but Tasnim's words helped ease Marni's disappointment, and she walked out to the car, slipped into the back seat and settled her beautiful new clothes around her.

Cinderella going to the ball, was her first thought, but if that had been the case she'd have been wearing one of the ballgowns.

And glass slippers!

She sighed and wondered just what lay ahead of her on this, the second momentous day in this new, and totally fantasy, life.

Lost in her thoughts and concerns over pretence, she barely noticed where the driver was taking her until she saw the palace looming up ahead.

'We're going to the palace?'

Duh!

'No, miss, we're going to Sheikh Nimr's home. His wife, Sheikha Alima, is preparing a special banquet in your honour.'

A special *banquet*! Great!

Fortunately Gaz was at the top of the steps as the vehicle pulled up and it was he who came down to open the car door for her, taking her hand to help her out, the light in his eyes as he took in her appearance enough, for a moment, to still her nerves.

'You are beautiful,' he murmured, for the second time that day.

'It's the clothes—the dressing up in this gorgeous gear—anyone would look beautiful,' she said, trying for lightness, although her fingers clung to his for support.

His smile told her he didn't agree, and it was the smile, plus the sensations firing through her that made her remove her hand and regain some common sense.

'A banquet?' she queried.

'Only a small one,' he assured her, smiling as she spoke. 'Having put all the sisters' noses out of joint by asking Tasnim if you could stay with her for a while, I have to start the conciliation process. Believe me, growing up with seven sisters is better training in diplomacy than any university degree.'

They had reached the top of the steps, and he paused, turning towards Marni to explain.

'I have to start with Alima because she is the eldest. She has invited two other sisters, Meena and Ismah, and their husbands, as well as Nimr's brothers and their wives, the married ones. A small party and you do not have to remember everyone's names and if I don't get you inside very soon I shall have to kiss you right here and scandalise everyone.'

Marni had been trying to get her head around the names and wondering why only two sisters had been invited—with Tasnim she would now have met four of the seven—when Gaz—in a business suit so definitely Gaz—had added the last bit.

About the kiss…

So it wasn't *all* pretence…

Of course not, there's still the lust, she reminded herself, dousing her re-smouldering embers.

They paused at the front door, Marni preparing to slip off her sandals and noticing the ease with which Gaz removed his highly polished loafers.

'You learn our ways,' he said quietly.

'This one's easy,' Marni retorted, unsettled by the lust reminder as well as by his nearness.

The lust wasn't pretence.

Neither was it love!

But love's not been any part of this, the sensible part of Marni's brain responded.

And the funny lump of pain sneaked back into the middle of her chest.

'Have you an extremely tidy mind that you need to reposition your sandals three or four times, or are you having second thoughts about meeting the family?'

Gaz was waiting for her to move away from the neat array of sandals.

Marni pulled herself together and looked directly at him, hoping all her doubts and inner discussions weren't visible on her face.

'Only two of the other sisters?'

He smiled and her heart turned over.

Love not part of this?

'I'm breaking you in gently. I think you'll find Tasnim has already asked the others to lunch one day next week. Alima set the limits—ordered them all not to crowd you—and what Alima says goes with the women.'

He took her hand and placed it on his forearm, tucking her close to his side as they walked through the wide entranceway. Marni glimpsed the huge majlis off to the left, and was relieved when a white-clad servant bowed them into a smaller, though no less opulent room.

Where shades of yellow from palest lemon to deep, rich gold had been the dominant colours in the rooms Marni had seen in the palace, it was red that struck her here. Swathed red silk curtains framed arched openings into what appeared to be a courtyard garden, while deep vermilion couches were pushed back against the walls. The floor, again, was marble, but a creamy colour, streaked with red, so Marni wasn't surprised to find the woman walking towards her, hands outstretched in welcome, was also clad in what must be her favourite colour.

'My sister, Alima,' Gaz said smoothly. 'Alima, this is Marni.'

Alima clasped Marni's hands and drew her closer, kissing her on both cheeks—air kisses really, although the warmth of the woman's smile seemed genuine.

'What I wonder,' she declared as she looked Marni up and down, then down and up again, 'is how our father knew his son would be so difficult to please as far as women went, so he solved the problem early on, betrothing him to you.'

'I think it was probably a joke,' Marni said, the words popping out before she realised it was probably the wrong thing to say. But Alima was unfazed.

'My father *never* joked and, believe me, having cast upwards of a dozen beautiful and intelligent women in my brother's path over the years, I am more than ever convinced of my father's prescience.'

'You do rattle on,' Gaz said to his sister, but Marni heard fondness in his voice. 'Now, do your duty and introduce Marni around. I've told her she needn't remember all the names—in fact, any of them except for Meena and Ismah, and I assume you've seated her near them for dinner.'

Gaz—why when he was with Marni did he think of himself this way—watched Alima lead Marni into the throng, seeing the way the fluid material of her tunic swayed about her body, noticing the strands of fine silvery hair escaping from the dark blue shawl she'd draped over her head.

His silver wraith!

His body had tightened the moment she'd stepped out of the car, and he was sorry he'd chosen to wear a suit tonight. His kandora hid far more than trousers.

A string of oaths echoed through his head. He'd brought this on himself, betrothing himself to her, so if he wanted her, and he did, he'd better organise a wedding, and soon!

'Well chosen, brother!' He turned to find Nimr standing beside him. 'But you'd better secure her before my boys are old enough to challenge you. Karim is already in love with her—he talks of nothing but the soccer-playing blonde he found in the gardens.'

'Surely he's too young to be thinking of women,' Gaz protested, and Nimr laughed.

'Don't believe it for a minute. They mature early, our boys, and didn't we, as youngsters, believe an older woman could teach us much?'

Gaz laughed but he was looking around the room at the same time, and realised that not only were all four of his nephews included in the party—very smartly dressed in miniature suits—but Karim was right now chatting up Marni, making her laugh at something he'd said.

He's twelve, he reminded himself as he moved away from Nimr, easing his way through the crowd, hopefully unobtrusively but heading for his fiancée nonetheless.

'We'll have to lead the way into dinner,' he said when he arrived, taking Marni's arm in a possessive grasp. 'It's the way things are done.'

'Oh, but dinner won't be for ages,' Karim told him, 'and there must be people you have to see.'

'People Marni has to meet as well,' Gaz said firmly, at the same time telling himself he couldn't possibly be jealous of a twelve year old boy.

He was leading Marni towards Ismah's husband when two youngish men swerved into their path—Nimr's youngest brothers, unmarried as yet and more than a little wild. He introduced Marni and was pleased at their manners, although, as they moved away, Marni smiled and said, 'The wild ones of the family?'

The effect of the smile left him floundering to catch up with the question, and he had to find an echo of it in his head before it made sense.

'What makes you ask?'

Even that was a stalling tactic—he was still trying to come to grips with why a smile would stir his blood and have his body thinking about ravishment.

Marriage or distance—they were the only two options—and hadn't he promised he wouldn't rush her into marriage?

Well, not actually promised…

Although marriage hadn't been an issue when he'd asked her to pretend to the betrothal!

'They look like young men who are constantly seeking amusement—the kind that usually leads to trouble. I've met young men like them staying as guests at the hotel, young men with too much money and too much time on their hands, always looking for what they call fun but which often translates into something illegal.'

He heard the words but his mind was still following his

body down the sex trail so he took little notice, although the word 'hotel' registered enough to give him the glimmer of an idea.

'Will you give me your grandfather's phone number? I should have asked before. I must phone him to—'

Marni giggled.

'To ask for my hand in marriage? Oh, really, Gaz! That is so old-fashioned. Besides, he is in hospital. Nelson emailed this afternoon to say the operation will be within the next few days.'

The giggle—such an inconsequential thing—had further activated the inappropriate desire he was feeling, but the idea was even better now. Out there, in Australia, anything might happen...

'Then we should fly out right away. You will want to be there when he has the operation and I can stay in the hotel so I don't put your Mr Nelson out at all.'

Pale eyes looked up at him, no mirth in them now, only fear and sorrow.

'He definitely doesn't want me there, Gaz,' she said softly. 'That's the main reason I'm over here. He's a proud man and doesn't want me to see him all weak and tied to tubes in the ICU, or have me around while he's recovering. I promised him I'd stay away.'

'But you'll be riven with worry and concern and feel helpless because you're so far away.'

She tried a smile but it wavered with apprehension and he wondered if the response that burned through his body might not be more than lust.

'I'll just have to deal with it, won't I?' she said, the smile getting better. 'I promised! Besides, I'd be just as helpless there! I know he's in the best possible hands.'

'Ghazi, you must not monopolise your betrothed in this manner!'

Alima had appeared and before he could object, she whisked Marni away.

He'd drive her back to Tasnim's later! At least that way they could kiss.

But wouldn't kisses make the longing worse, the desire stronger?

Maybe putting some distance between them would be better...

Marni allowed herself to be led through the crowd, introduced to this one and that, realising Gaz had been right, she'd *never* remember all the names. Meena would be easy. She was very like Tasnim in looks.

'We are full sisters,' the pretty woman explained, 'the daughters of our father's third wife, the one before Ghazi's mother.'

'I was just thinking I'll never remember everyone's names and now you're making me realise I'll have to remember relationships as well.'

Meena touched her softly on the arm.

'Do not worry. It will come to you in time. For the moment, it is more than enough for us all that Ghazi is happy—that he has found the right woman to love.'

The 'love' word had its almost predictable effect in Marni's chest, but she was getting used to it so ignored it, reminding Meena instead that it wasn't love but an arrangement made by her father.

'Ah, but the old ones know,' Meena said. 'My marriage was arranged but when I met my husband I knew my father had been right for there was no one else in the world I could love as much.'

Intrigued by a culture so different from her own, Marni couldn't help asking, 'Were all your marriages arranged?'

The question was probably too personal but Meena didn't seem to mind.

'Not really, although when Alima was about eight she decided she was going to marry Nimr, so then our father and our uncle betrothed them. Ismah met her husband at university in America. He is from a neighbouring country and will one day rule it so our father couldn't object to him. Tasnim, of course, just told our father she was going to marry Yusef and no one could ever argue with Tasnim.'

'I can understand that,' Marni put in, but if Meena heard her she didn't show it, continuing on down or up the family tree.

'Our other sisters, well, you'll meet them eventually, but Zahrah is married to a Westerner, the son of one of our father's old friends and advisors, Maryam is married to her work, she is a doctor like Ghazi, and Rukan is married to another of our cousins. They were both betrothed to others but ran away to get married and our father forgave them both because they were obviously meant for each other.'

Just as Marni decided it would be impossible to remember even the sisters' names, Alima rescued her, taking her off to meet other guests, including Ismah, a slight, plump woman with such beautiful eyes Marni could barely stop staring at her.

'She is beautiful, yes?' the man beside Ismah said, and Marni could only nod and smile.

'As are you,' Ismah said quietly, and Marni shook her head. Among these exotically beautiful women she faded into oblivion.

Gaz returned to lead her into dinner, explaining on the way that although all those present were family, the women would still sit together at one end of the table and the men at the other.

Marni smiled at him.

'Sounds like an Aussie barbeque,' she said. 'The men in one group the women in another.'

'Here it makes sense as most of the women live with their husbands, so at gatherings like this they enjoy gossiping with the other women, and the men enjoy catching up on politics or, more likely, the latest football scores and transfers.'

'*Most* of the women live with their husbands?'

His turn to smile.

'As against the old days when they would all have lived in the harem, visiting their husband in his tent, or later his palace, when invited.'

The teasing glint in his eyes made Marni's insides flutter. What had she got herself into, and where was this going?

Had he read the questions in her eyes that he gave her hand, where it rested on his arm, a slight squeeze before abandoning her to his sisters at the women's end of the table?

To Marni's great relief the meal was not a banquet in the true sense of the word, with endless plates of food laid out in the middle of the table. Instead, light-footed serving women offered plates of this and that, placing small or large spoonfuls of each dish directly onto the guests' plates.

And contrary to her impression that personal conversation was off limits in this country, she was peppered with questions about herself, her home and her family.

'We all remember that visit to the beautiful hotel,' Ismah told her. 'Alima and Rukan were betrothed already, but Maryam and Meena flirted shamelessly with the young man who worked on the concierge desk, flashing their eyes at him and teasing him so he blushed whenever one of us came near, because he couldn't really tell us apart.'

'You flirted too,' Meena reminded her. 'And remember the day Zahrah went out without her abaya, in Western jeans and a T-shirt and her hair in a ponytail for everyone to see.'

The sisters laughed.

'Oh, I remember that,' Alima said. 'She went to Sea World to ride on the big roller-coaster and she was so sick she had to ring the hotel and ask them to send a car to take her back there.'

'And Father said she'd shamed the family and would never get a husband.'

'That's probably why he sent her to America,' Meena said, and the women laughed, as if that had been a good thing, not a punishment.

The talk turned to other holidays, other places all the women had stayed at one time or another, London and Berlin apparently favourites with them all. Sitting listening to them, Marni realised how at ease with each other they all were, even the women married to Nimr's brothers.

Was this normal in all families?

Not having one—not an extended one—she couldn't judge, but their obvious closeness once again reminded her that her position was a false one, and the niggle of disquiet that rarely left her these days began to make itself felt more persistently.

'I will drive you home.'

Gaz appeared at her side as the women left the dining room. He took her hand once again and placed it on his arm in the formal manner he had used before.

She said goodbye to the women she had met, sought out Alima to thank her for the evening, then let Gaz guide her to the door, exhaustion nipping at her heels as the tension she hadn't realised she'd been feeling drained from her.

Pausing at the front door, she managed to get one sandal on but was having trouble with the second when Gaz knelt and slipped it on her foot.

'Oh, no!' she protested, not sure whether to laugh or cry, 'that is just far *too* Cinderella! Is your car a pumpkin?'

He looked at her, bemused, but at least it gave her something to talk to him about, explaining the story of Cinderella and her prince.

'They were real, these people?' he asked, driving through night-quiet streets, the engine in the big saloon purring quietly in the background.

'No, it's a children's fairy-tale,' Marni told him. 'It's just that I can't help thinking of it.' She paused, then added quietly, 'Probably because it's easier to be thinking of my life right now as a fairy-tale than be worrying over deceiving nice people like your sisters and their friends.'

He had pulled the car over as she was talking and she looked around, seeing a long wall with an arched opening in it, an ornate gate protecting whatever lay behind the walls.

'You have the photo,' he said, turning and taking both her hands in his. 'How is there deceit?'

'It's pretence—you asked me to pretend, remember, to get your sisters off your back.'

'And it is working,' he said, lifting her hands and kissing the backs of her fingers, one by one, so she had to struggle to keep her brain working while her body melted from something as unsexy as finger kisses. 'So much so they are asking about the wedding—about when it will be.'

If finger kisses had melted her bones, talk of a wedding sent such heat washing through her she could barely breathe.

Had to breathe!

Had to protest.

'But we're doing this to give you time to get to know your job,' she reminded him, hoping he wouldn't hear just how shaky her voice was. 'A wedding, even if we wanted to marry—well, the kind of fuss that would surely entail would interrupt your schedule far more than just being betrothed. It would be a terrible distraction.'

He didn't reply, simply using his grasp on her hands to draw her closer then dropping his head to kiss her on the lips.

'This particular distraction,' he said a long time later, tilting her head so he could look into her eyes, 'is interrupting my schedule more than you could ever know. If we were married there'd be *one* distraction less.'

She frowned at him.

'Are you talking about sex? Is that the distraction that's so hard to handle?'

He kissed her again, but lightly.

'Do you not find it so?' he teased, and just as she was about to admit she felt it, too, she remembered the virginity thing and was flooded with embarrassment.

Should she tell him now?

But how?

What would he think?

That she was frigid, or had something wrong with her?

Or decide she was pathetic, locked in adolescence, as the last man she'd dated had. Christmas cake, he'd called her, apparently a foreign insult for an older virgin, dried out the way a cake did after the twenty-fifth of December.

He'd laughed at the notion that there was anything special about virginity—not that she'd considered it that way. As far as he'd been concerned, it was nothing more than an embarrassing nuisance. Men, he'd told her, expected a woman to have had experience and be able to please a man in bed.

And that had been a man she'd thought she loved!

The thought of telling Gaz—of his reaction—made her tremble. It was one thing to think she could tell some man with whom she was having a virginity-relieving fling about it, but telling Gaz?

'I think we'd better just stay betrothed,' she muttered, her voice sounding like a very creaky gate in desperate need of oil.

CHAPTER EIGHT

'ARE YOU TIRED, or would you walk with me a little way?

Marni, who'd been expecting an argument, or at least further discussion, over the marriage business, was startled.

'Walk?

'In the oasis,' Gaz said, waving a hand towards the gate. 'Have you been there?'

'I remember going past the wall on my way somewhere, but haven't been inside it. Won't it be dark?'

'Wait and see,' Gaz said. He was already opening his door, coming around to open hers and offering his hand to help her out.

He led her to the gate and unlatched it, ushering her inside onto a path between what seemed like a jungle of palm trees. The path was lit by lampposts placed at intervals, and the palms were lit from below by soft floodlights.

'It's like an enchanted forest,' she whispered as they walked through shadows.

'It has been here for thousands of years,' Gaz explained. 'There is a spring, and our ancestors built a series of narrow canals out from it so the palms would thrive. It is here for all our people to enjoy, and the dates are free to anyone who wishes to pick one or many.'

The soft air smelled sweet, and a slight breeze ruffled the fringed palm leaves, so it seemed as if they walked through a world apart.

'Will you pick one?' Marni asked, enjoying the sight of the palms growing so closely, and the little paths that led this way and that but still wondering what they were doing here, given the late hour and the marriage conversation, which seemed to have been forgotten.

'Of course, that is why we are here.'

He held her hand and was leading her to the right then to the left, taking paths seemingly at random. Yet when he answered, she'd heard something in his voice—something that was Ghazi, not Gaz. This place must be special to him—like the desert—part of who he was...

Why?

'Dates and camels, these have kept my people alive down through the ages,' he said quietly, apparently answering her unspoken question. 'The date is especially miraculous as it can be eaten fresh, or dried and kept for months while the tribes travelled across the desert. The pulp makes sweets and bread, the seeds can be ground for flour, the fibrous mass that holds the dates is used for brooms, the palm leaves for thatch. But it is the legend that brings us here tonight.'

'A legend?'

'A story like your Cinderella. You reminded me of it when you told me your fairy-tale. The date grove is the one place a betrothed couple may walk together without a chaperone.'

Marni looked around and smiled.

'I can understand that—they can hardly get up to much with the narrow pathways and the little canals and the prickly fronds of the date palms pressing in on all sides.'

'Ah, but they walk together for a reason,' Ghazi said,

stopping by a heavy cluster of ripening dates drooping from a palm. 'Our legend says if they find the perfect date, ripe and ready to eat, and they feed it to each other, not only will their marriage be fertile but they will live long together.'

'Just live?' Marni queried. She knew she should be protesting the marriage thing again, yet here she was querying a single word.

Had she been hoping the legend would say live and love?

Of course she had! It was the silly lump that kept forming in her chest causing this sudden longing for—

Love? Get over it, Marni! Love was never the issue here! It's the marriage thing you should be worrying about!

She knew he was talking marriage now so they could go to bed together—a marriage dictated by lust. Although she hadn't seen much of her mother since she'd abandoned her daughter to Pop and Nelson, she had memories of her mother's desperate search for love, and understood now how lust could be mistaken for it.

Did she want that?

No!

'Of course live,' Ghazi said, his attention still on the cluster of dates. 'Aha! I have it.'

He plucked a date and turned towards her, holding it to her lips so she could take a bite.

'Just a bite,' he warned. 'You must then feed me.'

Ghazi was watching her, his eyes intent, his fingers moving closer to her lips.

It's only a legend, she told herself, but her heart was pounding and suddenly being fed a date—well, half a date—by this man was the most erotic thing that had ever happened to her.

Her body afire, she opened her lips and bit into the sweet, juicy flesh. Ghazi's thumb brushed her lower lip and she felt her nipples peak beneath her tunic and a near orgasmic heat between her thighs.

'Now you,' he said, his voice so husky it rasped against her sensitised skin.

He handed her the date and she lifted it towards his lips, her fingers trembling as he opened his mouth and his even white teeth bit into it, taking it and her finger and thumb into the moist cavern of his mouth, suckling at them while her body pulsed with need.

He released her fingers, disposed of the seed then drew her close so they embraced within the heady scent of the dates, and her body pressed against his, feeling his reaction to the tasting, wanting him so badly she was beyond all rational thought.

Never had he held such a responsive woman in his arms—never felt a need that matched his own in its ferocity, and he'd gone and betrothed himself to her and so put her off limits for the moment. He could not tarnish her name with his family or his people by sneaking in or out of lodgings or hotels, and both the palace and Tasnim's place were off limits for the same reason.

He could kiss her, but kisses made things worse—but he couldn't not kiss her…

Ghazi groaned and held her more tightly, pressing the softness of her body against his, fitting the two halves that were man and woman together to make a whole, aware she must know just how much he wanted her.

'It's like a madness, my desire for you,' he whispered, before his lips closed on hers, seeking to devour her, to draw her body into his, to make her his for ever.

For ever?

The words echoed in his head.

Surely he didn't mean it.

Yes, he desired her, and would marry her if only to assuage that desire, but such desire—lust even—did not last for ever. He knew that from experience. Marriage, then a suitable arrangement to end it and no one any the worse off. Marni, in fact, would be better off, although he was aware her grandfather must be a wealthy man. But her settlement would certainly include a house and enough money to live on without having to work—she'd take whatever jewels he gave her during the marriage, it would all be worked out by his advisors and—

She was pulling away from him, peering up at his face as if to read it in the shadows.

'You're not with me in this kiss, are you?' she asked. 'I think it best you take me back to Tasnim's.'

He didn't argue, couldn't, yet as he walked with her, back the way they'd come, he felt a sense of loss—not for the kiss, there'd be other kisses, but because of the conclusions he had reached.

Although they had to be the correct ones, the best for both of them, surely...

Tasnim had been in bed when Marni had returned the previous evening, but Shara had been waiting up for her and Marni had asked the young woman to wake her for breakfast in time for her to get to the hospital to do her shift.

She didn't know what Gaz might have arranged at the hospital, but she was due on duty and she'd decided that was where she most wanted to be. At least there she could concentrate on work and forget all the mind-boggling stuff going on in the rest of her life here in Ablezia, as well as her worries over Pop's imminent operation.

So, early next morning, reminding Shara to explain to Tasnim, Marni went out to the car Shara had arranged for her, feeling like her real self in her uniform and hospital shoes.

Cinderella back in the kitchen after the ball!

Jawa was surprised to see her, yet pleased.

'As far as we know, there's been no change in our work schedules so if you hadn't turned up we'd have been a nurse short. We're in Theatre Three with the Frenchman for the morning, then with a paediatric orthopaedic surgeon this afternoon.

'Good. We should be busy,' Marni said, knowing she needed something—anything—to distract herself from thoughts of Pop.

And Gaz!

And *marriage,* whatever that might have meant...

Not to mention memories of the last time she'd told a man she was a virgin...

Work went well, and Marni enjoyed the sense of teamwork that was typical of operating theatres—the moments of drama, the excitement when a tricky bit of cutting or stitching was successful, the quiet pleasure when a job was done.

As they finished their shift, she and Jawa left the changing rooms together.

'Coffee?' Jawa asked, but Marni shook her head.

'I want to sit with Safi for a while. I've been neglecting him lately.'

It was mostly true, but when she'd checked her phone for messages earlier she'd found a text from Nelson telling her Pop's operation was going ahead that day.

Working out the time difference, she knew he'd be in Theatre right now, and although she knew worrying about it was pointless she couldn't help feeling anxious, tense and sick-to-her-stomach nervous. Neither did she want to return to her current abode and have to explain her concerns or distraction to the ever-bubbly Tasnim.

'So I'm really hiding here,' she said to Safi when she entered his room and settled by his bed, taking his hand in hers. She knew he didn't understand her but the slight pressure of his thin fingers told her he was glad she was there.

She sang the songs she knew he liked and watched him drift off to sleep, before picking up his chart and checking what had been going on with him.

As far as she could see, he was doing well.

Pop would be, too! If she couldn't be there, the least she could do was send positive thoughts in his direction.

You *will* get through it! You *will* be well!

'I thought I'd find you here. Tasnim phoned to say you'd sent the driver home and would take a taxi later. Drivers will always wait, you know.'

Marni smiled up at the man who'd entered the room so silently he'd been standing beside her before she realised it.

And before her body reacted?

She *must* be distracted!

'No, I didn't know that,' she said, trying for lightness, although she felt strangely intimidated by the white-robed Ghazi.

'Is it your grandfather?' he asked, pulling over a chair and sitting beside her, taking her free hand in his so the three of them were linked.

Marni nodded.

'He's in Theatre now.'

Had he felt a tremor in her hand that his fingers tightened on hers?

'I could organise a hook-up to the hospital so you know exactly what's going on,' he offered, rubbing his thumb back and forth across the palm of her hand—distracting her in spite of her concern.

'Nelson has promised to contact me when it's over and he's spoken to the surgeon,' she said, turning to look at him, reading his sympathy in his dark eyes, feeling weakness all through her that this man should care enough to be here for her.

Not that she could let him see her reaction. He was being practical—sensible—and she could do both!

'I know the routine of the op, and that makes it both easier and harder,' she said. 'They'll open his chest and bypass the two stents in his coronary arteries before opening his heart to replace the valve.'

'You've seen the operation before?'

'I worked in the cardiac theatre for a while when I was training. It's a long, hard operation, but generally there aren't too many risks.'

Ghazi took both her hands now and smiled gently at her.

'Or so you keep telling yourself,' he said. 'Now come, you need to eat. We'll go to the restaurant at the top of the building again. You can turn your phone back on up there and be ready when your Mr Nelson calls.'

Marni stared at him, feeling a frown forming between her eyebrows.

'But you've no time for this,' she protested. 'You said yourself you've got a schedule from hell and I've already taken up too much of your time. I'll just sit here for a while then go on back to Tasnim's—even phone her to send a driver if that will make you happy.'

His smile was broader this time, and it started up all the reactions her preoccupation had held at bay.

'If the country's boss can't take time out to be with his betrothed when she needs him, who can? Besides, the dinner I was meant to be attending promised to be boring in the extreme—a meeting of some world soccer association organised by Nimr—and the men attending won't know one sheikh from another. To them we're all just men in long white dresses—so one less will hardly matter.'

Still holding her hands, he eased her gently to her feet, but before he left the room, he, too, looked at Safi's chart and examined the little boy who lay sleeping quietly in the big bed.

'He seems to be doing well,' Marni said, as they walked towards the lifts.

But Ghazi's, 'Yes,' was distracted.

'You're worried about him?' she asked as they waited in the foyer.

'Worried about his family situation,' Ghazi admitted. 'I really don't want to send him home while he recovers enough for another operation, but he's already been away from home for a month and that's a long time for a child. Also, he can't stay at the hospital. I can keep him at the palace, of course. The women would look after him and there are children he can play with, but his family—'

The lift doors opened in front of them and they stepped in, the three occupants inside nodding their heads towards Ghazi, while Marni considered the conversation they'd just had.

This man was the ruler of his nation, battling to come to terms with his 'job' and to meet the demands made of him, yet he had time to worry over one small boy, or made time to worry about him.

He was special—not the boy but the man! The realisation wasn't a total shock—Ghazi had shown his empathy with people before, his being here with her tonight being one example—but…

The warmth unfolding in her chest as she pondered these things was different—not lust at all!

Oh, surely not the other 'l' word,' she thought as they left the lift and a warm hand on her back, guiding her towards the restaurant, sparked her more recognisable reactions. To fall in love with this man would be madness! They were from different worlds, so different she doubted any marriage could survive, especially if the love was one-sided.

He'd spoken the truth when he'd said he wouldn't be missed at the sports dinner, Ghazi mused as he asked the waiter for a table overlooking the desert, but there'd been many other things he could have been doing.

So why was he here?

Kindness—Marni was a stranger in his land and at the moment needed some support.

Right! said the cynic within him. You couldn't have made sure Tasnim or one of your other sisters was with her?

And was support the only reason you wanted to be with her?

Honesty compelled him to admit it wasn't.

He'd *wanted* to see her.

Needed to see her!

Not only to see her but to touch her, even just minimally as touches must be in public.

This was crazy!

This was a betrothal of convenience and somehow he'd allowed himself to become attracted to the woman.

Allowed?

Did one *allow* such reactions to happen, or were they beyond human control?

Surely not! He'd always been able to control such impulses before.

'Sir?'

The waiter had obviously asked him a question as both he and Marni were looking at him, obviously puzzled.

'Sorry!'

He dragged his mind back to the present. This was hardly the time to be questioning his behaviour.

'This time you will choose what we eat,' he said to Marni. 'There is an explanation for all the dishes in English, so you decide.'

He smiled, hoping she'd forget his distraction.

Some hope! She'd no sooner finished ordering and the waiter had disappeared than she asked, 'Are you worried about something? Is it still Safi or was it more important than you made out, this dinner you're missing? Because if it is, or if there's something else you should be doing, I'll be fine on my own. I could even go to Jawa's rooms and wait for the phone call there. She'd understand.'

He gazed at the woman across the table from him, aware how worried she must be beneath her cool exterior, yet here she was worrying about *him*! When had anyone last concerned themselves about his welfare—apart from Mazur and a couple of his closest servants?

She disturbed him in ways apart from the purely physical...

'Ghazi?'

His name, softly spoken, reminded him she'd asked a question and deserved a reply. But there was more—the name itself—more internal disturbance.

'That is the first time you've used my full name,' he said, reaching out across the table to touch her hand where it rested beside her water glass.

Her smile stirred the more usual disturbances.

'That's because when you're in your prince gear I can't help but think of you as Ghazi. Gaz is just a bloke—an

Aussie term for an ordinary man—but in that get-up you have to be Ghazi.'

She paused then added, 'But don't think you've distracted me with this talk of names. You're obviously worried about something and if it's that I'm keeping you from where you should be, please believe I'll be okay on my own.'

He had to smile.

'I know you would. I am coming to realise just how strong and capable my betrothed is, but I want to be with you tonight.' It was his turn to pause, though what he added was, 'In many ways,' which made the colour rise in her cheeks and his own body harden.

Fortunately their dinner arrived, the waiter setting down plates and different dishes in the middle of the table, offering them first to Marni, who had chosen them.

They ate, and talked of food, but he could see her anxiety growing, and noticed the quick glances she was giving her watch.

'Come,' he said, 'we can get a snack at Tasnim's later if we're hungry, but for now we'd be better waiting somewhere quiet. I've an office here, on the floor below. I'll order some coffee and sweetmeats to be sent there and we can both be comfortable.'

The relief on her face told him he'd made the right decision, and although she smiled her thanks as she pushed back her chair and stood up, he knew all she wanted to do was be somewhere private when she heard the results of the operation.

He distanced himself when the phone rang, standing by the windows while she burrowed deep into one of his armchairs, the hand that held the tiny mobile to her ear trembling slightly.

He only heard her end of the conversation but could

tell from the relaxation in her voice that all had gone well, so he was surprised when she'd said goodbye to turn and see the tears trickling down her cheeks.

'Marni? It's all right, isn't it? I heard you saying "That's good" all the time. I realise it will be a while before he's out of the CCU but your grandfather's come through it well, hasn't he?'

Marni scrubbed at her cheeks, ashamed of her tears when everything had gone well. Far better than the surgeon had expected, according to Nelson.

'Are they tears of relief?' Ghazi asked.

He'd taken off his headdress and come to sit on the arm of her chair, his hand resting gently on her shoulder.

'Mostly relief, I suppose,' she admitted. 'I'm sorry to be such a wuss, but when Nelson said goodbye he called me "darling girl". Nelson hasn't called me that for years and I guess it just broke me up.'

'Darling girl! What a lovely phrase. He's something special, the man called Nelson.'

'He is indeed,' Marni responded, resting her head against Ghazi's side and remembering just how special Nelson had always been to her. 'Pop was very good with children but once they started to grow up, girls especially, he became...not embarrassed but less approachable somehow.

'He always blamed himself for how my mother turned out, always seeking love in the wrong places. So it was Nelson who had to check I knew about the birds and the bees—he actually used those words—and he'd call me darling girl when he talked about growing up, and give me little lectures about believing in myself, and about honour and respect and loyalty—all the things he felt were most important in the way we live our lives, all the things Pop lived by but couldn't put into words.'

She looked up at the man she'd been leaning on, suddenly embarrassed by all she'd revealed.

'Not that you need to know all that! It's just the words brought it all back. I'm sorry. You've already been so good, and here I am babbling on about Nelson bringing me up.'

The dark eyes were unfathomable, but as he moved she sensed what was coming and her body tightened as he dipped his head and kissed her on the lips.

'I think I owe your Nelson a big favour,' he said quietly, breathing the words against her skin, then his lips returned to hers and the kiss deepened, taking her away from the past and the present, to where sensation swamped all thoughts.

CHAPTER NINE

COULD SHE BLAME the relief that had set in after talking to
Nelson, or was it just that this man had been so good, so
kind and considerate, so *there* for her, that her response
was so heated when he kissed her the second time?

Somehow, as the kiss deepened, they'd moved, Ghazi
in the chair, she mostly on top of him, her arms wound
around his neck, her body snuggling against his.

His hands were on her breasts, brushing across them,
teasing them to a heavy longing, while his lips explored
her face, kisses brushing eyelids, temple, the little hol-
low beneath her chin.

Her hands explored his back, feeling the hard muscle
beneath the white robe, and ranged across his head, his
beautifully shaped head, dark hair cut close to the scalp,
her fingers teasing at his ears, wanting more contact with
his skin.

Now his lips found hers again, deep, drugging kisses,
while his hands travelled lower, fingers seeking sensitive parts while she squirmed against his hardness and
wanted more and more of him, wanted the feel of his skin
on hers, wanted to know him by touch, to tease him as
he was teasing her.

Could she?

Awareness that she had never felt this way before—

had never known she could—was somewhere in her consciousness, but buried deeply beneath the sensations she was experiencing.

The sensations she was enjoying!

Inflamed by his fingers, trembling on the brink, she heard him saying something but the words didn't penetrate the fog of longing enveloping both her body and her brain.

She moved and felt a shudder of release, a promise of things to come that she didn't fully understand but knew she wanted.

Her excitement must have stirred more arousal in him, for now they were joined in a macabre dance as they tried to strip each other's clothes off, while still kissing, still touching, still stoking the fires in both their bodies.

'There's a couch, for emergency overnight stays,' Ghazi said, half leading her, half carrying her towards an open door at the side of the office.

She glimpsed a small bathroom then an even smaller room, as plain as a monk's cell, one narrow bed against the wall, but Ghazi had stripped off his robe and stood before her, a snowy-white sarong tied around his waist—untied now, the full magnificence of the man revealed.

Her lungs jammed, she couldn't breathe—had to—

He drew her close, her trousers and tunic gone, her bra disposed of next, his lips suckling on her breast, her body in a torment of need as his fingers slipped beneath her knickers, touching her already sensitised nub, and she knew the little whimpering noises were coming from her, although an occasional groan suggested he was as aroused as she was.

Now on the bed, his fingers inside her, feeling the hardness of him against her soft abdomen, need outweighing any lingering doubt she might have had—need, and fear that he'd stop if she admitted—

He mustn't rush! Ghazi told himself.

How could he not?

Control was about the last thing on his mind now this woman who'd been driving him insane with desire was finally naked beneath, or nearly beneath him.

Yet he wanted to savour this first experience of the two of them together, for her sake as much as for his, and the way he felt now he'd be rushing towards a finish like an adolescent boy!

He cupped her flushed cheeks in his hands and pressed a kiss on her lips, slowing himself down, breathing deeply, allowing her time to...

To say no?

Could he stand it?

He didn't have to—not if the way she was returning his kiss was any indication. The kiss was surely her answer to his unspoken question, a kiss that burned along his nerves while her fingers teased his skin, trailing across his abdomen, his chest, brushing against his nipples.

He knelt above her, pressing kisses on her pale skin, sliding his tongue across her nipples while she squirmed beneath the attention, her breath rasping in her throat.

Trailing kisses down her chest, he teased her belly button with his tongue. Her hands were on his head, half holding him back, half urging him on.

He kissed her lower, felt a flinch of uncertainty and returned to use his lips and tongue in torment on her breasts while his fingers did the exploration.

He felt her tightness, warmth and slickness—heat—felt a tremble that told him she was ready, more than ready, her response to his attentions exciting him beyond reason—beyond control.

He took her hand and cupped it around his length, urging her to guide him in. Her fingers were shaking, and he slid his hands beneath her buttocks, easing her off the bed so he could slide inside that hot, moist sheath.

Slide inside now in one quick thrust, the idea of not rushing forgotten in his need to take her, make her his, and himself hers in the give and take of sexual pleasure.

Her fingers slipped away, he thrust again, heard her cry out but it was too late—far too late—her movement beneath him driving him on. Her cries were different now, asking for more, needing more, seeking her satisfaction as well as his.

Her body gripped him, her legs lifted to link around his back, they moved as one until he burst apart, collapsing on her, feeling the quivers in her body that told him she had found her own pleasure and release.

But as common sense returned he realised what had happened and anger surged through him—anger at himself.

He'd taken advantage of this woman at a time when she was most vulnerable, comforting her with kisses that had led to this, never for a minute dreaming she might be a virgin. Then he'd let the desire he'd held in check since he'd first met her take over, when he should have—

Well, there was a lot he should have done.

Al'ana! How was he to know? Women her age...

He heaved himself away from her, sat up on the very edge of the narrow bed, his back to her, searching for something to say.

'You should have told me,' he finally managed, then realised the words had come out as an accusation, not an excuse.

He felt her move behind him and watched as she slid off the bed, briskly gathering up her discarded clothing, her beautiful, slim body silvered by the moonlight through the window.

His body stirred again, almost ready, but she'd straightened now and faced him.

'And have you ridicule me?' she demanded angrily. 'Tell me men expect women of my age to be more experienced? Tell me you're beyond wanting to teach a virgin about sex? I wanted it as much as you did, and I'm sorry if I disappointed you. Now, I'm going to have a shower and get dressed and I'd be grateful if you'd call a driver to take me back to Tasnim's.'

He sat on the bed as the bathroom door closed behind her, trying to make sense of the situation. First the virgin thing, then the things she'd said—she'd been *mocked* because of it?

How hurtful!

How damaging to her.

And now *he'd* made things worse.

Or he thought he probably had.

Seven sisters and he didn't have any understanding whatsoever of women and the stuff that went on in their heads.

Seduced by tears in grey-blue eyes and lips as soft as rose petals, he'd done the one thing he'd been determined not to do—made love to Marni.

And having had her once…

It didn't bear thinking about, but he did know he couldn't sit in the back of a dimly lit limousine with her while his driver took her home.

He picked up the phone and asked Tasnim's major domo to send a car to meet Marni at the entrance to the hospital, but his phone call alerted someone to where he was, because now the phone was ringing, Mazur asking him if he could call in at Nimr's dinner on his way home.

He was arguing about the uselessness of that as Marni slipped out of the bathroom, nodded once in his direction then headed out through his office towards the door.

'Wait, I'll walk you to the car,' he called, while Mazur listed reasons he should do this one thing for his cousin.

Marni turned then shook her head and disappeared from view.

Lost in thoughts of what might have been, of should she have done it or shouldn't she, and all the other questions that had arisen out of their coupling, it took Marni a while to realise the car she was entering already had a passenger.

'Are you all right?' Tasnim asked. 'I know you phoned earlier to say you'd be late home, but I was a little worried, so when Hari, Nimr's youngest brother, who was visiting, offered to come and collect you, I came along as well.'

Marni took her hand and squeezed her fingers.

'You are far too kind to me,' she said. 'I visited Safi, the little boy I've told you about, then Ghazi kindly said I could wait for my phone call from home in his office.'

'Your grandfather's operation? It was today? It went well?'

'Yes, and, yes, and, yes,' Marni said, and for a moment in her pleasure and relief at being able to report that she forgot what had happened after the phone call.

But only for a moment.

What on earth must Ghazi think of her?

How could she have been so stupid as to think it would all be okay?

'What was that?'

She turned to Tasnim, aware the other woman had said something—had sounded concerned.

'We're going the wrong way,' Tasnim repeated, pointing out towards the road.

'I can't help you but surely Hari knows the way. Ask him.'

She hoped she didn't sound as distracted as she felt. As far as she was concerned, Hari could take her out into the desert and drop her there.

Tasnim rapped on the glass that separated the passengers from the driver but when Hari didn't turn, she picked up the handpiece for the intercom, talking into it, then yelling into it.

He didn't answer.

'The wretched boy! I don't know why I agreed to let him drive us tonight. It's just that his brother's away somewhere—Fawzi, the other young one he hangs around with—and I thought he must be lonely to have come for a visit. Then when he wanted to play chauffeur I went along with it. This will be some bet they've had, or some daft joke they've dreamed up. The two of them are always up to something.'

Tasnim was sounding angry and concerned enough to distract Marni from her morbid thoughts.

'Can you phone your home? Tell someone what's happening?' Marni asked.

Tasnim shook her head.

'I was only coming for the ride to collect you. I didn't think to bring my mobile. But you'd have yours.'

Marni felt around her on the seat then remembered Hari—only she hadn't realised it was Hari—taking her handbag as she'd got into the car. He'd put it on the front seat—behind that nice, impenetrable barrier.

A smidgen of concern sneaked into her already tortured thoughts but considering Tasnim's condition, surely it was best to pretend that it was all some kind of joke.

'Well, as there's nothing we can do, we'll have to relax and go along with it,' Marni said, almost pleased to have something other than Ghazi to consider. 'Think of the baby and don't let yourself get upset.'

'Don't let myself get upset? It's ten o'clock at night and I'm usually in bed by nine these days. I was only up because Hari was there and he seemed to want company.'

Tasnim's voice was becoming more and more strident, and concern for her and her unborn child soon outweighed Marni's guilt and anxiety over what had just happened with Ghazi.

'Breathe deeply,' she told Tasnim. 'Calm yourself down. We're in the car, we're safe, and we really can't do anything other than sit back, relax and wait to see what happens.'

'I'll kill him!' Tasnim declared, leaning forward so she could hammer on the heavy screen.

'Later!' Marni said, capturing Tasnim's hands and massaging them, forcing her to lie back against the seat, talking quietly until the distressed woman calmed down.

Forget the joke, Marni now felt almost as much anger and murderous intent towards Hari but she kept it hidden, knowing the most important thing was to keep Tasnim as calm as possible. Eight months into her first pregnancy, a bout of hysterics was the last thing she needed.

'We're out on the desert road,' Tasnim told her, and Marni looked out the car windows, surprised to see the city must be far behind them for there was nothing as far as she could see—well, nothing but the dunes and sand, lit by the headlights as the car raced up the broad highway.

'It's the road to the old palace. That's Hari's joke. He's taking us to join the harem—he probably thinks that's where all the women should be.'

The idea that they were going somewhere specific seemed to calm Tasnim and she rested her head back against the seat, wriggled around to get comfortable, and promptly fell asleep.

Leaving Marni alone with nothing but her memories of what had happened before she'd left the hospital—memories she didn't want, things she most definitely didn't want to think about.

She thought of Pop instead, of how he must be feeling, picturing him in the CCU, all wired up to machines, tubes anchoring him to his bed. How he'd hate it, being so helpless, so reliant on others. Hopefully he wouldn't be conscious enough to be aware of it.

Her heart ached for him, but Nelson would be there…

The car stopped, but definitely not at any palace for, looking around, Marni could see nothing but desert and more desert, and perhaps a cloud of dust, just visible in the distance, gradually revealing another vehicle as it came into the beams of the headlights.

Hari got out of the car and opened Marni's door.

'You will die in the desert if you do anything foolish,' he said, startling Marni so much she could only stare at him.

'Die?' she finally echoed weakly. 'But you're Hari, Nimr's brother, why would you want us to die?'

'I don't want you to die, I'm just telling you what would happen if you ran off into the desert,' he said, shifting uneasily, and looking anxiously towards the approaching vehicle. 'Fawzi will explain.'

'Have we been kidnapped?' Marni asked, and Hari looked even more embarrassed.

'Not for money,' he finally blurted out. 'We wouldn't do anything like that.'

'Is that supposed to make me feel better?' Marni demanded, but Hari had moved away from her and didn't reply.

The other vehicle was pulling up now, off the road but close enough for Marni to see it was a big four-wheel drive painted in the sandy camouflage colours of desert war vehicles.

'Here's Fawzi now,' Hari said, with such evident relief that Marni knew that whatever was going on, it was Fawzi who was the organiser—Hari was the weak link, should she and Tasnim need one.

'You're talking to her,' Fawzi said as he strode towards them. 'I said no communication.'

'But she asked—' Hari began.

'Bah!' his brother said. 'Just get her in the car and no talking. Where's Tasnim?'

'She's asleep.' Marni answered for the younger brother. 'And she's eight months pregnant so whatever arrangements you've been making, I do hope you've got an obstetrician or a midwife on hand because an upset like this could bring on the birth any minute.'

Even in the dim light shed by the muted headlights she could see Hari's face pale, but Fawzi only swore— well, Marni imagined he was swearing—and waved at his brother to get her into the bigger vehicle.

'No, I'll wake Tasnim and help her,' Marni said, thinking she could slide in beside Tasnim and they could both refuse to budge. She doubted the young men would drag them out forcefully, their inbred respect for women too powerful to overcome. 'You don't want her going into shock,' she added, for good measure.

Both brothers looked concerned this time, and Marni realised, whatever was going on, and whatever they intended doing, she could use Tasnim's condition as a weapon against them.

Weapon! Was that a gun stuck in the belt of Fawzi's tunic?

If it was, then refusing to leave this car and get into the other one was no longer an option.

Marni frowned at him.

'Is that a gun?' she asked, and heard the incredulity in her voice.

He glanced down at it, telling her all she needed to know.

'Then hide it somewhere else on your person. The last thing Tasnim needs is to see people with guns!'

Especially young foolish people, she thought but didn't say.

The two young men began muttering at each other, Hari obviously getting more and more upset about the situation, but Fawzi seemed able to calm him in some way.

Marni slid back into the car and shook Tasnim awake.

'We've met up with Fawzi and have to get into his car,' she told the sleep-bewildered woman. 'I'm sure they don't intend to harm us because every time I mention your pregnancy they get worried. Let's just go along with things for now. I'm here with you and I'll look after you, whatever happens.'

Tasnim's reaction was to burst into tears, which was hardly helpful, but eventually Marni got her transferred to the other vehicle, needing the help of both their kidnappers to get the heavily pregnant woman up into the high-set four-wheel drive.

Hari left them, no doubt to drive the limo back to the city, and Fawzi drove—carefully for one so young, Marni thought—across the desert, up and over sand dune after sand dune, reinforcing—as if she'd needed it—the desolation of the endless shifting sands.

Tasnim was asleep again and Marni dozed, aware there

was no point in watching where they were going because it all looked exactly the same. Finally, he pulled up beside what looked like a small thatched cottage, half-buried in the sand.

'We are here. There is food and water, a little camping stove, beds and bedding. You will stay there. We will be watching you, though you may not see us. Just remember if you venture out into the desert, you will surely die.'

Marni didn't argue. Tired, confused and still angry with Ghazi over his 'Why didn't you tell me' question, still hurt by it, she was beginning to think a comfortable prison cell might not be such a bad idea.

With Fawzi's help she got the still sleepy Tasnim out of the vehicle and into the little shelter, lit by two small gas lanterns that threw dark shadows into the corners of the room.

She could see a couple of mattresses against one wall, a pile of bedding in a corner, a table, where one lantern and a small gas stove, some plates and cups and a kettle stood, and a set of shelves packed with what was probably tinned food—the second lantern on the top of them.

'Lie down on that mattress,' she told Tasnim. 'I'll make you some mint tea. Assuming there is mint available for tea?'

She'd turned to Fawzi, hovering in the doorway, to ask the last question and a more hesitant or unhappy kidnapper she could not imagine.

'Of course,' he said abruptly, before walking out into the darkness. She heard the engine of his vehicle starting up then the noise gradually died away.

Tasnim was lying on the mattress, shivering in the night-cold desert air. Marni found a warm duvet and tucked it around the pregnant woman, thinking, as she did so, of her far-off obstetrics training.

How much did she remember?

'I'll get some tea,' she said. 'There might be biscuits. I'll have a look. We're quite safe here,' she added, reassuring both herself and Tasnim. 'And as soon as Ghazi realises we're missing, he'll find us.'

Given what had happened, she actually wasn't sure about that statement and had said it to reassure Tasnim.

It must have worked for Tasnim nodded and snuggled into the bedding. Satisfied that she was all right for the moment, Marni stood up to explore their temporary home. Water first, to boil for tea. Four large plastic containers of it suggested their kidnappers thought they might be here for a while. Fortunately, as she doubted she could lift a full container, she found a tap at the bottom of each of them so was able to slide a cup under it and get enough water to put into the kettle.

They'd thought of everything, she realised as she picked up a box of matches to light the little gas cooker. Beside the matches was a small gas firelighter but she was too tired to work out how to use it right now.

She set the kettle on to boil and began to check the shelves—sure enough, there were biscuits. Probably because the young men liked them, she decided, but she wasn't going to quibble over the reason for their choice.

Dried mint in a plastic container—she had no idea how much to use, having only made the tea with fresh mint when she'd been living in her little flat. She guessed amounts, realised there was no teapot so she waited until the water boiled then threw the mint into the kettle, adding sugar because that would help with shock.

But by the time she was done, Tasnim was asleep again, too deeply asleep for Marni to want to wake her.

Pouring herself a cup of tea, she carried it to the doorway of the hut, holding it in both hands as she sipped the sweet liquid, looking up at the billion bright stars and wondering if some combination or permutation of their movements had dictated the events of this most momentous day.

Well, at least you've achieved what you came to this place for, a cynical voice whispered in her head. Now perhaps you can get on with your life—go on dates, have some fun!

The realisation that she didn't want to go on dates—except perhaps with Ghazi—or have some fun—except, of course, with him—made her feel so miserable she gave up on the beauty of the night sky and crept back into the hut.

CHAPTER TEN

TASNIM WOKE UP irritable and unhappy, waking Marni, who'd settled on a second mattress nearby and had finally gone to sleep way past midnight.

'We have to get out of here,' Tasnim was saying, while Marni was still shaking off the heaviness of sleep. 'We've got to get away!'

'And go where?' Marni demanded, more concerned that she was going to have to find somewhere behind the shed to relieve herself in private.

And soon!

'If we walk out into that desert we're as good as dead,' she added, heading for the door then hesitating there. 'Do you think they're really watching us from somewhere? I mean, it's not as if we can escape, is it?'

'I went behind the shed,' Tasnim told her, guessing at her concern, 'not something that's easy when you're eight months pregnant. And I don't mean to walk out into the desert, but next time they come we'll have to overpower them some way and take the vehicle.'

I rather think that's a royal *we*, and she's meaning I will have to do the dirty work, Marni thought.

But right now she was beyond caring, hurrying around behind the shed, worrying now about how they'd wash themselves *and* their underwear.

Tasnim was ahead of her, for when Marni returned Tasnim had found a basin and filled it with warm water from the kettle, smelling of mint but very welcome nonetheless.

'I've found a couple of long gowns, like the men wear in the desert. I think the boys must use this place when they come out to hunt. They look clean enough so I'm going to have a wash and put one of them on. We can use the water we're washing in to wash our underwear.'

She must have read the surprise in Marni's face for she laughed and said, 'Being the descendant of a long line of desert women,' she reminded Marni, 'I know how precious water is. Out here we don't really need our underwear so we wash it this once then put it away until we're rescued.'

'Excuse me,' Marni said, 'but are you the same woman who was telling me, rather emotionally and only minutes ago, that we have to get out of here?'

Tasnim smiled at her.

'Pregnant women get very emotional,' she reminded Marni, 'but we're also very sensible under the hysteria because we've something very special to protect.' She patted her bulging belly. 'So now we have to be practical and look after ourselves, bathe and eat, and then we plan.'

The bathing and eating part went well, but planning? Tasnim's escape ideas became more and more impossible—finding a rock and hitting whoever came over the head, grabbing the gun, hiding in the sand then racing to the car while their kidnappers searched for them—until Marni grew tired of pointing out just why they wouldn't work.

'Well, we can't just sit here waiting to be rescued,' Tasnim complained. 'I mean, Yusef's still away, and is Ghazi likely to come looking for you?'

After the way she had stormed out of his office? Hardly! But Marni didn't share that thought.

'Your staff will know you're missing and they must know you went off with Hari,' Marni said instead.

'Yes, but if Hari's not in town—if he's somewhere out here, watching us—how can they ask him where I am? And if they've really thought things through, that pair, they'll have come up with some reason why we didn't go home. They'd have told my people we were going to stay with one of the sisters or something.'

'Would your people believe them? I mean, you didn't pack anything or make any arrangements.'

Tasnim's smile was rueful.

'I do tend to be a little impulsive so although they might mutter among themselves, I doubt any of the staff would be surprised enough to be suspicious. And everyone always has spare clothes and toiletries, even make-up, for visitors. Like the stuff in your bedroom suite.'

They were sitting on Tasnim's mattress, and now she stretched out and lay down on it.

'I'm going to sleep for a while,' she said, patting Marni's leg where she still sat on the edge of the mattress. 'You keep thinking.'

Marni was relieved her companion was sleeping, but without Tasnim's chatter and flow of ideas there was nothing to stop Marni's mind drifting back to Ghazi and the events of the previous evening.

'They cannot just have vanished,' Ghazi yelled, striding about his office at the palace, glaring at his closest friends and advisors.

Unfortunately, deep down he believed they could have done just that. Marni, upset with him—hurt—over what had happened, or what he'd said, could have told Tasnim and Tasnim certainly had the guile and resources to hide them both away somewhere. In fact, the little devil would delight in the intrigue!

'I don't want to alarm you further—' Nimr's voice brought Ghazi out of his dark thoughts. '—but Alima says there's no way Tasnim would put her unborn child in jeopardy by doing something rash, and as far as Alima's concerned, leaving her home voluntarily at this stage of a pregnancy counts as rash.'

'So they *are* in danger!' Ghazi stormed, as his cousin swept away his last hope that Marni might be safe. 'Why? Who? Is it to get at me? Who have I offended?'

'At least we know they've got Hari with them,' Nimr offered, and Ghazi snorted.

'That's hardly comforting, Nimr. Those two young brothers of yours have about as much sense as the rabbits they love to hunt.' He hesitated for a moment, then added, 'Although, where's Fawzi? Maybe he knows something.'

Nimr shrugged.

'He went off a few days ago. Hunting, as you said. The pair of them are obsessed with all the old ways. They believe we should still live in tents and roam the desert sands—in the newest and biggest four-wheel drives, of course.'

Ghazi shook his head. He had no time to be thinking of Nimr's irresponsible brothers now, not when Marni was missing, perhaps in danger.

His gut had been tied in knots since he'd first tried to contact her at Tasnim's house, phoning when he'd been on his way from the hospital to Nimr's dinner, phoning again every ten minutes, feeling more and more desperate until someone finally admitted that neither woman had returned to the house.

If she'd left voluntarily it was because of him, and if something had happened to her, well, that was probably to do with him as well.

Somehow they got through their first full day of captivity, although Tasnim's mood swings took more out of Marni than the desert heat when she ventured outside during the day. Tasnim's first idea had been to write the word 'help' in big letters in the sand so the searching helicopter Ghazi was sure to send would see the message.

Although not believing for a minute Ghazi would send any form of rescue, Marni did write the word in large letters in the sand a few metres behind their shelter. But the wind that came up in the afternoon obliterated the word in seconds—*and* gave Tasnim a new idea.

'We'll put up a flag—use one of the wuzars in the pile of clothing.'

She dug around and produced a snowy-white length of material and Marni felt blood flowing into her cheeks as she realised it was the kind of undergarment Ghazi had shed on that memorable night.

Did Tasnim see that blush that she laughed and said, 'It's only a strip of cloth!'

As they'd agreed Tasnim should stay inside out of the sun, so as not to overheat, once again it was Marni who searched the dunes around their shelter for a stick long enough to hoist a flag.

But a flag with no message? Would it mean anything on the slim chance someone *did* come looking?

She found a stick behind the shelter where some small branches and bunches of dried grass had been stacked, presumably to provide fuel for a fire on a cold night. Digging around, wary of the scorpions Tasnim kept telling her to watch out for, she discovered another, smaller, though thicker stick. Taking it inside, she put the little gas lighter under one end of it, charring it all around so she could use it as a writing implement.

Tasnim objected to the word 'help' this time. It had been chosen when Marni had written in the sand because it was shorter than the local word, but now they settled on the universal 'SOS'.

It took over an hour, charring the stick, writing, charring again, until it was done. But where to put it? Their shelter was nestled between dunes, and even on the stick and somehow attached to the roof, it would barely be seen above the sand.

'You'll just have to climb to the highest dune,' Tasnim told Marni, 'and if Fawzi and Hari really are watching us then you'll get caught but I don't think they'd shoot you.'

'Well, that's comforting,' Marni grumbled, although she was becoming used to Tasnim's cheerful fatalism.

Ghazi stared at Mazur in disbelief.

'You're telling me those two idiots are holding Tasnim and Marni because they want me to stand down and declare Nimr the ruler?'

Mazur shook the six-page letter he was holding.

'There's a lot more than that—all kinds of rot about you having stolen Nimr's birthright and brought shame to the family's name, and not having any honour or integrity or cultural importance.'

'What the hell is cultural importance?' Ghazi demanded, then shook his head at his stupidity. As if it mattered what the pair had said about him—the important thing was rescuing Tasnim and Marni, although Tasnim would probably be happier to see him than Marni would.

'Phone Nimr, get him here immediately. If anyone

knows where those two reprobates might be holding the women, he should.'

Ghazi hoped he sounded more in control than he felt. His mind had been in chaos since Marni's disappearance, and now this! His chest was tight with worry, his gut knotted, and his neck ached with tension. It was bad enough that he'd hurt Marni with his thoughtless words, but to have put her into danger purely because of her connection to him—a connection he'd shamelessly used for his own purposes...

He'd kill those two.

'There are two or three old hunting shelters they use as bases when they're hunting.'

Nimr was striding into the room, his mobile phone in his hand. He crossed to Ghazi and put an arm around his shoulder.

'I was in the palace when Mazur called. Man, I'm sorry about this. We'll get them back. The one thing we can he sure of, they won't hurt the women. They might be stupid and infantile in their pranks but they would never hurt a woman.'

Ghazi acknowledged his cousin's words with an abrupt nod, but Nimr's arrival had brought more than hope.

'Did you want the job?' Ghazi had to ask, although he'd been sure they'd discussed this many times and Nimr's answer had always been the same.

'No way,' Nimr assured him now. 'And those two lame-brains know that! I've told them times without number that I've other things I want to do with my life and, besides, I've always known, just as my father did, that you're the best man to rule our country at this time.'

He gave Ghazi another hug, then bent over the map he'd asked Mazur to find.

'A helicopter, flying low,' he suggested. 'I'll pilot it and you be the lookout. We'll take the little four-seater Bell. It can fly lower without disturbing the sand too much so we'll still be able to see.'

He nodded to Mazur, who left to arrange the helicopter while Nimr pored over the map then glanced up at Ghazi.

'What about Tasnim? How do you think she'll be holding up?' He grinned then added, 'Are your obstetric skills up to date?'

'Don't even think about it,' Ghazi said, watching as Nimr traced a line across the map with a red pen.

Obstetric skills? The words echoed in Ghazi's head.

Tasnim was eight months pregnant and had been through a major upset. He phoned the hospital and asked if they could have a midwife with her obstetrics bag standing by on the heliport in twenty minutes.

The little aircraft lifted lightly into the air, Nimr confident at the controls, Ghazi already working out logistics. He would send Marni, Tasnim and the nurse out on the first flight and Nimr could return for him.

Once they found the women…

If they found the women…

Marni had expected Tasnim to be asleep again when she returned from planting her flag on the dune. Tasnim dozed on and off all day because her sleep at night was restless.

But Tasnim was awake—not only awake but naked.

'There must be something in the clothes, either some kind of bug or they've been washed in something that disagrees with my skin. Look!'

She pointed to where little red weals were showing on her belly.

'They're itchy and they're driving me mad.'

Marni examined them, wishing she knew more about general medicine than she did.

'They look more like an allergy than a bug of some kind,' she said. 'And I've not been bitten by anything. Lie down on the bed with just the sheet on you and I'll see what there is in the supplies that might help soothe the itches.'

Cold mint tea? she wondered.

But Tasmin refused to lie down, believing now that whatever had bitten her could be in the mattress. She went outside and sat on the sand in the small amount of shade offered by their shelter, scratching at the weals and crying softly to herself.

Aware just how brave and held-together Tasnim had been so far, Marni knew she had to do something to help her friend before she fell apart.

She poured cold tea into a cup and tore a clean strip of cloth off a wuzar, then went outside.

'Let's try this to see if it helps, otherwise there's salt—we can try salt and water—or oil perhaps. She kept thinking of bicarbonate of soda, which had been Nelson's panacea for all ills. Bathing in it when she'd had chickenpox had definitely eased the itchiness. But their little hut didn't provide bicarbonate of soda...

And Nelson wasn't here...

Ignoring her own momentary weakness, Marni concentrated on Tasnim.

The rash was spreading, and Tasnim was getting more and more upset, undoubtedly because she was becoming more and more uncomfortable.

Ignoring the dune where she'd raised her flag, Marni climbed another dune, back in the direction they'd come in from. Once at the top she shouted for the boys, alternating their names, yelling that Tasnim needed help, they had to come.

Her voice seemed a pitifully weak instrument out there in the vastness of the desert and she was certain they wouldn't hear her. She slid and slithered back down the dune, persuaded Tasnim to come inside and put on her own abaya, which she'd been wearing over her clothes when they'd been kidnapped.

Too tired and upset to argue, Tasnim dressed, then lay down to sleep—on the floor, not on a mattress.

She was still asleep when Manir heard the engine of a vehicle break the endless silence in which they'd lived since they'd reached the shelter.

'Come on, we're moving you,' Fawzi announced, when Marni met him outside the hut.

'Did you hear me calling? Tasnim's ill. She has a rash across her stomach and it could be affecting the baby. She needs to get back to town and see her doctor.'

'No can do,' Fawzi said, although Hari looked only too happy at the idea of getting rid of their captives. 'But it won't be much longer,' Fawzi continued. 'The imposter has our letter of demand and he'll be giving in any minute now.'

'The imposter? You mean Ghazi? Why is he an imposter?'

'Because he took the throne from our brother,' Hari said, apparently repeating a lesson Fawzi had drummed into him.

'But I heard Nimr didn't want the job,' Marni argued.

'He should still have taken it,' Fawzi said. 'It was his birthright.'

'Well, I don't understand the politics of your country and even if I did I'd have no right to comment, but it's silly to be standing out here in the heat. Tasnim's asleep so we can't leave yet, but if you move around the side into the shade I'll bring you some mint tea and biscuits.'

Hari, appearing only too happy to indulge in tea and biscuits, led the way, and Fawzi followed, though, Marni felt, more reluctantly.

She set everything out on a makeshift tray and joined them in the shade, knowing it would be to their advantage if she could make friends with the young men, rather than hitting them on their heads with rocks.

And as they talked, relaxing quickly as young people did, she realised just how much they loved their country, especially the desert.

'I'll get some of Fawzi's photographs to show you,' Hari offered, when he'd finished his tea.

He raced over to the car, returning with a computer tablet, opening it up at a picture of an Arabian gazelle, a beautiful picture, taken so close up you could see the reflection of the camera in the animal's eyes.

'How on earth did you do that?' she asked, and Fawzi explained that they had many hides in the desert, like this place, only built for photography rather than for shelter.

'So you're still hunters, the two of you, but your gun is now a camera?' she said, and Fawzi looked pleased that she understood.

She slid her fingers across the screen, looking at one photograph after another, amazed at how good they were.

'You should put these into a book. I had no idea there was so much wildlife in the desert. It would be wonderful publicity for Ablezia.'

'This is what people are forgetting,' Hari said. 'That's what Fawzi and I don't like about the way our country is going. People move into the city and lose their interest in the desert, forgetting that the desert is part of their hearts and souls.'

'I can understand what you mean,' Marni said, but her visitors' attention had shifted from her, and as she watched the tension build in their bodies and their heads turn skywards, she heard the distant thud, thud, thud of a helicopter.

'It's Nimr, he's found us,' Hari said, looking as if he'd like to burrow deep into the sand and disappear.

'Quick, we have to leave!' Fawzi stood up and looked ready to flee but couldn't quite bring himself to haul Marni to her feet.

'Sit down again,' she said. 'You can't go rushing all over the desert with a helicopter chasing you. That's only for the movies and even in the movies the vehicle usually crashes. And there's no way on earth I'd let Tasnim get into the vehicle with you. She's too far gone in her pregnancy. Stay here, I'll talk to Nimr. I'll show him we're both quite all right and you've been very kind to us and that it's all just been a joke.'

'Except Fawzi wrote the letter to Ghazi, telling him we had you,' Hari reminded her.

'Well, we can get around that too,' Marni said above the now loud clatter of the helicopter rotors. 'Ghazi isn't going to throw you into a dungeon. In fact, I doubt he'll even throw you into jail. We'll work something out.'

She didn't add that he might well have given them a medal for getting rid of her, if his sister hadn't been involved as well.

Perhaps realising the futility of escape, the young men stayed put, all three of them bending their heads low over their knees as the sand from the rotors kicked up all around them.

The little aircraft touched down as lightly as a butterfly and when the engine was turned off and the rotors started spinning more slowly a door opened and not Nimr but

Ghazi dropped onto the sand, followed by a woman with a large black bag and, finally, from the other side, Nimr.

'I'll kill you two,' Nimr roared, then proceeded to yell at them in their own language.

'Where's Tasnim?' Ghazi growled, anger in every line in his body, rage radiating from his pores.

Marni pointed towards the hut where a still sleepy Tasnim had appeared in the doorway.

Ghazi—although clad in jeans and a polo shirt there was no doubt from the way he held himself that he was Ghazi—led the nurse in that direction,

So that's what he thinks of me, Marni decided sadly.

Ghazi thought he'd held himself together quite well through the ordeal of not knowing where Marni was, or even if she was alive. But when he jumped out of the helicopter and saw her sitting on the sand, chatting happily to her kidnappers the tension that he'd held in check erupted into searing, white-hot anger.

Not wanting to let fly at her in front of so many people, he held it in check and sought out his sister instead, taking her in his arms and holding her close while she sobbed onto his shoulder. Her cries of relief were rising towards hysteria, her babbled words barely understandable. He soothed and comforted her, taking his time to calm her down before peeling her off his body so the nurse could check her.

By that time Nimr had joined the little group sitting on the sand, and they had obviously calmed him down because both his brothers were not only still alive but didn't seem to have been harmed in any way.

Ghazi walked towards the group and now, finally, the woman whose disappearance had nearly ripped his heart out looked up and nodded acknowledgement of his presence. She was pale, her hair coming loose from a plait and sticking out in all directions, but her face betrayed no hint of relief that they'd been rescued, or delight at seeing him.

'Nimr tells me the helicopter only carries four, Ghazi, so I think you should go with Tasnim back to the hospital,' Marni said, so calmly he wanted to throttle her. 'I know you brought a nurse, but Tasnim's been really strong up until this morning when she came out in a rash across her belly. I vaguely remember something called PEP, poly-something eruption of pregnancy that can happen in the later months. I think that's all it is but she's getting very anxious and upset about it and is desperately worried that it could affect the baby. If you're with her, you'll be able to keep her calm until she gets back home and her own obstetrician sees her.'

Ghazi stared at the woman he'd come to rescue.

Was that all she had to say?

Apparently not, because she was speaking again.

'That way, I can get a ride back to town with Hari and Fawzi, or Nimr's said he'd be happy to fly back out to pick me up once he's dropped Tasnim off.'

She had it all organised, this pale, dishevelled devil he'd fallen in love with.

And not a *hello Ghazi, nice to see you, sorry if you've been worried* to be heard!

She was unbelievable and, heaven forbid, unbelievably beautiful to his eyes—even in an old kandora she must have found in the hut and smudges of exhaustion under her eyes.

Had he hurt her so much that she was treating him this way?

Like a passing stranger?

Or a *pretend* fiancé?

The pain in his gut suggested this might be so, but how could he say anything in front of Nimr and his brothers?

'Are you in agreement with this plan?' he asked Nimr.

His cousin nodded.

'I think Tasnim will need you as well as the nurse,' he said.

Knowing Nimr was probably right, Ghazi turned to the young men.

'As for you two,' Ghazi he said, 'can you be trusted to stay here with Marni until we return or will you get some other wild idea and take off again?'

'We'll be here,' Hari said, so promptly Ghazi had to wonder what threats Nimr had already made to his brothers.

'I think we should go right now,' the nurse called from the doorway of the hut, and Ghazi, after one last, despairing look at the woman he loved, turned back to help his near-hysterical sister into the helicopter.

'Well, that went well,' Nimr said to him when they were airborne once again. 'Some little glitch along the road to matrimony?'

'Just keep flying,' Ghazi growled. 'And don't think for a minute you'll be flying back there, unless you want to ride home with your brothers—which might not be a bad idea. With you there, I'll be less likely to murder them.'

Nimr flew.

CHAPTER ELEVEN

NOT A PRIVATE word, not a touch—he hates me!

With Hari and Fawzi chattering on in their own language, Marni was left with her own gloomy thoughts.

You didn't exactly rush into his arms yourself, she reminded herself, which only made her feel even worse.

The problem was that, being the honourable man he was, Ghazi would undoubtedly feel he was bound to her in some way—apart from the pretend betrothal.

Enough to make the betrothal not pretend?

Probably, Marni decided gloomily, then became aware the other conversation had turned to English.

'Do you think Ghazi will banish us?' Fawzi was asking.

Marni studied the young men and saw fear and despair in their faces.

'I doubt that very much,' she said gently. 'You did a very silly thing but no harm has come of it. And you did it for reasons you believed in your hearts were right. I'm sure Ghazi will understand that.'

'You will speak to him on our behalf?' Hari begged, and although Marni knew her words would achieve little, given Ghazi's current opinion of her, she agreed that she would.

'But you'd do better speaking to him yourselves—

apologising for causing alarm. And I think he'd be more willing to forgive you if you can come up with more than just an apology. What do the pair of you do, apart from kidnapping women?'

'We hunt,' came the chorused reply.

'Hunt animals for food?'

The young men laughed.

'No, for the camera,' Fawzi said. 'You saw the pictures, and that gun I had, well, it was an antique—no way would it harm anyone or anything. We love the old ways but some of our desert animals are almost extinct. Some we trap and keep to breed from—out at the old palace—then we set the young ones free when they are able to live on their own.'

'Your photographs are brilliant,' Marni told him, 'but would it not be better for people to see these animals and birds in the wild? Could you take tourists on trips to the desert—not just to eat dinner and watch the sunset, the way tourism operators do now, but run specialist tours for photographers and wildlife lovers. You could mix the old ways with the new, as tourists want comfort—set up luxury tents and provide good food. I am sure that kind of thing would really take off.'

She saw the growing excitement in their eyes so wasn't surprised when the talk again excluded her—not that she cared. If this pair could find something useful to do with their passion, they'd have no time to be thinking up wild schemes, like kidnapping pretend fiancées.

Which brought her thoughts back to Ghazi, but what he must be thinking she had absolutely no idea.

Flying the little aircraft was second nature to him. He and his boyhood friends and relations had been flipping around in them since they had been teenagers, so he had time to plan.

No matter that Marni might hate him, he had to do the right thing by her, his honour demanded that much. He'd sort out the rest later.

He phoned Mazur and gave him orders to have everything in readiness at the old palace, for that was where he'd take her—where he felt most at home, and where he knew she would be safe.

'I'll need someone qualified to marry us. With the photograph as proof of her grandfather's agreement to the betrothal, we won't need anyone to stand in place of her father, and I'll use Nimr's otherwise useless brothers as witnesses, then send them packing back to the city and deal with them later. I want my quarters prepared, clothing and toiletries for Marni, and food laid on, but no hovering servants. She'll need privacy and quiet, Mazur, to get over the ordeal she's suffered.'

He tried not to think about what would happen beyond the ceremony he was planning—what might happen in his quarters. He knew what he hoped would happen but feared he'd damaged the tender shoots of their relationship beyond repair, not with his lovemaking but with the rash words he'd uttered afterwards.

Nearly there, and now he saw the brave little flag flying from a dune beyond the shelter and knew she'd put it there. Kidnapped and left in the middle of the desert, she'd not only handled the situation but had done her best to get herself and Tasnim safely out of it.

He set the aircraft down, waited while the rotors slowed then dropped down to the ground.

Marni watched him walk towards them. Behind her, the two men stood, but she couldn't get her legs to move because this time Ghazi wasn't radiating anger. In fact, he appeared to be smiling and she was reasonably sure he wouldn't be smiling at Fawzi and Hari.

'You two get into your vehicle and get over to the old palace,' he said. 'I want you there as soon as possible. I've got a job for you to do.'

The pair looked shocked, but moved rapidly enough as Ghazi drew closer, his hand waving them away dismissively.

'But they wanted to talk to you about an idea they've had,' Marni objected, with only the slightest quiver in her voice betraying just how trembly she was feeling inside now she knew she'd have to face Ghazi on his own—be with him on *her* own!

'They can put it in writing—Fawzi's good at that!' Ghazi growled, coming closer and closer to where she sat.

She feared if she stood up her legs would give way on her, because just seeing him was causing palpitations, and quivering nerves, and goose-bumps on her skin, and too may other physical sensations to name.

'You,' he said, putting out his hand and hauling her unceremoniously to her feet and marching with her towards the helicopter, 'are coming with me.'

'Do you think this is the modern equivalent of one of our ancestors throwing his woman over a camel and riding off into the desert?' Hari whispered to Fawzi, loudly enough to bring another growl from Ghazi.

'Is Fawzi right?' Marni asked, because she had to say *something*. 'Are you throwing me over your camel and riding off with me?'

He had helped her into the helicopter and now stood outside, looking in at her.

'Would you like that?' he asked, his voice deep, his eyes, his face unreadable.

'I don't know,' she answered honestly.

Or was it honestly? she wondered as he marched around the chopper to get in behind the controls. She suspected that, somehow or other, she'd fallen in love with this man, without really knowing him at all.

Was that possible?

Or was it nothing more than the manifestation of the attraction that had flared between them from the beginning?

But would lust make her heart ache when she saw the tenderness with which he treated Safi?

Would it make her heart skitter when he smiled?

Not that there was any evidence of a smile at the moment. In fact, sneaking a sideways glance at him, she had to wonder if she'd ever see him smile again. Not any time soon, that was for sure.

'Are you all right?'

The demand came when they'd lifted into the air and banked as if to go even deeper into the desert.

She wanted to cry. Wanted to ask why he hadn't asked her that before. But he was all business, and she could do business.

'Desperately in need of a bath but apart from that, yes, I'm fine,' she said, and saw a slight frown mar the inscrutability of his expression, but it was quickly gone.

'You'll have time for a bath,' was all he said, or maybe he kept talking, but if he did, Marni missed it, too filled with astonishment at what lay ahead of them.

Rising out of the desert sands, barely perceptible at first, was what seemed like an immense building. High walls, sand coloured and seemingly endless, round turrets set at intervals, and where the walls changed direction, and within the walls, more walls, and domes, and spires.

'It looks as if it just grew up out of the desert sands like some fantastic plant.'

She breathed the words, lost in wonder as they flew closer and the immensity of the old palace—for that was all it could be—was revealed.

Now she could see colour—rugs hanging over balcony parapets to air, market stalls set up inside the walls, the sun glinting off brass and silver pots and pipes and urns.

Ghazi circled the building, allowing Marni a glimpse of an inner courtyard, green with trees and plants, then landed on a concrete pad at the back of the building but within the outer walls.

Speechless with astonishment and wonder, Marni followed Ghazi as he led her past a long row of stalls, with horses' heads poking out of some—horses here, not cars—and further on past different stalls—camels?—all the time heading towards the main building.

'You're late!' he said, as Mazur pulled up in a little electric cart so they could ride the rest of the way.

'You flew too fast,' Mazur countered, but when Ghazi slid in beside him in the front, Mazur clapped him on the shoulder.

'It's done?' Ghazi asked.

'All done, although Fawzi and Hari aren't here yet. Not that it matters. All you need are two adult males.'

Ghazi nodded but gave no explanation of this weird conversation. Not that Marni minded. Now she was finally somewhere civilised, all she could think about was a bath. She just hoped this place was stocked up with clothes and underwear, because second in importance to the bath would be clean underwear!

They drove through an arch into the courtyard, a wonder of green in the barren land. All around the courtyard Marni could see arched openings that led into the shade of the wide loggia, the covered outside sitting area.

Mazur stopped the cart at the bottom of shallow steps,

and Ghazi hopped out, turning to offer his hand to Marni. To her horror, she found that she was shaking—that the simple of touch of this man's hand had thrown her into a quivering mess.

She tried a smile and said weakly, 'I was doing fine up till now.'

He squeezed her fingers and she saw the familiar kindness in his eyes—kindness and something else she didn't recognise.

'You have been marvellous. Tasnim told me how you helped her remain calm.'

Marni shook her head, and tried a better smile.

'No, Tasnim did her bit. She told me it was the generations of desert women standing behind her that kept her going.'

Ghazi saw the bravery in her feeble smile and felt the tremors of post-traumatic shock shake her body. He wanted nothing more than to gather her into his arms and hold her close, tell her everything would be all right now—tell her things he barely understood himself.

But Mazur was there, servants appearing from inside the house, and a young woman, obviously chosen by his major domo here to look after Marni, was waiting in the doorway.

'This is Lila,' Mazur said, beckoning the woman forward. 'Lila, will you take Ms Graham to her suite and do whatever she needs you to do.'

So Ghazi had to hand Marni over to a stranger and hope she had the strength to keep going for just a little longer.

'Does the girl know what is planned?' he asked Mazur.

'Only that you wish to see Marni in the majlis in an hour.'

Ghazi heard the doubt in Mazur's voice—doubt and no little condemnation.

'I know she's exhausted but that's why I must do it now,' Ghazi told his friend. 'Once we're married she can rest.'

'Did you tell her?' Mazur demanded, and Ghazi shook his head, unable to explain that he hadn't been able to bring himself to mention marriage to Marni on the flight.

Because he was afraid she'd object? Refuse to go along with it?

'Then you should,' Mazur said firmly. 'I know you think you're doing the right thing, but you can't just drag the woman down the aisle with two witnesses—and why couldn't I be a witness might I ask?—and expect her to go along with marrying you.'

'It's for her safety and as for witnesses, she knows you and I need you to be there as her friend, not mine,' Ghazi snapped, then he strode away from his friend and mentor, angry, confused and heartsore.

'We must hurry,' Lila said as she led Marni along marble corridors and through jewelled archways, finally entering a room with a high domed ceiling, painted a deep, rich purple that matched the curtains around the huge four-poster bed.

'Why?' Marni managed to ask, as she took in the magnificence of this room, with its grilled windows looking out to the courtyard.

'Because we only have an hour. I have drawn a bath, it is all ready for you. I will wash your hair while you are in it, then perfume you and do just a little henna design on your hand because although no one is supposed to know, you will be marrying our prince today.'

'I will be *what*?' Marni demanded, the words muffled

as she'd been pulling the long tunic off over her head as she spoke.

'Getting married,' Lila said, obviously very excited about the upcoming event.

'No, and, no, and, no!' Marni stormed, although she did step into the bath. She could hardly argue with Ghazi stark naked—*dirty* and stark naked. 'I'll have the bath but I'll wash my hair myself and while I'm doing it you find whoever you have to talk to and get a message to your prince that I'll see him in my room in twenty minutes.'

'Oh, but you can't do that—not in your bedroom,' Lila protested.

'No?' Marni muttered. 'We'll see about that! You just get the message to him. And leave some underwear and something I can wear on the bed before you go.'

Sinking into the water, delicately scented and bubbling around her, was pure bliss, but having set her own deadline she couldn't lie back and enjoy it. She wet her hair and lathered it with shampoo that was handily placed on a shelf alongside the bath, rinsed it off and rubbed conditioner in, then let her hair absorb the treatment while she scrubbed her body clean of sand and dust and dirt.

Emptying the bath water, she stood up beneath the overhead shower and showered off the conditioner, then stepped out of the bath, wrapping herself in a super-soft towel and growing angrier by the minute that she hadn't been able to revel in the luxury of her first bath in three days.

The memory of when she'd last showered brought a rush of embarrassment, and she wondered if summoning Ghazi to her room might have been a mistake.

No! She had to talk to him. A pretend betrothal was one thing, but being rushed into marriage was just not on.

Wrapped in the towel, she went back into the bedroom, to gasp in wonder at the clothing Lila had apparently deemed suitable for her wedding.

Various packets of lacy underwear offered her a choice of colour and size, but it was the garment that would cover it that gave Marni pause. It was a simple enough gown, long and straight like the tunic she'd been wearing in the desert, but there any similarity ended, for this garment was apparently made with spun silver—fine and delicate silver—elaborately embroidered around the sleeves, neckline and hem.

It was something that should be in a museum, not about to be worn by any ordinary mortal.

She searched the walls of the bedroom, knowing there'd be concealed wardrobe and dressing room doors somewhere, and within those rooms there'd be other clothing—something else she could put on.

The doors eluded her, so she found underwear her size among the packets then returned to the bathroom, sure there'd be a robe there she could wear.

No such luck, but the towels were huge, and choosing a dry one she wrapped it around herself, then went across to a small sitting area by one of the windows to await her confrontation with her betrothed. Talking to him in the sitting area was slightly better than anywhere near the bed, but the bed still seemed to dominate the room.

And her thoughts!

Seeing her clad only in a towel was very nearly Ghazi's undoing. To hold her, smell her skin, feel her still damp hair against his face, peel off the towel—

'So, what's this all about?' the woman in the towel demanded, and he jerked his mind back to reality.

'No, don't bother answering that,' she added, before he could reply. 'It's your sense of chivalry, of honour that you're insisting on this marriage business. And sit down, I can't keep arguing with you when you're towering over me up there.'

For some reason he wanted to smile—perhaps because she should be at such a disadvantage in the towel, yet here she was issuing orders to him.

He didn't smile, knowing that would only make her angrier, but he did sit, and, sitting, could take in the clear pale skin of her shoulders—was that a bruise or the remnant of a love bite from the other night?—and the shadows of tiredness beneath her eyes.

His arms ached to hold her, to kiss away those shadows, to feel her body tight against his—where he was sure it belonged.

But was she sure it was where *she* belonged?

He had no idea, which was why he had to tread carefully.

'It's a matter of keeping you safe,' he said, forcing his mind to take control of his wayward thoughts. 'I need to have the right to protect you for as long as you remain in this country. As my wife, you would have a status that makes you, by tradition, untouchable. We don't have to stay married for ever or have a marriage in anything but name, but what has happened once could happen again, and next time your kidnappers could be more dangerous than a couple of stupid young men.'

She frowned at him and he wanted to wipe away that frown, to smooth the skin above her neat little nose, maybe kiss the frown away.

'They're not stupid, they just don't have enough to occupy them and that always leads to trouble with young people,' she said, and Ghazi was so lost in thoughts of kisses it took him a moment to catch up.

'You mean Hari and Fawzi? I've been telling Nimr that for ages, but we're not here to talk about them, surely?'

'Not exactly, but it's the same thing in another way. Those two, well, we've worked out what they can do—run wildlife safaris for photographers and animal lovers. But they did what they did because they could—because no one's ever said no to them or their wild schemes and I suspect it's just the same with you, no one's ever said no to you so you dream up this stupid idea of us getting married for whatever reason and don't stop to think what I might have to say to it.'

Now he did smile, and if the delicate flush of colour on her chest above the towel was any indication, he didn't think he'd made her angrier.

Marni had thought she was doing quite well with the conversation, considering she was sitting practically naked in front of the sexiest man in the world, and her thoughts were rampaging on about giving in to her body and letting the towel slip, and then he smiled and her mind went blank.

'What *do* you have to say to it?' he asked, the smile still lurking because she could see it shining in his eyes.

To what?

She'd totally lost the thread of the conversation, if it had ever had a thread.

And *she'd* summoned *him*, so presumably she was the one who was supposed to be in control.

'To us getting married,' he said in such a kindly manner she wanted to slap him—or perhaps kiss away the little quirk of a smile on the corners of his lips. 'After all, we are betrothed, and as I said earlier it needn't mean anything, but it would give me the right to protect you, Marni, and I think I owe that to your grandfather.'

'Pop! Oh, heavens, I'd forgotten all about Pop. I need to phone Nelson, I need to find out—'

Ghazi touched her gently on her knee.

'Your grandfather is doing well—far better than his surgeon expected. I have spoken to both the surgeon and to Nelson every day. It will be a long convalescence, as you already knew, but he's progressing extremely well.'

Marni wasn't sure if it was the assurance or the hand on her knee that brought a rush of relief to her body, and with the relief came a release of the tension she'd been feeling for days.

And a burst of gratitude to this man who thought of everything.

Except she didn't want to be feeling grateful to him—she didn't want to be feeling anything!

Not that she'd have a hope of stopping the physical stuff!

But right now she had to get past that and get her brain working again, so she could explain why she wasn't going to marry him.

Wouldn't it be easier to just give in and marry the man? Then she could sleep.

Except...

'You say we're getting married so you can protect me but if I go back to being plain Marni Graham, a theatre sister, and live in a flat at the hospital, go to and from work there, then there'd be no need for protection. Now I know you better I know you can handle your sisters, so we can dispense with the betrothal business and everything can go back to normal.'

Her heart grew heavier and heavier as she spoke, yet she knew it was the right thing to do.

'Can it?' he asked, while the strength of the attraction between them was such that she could feel his body against hers, his mouth capturing her lips, although a full metre of palace air separated them.

'Of course it can,' Marni said, but the words didn't come out as strongly as she'd hoped they would. In fact, they sounded feeble in the extreme.

She took a deep breath and tried again.

'It's not only the protection thing that's pushing you,' she told him. 'I know you well enough to understand you feel you have to marry me because it's the honourable thing to do, and that's just nonsense. What happened happened, and I wanted it as much as you did.'

'What *happened* was that I hurt you,' Ghazi said, his voice full of regret. 'Hurt you with my foolish words, but it wasn't that you'd disappointed me in any way, but that, had I known—'

'You'd have pulled back,' Marni said. 'Don't bother denying it, it's happened to me before.'

The pain in her voice was too much! He stood up, lifted her out of the chair and sat down again with her on his knee. He brushed the hair back from her face and kissed her gently on the lips.

'Maybe,' he said, running his hand over her hair, enjoying just holding her, 'but only until I could make it special for you, make it easier and more enjoyable—slower and more careful, so it was more pleasure than pain for you. But how was I to know?'

He looked into her eyes, filmed with tears, although a brave smile was hovering around her lips.

'That I might still be a virgin at my age?' she asked. 'Not many people would think it. It wasn't that I was keeping myself for someone special, or that I thought my virginity precious, or anything that definite at all—it just happened.'

She was studying his face as she spoke, as if hoping to read understanding there.

'You see,' she continued, 'I was brought up by two elderly men, who loved me as dearly as I loved them, so early on, at school and university when all my friends were experimenting with sex, I couldn't quite get into it, afraid Pop and Nelson would be disappointed in me, that they'd think less of me. I knew if someone did come along that they'd like and approve of, then probably it would happen, but no one did, and then I was older and suddenly it was embarrassing to be a virgin and that made it harder and harder and—'

He cupped his hands around her face and kissed her gently on her lips.

'And when you did tell someone you thought might be the right man, he mocked you, hurt you with cruel words and snide remarks?'

She nodded and rested her forehead on his chest while he wound his fingers through her hair and held her close.

'So, now that's sorted,' he said, 'how about we go and get married so I can show you just how wonderful it can be?

Marni eased her head off his chest and looked at him.

'You could show me anyway,' she teased. 'The bed's right there, and no matter what you say, you're marrying me because you feel it's the honourable thing to do, aren't you?

He was and he wasn't but how to handle it?

Could he, who'd never opened up his heart to anyone, not even his closest friends, open himself up to this woman?

Couldn't that lead to loss of power?

To vulnerability?

To pain?

Yet, holding her, knowing her as he now did, he knew nothing less would do.

He stood up and put her back in her chair then knelt before her, taking both her hands in his.

'You're right about the honour,' he said, trying hard to get the words he needed—to get them right. 'Yes, I believe marrying you is the right thing to do, and even if you feel you don't need it, I want to be able to protect you—to protect you, provide for you and care for you.'

Deep breath because this was it—this was where he laid bare his soul.

So she could trample on it?

He had no idea.

'But most of all I want to marry you because I love you more than I have ever believed I could love anyone. These last few days have been the vilest kind of torture, because not only did I not know where you were, or even if you were still alive, but because I'd hurt you before we'd parted, and not knowing if I'd ever be able to explain—to make things right between us—well, that was the worst agony of all.'

Marni stared at him in utter astonishment.

'But you never said—'

'Did you?' he countered, smiling up at her in such a way she felt her entire body melting.

'How could I? I was worried it might just be lust, although as I got to know you, saw your kindness, your love for your country and your people, the way you were with Safi, it felt like love, but what did I know about that? It was as foreign to me as Ablezia, so how could I tell? I just wasn't sure.'

'Not I until I lost you,' he admitted, then he lifted her hands and kissed the backs of them, before turning them and pressing a kiss into each palm.

'So we're good to go?' he asked, his voice shaking just slightly with what could only be nerves.

'I guess so,' Marni told him, although she was sad that Pop wouldn't be there on her wedding day. But then she leaned towards him, ready for the kiss that *had* to be coming.

Needing the kiss as confirmation of their love.

'If that towel falls off, we'll never make the wedding,' Ghazi told her, not kissing her at all but standing up and stepping back, needing space between them so the fires didn't start up again. 'Get yourself dressed. I'll send Lila back to help you.'

He headed out the door

EPILOGUE

MARNI WALKED THROUGH the suite of rooms she'd chosen for Pop and Nelson, checking everything was in readiness. This suite had a small kitchenette and she'd stocked it with their favourite snacks, brands of tea and coffee, and a refrigerator full of cold drinks.

It would make Nelson feel more at home if he could prepare small meals for himself and Pop and, as Pop was still convalescent, they'd both appreciate not having to join the family for every meal.

'Stop fussing, it's perfect, and it's time to leave for the airport.'

Ghazi had obviously known where to find her and he stood behind her, slipping his arms around her, one hand resting protectively on her belly where the surprise she had for Pop was just beginning to show.

She leant back against her husband, aware of him in every fibre of her being, aware of the love that flooded through her whenever he was near.

In six short months her life had changed so tremendously it still had a dreamlike quality. She'd soon learned the wife of the ruler had a multitude of duties to perform, but his family had been wonderful, even Tasnim, with her new baby—Marni—was constantly on the phone.

Like him, she was still learning 'the job' but it was

becoming easier every day—her reward for her dili-gence, the nights she spent in the arms of her lover—night after night of excitement, tenderness, raging lust and pure bliss.

Ablezia had certainly provided the answer to her 'vir-ginity thing'!

'I can feel you thinking about sex,' Ghazi whispered in her ear.

'Not here, and there's no time anyway,' she told him, but she pressed her body against his and enjoyed the ripples of excitement even such a casual embrace could cause.

'We have to leave—the plane's due in within half an hour.'

She spun around and kissed him, her excitement over the arrival of Pop and Nelson now quelling other kinds of excitement.

Like most of the guest suites, this one opened onto the inner courtyard and Ghazi led her out that way and through the gardens to the garages at the back. This told her he'd be driving them to the airport—no driver for this private family meeting.

The courtyard seemed darker than usual, and only a few lights shone from the rooms around it, although usu-ally the place was flooded with light.

'Austerity measures?' she teased, waving her hand towards the dark building.

'Probably a problem with a fitting somewhere,' Ghazi replied, 'and the electrician's closed off a whole section of the power.'

She forgot about it as they drove to the airport, al-though as they skirted the city, it, too, seemed to be less lit up. But Ghazi was talking about Safi, staying at the palace, in the harem, with his mother and younger brothers, awaiting his next operation.

One of Marni's projects was setting up a fund to raise money for the families of children who came to Ablezia for medical treatment—money that would allow family members to accompany the children and cover any loss of income they might suffer because of their absence from work back in their homeland.

They talked of it until they pulled up at the airport, driving to a private area where Ghazi's own plane would touch down.

Had touched down!

And there was Pop, using a walking stick but as upright as ever, Nelson right beside him, while a steward came behind them with their luggage.

Marni raced across the tarmac and threw her arms around her grandfather, tears coursing down her cheeks. She could feel his fragility as she held him, and that made her tears flow faster.

Eventually he eased away.

'See,' he said, 'that's why I sent you away. Couldn't have stood to have you weeping over me for six months. No more tears now. Say hello to Nelson then you'd better introduce this husband you seem to have picked up.'

Marni smiled through her tears and hugged Nelson, thanking him again and again for all he'd done, seeing Pop through his operation and recuperation.

'I know how difficult he can be,' she said, and Nelson smiled.

'And you also know I can handle him,' Nelson told her. He studied her for a moment then added, 'Ghazi being good to you, darling girl?'

Marni could only nod, the lump in her throat too big for speech. Then Ghazi was there, introducing himself, telling Nelson he remembered him, thanking them both for the gift they'd sent—the gift of Marni.

The steward had loaded the luggage into the car, and Ghazi seated Nelson beside him in the front, Marni and Pop in the back.

He drove slowly back towards the main road into the city, although maybe they were on another road for now all Marni could see that beyond the headlights was complete darkness.

'Is that desert out there?' Pop asked.

'Mostly, although this is a big highway and usually well lit.'

She'd barely spoken when the lights came on—and what lights! Strung between the tall lampposts were garlands of red and green, Christmas bells hanging from the centre of each one. The posts themselves were decorated with streamers, and along the road reindeer were picked out in fairy-lights.

'But you don't celebrate Christmas in Ablezia,' Marni protested, as more and more Christmas decorations came into view—huge banners hanging from high-rise buildings, streamers of coloured lights around the souk, Christmas trees in parks and gardens, and huge blow-up Santas atop any available chimney.

Ghazi slowed the car and turned back to look at her.

'I couldn't let you miss out on *your* celebration,' he said. 'Nimr took the idea to parliament, reminding everyone we have a lot of Western expats in our land. How better to welcome them and make them feel at home? he suggested. Then although Fawzi and Hari are busy with their safari plans, he got them busy organising it, seeing all the big corporations and explaining what we wanted.'

Marni shook her head, unable to speak for the wonder of what her husband and his people had done for her.

But the palace itself was even more breathtaking, for here everything was done in fairy-lights so the court-yard looked like a fairy wonderland, the tree in the maj-lis a miracle of silver decorations and tiny shining lights.

Still bemused by the whole thing, she showed Pop and Nelson to their suite, introducing them to the servant who would be on call for them at any time.

In Pop's bedroom they finally had time to pause, to hug each other again, and for them to study each other.

'How are you, really?' she asked, and he smiled his old, cheeky smile.

'Nearly there, my girl, nearly there. You know you can't keep an old dog down.'

Then the smile faded as he touched her cheek.

'And you? Are you happy? It's obvious he loves you, I can see it in his eyes. Do you love him?'

Marni smiled and hugged her grandfather again.

'With every breath I take, with every cell in my body,' she whispered, and Pop patted her on the back.

'That's good,' he said, then he held her at arm's length and she saw the twinkle in his eyes. 'So maybe two old men knew what they were doing, eh?'

'Happy?' Ghazi asked much later when she slid into bed beside him.

She shook her head and saw his frown. Kissed it away, and whispered, 'There has to be a better word than that for what I feel. Overwhelmed with love, that's what I feel, overwhelmed that you would do what you did for me tonight. You've given me so much with your love, and your trust, and bringing Pop and Nelson over for this visit, but to give me Christmas—that goes beyond everything I've ever known or expected or imagined.'

'So you *are* happy?' Ghazi pressed, as he gathered her into his arms.

'So far beyond it I can't explain, but maybe I can show you.'

And she did!

* * * * *

THE SURGEON'S
CINDERELLA

SUSAN CARLISLE

To Eric.

Everyone should have a son-in-law like you.

CHAPTER ONE

TANNER LOCKE NEEDED a matchmaker's help.

Two days earlier Whitney Thomason's hand had quivered slightly as she'd held the phone. He was certainly a blast from the past. Why would someone like Tanner require her help?

An hour earlier he had texted her that he needed to change their arrangements and asked her to meet him at a small airport outside San Francisco. As the owner of Professional Matchmaking, Whitney had made concessions for clients on more than one occasion, but this was the first time she'd been asked to meet one at an airport at dusk.

Tanner had said something had come up and that he couldn't join her at her office. He would appreciate her meeting him at the airport. If she hadn't been familiar with his status in the community she wouldn't have considered such a plan. She wasn't acquainted with the small airport but had agreed to do as he'd requested.

Having *the* Dr. Tanner Locke's name on her client list would be good for business. Even though it was unethical to publicize his name, she could say that an eminent doctor in the city had used her services. Who knew? He might even send her referrals. Either of those would make it worth her drive to meet him.

As the "big man on campus" when they'd been at

Berkeley, all the girls had had a crush on Tanner, including herself. But she hadn't been his style. He had been into thin, blonde, preppy sorority girls while she had been the heavy, dark-haired, mousy nobody. At least she already knew his type.

In the past couple of years she'd seen Tanner's name in the news a few times. He was an up-and-coming surgeon in the heart transplant field. So why did someone as good-looking and eligible as Tanner need her help in finding a mate?

Whitney chuckled drily. For the same reasons her other clients did. They didn't have the time or energy to weed out the unsuitable. She handled the nitty-gritty work of finding people with similar backgrounds so they only connected with the people most appropriate for them. It was a one-and-done process.

She rolled through the gate of the airfield minutes before she was due to meet Tanner. Would he recognize her? Why should he? She'd just been one of those people who had been a filler in a couple of his classes. Plus she'd changed a great deal since then. At least on the outside. She'd lost fifty pounds. She'd long outgrown having a crush on Tanner. Heavens, she didn't even really know him.

Pulling into a parking spot in the lot next to a red single-story, cement-block building, she turned off the engine. A gleaming white jet sat on the tarmac in front of the terminal. There were a couple of men working around it. Was Tanner going somewhere? Probably off to Hawaii for the weekend.

Normally Whitney liked to have her initial interview in a neutral and laid-back place. A local café, the park. Out of the client's high-pressure work world so that they were more relaxed, less distracted. She found that even though people's favorite subject was themselves, when it came to their personal life they weren't as forthcoming. Men tended toward telling about half of what she needed to know. The more successful her client was, the more insecure or demanding or both they were about their choices for mates.

At the sound of an ambulance siren, she glanced into the rearview mirror. The noise abruptly ended as the vehicle rolled through the gate at a normal speed and continued until the ambulance stopped close to the plane. A group of people dressed in green scrubs exited the back.

What was going on?

One of the men in the party broke away from the group and started toward her. That must be Tanner. It had been years since she'd seen him. He'd changed as well. His shoulders had broadened and his face had lost its youthfulness, having matured into sharper angles. He was still an extremely handsome man. Maybe even more so now.

With a wide stride that spoke of a person who controlled his realm and was confident to do so, he approached her. She stepped out of the car, closed the door and waited.

"Whitney?"

He didn't recognize her. Was she relieved or disappointed? She extended her hand when he was within arm's reach.

"Whitney Thomason."

Tanner took her hand and pulled her to him, giving her a hug.

What was he doing?

Her face was pressed into the curve of his shoulder. He smelled not of hospital antiseptic but of clean, warm male. Whitney was so surprised her hands fluttered at his waist. What was going on? She was released almost as quickly as he had grabbed her.

Tanner glanced over his shoulder. "Please just go along with me. First names only. No titles."

She looked beyond him to see the others in his party watching them. He made their meeting sound like a covert operation. She took a small step away from him. "Okay. I'm Whitney."

"I'm Tanner. I would prefer we keep my request between the two of us." His dark brown eyes beseeched her.

"I understand. I assure you I am discreet." Most professionals she worked with wanted their interactions with her to remain low-key. Either they didn't want others to know they needed help in their personal life or were just embarrassed they couldn't find someone on their own. Whatever it was, she respected their desires. But no one had gone to the extent that Tanner was to keep his secret.

So why was he meeting her in front of his colleagues? "Then why here?" She nodded her head toward the group at the plane.

"I didn't know I was going to have to go after a heart and I wanted you to get started on this right away."

"After a heart?" Her voice rose.

"I'm a heart transplant surgeon. I'm in the process of retrieving a heart."

"Oh." He made it sound like that was commonplace. For him it might be, but for her it was a little unnerving.

He looked over his shoulder as the jet engines roared to life. "So what do you need from me?"

And he wants to do this right now, right here?

"It usually takes an hour or so for me to get enough information from a client to form a good idea of the type of woman they are best suited to."

Tanner glanced back to where the others were loading the plane. "I don't have an hour. I have a patient who needs a new heart."

"Then I suggest we postpone this meeting." Whitney reached for her car door handle.

"I'd like to get the process started. I'm up for a promotion and the board is breathing down my neck to settle down. I've got to do something right away about finding a wife. But with my caseload I don't know when I'll be able to sit down and talk anytime soon." His voice held a note of desperation that she was confident didn't appear often. "What I'm looking for is someone who takes care of herself, is good in social situations, wants to be a mother and would be supportive of my career."

Really? That's all he wanted? He hadn't said anything about love. This would be a tough order to fill. "Those are pretty broad requirements. I like to know my clients well enough that I don't waste their or their potential partner's time."

"Hey, Tanner," the last man getting on the plane called. "We gotta go. This heart won't wait on us."

Tanner looked back to her. "I've got a patient that's been waiting for months for this heart. I have to see that he gets it. Look, I've heard you're the best in town. Do your thing. I'm sure you can find someone for me. Here's my contact information." He handed her a business card. "Call when you have something. Don't pull away. I'm going to give you a quick kiss on the cheek. I need for these guys—" he nodded toward the plane "—to think that you're my girlfriend."

Before Whitney could agree or disagree, his lips brushed her face and he jogged away.

The man's nerve knew no bounds!

Minutes later Whitney watched as the plane lifted off the ground and flew into the darkening sky. Somehow tonight the Tanner she'd had such a crush on and worshipped in college from afar had become a mortal man. The thing was she really didn't know this Tanner any better than she knew the old Tanner. If she did manage to find him a match, would he take the time to get to know the woman or just expect her to bow to his list of requirements? Whitney's goal was to find love matches, and Tanner had said nothing about wanting that.

And while they worked together there would be no more physical contact. She was a professional.

Tanner looked down from his window seat of the plane at the woman still standing beside her small practical compact car. She looked like a matchmaker. Simply dressed. Nothing sexy or suggestive about her clothing—he'd even characterize her style as unappealing. Her hair was pulled back into a band at her nape.

He didn't go around kissing strangers but he had kissed her. Little Ms. Matchmaker had the softest skin he'd ever felt. She was nothing like the women he was attracted to yet he found her no-nonsense, straight-to-the-point personality interesting. People generally didn't speak to him so frankly.

Did he know her from somewhere? Maybe she'd been a member of one of his former patients' families? But she'd said nothing about knowing him. He was good with faces. It could be her smile that drew him. It was one of the nicest he'd ever seen. Reached her eyes.

He hoped he'd made the right decision in calling her. There had been noises made by the powers-that-be at the hospital that he might be in line for the head of department position when Dr. Kurosawa retired. A subtle suggestion had been made that a settled married man looked more appealing on the vita than a bachelor.

For a moment he'd thought about doing the online dating thing but couldn't bring himself to enter his name. He didn't have the time or inclination to wade through all the possible dates. Make the dates and remake dates. The speed-dating idea came close to making him feel physically sick. Being thought pathetic because he used a dating service also disturbed him. The fewer people who knew what he was doing the better. Truthfully, he was uncomfortable having others know he needed hired help to find a partner. Even employing a matchmaker made him uneasy. But he'd done it. He wanted that directorship.

Finding women to date was no problem for him, but he had never found someone who met his requirements for a lifelong commitment. Tanner wasn't interested in a love match but in a relationship based on mutual life goals. Maybe with the help of an outsider, an impartial one, he could find a woman who wanted the same things he did? The search would be handled like a business, a study of pros and cons.

One thing he did know was that love wouldn't be the deciding factor. He'd already seen what that did to a person. His mother had loved his father but his father had not felt the same. In fact, she'd doted on him, but he'd stayed away more than he'd been at home. Each time he'd left she'd cried and begged him not to go. When he'd leave again she'd be depressed until she learned that he was coming home. Then she'd go into manic mode, buying a new dress and spending hours "fixing herself up." His father had never stayed long. Leaving two boys to watch their mother's misery as he'd disappeared down the drive. Finally he'd divorced her. Tanner refused to have any kind of relationship like that. His career demanded his time and focus. He had to have a wife who could handle that.

Maybe the executive matchmaker could help him find what he needed in a woman. If that woman was happy with what he could offer outside of giving his heart then she would suit him.

"Hey, Tanner," the kidney team surgeon said after a tap to his arm, "who was the woman you were talking to? Did you have to break a hot date?"

He shrugged. "Just a woman I met."

"You know one day you're going to have to settle down.

Hospital boards like to have their department heads going home to a family at night. I've got a friend of a friend with a sister. Pretty, I heard."

"I'm good, Charlie."

He grinned. "I'm just saying…"

Tanner was tired of being fixed up by friends and family. Everyone wanted their daughter or friend to marry a doctor.

He looked over at the nurse sitting beside Charlie. She was talking to a member of the liver team. They'd been out a number of times but nothing had really clicked. Tanner didn't want to date out of the nursing pool anymore. He wanted to go home to someone who wasn't caught up in the high adrenaline rush of medical work. A woman who gave him a peaceful haven where he could unwind.

He expected Whitney Thomason to find that person for him.

By the next morning, Tanner had put in over twenty-four hours at the hospital, but his patient, who had been at death's door, was now doing well in CICU. The life-giving gift of a heart transplant never ceased to amaze him. He was humbled by his part in the process.

Thankfully he'd managed to catch a couple of hours' sleep on the plane to and from the hospital where his team had retrieved the heart. Now he had morning rounds to make and then he was headed home to bed. His scheduled surgeries had been moved back a day or postponed. Sleep was the only thing on his agenda for today.

Knocking on the door of Room 223 of the step-down unit, he slowly pushed it open. "Mr. Vincent?"

"Come in." The man's voice was strong.

Tanner entered and moved to the bed. "How're you feeling today, Mr. Vincent?"

"I'd be lying if I said I wasn't sore."

Tanner smiled. Mr. Vincent was only a week out from

transplant. Where he'd hardly been able to walk down the hall in the weeks before his surgery, now he could do it back and forth with confidence. Transplants were amazing things. "Sorry about that but it's just part of the process. It should get better every day." Tanner looked around the room. "Mrs. Vincent here?"

"Naw. She had a hair appointment. She doesn't like to miss them." He sounded resigned to his wife's actions. "She'll be here soon, though."

"The plan is for you to go home tomorrow. There are a number of things that the nurses will need to go over with you both."

"Cindy doesn't like blood and all this hospital stuff."

"She'll need to help with your care or you'll have to find another family member to do it. Otherwise home health should be called in."

Mrs. Vincent's self-centeredness was just the type of thing that Tanner couldn't tolerate. This man's wife was so focused on her own needs that she couldn't be bothered to support her husband's return to good health. Her actions reminded him too much of his father's.

"I need to give you a listen, Mr. Vincent." Tanner removed his stethoscope from his neck. After inserting the earpieces in his ears, he placed the listening end on the man's chest. There was a steady, strong beat where one hadn't existed before the transplant.

"Can you sit forward, Mr. Vincent?"

"I can but I won't like it much." The middle-aged man shifted in the bed.

Tanner was listening to the man's lungs when a platinum blonde strolled through the door. She stopped short as if she was surprised to see Tanner.

"Hello, Dr. Locke," she said in a syrupy thick voice.

Tanner had only met Mrs. Vincent a couple of times but each time he had the prickly feeling that she was coming on to him. This time was no different. At least twenty years younger than her husband, she was overdressed and too absorbed in herself for someone who should have been concerned about a husband who had recently been at death's door. Wearing a tight top and pants a size too small, she sauntered up to the bedside, leaning over. Tanner had a view of her cleavage that had no business being shared with anyone but her husband.

More than once Tanner had seen his mother act the same way toward his father. The action then and now made him feel uncomfortable.

"Hi, sweetie. It's nice to see you." Mr. Vincent gave her an adoring smile.

"So how's the patient doing?" she cooed, not looking at her husband. His mother had used that same tone of voice when she'd spoken to his father.

"He's ready to go home after we make sure you both understand his care." Tanner wrapped his stethoscope around his neck.

"I'm not sure I can do that. I'm no nurse. I'm not good with blood and stuff." She gave him a wide, bright, red-painted-lips smile.

Tanner stepped toward the door. "I'm sure the nurses can help you practice so that you become comfortable with what you need to do."

"Cindy, sweetie, we'll figure it out together." Mr. Vincent took her manicured hand and gave her a pleading look. Just the way Tanner's mother had looked at his father before he'd left for weeks.

"I'll let the nurse know that you're ready for her instructions." Tanner went out the door.

The Vincents' marriage was exactly the type he didn't want. The one-sided kind. Tanner was afraid he would be too much like his mother. Give his heart and have it stomped on. A relationship where one of the partners couldn't see past their love for the other while the other cared about nothing but themselves. A bond based on mutual respect would be far more satisfying in the long run. With his executive matchmaker contacts, that should be just the type of arrangement he'd manage to find.

The censoring look in Whitney's eyes when he'd given his list of requirements had him questioning that she might have expected something more.

Whitney had spent the last two days working through her database in search of women who fit the description of what Tanner wanted. She had five names she thought might be of interest to him. Now she had to pin him down for a meeting so they could start the process.

She picked up the card he'd handed her and tapped it on her desk.

Why couldn't Tanner find his own mate? What was his deal with the passionless list of requirements? He had nothing in common with her in that regard. She was looking for true love. The kind of love that endured forever, no matter what the hardships. The till-death-do-us-part kind that her parents and grandparents had. She'd built her business on that idea. Believed her clients should have that as well.

Once she'd thought she'd had it. That love. With a business degree in hand, she'd taken a job in a corporation. There she'd met Steve. He'd worked in an adjoining department and had seemed not to care that she'd been heavy. That had been a first for her. She'd had no dates in high school and very few in college. When Steve had started giving her attention she'd been ecstatic. For once in her life someone had been interested. After dating for over a year, they'd started planning a wedding.

Two weeks before the ceremony he'd called and told

her he'd found someone else. The woman had turned out to be thin and pretty.

Whitney had been devastated. Again that inferiority she'd felt in high school and college had come flooding back. To fight the pain, she'd done whatever she could to keep busy. She'd spent her time walking whenever she'd been alone to prevent dwelling on her broken heart. After a while she'd become interested in wellness nutrition and had adopted a healthy lifestyle. Soon she'd joined an over-eating support group and continued to slim down. Men had started paying attention to her but she'd not yet found one that she trusted to stick with her. She wanted a man who cared about her and not just her looks. Those faded.

In college she'd introduced a number of friends to other classmates. The majority of those relationships had become long-term ones and many of the couples had gone on to marry. Whitney had gained the reputation of being a matchmaker. When her boss had confided in her that she was having trouble dating, Whitney had introduced her to a friend of her family. They too had married. A few years later, when the company she'd worked for had downsized and Whitney had been let go, she'd decided that if she couldn't find someone for herself she could at least help others find the right person. Opening Professional Matchmaking had been her answer.

Despite her own disappointments, she still believed that there was a soul mate for everyone. So what had happened in Tanner's life to make him not believe in love? Could she convince him it was necessary for him too? But that wasn't what he was paying her to do. He wanted the best mate possible and it was her job to see that she found that person, not change his requirements.

Whitney punched in Tanner's number from the card. Now it was time to help him do just that.

On the second ring he answered. "Locke."

"This is Whitney Thomason."

"Who?" His voice became muffled, as if he was speaking to someone else.

"Whitney Thomason of Professional Matchmaking."

"Uh, yeah. Just a minute."

She waited while he spoke to the other person, giving orders about what should be done for a patient.

Even with his abrupt speech he had a nice voice. Sort of warm and creamy. The kind a woman liked to hear in her ear when a man rolled toward her in the middle of the night. Heavens, that wasn't a thought she should be having about her newest client.

Seconds later the background noise quieted.

"I only have a few seconds. What can I do for you?"

She understood about being busy but he was the one requesting her help. "I have compiled a list of possible matches for you. I'd like to get together and discuss them. Start setting up some socials."

"Socials? I'm not interested in, neither do I have time for, tea parties."

That's why he didn't have anyone. He wouldn't put in the effort it took to develop a relationship. "Socials are when you have your first meeting with a potential mate. Before I can set those up we need to talk and sort out who you'd like to consider first."

"Can't you just take care of that?" He already sounded distracted. Maybe he was the same self-centered guy she'd known in college.

"Tanner, are you sure you want to do this?" Her voice took on a hard note. "You have to put some time and effort into finding the right person. Maybe you aren't ready yet."

There was a pause then a sigh of resignation. "What do you want me to do?"

"Can you meet me at Café Lombard at six this evening?"

"I'll be there." There was a click on the line as he ended the call.

Had she made him mad? Her time was valuable too. Tanner had come to her for help. He was going to have to meet her halfway, do his part to help find the perfect match for him. That required energy. If their conversation at the café didn't go well, she'd just tell him that he needed to go elsewhere for assistance.

Café Lombard was a small establishment at the bottom of Lombard Street, which was famous for being the curviest street in the world. Flowers bloomed between each of the curves, making it a fun street to look at but not to drive along. Tanner wasn't a fan of quaintness and this was one of the most picturesque places in San Francisco. When he arrived right at six, he spotted Whitney sitting at a table for two in the patio area.

Again her shoulder-length hair was primly pulled back into a controlled mass at the nape of her neck. She wore a simple blouse that gave little hint of her body shape and with that were a pair of black pants and flat shoes. There was nothing flamboyant about her. She looked as if she wanted to blend in, go unnoticed.

He started across the street toward her. She glanced up. A smile came to her lips as she waved at him. Now that expression stood out. It encouraged him to return it and he did.

Tanner joined her at the table.

"You're not going to grab me, are you?" She put a chair between them.

"Not unless you want me to. Look, I'm sorry about that. I just didn't want my colleagues asking a lot of questions. It was easier to pretend you were my girlfriend."

"I guess I can understand that."

He dropped into the chair across from her.

"Would you like something to drink or eat? It's on me, of course," Whitney offered.

She seemed to have already forgotten his invasion of her personal space. She was a good sport. "Thank you. I'm starved. But I can get my own."

The waiter came to their table.

"I'll have a cob salad and a water," Whitney said.

"And I'll have a steak sandwich with fries with a large lemonade."

The waiter left. Whitney quirked a corner of her mouth up as if perplexed by something.

"What?" Tanner asked.

"Lemonade? You seem more like a beer guy."

"I am, but I'm on call."

"Ah, that makes sense." She appeared to approve.

He leaned forward and crossed his arms on the table. "I'm sorry I was so abrupt with you on the phone. I've just been super busy this month. Under a lot of pressure."

She smiled. "I understand. I'll try to keep this short and sweet."

"So what did you need to see me about?"

"I've found some potential dates I think you might be interested in. I'd like you to review their files and see what you think. Then I'll set up a social with the one you like best." Whitney pushed a pink folder toward him.

Pink seemed an appropriate color for a matchmaker. At least her office supplies had some flair. Tanner opened the folder to find a printed page with the name of a woman at the top and information about her. He looked at Whitney. "No picture? I don't get to see what they look like?"

"Not until you meet them. I think a lasting relationship should be based on something more than looks. I want my clients to see beyond the surface."

"Interesting." Was there something peculiar about that belief? She no doubt believed in true love and happily-ever-after. He'd learned long ago not to believe in fairy tales. He flipped through the other pages. The women seemed interesting but a couple of them owned their own businesses. He picked up their sheets. "These don't look like they would have time to devote to children, take on social obligations."

"They both assure me that they would be willing to change their lifestyle for the right person. We can put them at the bottom of the list, if you wish, however."

"Have you spoken to them about me?" He didn't relish the idea of being discussed like a piece of merchandise. Yet he was doing the same thing in regards to those women.

She took the women's profiles from him and placed the open file on the table between them both. "I didn't disclose your name or picture but, yes, they have reviewed your profile as well."

"So this is how it works."

"Yes."

The waiter returned with their meals. Neither of them said anything until he left.

Whitney leaned forward with a reassuring smile on her lips. "It's not as painful as you might think. All my clients are interested in finding the same thing. Happiness with someone."

She made it sound like this was about a love match. A ride off into a beautiful sunset. "I'm more interested in someone who's compatible and interested in the same things as I am."

"I think if you spend some time reading this information—" she tapped the folder with her well-manicured, unpolished index finger "—you'll find these are all women worth meeting. They're all very lovely people."

Tanner took a bite out of his sandwich as he flipped the pages back and forth. He continued to eat and review the women's information. A couple of them sounded like they might work. He glanced at Whitney. She was sitting straight with one hand in her lap, eating her salad. Her manners were excellent.

He pushed two sheets toward her. "I think I would like to start with these."

She put her fork down and looked at the papers then nodded. "These are good choices. I'll see about setting up socials. I'll let you know when and where to meet."

"How will I know them?"

There was that reassuring lift of the lips again. "I'll be there to introduce you. It's very uncomfortable to wait for a person you don't know so I'll make the introductions and then leave you to get to know each other."

"So that's all there is to it?" He closed the folder and nudged it back toward her.

She moved her half-eaten salad away and took the folder. "That's it, except for the bill."

He raised a brow and grinned. "I thought you were getting the meal."

"I am, but there's the charge for my services so far." Whitney reached into her purse, removed an envelope and handed it to him.

"Did you add extra for meeting me at the airport and the hug and kiss?"

Whitney pushed the chair back. She looked dead serious when she said, "No. That came for free—once. Next time it will cost you."

"I hope it isn't necessary again. I'll have this in the mail tomorrow." He stuffed the envelope into his pants pocket.

Again she dug into her purse, came out with a couple of green bills and placed them on the table. "Thank you for that. Now, if you'll excuse me, I'll get started on setting up those socials. I'll be in touch soon."

Tanner watched her leave the patio and cross the street. Interesting person. Combination of quiet firmness and solid businesswoman. He grinned. She'd become a little flustered when he'd mentioned that hug and kiss again. There was a softness under that businesswoman tough exterior. His gaze moved to the swing of her shapely hips. That wasn't bad either.

CHAPTER TWO

IT HAD BEEN two days since Whitney had spoken briefly to Tanner about the social she had set up for him today. He'd assured her he would be there but he'd yet to show. She'd always had one of her clients meet her early so that they were waiting for the other one when he or she arrived.

Whitney looked around the coffee shop again. Still no Tanner. Picking up her phone, she texted him.

"Were you worried that I wouldn't show?" a deep voice asked from behind her.

She looked around and into Tanner's dark, twinkling eyes. He had nice eyes. Eyes she suspected saw more than he let on. "I was more worried about your tardiness hurting your chances with Michelle Watkins. After all, we're doing this for you."

"And I appreciate that. It's the reason I am here. So I'm going to be meeting Michelle. Five-six, brown hair, educated at UCLA and likes the outdoors." He came around the table and took the chair across from her.

"I see you remember your facts."

"So what happens now?" He leaned toward her as if what she was going to say was super important. She'd bet he had a great bedside manner.

"When Michelle arrives, I'll introduce you to each other, then I'll leave you to charm her."

His focus didn't waver. "How do you know I can do that?"

Tanner's intense attention made her nerves jump. She'd said more than she'd intended. Would he see the weakness and insecurity she worked to keep at bay? Since he hadn't remembered her she hadn't planned on bringing up their college years. Now she either lied to him or admitted she'd recognized him. She wasn't a liar. With her ex, Steve, she'd lived a lie and wouldn't ever treat anyone that way. "You and I had a few classes together at Berkeley."

He looked truly surprised. Cocking his head to the side, he asked, "We did?"

"Yeah. They were lower-level classes." From there she'd gone into business classes, he into sciences. She'd still seen him around campus, though.

He appeared to give that thought, as if searching back through his memories of those days. "I'm sorry, I don't remember you."

His tone led her to believe he was sincere. "There's no reason that you would."

Tanner leaned back in his chair and studied her. "So how does a woman with an education from Berkeley become a matchmaker?"

"Mostly by accident. I helped some people in college meet someone and then later did the same thing for my boss, and the rest is history."

He nodded sagely. "Just that easily you started a business matching people up?"

"It wasn't all that easy at first. But the word got around that I am discreet and, most of all, successful." She glanced toward the front door then raised her hand, drawing Michelle Watkins's attention.

Tanner looked over his shoulder then quickly stood. Whitney gave him points for being a gentleman. But she wasn't the one he needed to impress. Michelle was. She was smiling, which was encouraging.

When the woman reached them Whitney introduced them. "Michelle, I'd like you to meet Tanner Locke."

Tanner offered Michelle his hand, along with a warm smile that Whitney recognized from their college days when he'd been charming a crowd of women. "It's a pleasure to meet you, Michelle. Please, join us."

Michelle couldn't seem to keep her eyes off Tanner. Was she already bowled over by him? Whitney was tempted to roll her eyes. The man's magic knew no bounds.

"Thank you," Michelle cooed, and took the chair Tanner held for her.

"Why don't I order us all something to drink?" Whitney suggested as a waitress came to the table.

"That would be nice," Michelle agreed, not taking her gaze off Tanner.

Whitney placed the order and the waitress left.

Tanner looked at Michelle. "I understand you like the outdoors."

"Yes," Michelle simpered. "I love to hike when I have the time."

Whitney sat back and listened as the two traded stories about their favorite hikes. They seemed to have forgotten she was there, something that had happened to her more than once in her life. She'd learned to live with it. This time it was part of her business.

The waitress brought their drinks, which swung Tanner's attention back to her. "Thank you for the lemonade. I'll get these this time," he said to Whitney, then his attention returned to Michelle.

Whitney took a long swallow of the cool, tart liquid. Setting the glass on the table, she said, "I'll leave you both to get to know each other better. I'll be in touch."

Tanner nodded.

Michelle said, "Thank you, Whitney," before her attention went straight back to Tanner.

Whitney walked to the front door. She looked back at them. They made a nice-looking pair. Two dark-haired, well-groomed, professional people who looked as if they were enjoying each other's company.

That was what her matchmaking was all about. So why couldn't she do that for herself?

Two days later, Whitney answered the phone.

"We need to talk."

Whitney didn't have to question who she was speaking to. She knew that voice at the first roll of a vowel. This time it wasn't warm and creamy. It was icy and sharp.

"Tanner, is something wrong?" She kept her voice low and even. She didn't often have to talk a client down after a social or a date.

"Michelle won't do. We need to meet again. Bring that file."

Whitney stiffened. She wasn't one of his OR nurses to be ordered around. "What's wrong?"

"I don't have time to talk about it now."

And he thinks I do?

"Let me see. How about the coffeehouse on Market Street tomorrow morning around nine?"

"I have surgery then. Could you come to the hospital in about an hour?"

What? She wasn't at his beck and call. She'd already gone out of her way for him once and now he wanted her to drop what she was doing and drive downtown. "I don't know. That isn't how I like to conduct business. I thought you didn't want anyone to know you were using my services. Aren't you afraid someone might ask you questions?"

"They might but I don't have to answer. Whitney, it

would really help me out if you could come here. I'm tied up with cases but I'd really like to get this other stuff rolling along."

Other stuff rolling along.

Was that how he thought of the woman who would share the rest of his life? She was glad she didn't fit his list.

Unfortunately, she didn't really have a good excuse why she couldn't help him out. "Okay, but I won't be doing this again."

"Great. Just give me a call when you get here." He hung up.

Tanner hadn't even said goodbye. It was time to have a heart-to-heart with him about whether or not he was really interested in doing the work needed to find a soul mate.

The traffic was light so she made good time going up and down the hills of San Francisco. The city could be difficult to drive in but the views of the bay made it worth it. She was just sorry a streetcar didn't run close enough to the hospital for her to take one of those.

She found a parking spot in the high-rise lot next to the hospital. Crossing the street, she entered the towering hospital. In the lobby, she pulled out her phone and called Tanner's number. Never in her wildest dreams would she ever have imagined having it at her fingertips. She and Tanner didn't move in the same circles and never would.

He answered as he had before. There was an arrogance to how he responded but the crisp sound of his last name seemed to suit him.

"It's Whitney."

"Hey." His tone changed as if he was glad to hear from her. She liked that idea too much. Obviously since he'd gotten his way he had calmed down. "From the main lobby door continue down the long hallway to the second bank of elevators on your right. They'll be about halfway down the hall. Take one of them. Come up to the fifth floor. I'll meet you at the elevator."

Tanner didn't wait for her to answer before closing the connection. That she wasn't as accepting of. She'd rather be told goodbye.

Whitney found the bank of elevators and took the next available car. At the correct floor she stepped off. As good as his word, Tanner stood there, talking to another man also dressed in scrubs. When he saw her he left the man and strolled over to her.

He was the epitome of the tall, dark and handsome doctor. He still had the looks that drew women's attention. What had happened between him and Michelle she couldn't fathom.

Michelle had called yesterday morning all but glowing about the social and the date they'd had the night before. How she could have seen it as being so wonderful while Tanner was so unhappy was a mystery to Whitney.

"Thanks for coming." Tanner ran his hand over his hair. "I know it wasn't what you wanted to do. I had to come in last night to do an emergency surgery. I just couldn't get away today. I have one more patient to see. Would you mind hanging out for a little bit?"

If he'd asked her that in college she might have fainted. Now Whitney only saw him as a man who needed her services. "Sure. I wouldn't mind watching what you do. It might help me better understand you, which would assist me in matching you."

"All business, all the time."

"You're one to be talking," she quipped.

He grinned. "You're not the first person to say that. After I see this patient we'll go to my office to talk."

They walked down a hall until they came to double doors. Tanner scanned a card and the doors opened from the middle out. They entered a hallway with patients' rooms. He stopped at the third doorway along the passage. "This is Mr. Wilcox. Let me get permission for you to come in."

"I don't mind waiting out here."

Tanner touched her arm when she started to move to the other side of the hall. A zing of awareness traveled up her arm. "He's rather lonely. He'd like to have the company. See a face that has nothing to do with the hospital."

That was a side of Tanner she hadn't expected. Compassion beyond the medicine. "Then I'll be glad to say hi."

Tanner raised his hand to knock on the door but turned back to her. "He has a lot of pumps and drips hooked to him. That stuff doesn't bother you, does it?"

She smiled. "No, I promise not to faint or stare."

"Good." Tanner appeared pleased with her answer. Had other women he'd known acted negatively to what he did for a living? He knocked on the door and stuck his head around it. There was a rumble of voices, then Tanner waved her toward him.

"We'll need to wear masks." He pulled a yellow paper one from a box on a table outside the door and handed it to her before entering the room. She followed.

Mr. Wilcox was about her father's age, but his skin was an ash gray. Beside him was a bank of machines with lights. There was a whish of air coming from one. A clear rubber tube circled both the man's ears and came around to fit under his nose.

"Mr. Wilcox, I brought you a visitor," Tanner said.

The man's dull eyes brightened for a second as he looked at her.

"Whitney Thomason, I'd like you to meet Jim Wilcox."

"Nice to meet you, young lady," Mr. Wilcox wheezed as he raised a hand weakly toward her.

"You too, Mr. Wilcox." Whitney stepped closer to the bed.

"So how're you feeling?" Tanner asked, leaning forward, concern written on his face.

Whitney was impressed with the lower timbre of his voice, which sounded as if he truly wished to know. She could grow to admire this Tanner.

"Oh, about the same. This contraption—" Mr. Wilcox nodded toward the swishing machine beside him "—is keeping me alive but I'm still stuck in this bed."

"Well, maybe there'll be a heart soon."

"That's what you've been telling me for weeks now. I'm starting to think you're holding out on me." Mr. Wilcox offered a small smile and perked up when he looked at her. "At least you were kind enough today to bring me something pretty to look at."

Whitney blushed. "Thanks but—"

"Aw, don't start all that stuttering and blustering. I have a feeling your beauty goes more than skin deep."

Whitney really did feel heat in her cheeks then. "I think that might be the nicest compliment I've ever received."

Tanner's eyes met hers and held. Did he agree with Mr. Wilcox? Did he see something that others didn't?

The older man cleared his throat.

Tanner's attention returned to him. "Okay, Romeo. I need to give you a listen." He pulled his stethoscope from around his neck. "I might have done a bad thing by inviting Whitney in."

"If I promise to be nice, will you bring her back again?" Mr. Wilcox asked with enthusiasm in every word.

Whitney touched the older man's arm. "Don't worry, he doesn't have to invite me for me to come again."

She felt more than saw Tanner glance at her.

"Then I'll look forward to it. So tell me how you know this quack over here?" Mr. Wilcox indicated Tanner.

Her gaze met Tanner's. There was panic in his gaze.

He probably didn't want the man to know she was helping him find a wife. "Oh, we were in college together."

Tanner's brows rose. He nodded as if he was pleased with her response.

"Where'd you go?" Mr. Wilcox rasped.

"Berkeley," she told him.

"Then you got a fine education."

Tanner interrupted them with, "So, are you having any chest pains?"

Mr. Wilcox paused. "No."

"That's good. You seem to be holding your own." Tanner flipped through the chart he'd brought in with him and laid it on the bed tray. "You need to be eating more. You have to keep your energy up."

"I'll try but nothing tastes good." Mr. Wilcox pushed at the bed table as if there was something offensive on it.

"Not even ice cream?" Tanner asked.

"I've eaten all those little cups I can stand. I'd like a good old-fashioned banana split that I could share with someone like your young lady."

Tanner chuckled. "When you get your heart and are out of here I'll see if I can get Whitney to come back and bring you a fat-free split."

"Fat-free," he spat.

"That's it," Tanner said with a grin.

"Well, if Whitney shares it with me maybe I can live with it. She has nice eyes. Windows to the soul, they say." Mr. Wilcox smiled.

"That she does," Tanner agreed.

Whitney looked at Tanner. Did he really mean that? She'd had no indication that he'd noticed anything about her.

"So is she your girlfriend?"

"Just friends," she and Tanner said at the same time.

Whitney wasn't sure that their professional association

qualified as friendship. Tanner wanted his personal business kept private, so "friends" seemed the right thing to say. Could they be friends? She didn't know. What she did recognize was that she liked the Tanner who was concerned enough about his patient's loneliness to invite her to meet him just to cut the monotony of being in the hospital day after day. That was a Tanner she could find a match for. Sad that the other Tanner wouldn't let this one show up more often.

"Even behind that mask I can tell she's pretty enough to be your girlfriend. You can always tell a special woman by her eyes. My wife, Milly, had beautiful eyes."

Tanner put his hand on the man's shoulder. "I think we'd better be going."

Whitney touched Mr. Wilcox's arm briefly. "I hope to see you again soon. It was nice to meet you."

He lifted a hand and waved as she reached the door. "You too. You're welcome to my abode anytime."

Whitney smiled. She liked Mr. Wilcox. "Bye, now."

Tanner joined her. "See you soon, Mr. Wilcox."

"You too, Doc."

Whitney stepped out into the hall and Tanner followed, pulling the door closed behind him.

As they removed their masks Tanner said, "I'm sorry if he made you feel uncomfortable in there or put you on the spot about being with me. Mr. Wilcox can be pretty cheeky."

"I didn't mind. He seems like a nice guy who's lonely."

"He is. As a doctor I'm not supposed to have favorites but I really like the man. He's been waiting too long."

She watched for his reaction as she said, "That's why you took me to see him. You knew he needed something to prick his interest. You didn't mind him assuming I was your girlfriend because that would give him something to figure out, live for."

"Why, Ms. Thomason, you are smart."

Whitney couldn't deny her pleasure at his praise. She also couldn't help but ask, "I know you can't tell me details, but what's going on with Mr. Wilcox?"

Tanner's eyes took on a haunted look. "Most of it you heard. He's waiting for a heart. He needs one pretty quickly."

"Or he'll die," she said quietly.

Tanner's eyes took on a shadowed look. "Yeah."

"You seem to take that in your stride." She sounded as if she was condemning him even to her own ears.

"It's a part of what I do. Medical School 101. But that doesn't mean I like it." His retort was crisp. He started down the hall and she followed. At the desk he handed a nurse Mr. Wilcox's chart and continued on. "My office is this way. I'm on call tonight."

Whitney had to hurry to keep up with him. They walked down a couple of hallways to a nondescript door. Again Tanner swiped his card. There was a click. He turned the doorknob and entered. She trailed him down a short hall to a small sterile-looking office. It became even smaller when Tanner stepped in.

There was a metal desk with a black high-backed chair behind it and a metal chair in front. What struck her as most interesting was the absence of pictures. Didn't he have family? Nieces or nephews? A dog?

"Please, come in." Tanner walked around the desk and settled into the chair. Was his home this cold as well? Could he open his life enough to have a wife and family?

Whitney sat in the uncomfortable utilitarian chair. Apparently whoever visited wasn't encouraged to stay long. "I understand from Michelle that she had a wonderful time the other night. So what's the problem on your side?"

Tanner picked up a pen and twisted it through his fingers, a sure sign he wasn't comfortable with the question. "She wanted something that I won't give."

There was a chilly breeze in the words. "That is?"

"Let's just say she was already getting more emotionally attached than I want to be. You need to go through your file and find me some women who are interested in security, financial comfort, social status, not whether or not they are loved. I'm looking for something far more solid than love. Companionship."

Whitney felt like she'd been punched in the chest. She'd never heard anything sadder. All the compassion she'd just seen Tanner show Mr. Wilcox was gone. Now all she saw was a shell of a man. For him a heart was nothing more than an organ that pumped blood. Not the center of life she believed it to be. "The women I represent all want to be loved."

He put his elbows on the desk and steepled his fingers, giving her a direct look. "For the amount of money I'm paying you I expect you to find someone who suits my needs. I thought I'd made it clear what I wanted in a relationship. It's your business to find me that match."

If he had slapped her she couldn't have been more insulted. "I assure you I know my business. I'll set up a social with the next client on my list for as soon as possible." She looked him in the eyes. "But you should know, Tanner, it's my experience that most people see marriage less as a business deal and more as an emotional attachment."

Tanner's face turned stern. His voice was firm when he said, "That might be the case but that isn't the type of person I'm looking for. I've made my request and you've stated you can fill it, so that's what I expect."

What had happened to the man? How could he be so compassionate toward his patient but so calculating about the type of wife he wanted? Whitney stood. "I'll be in touch soon."

He got to his feet as well. "Good. If you take a right out of my door you'll come to a set of elevators. It'll take you down to the lobby. Thanks for coming here."

She'd been dismissed. That was fine with her. Whitney turned on her heel and left. Right now she wasn't sure if she should keep Tanner as a client. Truth be known, she wasn't certain she even liked him.

Tanner was at Café Lombard for the "social" before Whitney or the woman he was to meet. When Whitney had left his office the other evening she hadn't been happy. Her lips had been pinched tight and her chin had jutted out. Somehow what he had said she had taken personally. Hadn't he made it clear what he was looking for in a relationship during their earlier interview? Couldn't she understand that he had no interest in a love match?

Those only led to pain, not just between the husband and wife but for the children as well. He and his brother were a prime example of that. They hadn't seen each other in years. Tanner wanted a marriage based on something solid and not fleeting, like an emotion.

His date with Michelle had been wonderful. They'd had a number of things in common. They both enjoyed the outdoors, liked baseball and traveling. It wasn't that he didn't like Michelle, but he could tell by her speech and her body language that she was looking for more than he could give. There had been hopeful stars in her eyes. He wanted someone whose expectations were less dreamlike and more firmly rooted in reality.

Statements like "Children should know that their parents care about each other. It makes for a more stable child," or "I want a husband who can be there when I need him," showed him that Michelle needed emotional support that he just couldn't give. Tanner wanted someone who could handle their own ups and downs without involving him.

He looked up to see Whitney entering. The displeased expression she'd worn the other day was gone but there was still a tightness around her lips, indicating she might not be in the best of moods. When had he started being able to read so well someone he hardly knew?

He half stood. She flashed a smile of greeting. It was an all-business tilt of the lips instead of actual gladness to see him. Tanner didn't much care for that. Yet why did it bother him to have her disgruntled with him?

Today Whitney wore a flowing dress with a small pale pink rose pattern on it that reached just past her knees. A sweater was pulled over her shoulders and the sleeves tied across her chest. She was dressed like an old-maid schoolteacher. Why did she wear such nondescript clothing? Did she do it because she thought people believed that was how a matchmaker should dress? She was too young and too attractive not to flaunt it some. What would she look like in a tight, short skirt? He'd be interested to see. Great, would be his guess. But why should it matter to him how she dressed?

"Hello, Tanner." She took the chair across from him. "You're early."

"My last case was canceled due to a fever so I got away from the hospital sooner than I thought I would."

Whitney clasped her hands in her lap and looked directly at him. "I think you work too hard and too many hours." It wasn't an accusation, more a statement of fact. She didn't give him time to respond before she continued. "You're going to meet Racheal today. I think you'll really like her. She has a master's degree in business and loves children."

"I remember reading her profile. Did you make it clear to her what I am looking for?"

"I did. She's interested in a family but doesn't want to give over her freedom just to have that. She's looking for the same type of relationship that you are." Whitney made it sound as if the idea left a bad taste in her mouth.

"Do you have a problem with that?"

She shrugged then leaned back in the chair. "Not if that's what you both want."

He leaned forward, piercing her with a look.

She shifted in the chair.

Tanner crossed his arms on the table. "Tell me what you think this should be about."

Her eyes widened. She did have pretty ones. Like green grass after spring rain. She blinked. "It isn't about what I think but about what you want."

"Spoken like a true matchmaker, eager to please. Are you married, Whitney?"

Her chin raised a notch. "I don't believe that has anything to do with your case."

"It might not but it gives me an idea of how good you are at this matchmaking business."

She shifted in her chair. "If you don't have any confidence if my ability then I'll be glad to refund your money minus five hundred dollars for the work I've done so far."

He'd hit a touchy spot. "And add the charge for the hug and kiss after all?"

She relaxed and shook her head. "No. I wouldn't do that. This isn't a joke."

He leaned back in the chair and watched her for a long moment. Her direct look challenged his. This was a woman who wouldn't give up until she had succeeded. "You're right—it isn't. I'm not ready to throw in the towel yet."

"Then you do understand that I have the same responsibility to the women I introduce you to as I do to you?"

She had backbone and a moral line. What you saw was what you got with Whitney. That was refreshing. Most women he knew were only really interested in themselves. "I realize that. I'll try to be on my best behavior."

"I'm starting to wonder what that is. I also expect you to give them a fair chance." Her tone had become school-marmish.

"You don't think I gave Michelle that?"

She didn't immediately answer. "Truthfully, I'm not sure you did."

It didn't matter to him if she thought so or not. He knew what he wanted better than she did, matchmaker or not. It was his life they were talking about. He'd seen what uninvited and unrequited love did to a person. He wanted none of it. Good, solid, practical thought was what his marriage would be based on.

A blonde woman stepped up to their table. Whitney jerked around as if she'd forgotten all about her joining them. Tanner smiled. She'd been too flustered by his questions to remember why they were there. He liked the idea that he'd rattled Whitney. Too much.

"Hello, Racheal. I'm sorry I didn't see you when you came in." Whitney's voice sounded a little higher than normal.

Once again, Whitney was a contrast to her female client. Racheal had a short haircut and every strand was in its place. Her makeup was flawless and she wore the latest fashion with ease. She certainly looked the part of the woman he thought he would like to share his name. He looked at Whitney and somehow he found her more to his taste. Shaking that thought away, Tanner returned his attention to Racheal.

He stood and offered his hand to her. "Tanner Locke. Thanks for joining us."

He held a chair out for Racheal and she gracefully slipped into it.

"It's nice to meet you." Racheal had a no-nonsense note in her voice.

He looked at Whitney. "I've already ordered drinks."

"Thank you, Tanner. I think I'll leave you and Racheal to get to know each other better. I'll be in touch soon."

Tanner remained standing as she left. A tug of disappointment went through him to see her go. Why?

Whitney hadn't heard from Tanner in three days. Far too often she had found herself wondering how things were going between him and Racheal. She liked to give her clients time to get to know each other and digest their thoughts on the new match before she asked. This time she was particularly anxious to know.

Racheal had already checked in. She seemed pleased with Tanner. According to her, they'd had a wonderful time talking at the social and had enjoyed their first date. Maybe she had found the right one for Tanner after all. But she had thought that with Michelle. She would wait until tomorrow and give him a call. See if he was as pleased as Racheal.

That evening Whitney was just slipping into bed when her phone rang. A call this late usually didn't mean good news. Was her father ill again? "Hello?"

"It's Tanner."

His voice was low and gravelly. There was no apology for calling so late. She wasn't surprised. But with his schedule he probably thought nothing of it. "Yes?"

"You told me to call and let you know how things are going."

She had indeed told him that but had assumed he would do so during business hours. An edgy feeling washed over her, knowing she was in bed while talking to Tanner. It seemed far too evocative. She flipped the covers back and stood beside the bed.

"Racheal seems to be working out. We went out last night. I have a party on Friday that I've invited her to." His voice was low and calm, as if he had all the time in the world to talk.

"I'm glad to hear it. I'll check in with you both next week. I look forward to hearing how the relationship is progressing."

"How have you been?" His voice was warm and silky.

Whitney walked to the window. "I'm fine."

"That's good. Goodnight."

Whitney listened to the click on the other end of the line. She returned to her bed and pulled the covers over herself again. Somehow the sheets didn't feel as cool anymore.

Maybe Racheal was it. Had Tanner found the one he wanted? Whitney wished she felt happier about that idea.

Even if he hadn't, he wouldn't look at her that way. Did she want him to? Turning off the light, she settled under the covers, but it took her far too long to fall asleep.

Whitney continued to wonder how things were going between Tanner and Racheal. More than once she'd been tempted to call him but had held back. She'd never had that problem before. Normally she let her couples go without thought or overseeing them, but Tanner's case held too much of her attention.

Whitney was already asleep a week later when the phone rang. She picked up the phone and a man's voice said, "Just what type of women are you introducing me to? You're supposed to be the best at this."

"Tanner, what's going on? Do you know what time it is?"

"Yes. I know what time it is." He sounded angry.

At this point the time didn't matter. She was awake

anyway. Despite that, she found herself happy to finally hear from him. "What's the problem?"

"The problem is that Racheal backed out of a weekend we had planned in Napa. It's a hospital retreat and I had already said I would be bringing a guest. I'm trying to make a positive impression on the board. This situation could hurt my chance for a promotion."

"I'm sorry." And she was. He was a good doctor and deserved it, she was sure.

"You should be. I hold you responsible."

"Me!" Whitney squeaked and set up in bed.

"I'm paying you to provide me with women who understand the importance of my job and position."

What was he raving about? "Racheal didn't?"

"I guess not. She agreed to go and now at the last minute she's backed out."

Whitney worked to keep her tone even. "Did she give you a reason?"

"She just said she wasn't ready for this step."

That sounded reasonable to Whitney. "You can't expect her to do something that she isn't comfortable with."

"I damn well can expect her to keep her word."

He had a point there, but what did he imagine she could do about it? She couldn't make Racheal go with him. "I have to honor what my clients feel they need to do."

"And you have to honor our contract. I need someone as my girlfriend this weekend."

It was Thursday. How was she going to find someone who would go away with a perfect stranger on such short notice? "I wish I could help you, Tanner. At this point I don't know what I can do."

"Well, I do. If you can't find me someone then you have to come. At least that way I'll be bringing a guest. I can make up a story about how we broke up later."

What? Is he crazy? Spend a weekend with him?

"That's not possible. It's unethical. You're my client."

"One you're expected to keep happy. You were supposed to vet the women you introduce me to. You failed in determining Racheal's true character. I expect you to meet your professional obligation."

How did that logically extend to her personally replacing a client?

"Look, this weekend is important to my career, just as finding the right woman is. There will be no expectations on my part except for you to be pleasant and act as if we're a couple." His voice was firm and determined, as if he wouldn't accept no as an answer.

Whitney's heart pounded. Was she seriously going to consider it? "You can't just demand that I spend the weekend with you."

"Sure I can." His voice had turned hard. "We have a contract for services and you need to hold up your end. It was your suggestion that I pick Racheal. She didn't hold up her end so that defaults to you."

Whitney wasn't sure she agreed with his reasoning but she didn't need him bad-mouthing her around town. She'd taken Tanner on as a client to increase her professional profile, not to hurt it. Plus, she hated that he was in a spot.

If she agreed to his demand she couldn't imagine the weekend being anything but long and miserable. She didn't belong in his social group. She was an outsider. Tanner wanted someone who could make a good impression. More than once she'd been judged by her looks. He needed someone who could influence. That wasn't her. She was good with people one on one but not as a member of a house party. To run in Tanner's world…

"I'll pick you up at nine in the morning. What's your address?"

"Tanner, I can't do this."

"Oh, yes, you can," he all but hollered down the phone.

He wasn't going to allow her a way out. Apprehension bubbled in Whitney as she gave him her address.

"You'll need a cocktail dress, swimsuit and casual clothes." There was a click on the other end of the line. Tanner had hung up. Once again.

Whitney lay there. What had just happened? She'd just gotten press-ganged into a weekend with Tanner as his "plus one." What was he thinking? What *was* she doing?

Those bubbles combined into a heavy mass of dread in her chest. She wasn't part of Tanner's world. What if she made a mistake and embarrassed him?

If she had really changed from that insecure girl from years ago it was time to prove it.

CHAPTER THREE

TANNER DIDN'T KNOW what had gotten into him when he'd insisted that Whitney join him on this weekend retreat. He had been so angry when Racheal had called and told him that she wouldn't be going that he'd picked up the phone and dialed Whitney's number without a thought. But to insist she attend a weekend with him might have been overreacting. Desperation had fueled his demand. He needed a woman on his arm.

Well, it was done now.

For him to have a "significant other" with him for the weekend was an unwritten requirement. Besides, he might have hinted to one or two of the board members that he'd become serious about someone. It mustn't look like he'd been lying or he could kiss that promotion goodbye.

He pulled his car to the curb in front of Whitney's home. To his surprise, he'd known the address. She lived in one of the famous "painted ladies." Whitney stood waiting in front of a light blue Victorian row house with a yellow door and white gingerbread trimmings. Pink flowers grew in pots on the steps. The house was an obvious reflection of Whitney. He'd always liked these old homes. Something about them said life was peaceful inside.

Whitney looked small compared to the towering three-story home. His heart fell. This wasn't good. She wore a full shirt that hung almost to her knees and underneath she wore baggy pajama-style pants and flat slippers. Her hair was pulled back into a bun. Whitney couldn't have looked more nondescript if she had tried. He really couldn't force her to dress better, or could he?

Stepping out of the car, Tanner went to the trunk and opened it.

Whitney joined him with her bags in her hand. "Tanner, I think we should really reconsider this idea."

"I've already done that a couple of times and I don't see another way. I need a girlfriend for this weekend and you are it." Even if her sense of style was missing.

Uncertainty filled her eyes. "This type of thing really isn't me."

"You'll be fine. Sitting by the pool and reading all day works for me. I just need you to attend the dinner this evening and tomorrow evening and all will be good."

She didn't look any more enthused but she let him take her bags and climbed into the car.

Yet again he felt bad about insisting she come with him, but he needed her. The board members would be at this retreat and he had to give them the impression he was getting close to settling down. "Do you mind if I put the top down? It's a beautiful day."

"Not at all. I love a convertible."

Tanner leaned over her to unlock the roof from the windshield. A floral scent that fit her perfectly assaulted his nose. Maybe the weekend wouldn't be so bad. He flipped the other lock above his head. When he pushed a button, the roof slowly folded down behind them.

"I like your car. It suits you," Whitney said.

"Thanks. I grew up wanting one of these and when I finished medical school I bought one."

"I've always loved two-seaters. I'm going to enjoy riding in this one." She gave him a weak smile.

So at least they had that in common. As Tanner started the car, Whitney pulled a long multicolored scarf out of her purse. With deft efficiency she wrapped it around her head and tied it under her chin. Great, now he had Old Mother Hubbard with him. Why did she dress like she did?

"The only complaint I have about having the top down is that it's hard on a hairdo."

He'd never really thought of her as having a hairstyle. Her hair had always been just pulled back behind her neck when he'd seen her. Today was no different. She didn't seem to make any real effort to stand out where her appearance was concerned. What was she hiding from? Now with the scarf around her head she looked drabber than ever. That was with the exception of when she smiled. At those times she captured his attention completely.

It disturbed him on a level he didn't want to examine how much time he'd spent thinking about his matchmaker in the past few weeks. Even when he and Racheal had been dating he'd wondered what Whitney would think about this or that, or what she was doing. These were not things his mind should have been contemplating. Racheal had seemed perfect for him, just what he'd asked for, so why had he been thinking about another woman?

Especially Whitney. There could never be any real interest there. They clearly didn't want the same things out of a relationship. He had no plans to ever love a woman. His parents had seen to that.

Tanner's attention remained on his driving as he made his way up and down the steep streets of San Francisco lined with houses and businesses. He glanced at Whitney a couple of times. She seemed absorbed in the city life around them. Once he caught her looking at him. She made him feel both uncomfortable and pleased.

As they waited at the toll booth at the Golden Gate

Bridge she said, "I love this bridge. It's like this big smiling sentinel standing over the bay, protecting it."

"I've never thought about it like that. For me it's a feat of engineering, from the rock foundation to the suspension towers to the length of the wires."

"Or maybe it's like a big swing. Either way, it's amazing."

Tanner looked at her and grinned. "Agreed."

"Did you know that as soon as they finish painting it they have to start over again?" Whitney had her neck craned back, looking up at one of the three soaring towers.

He smiled. "I did. That's a lot of red paint."

Tanner paid the toll and they started across the bridge.

Halfway over the bay Whitney said, "The thump-thump of the tires reminds me of a heartbeat." A few seconds later she continued, "It's mind-boggling to me that I actually know someone who has held a heart in his hand."

Tanner grinned. "I'm glad I can impress." He wasn't sure he had so far during their acquaintance.

Traffic was heavy, even for a Friday morning, as people were leaving the city for the weekend. The road widened and the driving became easier after they were over the bridge. Tanner had been accused of being a fast driver but Whitney didn't seem bothered by his weaving in and out of traffic. Her hands remained in her lap and her chin up as if she were a flower enjoying the sunshine.

As they headed off the bridge toward the green rolling hills on the way to Napa she asked, "So what's expected of me this weekend?"

"Mostly to act as if you like me."

She met his eyes. "I'll try."

For some reason it disturbed him that she didn't already like him. "I know I've been a little high-handed a couple of times—"

Her brows rose. "A couple? How about all the time?"

Tanner shrugged a shoulder as he changed lanes. "Okay, maybe I deserve that, but I really need your help this weekend."

"You could have asked."

He glanced at her. "Would you have done it?"

"No…" The word trailed off.

Tanner's focus went back to the black sedan he was following. "So I would've had to apply pressure anyway. How about I double your fee for your trouble?"

She shook her head. "Let me think about it. No. That would make me feel like a prostitute."

He didn't like her accusation at all. "Whoa, that isn't what this is about. You won't be expected to sleep with me. In fact, I don't expect you to do anything more than hold on to my arm and pretend to be my girlfriend." Turning left, he followed a sign to Napa.

"Sleeping with you wasn't what I was referring to. I have no intention of doing that."

She made it sound as if he wasn't good enough for her. That was a first for him. Women were usually more than eager to climb into his bed. Why wouldn't she be? Was she holding on to her favors until she found that "love" she was so fond of believing in? Maybe he was just the person to change her mind.

Wait, that wasn't what this weekend was about. He'd promised sex wouldn't be on the agenda. He had no business thinking that way. Whitney was his matchmaker, and only with him because he had insisted. This wasn't some weekend fling. He had to remember that.

"So what're the sleeping arrangements?" Whitney asked in the matter-of-fact way he'd come to expect from her.

"We'll have to share a room but I'll give you as much privacy as possible. I'll sleep on the floor if necessary." That he wasn't looking forward to. But she was doing him a favor so it was the least he could do to try to make her as comfortable in the situation as possible.

"And what're the other plans for the weekend?"

"There is a round of golf organized for this afternoon and tomorrow." The land flattened as they entered the valley, allowing him to look at Whitney more often.

She met his look. "Do you play golf?"

"Not really. But I'll make a showing just to be a team player." Why did he feel like she was accusing him of being dishonest?

"I wouldn't have thought that was your style. Impressing the board really is important to you, isn't it?"

"It is." Tanner straightened in the seat a little. He wasn't ashamed of it. The promotion meant everything to his career.

"Is the department head position so vital?"

He felt her studying him. "Yes. It's my chance to make a difference in my field. Help people. I can influence the way we do transplants, lead the development of new skills."

"That's to be admired." He heard the approval in her voice.

Tanner glanced at her. He rather liked the glow of respect in her eyes.

Whitney couldn't keep the sigh of pleasure from rushing out of her as they drove up a long lane lined with neat row after row of vines for as far as she could see. The contrast of the deep brown of the rich dirt, the vivid green of the grape leaves and the tranquil blue of the sky was almost breathtaking. She glanced at Tanner.

And she was spending a weekend here with him. Her life had become surreal. She was off with a man that she hardly knew, pretending to be his serious girlfriend, and in a social situation she wasn't comfortable in. How was she not going to make a mess of it?

"Ever been to Napa?" Tanner asked, without taking his eyes off the road.

"Not really."

"I think you'll like it. We're staying at a vineyard with a hotel attached. One of the board members owns it. I understand there's a pool, tennis courts, a spa and just about anything else you might like. And, of course, there's wine."

He made it sound like she would be on her own most of the time, which suited her just fine. She didn't consider herself much of an actress so trying to convince people of the improbable idea that she and Tanner were a couple was distressing.

Finally they drove out of the vines into an open space where a huge structure that looked like a French château stood. Tall, thin trees flanked it on both sides and a manicured yard begged for Whitney to lie in the emerald-colored grass. If she'd been impressed with the landscape on the drive here, this view made her catch her breath. It was picture-perfect and despite the reason she was there Whitney could hardly wait to see inside.

Tanner leaned over and said close to her ear. "See, it's not going to be all bad, being here with me."

Whitney turned. Her mouth stopped only inches from his. Her heart fluttered. She looked into his velvety brown eyes. They could swallow her up if she let them and she would never know how it had happened. For long moments, though far too short for her, she waited, watched. Dreamed. Tanner's head lowered a fraction. He was going to kiss her. No, this wasn't what this weekend was about.

She blinked and quickly pulled back. She wouldn't be his plaything. She wasn't in his league when it came to casual affairs, she was sure. He would win every time. "I didn't say it was going to be bad. I just don't like being told what I'm going to do."

He leaned back and looked at her. "Noted. With that in mind, I'm asking you, not telling, would you please take off that hideous scarf before someone comes out?"

Whitney didn't have time to reply before the door to the hotel opened and a sophisticatedly dressed woman started their way. Quickly Whitney removed the scarf and the band securing her hair. Shaking it loose, she ran a hand through it. She looked to Tanner. "Better?"

A strange look had come over his face and he said softly, "Much." Seconds later a crease marred his forehead. "Can we keep what you do for a living between ourselves?"

"I won't lie."

His look held hers. "Maybe just evade the question."

A young man in a knit shirt and khaki pants followed close behind the woman. This was a far fancier place than Whitney had expected.

"Hello, Tanner. Welcome to the Garonne Winery," the woman said warmly as Tanner stepped out of the car.

The young man opened Whitney's door for her. She said, "Thank you," and received a warm smile.

"Marie Jarvis, I'd like you to meet Whitney Thomason," Tanner said from the other side of the car.

Marie stepped to Whitney with a well-manicured hand extended. "It's so nice to meet a special friend of Tanner's."

Whitney smiled and took her hand. Marie had no idea just how *special* a friend Whitney was.

Marie waved Tanner away from the trunk of the car. "Kevin will see to your bags and park your car. Just come join us by the pool. We have cool drinks waiting."

"That sounds lovely," Whitney said.

Tanner offered her an encouraging smile. On their way to the door he took her hand. His touch sent a tingle of awareness through her. It was so powerful that for a second she almost jerked away. Remembering they had to pretend they were a couple, she got control of herself. She hadn't counted on her body's reaction to being in such close contact with Tanner. Or how hard she would have to work to remember his touches were just for show. She tried to appear relaxed but her insides were a jumble of knotted nerves. Tanner gave her fingers a squeeze. Did he sense the effect he was having on her?

He allowed her to enter ahead of him through the tall double doors that opened into the cool dimness of the château. The entrance hall was every bit as astounding as the outside. A wrought-iron staircase circled up on both sides of the foyer to a landing. On each side of the landing were large windows with heavy drapes. From there, the stairs climbed again to branch off right and left. To one side of the foyer there was a small Queen Anne–style desk with an attractive young woman seated behind it.

Marie waved in the woman's direction and she smiled before Marie said to them, "Don't worry about checking in. I've already taken care of everything."

Kevin moved across the gray tile floor past them, laden with baggage, and headed up the stairs.

"The pool is this way." Marie walked toward the back of the building.

As they stepped out into the bright light once more, the scene reminded Whitney of a 1940s picture of a movie star's pool. The men stood in groups, talking, with drinks in their hands while the women sunbathed on loungers.

A flutter of anxiety went through her. She was in over her head. Could she get out of this now? What did she have in common with these people? Tanner expected her to mix and mingle. How was she supposed to do that?

When she would have pulled her hand out of Tanner's

he gripped it tighter. Had he read her mind and been afraid she might run? Somehow his clasp gave her confidence. Taking a deep breath, Whitney reminded herself that she was no longer that overweight girl who'd felt inadequate for so long. Or at least she didn't plan to let anyone make her feel that way. She was educated, owned her own business and paid her bills. There was nothing for her to feel ashamed of.

Marie said, "Tanner, why don't you introduce Whitney around then you both can change into your bathing suits and join us."

Whitney scanned the area. Even the women who were twice her age seemed to have better bodies than she did. Stretch marks and extra skin still plagued her, despite the number of years that had passed since she'd lost so much weight. Wearing a swimsuit in front of these people, particularly Tanner, wasn't something she was interested in doing.

Tanner's hand on her waist directed her toward the closest group of people. She wasn't used to his touch and certainly not to her reaction to it. If the situation didn't make her nervous enough, Tanner's close proximity did. Why? She wasn't even sure she liked him.

As they approached the group the circle opened to include them.

A man with more white than dark hair and a round belly stepped forward. "Tanner, glad you could make it."

"Malcolm, thanks for having us." Tanner gave her a slight nudge. "I'd like you to meet Whitney. Whitney, this is Malcolm Jarvis, the chairman of the hospital board and the owner of the Garonne Winery. Best known, though, as Marie's husband."

"Yes, yes. Good to meet you." Malcolm smiled at her.

Whitney couldn't help but return one of her own. "Nice to meet you as well. You have a beautiful place here."

"Thank you. Please, make yourself at home this weekend. All the hotel amenities are open to you while you're here."

Tanner faced another man. "This is Dr. Russell Karr, the medical chair and my boss."

Dr. Karr offered his hand. She took it and received a firm shake as he said, "Nice to meet you, Whitney. I look forward to getting to know you."

"And I you." To her amazement she'd managed to say that without her voice wavering.

His hand still on the small of her back, which was surprisingly reassuring, Tanner guided her around the pool. He introduced her to each guest, which included Sue Ann, Russell's wife, Ellen and Carlos Gonzales, and Lucy and Rick Hunt.

A woman close to their age, wearing a skimpy yellow bikini, stood as Whitney and Tanner came around the end of the pool toward her lounger. She rushed to Tanner and threw her arms around his neck.

Something about their friendliness said there was history between them. Whitney's radar went off. She wasn't going to like this person. Why should it matter what their relationship had been? Tanner didn't belong to her.

"Hello, Charlotte." Tanner's voice didn't sound as warm as her hug would suggest. He removed her arms and stepped away. "I'd like you to meet my girlfriend, Whitney Thomason."

The word *girlfriend* had rolled off his tongue as if it were the truth. Had he put extra emphasis on the word as well? It took all of Whitney's willpower not to stare at him as he continued, "Whitney, this is Charlotte Rivers. Her fiancé is Max Little and *he* is a member of the board. By the way, where is Max?"

Charlotte looked at Whitney as if she were something she would pull off the bottom of her shoe. "He'll be here later this evening. There was a last-minute case."

Not a good history, would be Whitney's guess.

"I know about those. We're going in to get settled. Maybe be out for a swim later." Again, Tanner's hand came to Whitney's waist. For some reason it gave her a sense of satisfaction to know Tanner was leaving with her. She held her head just a little bit higher.

When they were out of hearing distance from anyone Whitney said, "I don't think Charlotte likes me too much."

"I wouldn't worry about it."

"She's not going to sneak into our room in the middle of the night and take a knife to me and hop into bed with you, is she?"

Tanner stopped walking, threw his head back and let out a huge belly laugh. Hardly able to contain his mirth, he said, "Why, Ms. Matchmaker, I had no idea you had such a sense of the dramatic. I promise to be the one to open the door if anyone knocks. Feel safer now?"

She grinned. "A little." After a moment she dared to ask, "So what's the story with her?"

"Let's just say she doesn't like being turned down when she wants something." Putting his arm around her shoulder, he pulled her to him. This was a friendly action of two people conspiring together.

Maybe they could be friends.

Warmth entered Tanner's voice when he said, "I don't know if I said it but thanks for coming with me this weekend."

"I didn't know that I had a choice."

He held the door as they stepped inside. "I'm afraid you're right about that. But I do hope it isn't too awful for you."

* * *

Tanner was pleased with Whitney's reception by his colleagues. They had seemed to like her and she'd handled herself well, even with Charlotte. She had easily read the tension between Charlotte and him and had managed to make a joke out of it. That was a talent he admired. At his guffaw of laughter everyone had looked. To them they must have appeared as two lovers enjoying themselves.

In the house again they passed Kevin going to the front door and he told them what room they were in. Tanner led Whitney up the stairs, to the right and down the hallway to a door at the end. He opened it wide in order to allow her to enter first. When she hesitated he looked back to find her staring at the opening.

"I'm not so sure about this," she said, shaking her head slightly.

"The weekend, the room or staying with me?"

"How about all of it?"

Tanner glanced down the hall. Thank goodness no one was around. "At least come in to talk about it."

He reached for her but she stepped away. His hand fell to his side. After a moment she entered. He joined her and closed the door. Unsure what to do to make her feel more comfortable, he simply waited near the door.

Whitney's attention appeared fixated on the queen-size four-poster bed against the far wall. Thankfully there was a small sofa under one of the windows. That would be his sleeping spot for the next three nights. Not that he was looking forward to it.

"Why don't we have a seat?" He pointed toward the sofa.

She moved as if her shoes were weights. There she sat on the edge of the cushion, looking as if she would run at any moment. Finally she said, "I'm not particularly comfortable with lying to all these people."

A little charm and persuasion was needed here. "Have we lied? I introduced you as a girlfriend. I don't think that's such a stretch."

"We're really more like colleagues, though."

Whitney wouldn't be an easy sale. "Okay, colleagues. Still we can be friends."

"Those usually know more about each other than we do. I know little about you and you know nothing about me."

"Sure I do. You're a businesswoman with the ability to read people. You understand what helps people relax. You know how to put them at ease. And you like nice cars. You did great back there, by the way." Why was she all of a sudden so antsy? She'd seemed confident at the pool. Was she afraid to be alone with him? Did she sense his physical reaction to her?

When he'd initially placed his hand on her waist it had been for show, but as they'd made their way around the pool, and especially in front of Charlotte, it had become a protective action. Whitney pulled at something in him that he had no intention of examining or exploring.

She scooted back on the sofa, resting more easily in the cushions. "If you don't mind, I would rather not go to the pool. I'll just stay here and unpack."

He wouldn't push her. For now he'd just let her get used to the idea of being here with him. "That's fine. I'll see what Marie has planned for this evening and come back to get you."

"Okay."

"Is there anything special you would like to do while we're in Napa? We don't have to be underfoot here all the time." Maybe if they did something she enjoyed she would settle down some. He certainly didn't need her panicking and heading back to San Francisco.

"I don't know." She pursed her lips. "Maybe a tour of the winery?"

"Sounds good to me. If one isn't planned then we'll take one ourselves."

She smiled but it didn't reach her eyes.

"I'll leave you to unpack." He headed for the door. "I'll see you in a little while."

Tanner returned an hour later to find Whitney asleep in the middle of the bed. It was early for a nap. Had she been up the night before, worrying about coming with him this weekend? Through their meetings she'd proved herself intelligent and a woman who took little guff from people, or at least him. So why wouldn't she take the weekend at face value? Was she that distrustful of men or just him? She didn't strike him as insecure.

Why did he care? He had no intention of becoming emotionally involved with Whitney. The more he knew about her the more invested he would be in her life. He didn't want or need that. In fact, that implied caring and he wasn't going to take that step. Caring equated to hurt. He'd seen that clearly with his parents.

They'd get through this weekend and go back to being matchmaker and client.

Whitney looked so peaceful that he hated to wake her but Marie had made plans for everyone that afternoon. He placed a hand on Whitney's shoulder and gave her a gentle shake. She blinked then her eyes popped wide open. They were pretty eyes, almost as nice as her smile. The kind that saw into a person.

"Hey, the women are going into town for lunch and some shopping while the men go to the club to play golf."

"Is it necessary for me to go?" she asked after a yawn.

"If you don't mind, I wish you would. I wouldn't want to hurt Marie's feelings." Tanner wouldn't make it a demand. He'd made enough of those.

"Oh, of course." Sitting up and trying to unrumple her

clothing, she said in a convincingly sincere tone, "I don't want to do that either."

If anything, Whitney had a kind heart. Maybe that was why her business as a matchmaker was so successful.

"I'll tell you what—" he reached for his wallet in his back pocket "—why don't you buy something nice for yourself? It's the least I can do for you helping me out this weekend."

"That's not necessary."

"Maybe not, but I'd like to. You could maybe get a new outfit." He shrugged a shoulder. "Something more fitted."

Whitney raised a brow. "Thank you but I don't need you to buy clothes for me."

"I just thought you might enjoy going more if you could buy something new."

She rolled off the bed and faced him. "I don't need your money."

Tanner held up a hand. "Whoa, whoa. I didn't intend to insult you. Whatever you wear is fine with me. I was just thinking you must be covering up some nice curves under those loose-fitting clothes." He handed her a few bills. "Just take this. Get whatever you want. Or don't. Marie said to meet in the lobby in half an hour. I'll see you later."

He was out the door before she could argue more. Had he touched an exposed nerve?

Whitney stood in the lobby, waiting for the other women. She wasn't looking forward to the foray into town, especially if Charlotte was going. Whitney had known more than her share of Charlotte's type growing up but she refused to revert back to that timid, sensitive girl who had hidden behind her weight. She'd worked too hard to let the Charlottes of the world control her life anymore.

She clutched her purse. The money Tanner had given her was inside. He'd paid enough attention to her that he'd noticed her clothes? Had wondered about her curves? Heat filled her at the idea. But he'd said he wanted her to have something that fit her better. She looked at herself in the large mirror in the grand hallway. Did she have the confidence to wear a tight dress? Have him see her in it? She'd spent so many years covering up, could she let go enough to do that?

Soon she was in a limousine with Marie, Charlotte, Lucy, Ellen and Sue Ann, all of whom she had met at the pool. To Whitney's great distress, Charlotte took a seat next to her.

With her nose pointed down, Charlotte said as if they were new best friends, "So what brought you and Tanner together? You don't seem his type."

Marie came to her rescue. "How about a glass of champagne on our way to town?"

Whitney didn't normally drink much and certainly not in a limo. Still, she gratefully accepted Marie's offered glass of the bubbly liquid.

"So where did you meet Tanner?" Charlotte persisted.

Her tone was far too condescending for Whitney. In the past women like Charlotte had made her life miserable. Now it was happening again. Why she'd ever agreed to this weekend Whitney didn't know. It wouldn't be over soon enough to suit her. She took a sip of champagne in the hope it would fortify her. "We met in college."

Charlotte gave her a sly smile, as if she had set her trap. "Really? I knew Tanner in college as well. I don't remember you."

She wouldn't. People like Charlotte didn't notice people like her unless forced to.

"I was there nonetheless. We had a couple of undergrad classes together."

Thankfully Marie gained everyone's attention, wanting to know where they would like to shop. When Whitney voiced no opinion she said, "Whitney, is there someplace special you would like to go?"

"I've never been to Napa so I really can't say."

"Then is there something you're interested in shopping for?" Marie asked.

After her conversation with Tanner there was. "Yes, I need a new cocktail dress and I didn't have time to get one before I left San Francisco. Do you know of a good place to buy one?"

A large smile came to Marie's lips. "I know just the boutique." She picked up a phone attached to the side of the car and instructed the driver where to stop. "There's plenty of other places nearby for the rest of us to enjoy while you're getting your dress."

Minutes later they were stepping out of the car in front of a store with two windows on each side of a glass door. In one of the show spaces was a beautiful red dress. The bodice was seamed in panels so that it would fit tightly above the waist, while the skirt flared and flowed around the mannequin's legs. It was so unlike anything Whitney owned yet for some reason she wanted to surprise, even shock, Tanner. What was happening to her? All her life she'd been in the background, had worked hard to stay there, and yet everything about the dress screamed, *Notice me*.

"I can see the red dress has caught your attention. Let's go in and you can try it on." Marie all but pushed her into the store.

The other ladies, including Charlotte, headed down the sidewalk with a wave of their hands. One said, "We'll meet you in an hour at the café for tea."

A small bell tinkled as she and Marie entered the shop. A saleswoman greeted them. Marie wasted no time telling her that Whitney wanted to try on the dress in the window.

Minutes later Whitney was standing in front of three mirrors, wondering who she was looking at.

"It's lovely on you." Marie's words were soft and reassuring.

Whitney moved from side to side, watching the folds of the dress sway around her legs. "You don't think it's too much?"

"No. Tanner won't know what's happened to him when he sees you."

Did she want that? They weren't lovers. She was looking for a woman for him, not *to be* his woman.

"Yes, and even better, it'll get Charlotte's goat."

Whitney gave Marie a sharp look. "Why?"

"Because she seems to think she has some claim on him."

Watching Marie's face closely, Whitney responded, "Tanner said she's engaged."

Marie curled her lip in distaste. "She is, but that doesn't seem to mean much to her. Max doesn't spend enough time with her to keep her happy so she goes after other people's husbands."

Had Charlotte gone after Malcolm?

Marie picked out a necklace with a small pearl on the end of a stand on the table near them. "Turn around," she ordered then fastened it on Whitney's neck. "I'd like to see her put in her place. You might just be the person to do that." Marie patted her shoulder. "Perfect. He'll never know what hit him."

Her? She'd never outshined someone like Charlotte. Cautiously Whitney asked, "If you don't mind me being nosy, if you feel that way about her, why is she here?"

"Because she's Max's latest young thing." Marie didn't sound at all pleased. "His wife, Margaret, was my best friend. She died of cancer a couple of years ago."

Whitney touched her arm. "I'm so sorry to hear that."

"Thank you. It was a dreadfully hard time on everyone. Enough of that. Let's get this dress paid for and go have tea." Marie started toward the desk.

Did Whitney dare buy the dress? Tanner's comment about her clothing compelled her to say yes, but she sure didn't want Charlotte goading her into doing something to prove a point. But just this once it would be nice to indulge herself, wear something that made her feel confident, feminine.

"Okay."

It wasn't until she was taking the dress off and looked at the price tag that she almost fainted. It was half her house payment for a month. If she could just find the right woman for Tanner his fee would help her afford it. Even though she had his money in her purse, she wasn't about to use it. Only because of the idea that wearing the dress would give her enough poise to pull off the rest of the weekend and deal with Charlotte's barbs did Whitney have the courage to give the saleswoman her credit card.

She and Marie stepped out into the sunshine again. They gave her dress to the driver, who was waiting nearby, and started down the street. The honk of a car drew their attention. It was Tanner. He pulled into the nearest parking place and got out.

"What're you doing here? I thought you were playing golf." Whitney didn't take the time to examine the little skip of her heart at seeing him.

"Turns out I was odd man out and not needed for a foursome. I tried to catch you before you left but apparently you have your phone off, so I thought I'd drive in and find you. Maybe see if I could join you ladies for lunch."

"Sure. You're welcome," Marie said, then started down the street toward where the others sat on a patio of a café.

Whitney whispered, "So why are you really here?"

"I got to thinking it was unfair of me to throw you to

the wolves by pressuring you into coming into town without me to run interference. So when I wasn't needed for golf I came to save you."

"Just like a knight of old," Whitney jested. In reality she found it rather sweet that he'd been anxious about her welfare. Or was he just afraid she might slip up and tell everyone she was his matchmaker? Despite his high-handed method of getting her to come with him, he seemed genuinely concerned for her. It made it hard not to like him.

"Are you making fun of me?"

"I would never do that," Whitney said with pretend sincerity and then followed Marie.

Tanner caught up with her. He took her hand and leaned in close. "We need to make this look good."

A tingle of pleasure rippled through her. Just having him near made her feel warmer than the day indicated. She had to get a handle on her reaction or she would soon be swooning over Tanner like she had in college. That was a stage in her life she wasn't returning to.

Minutes later they had taken a seat at the table on the patio with the other women.

"I don't know if I've ever had afternoon tea. I might do this again soon," Tanner remarked as he picked up a sandwich that almost disappeared between his large fingers.

"You don't know what you've been missing," Whitney said. "It's one of the most relaxing things I do for myself."

"You've had afternoon tea before?" Tanner sounded surprised. Did he think she wasn't interested in anything that cultured?

"Many times."

"I prefer other diversions," Charlotte purred, giving Tanner a speculative look.

He ignored Charlotte and said to Whitney, "I'm going to count on you taking me to your favorite place. My treat."

The look he gave her created a low glow in her. He was

putting on a show for the women but she was still enjoying his attention, no matter what the reason.

Tanner was a perfect charmer during lunch. He spread his attention around each of the women, including Charlotte, but he made it clear Whitney was special. Where some men would have felt out of place as the only male at the meal, Tanner seemed to be enjoying himself.

When he wasn't eating, his arm remained across the back of her chair. That element of his personality Whitney had seen when they'd been in college was now very evident during the meal. Occasionally his thumb would drop down and brush her shoulder.

When she shuddered he leaned in too close and asked with his lips just touching her ear, "Are you cold?"

He knew full well she wasn't. If anything, she felt compelled to fan herself.

Tanner entertained with stories of his exploits during med school and shared one very poignant one about a patient. Whitney envied his ability to fit in wherever he was. He even paid for everyone's meal, stating, "That's what a gentleman does."

"So, Marie, what do you have planned for us this evening?" he asked as they were leaving the café.

"Tonight we're having a wine-and-cheese tasting at the winery, then taking a tour and ending with dinner in the wine cellar."

They had arrived at the limousine and the women started taking their seats. When Whitney ducked her head to get in Tanner said, "Aren't you going to ride back with me?"

He almost sounded hurt. "Uh, sure." Whitney joined him on the sidewalk again. They watched the limo move away from the curve.

"Do you need to get anything else while we're in town?" he asked.

"No, I'm good." She already had a stunning dress that Marie would take care of.

"Okay. Then how about a ride through the valley since you've never been to Napa? It's a beautiful day."

Secretly pleased, she admonished, "You know you don't have to entertain me. Don't you need to be hanging out with Malcolm and the other board members?"

"Nope. I have you here and I understand the need to appear ready to settle down, but I'm not going to pander to anyone for a job."

She was glad to hear that Tanner had a moral line that he wouldn't cross.

"Let's take that ride. Do you have a hat?"

"No, but I have a scarf." She gave him her best mischievous grin.

"We're going to find you a hat." He grabbed her hand and pulled her toward a boutique with hats in the window.

A few minutes later, they came out with her wearing a tangerine-colored wide-brimmed hat that was far more attention-getting than anything else she owned. But she loved it. Between it and the dress she was really stepping out of her comfort zone. Somehow Tanner was bringing out her inner diva.

"That color suits you," he said as they settled in the car.

"Thank you. You do know you don't have to compliment me when there's no one around to hear?"

"Has it occurred to you that I might like complimenting you?"

It hadn't, but she had to admit she liked the attention from him.

Over the next couple of hours they just drove at a peaceful speed along the main road through the center of the valley. The vineyards they passed were impeccably groomed and endless. Tanner pulled over at a little roadside stand and bought them bottled drinks.

"This is so beautiful." Whitney stood beside the car, looking off toward the east where the hills created one side of the valley.

Tanner leaned against the car and crossed his ankles. "I was impressed the first time I visited as well. It's like a little piece of France at your back door."

"I would love to visit France one day." Whitney took a sip of her cola.

"I think you would like it. I'd heard so much about Paris that I didn't believe it could live up to the hype, but it was everything I had expected and more."

"Do you travel a lot?" She couldn't help but look at him. Even his body movements captivated her. She was so on the road to trouble. Heart trouble.

"When I can. It takes some reconfiguring for me to get away from the hospital." He didn't sound disappointed, just resigned.

She met his gaze from under the brim of her hat. "So what about this weekend? Who's watching over everything?"

"I'm close enough to be there in an hour or so. I have good staff who will help out until I can get there."

Their lives were so different. Her career almost seemed frivolous compared to his yet he'd asked for her help. No matter what people did in life they wanted to share it with someone. The more she was around Tanner the more she could understand why he would be considered a catch.

But why was he so against a relationship that involved love? She had a feeling he had a lot stored up to give.

They were in the car again and Tanner was about to turn into the road to head back the way they had come when Whitney said, "Thank you for making the afternoon nice for me. It was sweet of you. I would have made it through tea by myself but it was good to have your support."

"You're welcome. If you have any issues with Charlotte, just let me know. Max will be here this evening and most of that will stop."

"Is she always so catty?"

He glanced at her. "Only when she can get away with it."

Whitney watched his capable hands on the wheel. He had nice hands. What would it be like to be intentionally touched by those fingers? That wasn't a safe subject. Charlotte was a more benign one. "She said she was at Berkeley at the same time we were."

"She was. We dated awhile in my senior year." He slowed and let a car go around them.

"I don't remember her."

"She transferred in." Tanner looked up into the rear-view mirror.

So that was why she hadn't recognized her. Charlotte had been around during those years she hadn't seen much of Tanner.

They returned to the château around four that afternoon. Whitney pulled off her hat and shook out her hair as they walked toward the main entrance.

"You have beautiful hair. That chestnut color is so unusual."

"Thank you." Oh, yes, the man had charm. And was laying it on thickly.

He pushed a strand off her cheek. "You should wear it down more often."

If she let him keep this up he would have her in bed in the next fifteen minutes. "Tanner, I think we need to make a rule that you only touch me if it's necessary."

"Do I get to decide what's *necessary*?" He fingered her hair.

She stepped out of reach. "No, I think I should make that decision."

"What're you afraid of? That I'll uncover the true Whitney?" He waited for her to join him on the stairs.

Tanner was perceptive, she'd give him that. Was that the part of his character that made him such a good doctor? But he was her client and she had no intention of confessing any of her secrets.

CHAPTER FOUR

TANNER COULDN'T REMEMBER when he'd spent a more relaxing few hours with a woman. Whitney didn't need to be entertained. She seemed happy just being along. Few women he knew would have been glad to spend hours riding in a car. There was something reassuring about having Whitney in the seat next to him. It was an odd feeling. It was nothing like what he'd seen in his mother and father's relationship. He wasn't going into that emotional minefield. They had nothing to do with him and Whitney.

Now she was in the bath, preparing for the evening. He was confident from her no-nonsense personality that he wouldn't be left waiting long. After showering and shaving, he'd given the bathroom over to her. He had no idea what she planned to wear that evening but he was determined that his response would be positive, no matter what her attire.

There was a knock at the door. He opened it to find one of the bellboys.

"Mrs. Jarvis sent this up for Ms. Thomason." The young man handed Tanner a dress bag and was gone before Tanner had time to tip him.

Tanner closed the door. So had Whitney taken his suggestion and bought something for herself after all? He tapped on the bathroom door. "Marie has sent you something."

Whitney opened the door a crack. Her eyes widened when she saw the bag. "I forgot." She reached out and took the bag. "Thank you."

Seconds later Tanner was left looking at the panel of the door.

It had been twenty minutes since he'd heard anything coming from the bathroom. He checked his watch again. What was Whitney doing? They would be late if she didn't hurry up. He tapped on the door. "Is everything all right in there?"

A muffled sound reached his ears. That wasn't good.

The door barely opened. Her voice held a note of misery. "I can't zip my dress."

So that was what this was all about. "Step out here. I can help with that."

Tanner registered a flash of red as she came only far enough into the room to present him with her back. For a moment his focus was on nothing but the bare V of skin between the two sections of the zipper. Whitney wore no bra. He made himself swallow.

Stepping up to her, Tanner took the tiny pull of the zipper between two fingers. Why were his hands trembling? He'd seen many bare backs. The zipper didn't move when he tugged so he had to hold the material below it snugly, which brought his hand into contact with the curve of her back.

Tanner didn't miss the sharp intake of Whitney's breath. He was breathing harder as well. Getting hard. This simple action of closing a zip was turning into something personal, sensual. With the zip closed Tanner stepped away, shoving his hands into his pants pockets.

What was going on here? He had no particular interest in Whitney. Still, what he wouldn't have given to run the tip of a finger over the exposed creaminess of her back. Or to taste the ridge of her shoulder.

He cleared his throat and stepped back until the backs of his legs touched the bed.

"Thank you," she said as she turned.

That scalding desire Tanner had felt had been fading and now it ignited to explode throughout his body as he took in the full view of Whitney. Her dress was demure by most standards but sexy on Whitney. With a V neckline that only showed a suggestion of cleavage and a length that stopped at her knees, she looked amazing. Just as he had suspected, there were curves under those baggy clothes she usually wore.

Her hair flowed thick and free around her shoulders. Tanner fisted his hands in his pockets so he didn't reach out and grab a handful. "Whitney, you look lovely."

A shy smile covered rose-tinted lips. "Thank you. I'm ready when you are."

His desire intensified. He was ready all right, but not for something that involved anyone but them. He stepped closer to her. "We should be going or we'll be late. But before we do, I think we need to take care of something."

Whitney looked around the room as if she had forgotten something then back at him with a questioning look on her face.

"I know you said only when necessary but I might need to kiss you tonight in front of the others so I think we should practice. Get that first uncomfortable one out of the way. Settle the nerves, so to speak." Yeah, like that was going to happen. Nothing about the reaction she was creating in his body was settling.

"I guess we could do that…"

He found Whitney's lips with his.

They were soft and inviting. Plump and perfect. He

pressed more firmly and a shudder went through her. Her fingers gripped his biceps yet she didn't return his kiss. Tanner pulled back and searched her face. Her eyes were wide and she looked dazed.

"It might be more believable if you kissed me back. Should I try again?" He waited. This he wouldn't push.

"Yes, please. I think it's necessary." Her lips hardly moved as the soft words left them.

Tanner chuckled softly. What little taste of Whitney he'd had made him want more. She lifted her mouth to his. This time he placed his hands on her waist and brought her against him. When her lips stirred, his heart drummed faster. Her hands tightened, fisting in his shirtsleeves.

The kiss was quickly moving away from practice to pleasure.

Seconds later, with one sharp movement Whitney broke away, turning her back to him. "I think that was enough practice. We should go." She picked up a shawl from the bed and draped it over her arm. The tightly controlled woman had returned.

Their simple kiss had left him rock hard. Staying where they were was more of what Tanner had in mind. But he was a man of his word. He'd promised not to ask her for anything physical. Their kisses might be considered bending the rule but he'd not push further. Nothing about Whitney struck him as someone who didn't invest emotionally and he certainly wasn't looking for anything that involved his heart.

"I guess we should." Even to his own ears he sounded disappointed.

Tanner's kisses had been sweet and nonthreatening yet they sure had rocked Whitney's world. Even now as they walked across the parking area toward the winery she still trembled. She'd been kissed before but none had been as divine as those Tanner had gifted her with. The problem now was that she wanted more, but she wouldn't let that happen.

She could be in trouble on so many levels. He was her client. He didn't believe in love. He was looking for a wife. She was nothing like what he wanted. He would break her heart. Of that she was confident. She had to get through this weekend and see to it that they returned to their business relationship.

When she stumbled, Tanner's hand was on her elbow to steady her instantly. "I'm sorry, Whitney. I promised nothing physical. I shouldn't have kissed you. It won't happen again. It'll be your call from now on."

Was that statement supposed to make her feel better? It sounded as if he regretted their kisses. Here she was trying to hold herself together while it hadn't had any effect on him. She couldn't have him thinking that she was some ninny who fell apart when a man kissed her.

Long ago she'd learned to cover disappointment and hurt. She'd just do it once more. "Not a problem. I won't hold it against you. It's no big deal."

Had she felt his fingers flinch?

"I'm glad you understand." His hand remained on her arm until they stepped in front of the tasting-room door to the winery. When he let go she felt the loss in more ways than one. That tentative friendship they were building had lost some stones.

"I hope I don't slip up and say anything wrong," she whispered.

"Don't worry about it. Let's just concentrate on having a nice evening."

Tanner seemed far too laid-back for someone who was worried about his friends finding out she was actually his matchmaker. She sure wished her nerves weren't jumping. If it was from Tanner's kisses or her worry over disappointing him, she couldn't say.

He held the large curved door open for her to enter. Inside, the lights were turned low, giving the stone-walled space a cozy feel. It reminded her of pictures of a French farmhouse. To one side there was a bar with a full wine rack behind it. To the other side was a small, tastefully arranged shop area where shelves held wine flutes, cork removers and other paraphernalia. An upright, glass-doored cooler containing small packages of meat and cheese was discreetly positioned in a corner.

Sharing the other half of the room was a grouping of café tables and chairs. Each table was covered in a bright yellow cloth with a white dahlia in a vase. They were a pop of sunlight in the otherwise dark area. Greenery and tiny lights were draped above the doors and along the shelves. Whitney was instantly charmed.

"I love this place." Whitney couldn't help but be impressed. She glanced at Tanner. He was giving her an indulgent look.

"Has anyone ever told you that you have a beautiful smile?"

"No."

He held her gaze as he said softly, "They should have because you do."

Tanner's voice vibrated through her. Had anyone ever looked at her like that before? Like she was the most special thing in the world?

"I think if you continue to look at me that way I'll forget my promises," he said quietly. "Maybe we should join the others? I've been told that the Garonne Winery has a remarkable white."

Whitney didn't drink much but she was in the mood to enjoy some wine with Tanner. She would *not* get any ideas where he was concerned. The only reason he was paying this much attention to her was because he was putting on a show. But that kiss had felt real. That moment just now had felt real too. She was going to enjoy this feeling while she could.

He took her hand and wrapped it around his elbow and they walked toward the others gathered near the bar.

Marie met them, her hands out in welcome and a wide smile on her face. "Whitney, you look wonderful. I knew that dress was just the thing for you." She regarded Tanner. "I hope you told her how beautiful she is."

He nodded. "I did."

"Did he?" Marie looked at her.

Whitney smiled up at Tanner. "He did. He was very complimentary."

Thankfully, Marie didn't waste any time directing them to the bar. "You must try the white."

"Tanner said it was good," Whitney remarked.

Marie smiled with obvious pride. "It's our first award winner."

"Then no wonder you're proud." Whitney watched as the middle-aged man behind the bar dressed in a white shirt, black vest and pants poured the liquid into a glass.

"I must check on our meal. The tour will begin in a few minutes," Marie said, and whirled away.

The bartender handed Tanner a tall fluted glass and he gave it to her, then took his own. He tapped his glass against hers. "To a nice weekend."

Their looks held as they took a sip of wine.

"Nice," Tanner said. "What did you think?"

"I'm not much of a wine connoisseur so I can't really say." Once again she was out of her element.

"That's okay. You either like it or not."

She paused a moment. Was he talking about more than wine? "I like it."

Tanner smiled. "Was that so hard?"

"No."

"Would you like a lesson on how to taste wine?" He made it sound like it was something intimate between them.

"I'm always willing to learn something new." Had she really said something that flirtatious?

Tanner's eyes darkened but his grin was an easy one. "That's good to know. Okay, let me show you. First, you look at it." He brought his glass up so that it caught the light. "Then swirl it gently so that you can get the bouquet." Tanner put his nose to the rim.

Whitney followed his lead, doing exactly as he did.

"Next you take a sip in your mouth and swish it around, letting each taste bud have its turn."

Whitney watched, enthralled, as Tanner's lips moved against the edge of the glass. Those same lips had just touched hers. She had tasted their fullness and she wanted more.

"Appreciate the richness of it. Then swallow."

She watched the long length of his neck as he drank. He was making the process a seduction. Heaven help her, he was a temptation she was having a hard time resisting. She no longer needed her wrap in the cool, dark room. It had turned far too warm for her. Tanner had an effect on her like no other male. He wasn't what she needed but she couldn't seem to stay away.

His gaze met hers. Tanner asked in a low raspy voice, "Do you still like it?"

He wasn't referring to the wine. The innuendo was clear. She licked her bottom lip.

Tanner's nostrils flared. He looked as if he might grab her. This time the kiss wouldn't be a practice one, she was sure.

The moment was shattered when Malcolm slapped him on the back. "Tanner, how're you doing this evening? We missed you on the course. I'd hoped we would get a chance to talk."

Tanner's attention went to Malcolm and that suited Whitney fine. She wasn't sure she could have handled the intensity she'd seen in Tanner's eyes if they had continued uninterrupted.

The two men talked about general hospital business and Whitney stood by listening but not really understanding the nuances of the conversation. Still, she enjoyed the rumble of Tanner's voice as it became animated about an issue. She was content to just listen to him. Mercy, she had it bad. Just like trying to return a cork to a bottle once it was out, there was no going back. She was falling for Tanner.

Marie had just touched Malcolm's arm, reminding him it was time for the tour, when Charlotte, hanging on the arm of a distinguished-looking man with snow-white hair, entered the room. Everyone in the room looked in their direction. The atmosphere took on a tense air.

"Well, it looks like we can start now that all the guests are here." The distaste in Marie's voice was unmistakable.

"Yes, it's time," Malcolm said in a pacifying voice as he took her hand. "Ladies and gentlemen, I believe they're ready to show us the winery now."

As if on cue, a young man dressed identically to the bartender came to stand at Malcolm's side.

"Please follow me," the young man said as he opened a wrought-iron door and walked along a passage. Whitney, Tanner's hand at her elbow, followed the other members of their small group through the stone opening into a modernized cement-floored room with large aluminum vats.

The guide began telling them how the grapes were harvested and pressed. Charlotte and her partner, who Whitney hadn't been introduced to, came to stand beside her and Tanner. The entire time the guide was talking Charlotte was busy whispering in the man's ear and giggling.

Once Whitney saw him give her butt a squeeze and was disgusted by the display. It was as if Charlotte wanted everyone to pay attention to them. A few times she noticed Tanner glancing in their direction. Did this show bother him as well? Was Charlotte putting it on for Tanner? As if he knew what she was thinking, his arm came around her waist and brought her close.

"Now, if you'll follow me," their guide announced, "we'll go into the cellar where the wine is stored in oak barrels to let time create our award-winning vintages."

They entered another room where barrel after wooden barrel were piled on top of each other in ranks. They were stacked well above Tanner's head.

Whitney pulled at her shawl, trying to bring it up over her bare shoulders as the coolness of the windowless wine cellar surrounded her. Tanner's fingertips brushed her arm. Why did she have to love his touch so much? The wrap was lifted off her. Seconds later, it came to rest across her shoulders.

"Thank you."

"You're welcome." His voice warmed her as much as the material around her.

They continued down the wide aisle until they came to an area where three formally dressed tables were set for dinner. A single candle flickered in the center of each.

"Everyone." Marie gained their attention. "This is where we'll be having dinner tonight.

"Charlotte and Max, you'll be at this table." She pointed to one to her right. "Ellen, you and Carlos will be joining them. Lucy and Rick, you'll be at this table with Whitney and Tanner." She touched the table closest to her. "Sue Ann and Russell, you'll join Malcolm and I here." She indicated the table off to the right.

Whitney couldn't deny she was relieved not to have to spend the entire dinner with Charlotte. The woman rubbed her up the wrong way for more than one reason. What Tanner had ever seen in her Whitney couldn't imagine.

Tanner held the chair for her to sit. His hand brushed her neck as he moved to take the chair at her left. A shiver of pleasure went through her. Had he done that on purpose? Her reaction to him was on overload tonight. The romantic setting must be getting to her.

A waitress came to stand beside the table and popped the cork off a bottle of red wine. She presented a glass to Tanner. He sipped and nodded. She then poured each person at the table a glass.

Whitney liked their tablemates, Lucy and Rick. She had gotten to know Lucy a little during the trip to town but found Rick an interesting yet bookwormish type. Their conversation was steady and often drew laughter. Whitney felt herself relaxing. Midway through the meal she'd forgotten all her worry over whether or not she might fit in.

"I can't believe I've found someone as interested as me in growing violets," Lucy commented.

"Just goes to show you never know about people until you get to know them," Tanner said as he looked at Whitney. "We always get surprised."

Was he talking people in general or her in particular? How had she surprised him? Why would he be interested enough to notice? After all, she was only his matchmaker.

"Yeah, and after this weekend I'd be surprised if I get that promotion as Director of Infectious Diseases," Rick said.

Lucy placed her hand over his. "Now, you don't know that."

"I just have a feeling," Rick said.

"What do you mean?" Tanner asked.

Rick lifted his glass. "I don't think you need to worry. You're the perfect person for the cardiothoracic department. It's just something Malcolm remarked that Max had said."

Tanner turned in Charlotte's direction. She was laughing loudly. "He does seem distracted."

"Don't give up hope yet, honey," Lucy encouraged.

Rick shrugged and took a sip of his wine. "Let's talk about something else."

By then the salad had been removed and the entrée of prime rib and roasted potatoes with green beans was placed in front of them. As they ate they discussed a recent movie.

Whitney enjoyed the delicious food too much. Tanner smiled at her as she put the last bite in her mouth. "Good?"

"Yes."

"I like a woman who enjoys eating." Tanner's attention returned to his plate.

A sick feeling formed in Whitney's stomach. Her fork hit the edge of the plate with a clink. Tanner glanced at her. His expression turned from one of happiness to distress. His hand took hers under the table and squeezed. "Did I say something wrong?"

He truly looked perplexed. Whitney felt sorry for him. "No. I'm fine." She made herself smile. Would she ever reach the point where she didn't think every remark regarding her and food was a negative one?

Minutes later the waitress removed their plates and brought another with chocolate à la mode on it. Whitney stuck the tines of her fork in it and put a bite in her mouth. The shot of chocolate tasted wonderful but she took no more of the dessert. She saw Tanner look at her uneaten sweet but he said nothing.

With dinner finished, Marie stood. "Before we all go on our separate ways for the evening I'd like to give you a little idea of what we have planned for tomorrow. First, we're going on a hot-air balloon ride. We'll have to be up before daylight but I promise it'll be worth it. If you haven't seen Napa from the sky you haven't seen Napa. Cars will be outside the main entrance to take you to the field at six thirty." Charlotte groaned loudly as Marie continued, "The rest of the day is yours. Dinner is at eight beside the pool. Casual dress is fine. Malcolm and I have enjoyed having you here."

She and Tanner said their good-evenings to Lucy and Rick then thanked Marie and Malcolm for the nice dinner. Tanner pushed the door of the cellar open for her to precede him out. It had turned dark. The moon was big and full against the night sky and the air was cool.

"The hot-air balloon ride sounds awesome. I've always thought they were so beautiful." Whitney pulled the shawl up around her shoulders. Tanner helped her adjust it.

"It should be fun." Tanner's words didn't sound all that heartfelt. Whitney didn't have time to question him before he said, "It's a beautiful night. How about a walk?"

She wasn't sure she should take the chance on being alone with him on a moonlit night but after the meal she'd just eaten she could use some exercise. She wasn't looking forward to returning to the room where they would be closed up together. He had too much sex appeal to ignore. Feelings that had nothing to do with looking for a wife for him had crept in, feelings that would only break her heart in the long run if she were to let herself act on them. It might not be a safe idea but she agreed. "I guess so."

Tanner offered her his arm. She placed her fingers in the crook and he set a leisurely pace toward the rows of vines to the left of the winery. The paths between the rows were so well maintained the walking was easy.

The night was still enough for her to hear herself breathing. They had walked some distance away from the hotel when she said, "I love this. It makes you want to take off your shoes and run."

"Go ahead." Tanner's voice was as deep and smooth as the night.

Whitney glanced at him. Suddenly she felt like doing just that. He made her feel special. She kicked off her shoes, grabbed a handful of her dress and ran. The soft dirt, still warm from the sun, surrounded her toes. She threw up her arms and twirled.

A deep chuckle filled the air, bringing her to a halt. She looked at Tanner.

"Don't stop on my account."

She studied him for a moment. He looked handsome and sturdy standing with his back to the moon as if he were a warrior of old. She wanted to reach out and take his smooth-shaven face in her hands and kiss him for all she was worth.

She didn't have to. He came to her, standing so close she could hear him breathe but he didn't touch her. "Whitney, I need to kiss you."

Needed to? Had anyone ever needed to kiss her? She stepped to him. His lips found hers. This was no practice kiss, this was a man wanting a woman and telling her so.

Tanner pulled her against him, lifting her until her toes barely met the ground. His tongue joined hers and danced a measure that Whitney recognized as theirs alone. She held on and took the spine-tingling, heart-revving and mind-blowing ride. Her arms circled his neck as her mouth begged in desperation for more. She clung to him.

Tanner broke away, inhaling before he took her lips again. This time his hands moved to cup her breasts. They tingled, became heavy. His arousal was evident between them. The pleasure of having Tanner touch her made her feel weak. She clung to him as if he were her lifeline.

In a low growl he said, "Let's go inside. I want you."

Whitney was tempted to throw caution away and act on the fiery emotions boiling within her. She'd had no business agreeing to a walk with Tanner. It was too romantic, too perfect, too much Tanner. He filled her thoughts, filled her days, and if this continued he would fill her heart. That would be a road to nothing but misery.

If she agreed to his request what would happen to her self-respect, her business? What would happen to what she wanted out of life? A husband who loved her. Someone who invested his life in hers, theirs. She wanted a loving marriage, something Tanner wasn't willing to give. What was between them would only be a weekend fling. That wasn't enough.

"I can't." She stepped back, her mind forcing her body to move away when it yearned to cling to him. "I need to go in by myself."

"Are you running, Whitney?"

She looked at him. He stood with his legs apart and arms at his sides. "I guess you could call it that. I know when something isn't going to end well. We aren't meant for each other. We are looking for different things out of a relationship."

Tanner watched as Whitney became a shadow among the vines. He knew she was right. Heck, he wasn't even sure what she wanted was real. He'd seen his mother fawn over his father, but was that love or obsession? His father had certainly not cared for his mother in the same way. Was his son even capable of loving someone?

He followed Whitney at a distance, making sure she safely entered the front door of the château. Along the way he picked up her shoes. She had such tiny feet for a woman who had such a strong will.

Once again he was pushing when he'd said he wouldn't. He'd apologized to Whitney more than he had to anyone in his life and here he was needing to do it again.

He went to the library off the entrance hall and poured

a drink. Taking a seat in a chair near a window, he nursed his drink, giving Whitney time to get ready for bed and for him to get his libido under control.

It was late when the sound of footsteps drew his mind away from the woman upstairs. He glanced behind him. Disappointment washed over him. It wasn't Whitney looking for him but Charlotte. He returned his attention to the window, hoping she hadn't seen him. Sadly, that wasn't the case.

"Why, Tanner, is that you? I thought you'd be upstairs with your plain little woman."

If his hackles hadn't already been up they would have stood on end at that remark. The need to defend Whitney ran hot and rapid through him. He made no attempt to keep the aversion out of his words. "You know, it's been a long time since it's been your business where I am or what I am doing."

"Or who you are doing, is my guess."

"Or that either. You've found who you want in Max. Leave me alone."

She sauntered toward him. "The question is, have you found what you want in Whitney?"

Had he? "That's between us. It has nothing to do with you."

Charlotte leaned toward him, giving him an impressive view of her full breasts. "You used to think I was pretty important."

"Those days are gone and I've moved on. Now, excuse me." He put his hands on her shoulders and pushed her away as he stood. "I have other people and things that interest me more now."

"Like that nondescript woman upstairs waiting patiently for your return."

What had he ever seen in her? "As a matter of fact, yes."

Charlotte stepped to him so fast he had no time to react.

Her mouth found his. Forcing himself not to squeeze her waist to the point of pain, he set her away from him. "If you ever touch me again, I promise Max will learn in no uncertain terms what a witch you are." He didn't wait for her reaction.

When Tanner entered their bedroom Whitney was in the bed, asleep. One lone light near the sofa burned. On the couch was a pillow, sheet and blanket. Tanner looked longingly at the bed and the soft, warm woman in it. After muttering a few expletives that he was sure would make Whitney blush, he shook out the sheet and let it drop haphazardly over the sofa. By the size of the piece of furniture his feet were going to hang over one end. Removing his jacket and shirt, he threw them on a chair nearby. His hands went to his belt. Normally he slept in the raw but he would defer to Whitney's sensibilities and wear his underwear. She would just have to deal with them.

He was on the sofa, curled up the best he could, when a soft voice said, "Goodnight, Tanner."

Had she been watching him undress?

CHAPTER FIVE

WHITNEY LOOKED DOWN at Tanner sprawled across the sofa. He'd thrown the blanket off his chest. His head was on a too-small pillow and one leg rested along the back of the sofa. Despite the unusual position, he was snoring softly.

Their kiss in the vineyard had kept her awake into the early hours. The passion behind it still had her feeling fuzzy all over. She'd been kissed before but not with the magnitude of Tanner. It made her forget all her reasonable thoughts where he was concerned. For once in her life she understood that "heat of the moment" concept. Tanner, the cool night, the warmth of the earth beneath her feet, the yellow moon above had all conspired against her. She had to see that she didn't get into that position again.

She was thankful for the second of reality that had crept in, for she had no doubt she was on the fast track to heartache. She knew rejection too well. Most of her life had been that where men were concerned. As a chubby child, overweight teen and college student she'd always been picked on in some form. She wouldn't set herself up for disappointment. Anything she might feel for Tanner would turn into just that. Letting a simple kiss change her entire life was ridiculous. Only it hadn't been a *simple* kiss.

She'd known the second Tanner had entered the room. Her body vibrated with awareness when he was near. She probably should have let him know she wasn't asleep but instead she'd watched him remove his clothes. No doubt she had been invading his privacy but she'd been unable to help herself. Worse had been the urge to touch him. When she'd said goodnight she'd seen the small smile form on his lips. He must have liked the idea she'd been watching him. It had been an enticing show.

When the alarm had gone off she'd quickly turned it off. There had been no movement from Tanner's side of the room. She'd lain there listening to his soft snoring for a few minutes before she'd looked at the clock. They needed to get up and get moving. Marie would be expecting them.

Delaying no more, she reached out to touch Tanner then pulled her hand back. For just a second she wanted to admire him a little longer. His shoulders were wide and the muscles of his chest defined. He must work out when he could. A smattering of hair surrounded each nipple before it formed a line down the middle of his belly to dip under the elastic band of his boxers. Tanner's manhood rose high beneath the material.

She sucked in a breath that sounded loud in the almost silent room. What would it be like to be loved by him?

Heaven.

In a raspy voice Tanner said, "When you stare at a man in the morning, you should be prepared for what happens."

He grabbed her hand and jerked her down to him. Whitney's hands came to rest on the warm skin of his chest. Tanner kissed her. A now familiar heat built low in her. Without thinking, she leaned in for more. Before she could register what was happening he'd pushed her away. She quickly moved to sit on the end of the sofa where his feet were. A foot brushed her back as he came to a seated position as well.

Whitney blurted, "I was only trying to wake you. It's almost time for us to be downstairs."

He didn't look at her as he snarled, "Then go get dressed. I'll do the same."

"Are you always this grumpy in the morning?" she asked.

"No, just mad at myself. Now, go."

Was he mad because he'd kissed her? Even though she shouldn't, she'd like more. She'd promised herself when she'd gone to bed that their kissing was done. All he'd had to do was pull her against him and she'd forgotten that promise. What had happened to her self-respect?

She felt his gaze on her as she crossed the floor to the bathroom. A few minutes later when she opened the door, Tanner stood there wearing only a pair of well-worn jeans. He pushed past her, brushing her shoulder with his bare chest. "I need to shave then we can go."

"I like the stubbly look on you."

Tanner stopped and turned to her as if she had said something of world importance. "Then I'll leave it." He went to a chair and snatched up a sky blue polo shirt, pulling it over his head. She hated to see all that gorgeous physique disappear.

"Ready?"

"Yes." He held the door as she entered the hall. Thankfully his mood had improved since he'd woken.

Minutes later they were joining the others as they climbed into the limousines waiting in front of the hotel. Whitney sat beside Tanner, close enough that she could feel the tension in his body. She wasn't vain enough to think it had anything to do with her, so what was wrong? True, she had led him on when she'd returned his kiss then ran, and again this morning, but he'd seemed to have forgiven her before they left their room. Yet now he was uptight again.

As she climbed out of the car, Tanner offered his hand

and she accepted it. He didn't release it as they walked toward the six hot-air balloons waiting in a field.

"They're beautiful. I love the colors against the morning sky." Whitney couldn't contain her amazement and the excitement bubbling within her. When Tanner said nothing she glanced at him. His gaze was fixed on the balloons. "Don't you think so?"

"Uh, yeah."

A man greeted their group and gave each couple instructions on which balloon basket to climb into. Thankfully there was a stool she could use for help getting in the basket but she didn't need it. Strong, sure hands came around her waist. She glanced back to see Tanner standing behind her. He seemed to lift her with no real effort. He waited until she had swung her legs in and was standing before he climbed in himself.

Minutes later the pilot released the tether and the balloon lifted. She watched in fascination as the ground moved away from them as they floated into the blue morning sky. The other balloons slowly joined them. It was a sight to see. Two rainbow-colored balloons, two shaped like a sunflower, another like a bunch of grapes and theirs in a harlequin pattern all floated above the green valley lined with vineyards with mountains to one side. Picture-perfect. She closed her eyes and took a deep breath of the fresh air. This was turning into an amazing weekend.

She turned slightly, wanting to get Tanner's attention to point out something on the ground. One of his hands had a white-knuckled grip on a support while the other grasped the edge of the basket. His body was rigid and his face was pale. Compassion filled her. She diagnosed the problem right away. Tanner was afraid of heights. Knowing how proud he was and not wanting to embarrass him in front of the pilot, she shifted toward him and whispered, "You okay?"

"I'm fine."

That was a lie. "You don't like heights?"

He glared at her as if she had discovered a shameful secret. "No."

The word sounded forced. She placed her hand over his on the basket edge. "Do you mind if I stand close to you?"

Tanner barely nodded agreement.

"Look at that winery over there." Whitney pointed to one in the distance, hoping that would take his mind off how far up in the air they were. She continued to point out landmarks and Tanner slowly relaxed. He even made a comment or two about different views.

"Why didn't you say something? We didn't have to do this," she whispered, looking at him for an answer.

"I thought I could handle it."

She chuckled. "Stupid male ego." For the first time on the flight Tanner's eyes held no terror. He gave her a sickly grin but at least it was a step away from the grimace he'd been wearing.

"I guess you're right. Thanks for helping my ego remain intact, at least where the others are concerned. I may never recover my knighthood in your eyes, though."

"I wouldn't worry about that. Your knighthood is in good shape where I'm concerned." She'd seen the care he gave his patients. She'd also been protected and complimented by him. His armor was still shiny.

He whispered, "Even after last night?"

"Yes." What he didn't know was that, given a chance, she would have liked that kiss to happen all over again.

"I'm glad." He sounded truly relieved.

Too soon for Whitney they were back on the ground again. Tanner wasted no time in climbing out of the basket. He offered her his help. She didn't hesitated to place her hands on his shoulders and let him lift her. Swinging her legs out, she slid down Tanner's body.

He kissed her forehead. "Thank you."

Heat washed over her that had nothing to do with the sun. Tanner Locke had needed her. Not as a pretend girlfriend but as someone who understood and cared about him. Hadn't he had that before? Why wouldn't he want it all the time in his life? As they walked back to the limo her hand remained securely in his. She was going to enjoy the feel of him while she could.

On the ride back Tanner continued to hold her hand and the old confident Tanner had returned. He talked and laughed as they joined the others in the car. He continued to touch her as if she had become his lifeline on the balloon ride and he didn't want to let her go. The one time he did release her hand, his arm came up to rest on the seat behind her. For once she felt that the actions were genuine instead of for show.

Her feelings for him were getting the better of her. She wanted to shout, *No, no, no, you are headed for disaster*, but her body said, *Yes, yes, yes, I want more*. Her body was winning.

When their party once again stood in front of the château Marie announced, "There is a brunch set up in the library if you would like something to eat. The rest of the day is yours. Sleep, swim, golf, go into town. Do as you wish. Dinner is at eight."

Whitney said to Tanner as they trailed the others inside, "I'm not really hungry. I'm going up to check in with a few clients. Don't worry about me."

"If you don't mind, I'd like to come with you. I didn't get much sleep last night. I promise to be quiet while you work. We can eat later."

Guilt filled her. He probably hadn't got much rest because he'd been trying to fit his large frame on the small sofa. "I don't mind. It's your room too."

With a wry smile he said, "Thanks."

Had he not liked her statement? Did he want her to refer to it as their room?

They climbed the stairs and walked down the hall to their room with not a word between them. She hadn't meant to make him unhappy. The less restrained Tanner was fun. Cautiously she said, "Tanner?"

"Yeah?"

"Did I say something wrong?"

He stopped and faced her. "It's just that you're always putting walls up between us."

"Walls? What walls? The only one I know of is that you are my client."

Tanner looked around and then walked to the door to their room and opened it. She followed him in. He shut the door with quiet control. "What if I don't want to be your client anymore?" He focused on her as if her answer meant whether or not the world would come to an end for him.

"Then I'll be sorry to see your business go." And her contact with him.

His look was one of disbelief. "Just my business?"

"Tanner, I'm not very good with word games."

He stepped toward her. "I'm not playing a game. I want you. Badly. Haven't my kisses told you that?"

He wanted her? His kisses had made her know she wanted him. Didn't a man like Tanner just play with someone like her? "I guess so."

Tanner came toward her. One of his arms wrapped her waist, bringing her close but not so near she couldn't see his face. "How little experience have you had that you don't recognize when a man desires you? Can't survive an hour without touching you?"

She looked at the rug beneath their feet. "Truthfully, not much."

Her few times had been short and sweet. Steve had left

her bed saying, "There's not enough room here for me to sleep well."

"May I show you how much I want you?" Tanner nibbled at her neck.

She turned, giving in to the divine pleasure. The mere idea of Tanner wanting her pushed every thought of self-preservation out of her mind. Just being desired by him was more than she'd ever dreamed of. "I guess so."

"'I guess so'?" he mumbled against her skin as he continued to leave little kisses across it. "I've had more encouraging invites."

"Then you might want to go and find them." She made an effort to leave his hold but he held her in place. "Or Charlotte."

He pulled back. There was a look of disbelief on his face. "I don't want them or Charlotte. I want *you*."

Tanner's gave her a gentle and chaste kiss on the lips. Then another. Another. He was testing and teaching at the same time. His lips brushed across hers until she couldn't help but rise on her toes, asking for more. When his mouth left hers she whimpered in disappointment. Eyes as dark as coffee studied her. There was a flare of light in them before both his arms circled her waist and jerked her against him. Tanner's mouth crushed hers.

Whitney's hands found a life of their own and pushed up his arms to circle his neck.

He didn't ask for entrance, his tongue took it. At first he teased until she joined him in the excitement of tasting, tempting and tantalizing. Whitney's heart thumped as her blood rushed to become a throbbing between her legs. She squirmed against him, unable to get close enough. Her fingers weaved through his silky hair, wanting to feel all of him. This was what she'd been wanting for days.

She had become someone she didn't recognize. Tanner made her feel special. Sensual. Confident. Wild.

Tanner's lips left hers and moved to the pulse point beneath her ear. His tongue flicked across it. She shuddered. He was jumbling her thoughts. They centered only on him. He held her mind and body in his control.

His hands moved up her sides to cup her breasts, gently fondling them. His fingers found a button of her shirt and opened it. He kissed the curve of a breast. She clung to his shoulders as her legs almost failed to hold her.

Tanner released another button, pushing her top away so that most of her bra was revealed. Fear drummed in her chest. She couldn't let him see more. Know. Her hands stopped his when they moved to the next button. "Close the curtains."

His head jerked up. "Why?"

"Tanner, I'm sorry. I don't think this is going to work." She didn't miss the flash of anger that entered his eyes before concern covered it.

He backed away and, taking her hand, he led her to the edge of the bed. Sitting, he pulled her down beside him. "Tell me."

Whitney looked down at his large feet and her smaller ones beside them. They were so different. She the blend-into-the-crowd person, and he the shining star. How could he comprehend the pain she'd known? "You wouldn't understand."

His thumb rubbed the back of her hand. "Try me."

She'd seen him with Mr. Wilcox. His compassion, empathy. Could he?

"Please tell me. I know you like me as much as I like you. We're friends, right?"

He was right. They had at least become that. "I was heavy. Fat."

Tanner waited, as if there was more.

"That's part of the reason you didn't see me when we were in college. I wasn't one of those thin pretty girls you hung out with. You might not be interested in me now if I hadn't lost weight."

He shifted away. "You really don't have a very high opinion of me or yourself, do you? Has it occurred to you that I might have grown up? Can see beyond a woman's looks? Appreciate her intelligence? And you, can't you see what you have accomplished, not only in losing weight but starting your own business? You have a heart for people. Mr. Wilcox saw that. Marie as well. Is there some reason you think me incapable of doing so too?"

Whitney's heart swelled. She couldn't believe it. Tanner sounded hurt. "I didn't mean—"

"If I wanted anyone in my bed I could have Charlotte. You're my choice."

"You have no idea what it means to me to have you say that. But, you know, I have stretch marks. I still sag in places."

He gave her an incredulous look. Taking both her hands in his, he leaned toward her. "I don't care about that stuff. I want you. Just the way you are. I'm not going to close the curtains. I'm not going to let you do it either. You trust me or you don't."

"I don't know…"

He brushed her hair back from her face and cupped a cheek. His gaze never left her face. "Honey, I don't care about who you were. All I care about is the desirable woman you are right now. You're not running me off. I'm staying right here." He stood and kicked off his shoes. Pulling his shirt over his head, he let it drop to the floor. On the bed again he lay back on the pillows and crossed his feet. He patted the space beside him. "When you decide you want me, I have a spot for you. I'd be glad to share my nap with you anytime you're ready."

Could she trust him? Expose her vulnerability? What would she miss if she didn't? Minutes later Whitney watched as the dark fans of his eyelashes rested against his cheeks. She was tired too. They'd had an early morning. Maybe if she just lay down for a minute next to him she could accept what he offered.

If she did trust Tanner, act on her need, would she regret it?

Tanner woke to a warm body curled against him. Whitney lay spooned along him. At least that was a step forward. Except for the time she'd remarked about his facial hair and the moment in the balloon, had she shown him any real attention? Her kisses told him otherwise but she fenced him off when she wasn't in his arms.

It had been her choice to lie next to him. Progress. Good progress.

He brought his free arm over her waist and shifted toward her. Even now his libido was stirring, just being this close to her.

Whitney let out a small sigh as she wiggled her behind. He was in real trouble now. With a resolve he hadn't known he had, Tanner closed his eyes and went back to sleep.

The movement of the bed brought him awake again. Whitney had rolled to face him. She slowly opened her eyes.

His gaze met her green, unsure one and saw the second she registered where she was. "Whitney, if you don't want me to take you here and now in broad daylight, I would get off this bed," he said in a soft but firm voice.

She blinked then her look returned to his clear and confident. Her hand came up to rest on his chest. "What if I do?"

Her touch almost scorched his skin. "I want to see all of you. Appreciate everything about you." She waited so long to respond he was afraid all his desires would be dashed.

"Okay," she said softly.

Tanner reached to undo the button he'd undone earlier. His fingers moved to the next one then the next until he could push the shirt away from her shoulders. Sitting up, she let him remove it. He held her gaze as he reached around her and flipped the hook to her no-frills bra open.

She slowly let the bra drop to the floor.

"Now lie back so I can take in your beauty."

Tanner held her uncertain look as Whitney slowly lowered her head to the pillow. His gaze left hers to take in the view of her plump and perfect breasts. He touched the tip of one and heard the intake of her breath. His eyes lifted to her face. With her mouth forming an O and her eyes wide in wonder, he was sure Whitney was the most astonishing creature he'd ever known. "I don't know what you were worried about. You're beautiful."

"Don't look too close."

"Aw, honey, too late for that." His hand cupped a globe and lifted it so that he could take the nipple into his mouth. As he sucked and swirled his tongue, hissing sounds came from Whitney.

He raised his head. Her eyes were closed and she bit part of her bottom lip.

"Whitney."

Her eyes gradually opened. "Yes?"

"Please don't abuse that beautiful lip of yours. I wish to kiss it." He claimed her mouth as he continued enjoying the feel of her breast. She returned his kisses. Her hands traveled over his back and shoulders as if she were hungry for him. He sure hoped so because he was starting to hurt for her. "I need to see all of you."

The worried look returned to her eyes and she started to turn away from him. Tanner kissed her, stopping the move.

"You must think I'm some prima donna who is so up-tight she can't let go enough to let a man see her."

"You certainly have nothing to be ashamed of. Don't you remember me being scared of heights this morning? You came to my rescue. I'm just coming to yours this time."

She looked at him then. "But you got in the balloon despite your fear."

"And aren't you here despite yours?"

She nodded.

He ran his hand along her ribs to her waist. "How about we do this together?" Tanner stood beside the bed and offered her a hand. Much to his delight, she didn't hesitate in taking it. As she stood he couldn't help but enjoy watching her ripe breasts moving freely. His gaze found hers. Whitney was waiting for his reaction. He took her hand and placed it on his length. "See what you're doing to me?"

A spark he'd only seen in her eyes when she was emotional about something he had said or done flared just before she stroked him softly.

Tanner stepped out of her reach. "Any more of that and I won't wait until you take off your clothes, I'll tear them off."

Her smile was a wicked one. His Whitney was gaining confidence. His Whitney? The idea was far more possessive than he liked.

With her hands at the button at her waist she said, "On three."

Tanner forgot all about his mental slip and watched her undo the button. He soon caught up with her actions and they both stood naked before each other.

"Whitney, look at me." He chuckled. "Not that part of me. Up here."

Her gaze rose to meet his. A delightful rosy color covered her cheeks.

"That wasn't so bad, was it?"

"No-o-o…"

"Now I'm going to look at you and you can look at me."

Whitney couldn't believe she was standing in a room naked before Tanner with the sun streaming through the windows. What had happened to her? Who was she becoming?

Trembling, she watched as Tanner's gaze left hers and started downward. His nose flared and his eyes darkened. With an index finger he lightly traced the curve of her hip. Almost reverently he said, "I see nothing that should be hidden."

Relief, desire and an emotion that went deeper filled Whitney. For once in her life she felt she measured up. She took that confidence and found her own pleasure. Studying Tanner's shoulders and chest, she let her look rove over his flat stomach to his slim hips. He stood strong and proud, and incredibly large. Her gaze continued down to his feet, where he wiggled his toes.

She looked at him and smiled. "There was a time I thought you had no sense of humor."

"I'm a man of many surprises. And right now I'm going to show you some of those." He grabbed her and lifted her onto the bed. "And I plan to touch every part of that lovely body."

"Shouldn't we get under the covers?"

"No. I want to experience you. Watch the light dance off your skin. See your expression as you climax."

"Oh!"

"I bet we can do much better than 'oh'…" Tanner kissed her deeply as his fingers caressed her breasts. Heat began to build. Involuntarily she flexed her hips.

Tanner continued to kiss her as his hand left her breast and moved to lie over her belly. Slowly, his hand lowered to her curls and over them. His lips moved over her cheek to nip at her earlobe. He whispered, "Open for me, beautiful Whitney."

She released the tension from her legs, let them part. Tanner didn't pause before he cupped her hot, throbbing center. A finger teased her, then pushed inside. Whitney bucked.

"Easy," Tanner said, then he kissed her and his tongue started making the same erotic motions as his finger.

Whitney sucked in a tight breath and arched her back. Tanner thrust his finger again and she wriggled against it. She squeezed her eyes closed. A heated swirl grew deep in her, built and curled into itself, tightening, growing. Tanner eased deeper and the spring popped. Pleasure flowed throughout her. She rode a sunbeam down with a sigh.

Her eyes opened and she looked into Tanner's grinning face. He teased, "You liked that, didn't you?"

"Mmm…"

"I think you'll like this as well." Tanner reached for the foil packet he'd pulled out of his wallet earlier and placed on the bedside table. He opened it and covered himself before he leaned over her, supporting his torso with his hands. Hers came to his shoulders. He kissed one of her breasts and she felt the pull deep in her center. Moving to the other nipple, he gave it the same attention. His length nudged her opening. He flexed his hips forward and Whitney allowed him passage. Tanner eased into her. With each push-pull her fingers contracted into the muscles of his upper back. With one final plunge he filled her completely.

After a few seconds Tanner withdrew and then pushed forward, then followed the same pattern until that fist of heat started tightening again. She squirmed, wanting more of him. He kissed her then pushed hard and sent her soaring once again. Whitney was on her way down when Tanner made three quick forward motions. He groaned deep in his throat then collapsed beside her.

His arm circled her waist, pulling her to him. He brushed the hair from her forehead. "That was far better than 'oh.'"

Whitney smiled. It was. Much better.

CHAPTER SIX

TANNER POPPED ANOTHER grape into his mouth and watched as Whitney bit into a cube of yellow cheese.

He wasn't by a long shot inexperienced where women were concerned, but he'd never enjoyed giving or watching a woman receive pleasure as much as he had with Whitney. She was so responsive to his touch. To his amazement he'd appreciated her to the point of pain. He wasn't used to that kind of connection. What was she doing to him?

She had crawled under the sheets as soon as she could, saying she was cold. When he'd gone to the bathroom she'd pulled on his shirt. Why was she so uptight about her body? What had happened to her? No one was perfect. Where had she gotten the idea he was only interested in looks? He certainly hadn't been focused on that aspect when he'd listed what he wanted in a wife.

He looked at Whitney. Wife? What kind would she make? She'd certainly represented herself well this weekend. He already knew she had a kind heart. Did she like kids?

"Do you want children?"

She gave him a quizzical look. "Yeah, why?"

"Just wondering." This wasn't a discussion they needed to get into right now. She'd been so unsure of their attraction he didn't want her to backslide to that point again.

He sat up. "As much as I hate it, I think we should make an appearance down by the pool."

Her face turned unsure.

"Something wrong? You didn't bring your suit?" He ran a finger over the top of her hand.

"I've got my suit." Whitney scooted off the bed.

"Then what's the problem?"

She stood beside the bed. "I just don't like wearing it."

"Why not? I bet you look cute in it." He liked the way she looked in his shirt.

"And I bet you need glasses."

He chuckled. Something he found he'd done more of around Whitney. "I'm a surgeon. Don't let the rumor I can't see get started."

A smile tugged at the corner of her mouth. "You go on without me."

"I don't think so." He leaned across the bed and reached out, letting the pad of his finger travel down the opening of the shirt. He reveled in her shiver. "Come on, for me." Tanner saw her indecision.

"And what're you going to do for me?" she came back in a saucy tone.

He wiggled his brows up and down. "What do you want?"

She looked at the ceiling, revealing her long creamy neck, then back at him. "I get to drive your car home."

"Done."

Whitney looked surprised. "I should have asked for something more."

He came to stand beside her. "Hey, I can count on one hand the number of times I've let someone drive my car. Three of those were my mechanic."

"The others?"

"My mother. My brother."

"Tell me about your mother." Whitney sat on the bed and patted the space beside her.

"Trying to stall about going to meet the others?"

"Maybe a little, but I do really want to know about your mother."

Tanner shifted around to sit beside her. He looked at the floor as he said, "She was a good mother. Did the usual things mothers do."

"No, tell me about her." Whitney leaned forward. "What does she like? Do? Her favorite things?"

His father, his father, his father. Tanner thought for a minute. "She likes sitcoms, pink lemonade, dressing up and going to the beach. But most of all she loved my father beyond reason. To the point it broke her heart."

Whitney's gaze was intent. "How's that?"

Tanner knew better than to start this conversation. He also knew Whitney wouldn't let it go. "She would do anything for him. Forgive him for anything, and he treated her like dirt. He had a traveling job that she hated. She desperately wanted him to stay at home. He refused. More than once I heard them fighting, her crying, and the next morning she was hugging and kissing him. She was always begging him to stay."

"That must have been hard on you."

"She just adored him. He could do no wrong. I've never understood why she stayed in the marriage. Let him treat her that way."

"She must have loved him deeply," Whitney said softly.

Tanner made a scoffing sound. "If that's love, I want none of it. Obsession was more like it. It wasn't healthy for her, or my brother and I. And my father didn't care one way or another." He could hear the anger building in his voice. "Look, that's enough on that subject. Let's go put in that appearance at the pool then we can find something else that we can do, just the two of us." He gave her a wolfish grin, took her hand and pulled her off the bed.

"Okay."

Despite him having seen all of her, she still went into the bathroom to change. When she returned she wore an orangey, flowy thing over her swimsuit. Her hair was pulled back at the nape of her neck. Going to the dresser nearby, she picked up the hat he'd bought her the day before in town.

He'd already put on his swim trunks and his polo shirt. "You ready?"

She nodded but there wasn't much enthusiasm in it.

Tanner reached out his hand and she placed hers in it. He pulled her to him and gave her a kiss. She had a smile on her face as they walked through the château. One that he knew he'd caused.

There was no one at the pool when they walked out of the hotel into the afternoon sunshine. Tanner not only heard Whitney's sigh of relief but saw her physically relax. He didn't mind them having the place to themselves, glad to have more time alone with her. His obsession with Whitney was starting to concern him. Was this how his mother had felt about his father?

No, no, no. He wouldn't care about anyone to that magnitude!

"I'm going in. Join me," Tanner said as he pulled his shirt over his head and threw it on a lounger.

"I think I'll sit in the sun for a few minutes. It feels good out here." Whitney took the lounger next to the one he'd tossed his shirt on. She lifted her feet and rested them on the cushion.

Whitney had pretty legs. Ones that had been wrapped around him only an hour ago. His body reacted to that thought. She'd already made it clear how she felt about public displays. He was going to make one of his own if she didn't get in the pool soon.

After swimming a few laps in the pool, he came to the edge where Whitney sat. Splashing water with accurate aim, he was rewarded with a yelp.

Whitney jerked forward and glared at him. "What do you think you're doing?"

Tanner grinned. "I'm lonely. Come in."

"After that I'd like to drown you!"

He pushed away from the side, backstroking to the middle of the pool. "Why don't you come in and try?"

Seconds later she stood, dropped her hat to the lounger, pulled the band from her hair, jerked the cover-up over her head and let it flutter to the chair. He liked this side of her. It reminded him of the Whitney he knew in bed.

He couldn't keep his eyes off her. Whitney wore a plain, navy one-piece suit that showed her curves to their best advantage. Her middle was charmingly rounded, which attested to the fact that she had once been heavy. It made her a real person instead of a stick figure.

There wasn't much time for him to admire her before she startled him by diving into the pool. Seconds later she was swimming toward him. He didn't move, thinking she was just swimming out to him. Instead, when she reached him she put a hand on his head and pushed him under the water.

Seconds later he came up, spluttering. "Hey, what was that for?"

"For splashing me." She had moved beyond his arm length.

He swam after her slowly, much as an animal sought its prey. "What if I dunk you?"

"I don't think you can so it doesn't matter." She moved farther away.

"Cocky, aren't you?"

She grinned. "You could call it that or maybe I'm just confident."

"I think I'll find out which." Tanner dove after her and to his surprise he came up empty-handed. As he surfaced he looked around. She was behind him in the deeper end of the pool.

Whitney just smiled. He'd be able to catch her against the wall. Diving again, he reached out and his hand skimmed one of her legs but couldn't hang on. Once again he came out of the water to glare at her. This time she was swimming toward the other end of the pool.

"I'd say *confident* was the word." She splashed toward him.

Now she was taunting him. He didn't know anyone who dared to do that. It seemed as if everything with Whitney was a new experience. This time he would have her. She was in the shallow end, easier to trap. As he came closer she moved to one side. He shifted to face her. She moved again. Tanner followed.

She giggled. It might have been the most pleasant sound he'd ever heard. They were playing like kids, something that he'd never seen his parents do. He laughed. "This time you're mine."

Whitney had a surprised look on her face for a second and he took advantage of that weakness to pounce. When he did she flipped onto her back and shoved a foot into his chest, pushing him away. Before he knew what had happened she was gone. Seconds later, her hand was on his head and he went under.

Tanner came up to her laughter and her taking a seat on the steps in the shallow end. "You've had enough?"

He swam to join her, sitting beside her. "You're good in the water."

"I've always liked it so when I decided to lose weight

I started swimming for exercise. Even took a lifesaving course for the fun of it."

"I've been had."

"You started it." She pushed a handful of water toward him.

"I guess I did." This was nice. Just teasing each other. With his high-pressure job he didn't just have fun very often. "So what can I do to make it up to you?"

"Well, I'm already getting to drive your car, so how about you be my sex slave for a night?" A stricken look came over her face. "I'm sorry. I can't believe I said that."

Tanner shifted to one hip so he faced her. One hand went under the water to her calf then slid up her leg to her waist. Looking into her wide eyes, he said, "It would be my honor." His lips found hers.

The sound of someone clearing his throat broke them apart. It was Malcolm, standing at the other end of the pool. "I hate to interrupt, Tanner, but you and I haven't had much time to talk. I was wondering if we could do that now. Sorry, Whitney."

Tanner looked at her, unsure whether or not he wanted to leave her.

"Go on," she said quietly as her hand gently pushed against his chest. "This is what you came for. Wow him. I'll be fine. If I'm not here I'll be in the room when you get done."

It was nice to have someone being supportive of him, not just wanting something from him. He stood and climbed out of the pool. "I'll see you later then."

"Okay." She smiled. "I'm not going anywhere." She looked at Malcolm. "You know Tanner really is a great doctor."

Tanner looked down at her and winked. "Thank you." For some reason he walked away thinking he could conquer the world.

* * *

Whitney went back to the room after a brisk swim that ended when Charlotte showed up. She shouldn't let her affect her life but Whitney was in a good mood and the woman would poison it. She'd just as soon read as spend time in Charlotte's presence. Sitting in the corner of the sofa with a book in her hand, Whitney was surprised when Tanner returned and came straight to her, giving her a kiss. Demonstrative actions from a man were something she wasn't used to. She rather liked them coming from Tanner.

When he pulled back and sat beside her she said, "That must have been a good meeting."

"Yes, it was. Malcolm said the board was pleased with my work. He and Marie really like you."

"I'm glad I could help." She just hated that they were not being truthful about their relationship. Even more, she wished it was true. She knew better than to let that happen yet she'd done it.

"How about we celebrate?"

"How're we going to do that? We're supposed to be at dinner in a couple of hours."

Tanner gave her a wicked grin. "I have a few ideas." He leaned toward her again. "To start how about we get it on here on the sofa?" He kissed her and his hand ran up her leg and under the sundress she was wearing. "Then we move to the floor."

"Floor?"

He nibbled behind her ear. "You can be on top if you want."

A flash of heat went through Whitney at the thought.

Boldly cupping her breast, Tanner said next to her lips in a voice that had turned rough with desire, "Then it'll be time for us to shower for dinner. I'll be glad to scrub your back."

* * *

Tanner took Whitney's hand and held it as they waited to fill their plates at the buffet dinner arranged in the grassy area surrounding the pool. She'd picked out a flowing blue-and-gray dress to wear and Tanner didn't even think to complain. He knew well what was under it. A satisfied smile he couldn't control came to his lips. They had celebrated just as he had suggested, to the point of exhaustion. Still he looked forward to taking her to bed later that night. Whitney was weaving a web around him that he wasn't sure he could find a way out of.

With plates filled, they were on their way to a table when his cell phone rang.

"I'll take that," Whitney said, reaching for his plate, "while you answer that."

Tanner gave her his plate and walked off so he could talk privately. "Locke."

"Williams here."

Tanner knew the minute he heard his physician assistant's voice that the call was important.

"We believe we have a heart for Mr. Wilcox," Williams said. "Won't know for sure for a few more hours but things look good. Thought you might want to do this one."

"I'll be there in an hour and a half. Keep me posted." Tanner rang off. As he walked back toward where Whitney was already sitting at a table, she turned and looked at him with concern.

She excused herself and met him. "Is everything okay?"

"No, but it will be, I hope. They think we have a heart for Mr. Wilcox. I've got to go back to town."

"Of course you do. Let's say our goodbyes to Malcolm and Marie. I can be packed in five minutes."

That's one of the many things he liked about Whitney— she didn't require convincing that his work was important. She understood and supported it. Other women he had dated had resented his job when it had interrupted their plans. His mother had certainly resented his father's job.

Less than ten minutes later he and Whitney were packed and going out the door of their room. Tanner stopped and looked back at the bed.

"Did you forget something?" Whitney asked.

"No, I was just thinking I had other plans for tonight." For once he was the one hating the interruption.

Whitney turned an appealing deep shade of red and headed down the hall.

Marie saw to it that his car was waiting outside the front door. As a bellboy loaded their baggage Tanner said to Whitney, "I'm sorry but this time I think I should drive. I promise you next time. If one of us gets a ticket, I want it to be me."

"I understand."

They were pulling out onto the main road when Tanner's phone rang. "I've got to get this." He put in his earbuds, not waiting for Whitney's response before he clicked the button.

Over the next few minutes he listened and gave instructions as they sped through the countryside and then onto the four-lane road back to San Francisco. He drove fast but not carelessly.

He rang off and glanced at Whitney. "I hope I'm not scaring you."

"No." And she appeared at ease.

"I hate it but I won't have time to take you home. I'll see that one of the security guards drives you."

"Would you mind if I stayed for the transplant? I think Mr. Wilcox needs someone in his corner. Maybe I could visit with him before he goes in."

Tanner glanced at her. "I think he'd like that."

A mile farther on his phone rang again and he spent the rest of the time on it with his team. Almost to the minute of the time he'd said he would arrive he eased into his parking space beneath the hospital. Whitney didn't wait on him to come around and open her door. She was at the trunk when he opened it to remove her bags.

"I'll put these in my office so that you can get them before you go home. I won't be leaving the hospital until I know that Mr. Wilcox is stable."

"I understand."

She walked beside him as they took the elevator up from the parking garage. They entered the hospital through a door that required him to swipe a card for it to open and rode another elevator up to the fifth floor. There they went down a couple of hallways and arrived at his office. Whitney waited outside as he set her bags inside the door and grabbed his lab coat.

"Now we'll go see Mr. Wilcox. He'll be in his room for a little while longer. I'll need to examine him then you may visit until I send someone to bring him to surgery."

"Will he be awake or will he have already taken some presurgery medicine?"

"He might be groggy from premeds but he should be awake enough to know who you are." Tanner started down the hall at a brisk pace. The retrieval team was on their way to get the heart. The clock was already ticking.

"Either way, I'll stay with him." Whitney hurried along beside him.

Soon they turned a corner and Tanner scanned his card again. Double doors opened. She followed him to the door of Mr. Wilcox's room. Tanner donned a mask and pulled his stethoscope from his pocket. Without looking at her or saying anything, he entered the room and closed the door. Now wasn't the time to think about what was happening between him and Whitney. He had a life to save.

Whitney was leaning against the wall opposite the room when he came out. He pulled off the mask and dropped it into a garbage can. "You can go in now. I told him I had brought someone to keep him company. I've got to go."

"I know."

He hated to leave her this way but if he kissed her... His focus had to remain on what was going to happen over the next few hours.

Whitney watched Tanner's long stride toward the double doors. He was a man on a mission. His shoulders were broad enough to carry the world. And he was about to do so with Mr. Wilcox's life. What would it be like to have Tanner watching over her with such single-mindedness?

They had shared far more than she had ever expected or anticipated. Tanner had opened up to her about his past. She was confident he didn't make a habit of telling people about his parents. Whitney felt honored he trusted her that much. No wonder Tanner felt the way he did about relationships. He'd never seen a healthy one up close.

But she knew what one looked like and that's what she wanted. To love and be loved. To have that closeness that came from understanding and caring. They were fundamentally different. Tanner wanted a business deal and she wanted happily-ever-after.

Whitney put on a mask then knocked lightly on Mr. Wilcox's door. Unsure if he was strong enough to call to her to come in, Whitney pushed the door open slightly. The lights were low in the room and the only sound came from the oxygen machine. Mr. Wilcox's eyes were closed. Maybe this wasn't such a good idea. She started to back out the door.

"Come in, young lady. It's nice to see you again."

Whitney smiled and said softly, "It's nice to see you too." She entered and closed the door before going to his bedside. She stood so he could see her without straining his neck. "I hear you have a big evening planned."

"That's what they're telling me. What brings you around at this time of night and on a weekend?"

"I was with Dr. Locke when he got the call about your heart." That made it sound like she and Tanner were a couple. That was the furthest thing from the truth. They'd enjoyed each other's bodies but there was no emotional attachment. "I thought you might like some company while you're waiting to go to the operating room."

"That's mighty nice of you. Pull up a chair."

Whitney tugged one of the bulky chairs around so she faced Mr. Wilcox and sat.

"So what were you and Dr. Locke doing this evening that I interrupted?"

Whitney was glad for the dim light to cover her blush. Making love everywhere they could. She couldn't say that. Making love? That's what she had been doing. Emotion was involved on her side. She was in love with Tanner. In love with a man who had no desire to love or be loved. She'd known better but there it was.

Whitney finally managed to get out, "We were in Napa for the weekend." One she would never forget.

"I'm sorry that I messed it up."

"Hey, getting a new heart is a big deal. Well worth messing a weekend up for."

"You're sweet. You remind me of my Milly. She always thought of others first. If she was here she would be holding my hand, telling me everything was going to be all right. She always saw the good side to everything."

"She sounds like a great person."

"She was." He said it as if he were thinking back over the years.

"Would you like me to hold your hand?" Whitney asked.

"That would be nice. I know it isn't very macho, but I'm a little scared."

Whitney pulled the chair closer to the bed. She took the thin hand of her new friend and held it gently. "That's understandable."

Half an hour later a nurse came in and flipped on the overhead lights. "Mr. Wilcox, Dr. Locke is ready for you in the OR."

Whitney stood and pushed the chair away from the bed. "I'm going to say bye now. I'll wait around and see how you're doing. I'll be by to visit again soon." She leaned over and gave the man a kiss on the forehead.

"And I'm going to look forward to dancing at your wedding."

That was an odd thing for him to say, especially since she'd said nothing about getting married, but she didn't question his statement. Maybe his mind was fuzzy.

The nurse gave her an odd look. "Dr. Locke said you could wait in the surgery waiting room on the first floor."

"Thank you," Whitney told the nurse. "See you soon, Mr. Wilcox."

Over the next few hours Whitney watched the weather channel on the TV in the waiting room, read a three-month-old magazine and dozed on and off, but otherwise remained anxious about what was happening in the operating room. She was concerned on two levels. Knowing what Mr. Wilcox meant to Tanner, she was sure he would take it hard if the transplant didn't go well. Then there was her fondness for the older man as well. With her nerves in a jumble, she also paced the room.

She'd been in the waiting room almost six hours when Tanner appeared at the door. He looked tired but it was wonderful to see him. He still wore his surgical cap and scrubs.

Whitney hurried toward him. "How's Mr. Wilcox?"

Tanner smiled. "He's in ICU and doing well."

Whitney hugged him and he returned it. "Now it's time for you to go home. I'll walk you to the front door and one of the security guys is going to drive you."

"What about you? You need to rest." Guilt washed over her. He'd had to sleep on the small sofa the night before, had been up early for the balloon ride and when he could have napped more they had been making love. Tanner had had little rest because of her.

He directed her toward the lobby door with his hand at her waist. "I'll be fine. I'm used to this."

The security man was waiting when they arrived. "What about my bags?"

"They're already in the van."

She grabbed his arm. "You'll let me know how Mr. Wilcox is doing?"

"I'll call you if there's any change," Tanner assured her. "Now go home and get some sleep." He gave her a hug and kissed her forehead.

By the time she was seated in the passenger seat of the hospital van Tanner had already disappeared. It was three in the morning and she paid little attention to what was going on around her on the way home. What had happened to her life? The one she understood? Tanner had entered it and spun it in a new direction. More than that, when he left, and he would, it would come crashing down. She was a woman in love who was destined for heartache.

Love. Heaven help her but she had stepped over the line. She had to stop this now. Next time she saw Tanner she would return his fee and give him the name of another matchmaker. She couldn't continue setting him up with other women. That would be more than her heart could take. Covering up her feelings would be impossible. If she told him now, maybe she would have a chance to recover, heal. But breaking it off would be the most painful thing she'd ever had to do.

It. There was no *it* between them. They'd just enjoyed sex as far as Tanner was concerned. What was there to break off? As far as he was concerned it would be no big deal while her heart would be crumbling.

Most of the day had come and gone when there was a knock on her front door. Whitney answered it to find Tanner standing there. Wearing the jeans and shirt he'd gone to the hospital in, he looked haggard.

"Hey," he said.

Concern gathered in her chest. "Is something wrong? Did something happen to Mr. Wilcox?"

"No, he's doing fine. Even asking when you're coming to see him again."

Relief filled her. So why was Tanner there? "That's good news."

"Can I come in?"

"Oh, yeah. Sure." She couldn't turn him away now. Moving out of the entrance, she allowed Tanner to step in. He continued into the living room. Whitney closed the door and joined him.

"You look like you should be at home, getting some rest. Can I get you a cup of coffee?"

"At this time of the day maybe a soda or an iced tea." He was looking around the room as if evaluating it.

She waited, unsure if he would appreciate her shabby-chic style.

"Nice place. Comfortable. Like you."

Whitney wasn't sure that was a compliment but it didn't matter. Tanner would be gone from her life soon. "Thanks. I do have some iced tea made. Have a seat and I'll get a glass for you."

Gone only minutes, she returned to find Tanner with his head resting against the sofa back sound asleep. He looked out of place on the pink rose-printed fabric that covered the sofa, yet in an odd way he seemed to belong there as well. Pulling the thin white curtains over the windows to keep the sun from beaming in, she then took the crocheted throw, which her grandmother had made, off a nearby chair and covered him. The man had earned his rest.

She couldn't resist placing a kiss on his cheek. It was nice to have him near.

Tanner woke to the smell of something delicious. When was the last time he'd had a home-cooked meal? His mother used to prepare them in the hope his father would be home to eat them. Which had rarely happened.

Where was he? He looked at the blanket over him. *Whitney's*. The entire place reflected her. Simple, floral and comfy. All the things he hadn't had in his life until she'd come along.

Sitting up, he stretched, trying to remove the kink from his back. He'd been almost as surprised as her that he'd turned up on her doorstep. After leaving the hospital he'd just needed to see her. Whitney was like a balm to his tired spirit. Getting to his feet, he followed the smell down a hallway with a multitude of pictures on the wall. Many of them must be members of her family.

Humming, mixed with a song playing on the radio, came from the back of the house. He found Whitney standing in front of the kitchen sink. Her back was to him. Once again she wore a flowing dress but it was belted at the middle, giving her shape. The kitchen was yellow and had bright modern pictures of roosters on the walls.

He leaned against the door frame and watched her for a minute. What would it be like to come home from a hard day to this scene? Somehow life would be better just being a part of it.

A faster song filled the air and Whitney swung her hips to the music. She moved to the stove and must have seen him out of the corner of her eye. She turned. "Hey. Feeling better?"

He started toward her. "A little, but I'll be a lot better after this." Tanner pulled her to him and his mouth found hers. She briefly returned his kiss then stepped back.

Had something changed between them?

"I need to check our supper. I thought you might be hungry."

Was that all there was to it? He wasn't buying trouble until it came. "It smells wonderful. I'm starving. I've not had anything since we left the château."

"Really? That's not good for you."

He liked her being concerned. "I'm used to it."

"I guess with your profession you would be, but that doesn't mean it's healthy."

"I'm sorry I had to dump you off with Security. I know that wasn't a very gentlemanly thing to do."

Whitney held up a hand. "Stop apologizing for that. You had a more important job to do. I'm not so incapable that I can't take care of myself."

She was so insecure about her body and so confident about other areas of her life. "Not everyone thinks that way."

"Then they're wrong. Have a seat." She indicated the table. "The lasagna is ready."

Tanner took a seat in front of a square wooden table already set with mismatched plates and crockery. A glass of iced tea was there as well.

Whitney brought a steaming hot casserole dish to the table and placed it on a hot pad in the middle. She went back to the stove and returned with a basket of bread. She was half seated when she jumped up. "I forgot the salads." She hurried to the refrigerator.

She'd done all of this for him. He'd never dated anyone

who showed they cared by cooking a meal. "You have gone to too much trouble. We could have gone out."

"I like to cook and don't eat out much." She put the salads beside their plates and then picked up his dinner plate and started spooning a portion of lasagna onto it. Placing it in front of him, she then put a small amount on her own.

"Where did you learn to cook?" Tanner picked up his fork.

"From my mother and grandmother. They said a way to a man's heart is through their stomach. I don't know if that's true but my father and grandfather seem happy enough."

Tanner put a forkful of the lasagna into his mouth. "If what they eat is anything as good as this then no wonder they're happy. This is delicious."

"Thanks."

Tanner filled his mouth again. The lasagna might be the best he had ever tasted. Whitney offered him the bread basket and he took a piece. Even that he savored. After eating in silence for a few minutes he said, "So tell me how you happened to live in one of the 'painted ladies' on 'postcard row.' It suits you, but they don't come on the market often."

"This one didn't come on the market. It was my grandparents'. They're letting me slowly buy it. They wanted something smaller and moved to a retirement community. I begged them to let me buy it."

"I have a nondescript place that I almost never see. When I marry, the first thing my wife will have to do is find us somewhere to live." What had made him bring up that subject? He poked at his salad full of fresh vegetables.

"Uh, there's something I'd like to talk to you about."

He didn't like the sound of that. Suddenly his food wasn't as appetizing. "What's going on?"

"About this weekend, I, uh, don't think I can be your matchmaker any longer." She reached into her pocket and pulled out a check. Placing it on the table, she pushed it toward him.

"What's this?"

"It's your fee and the amount you gave me to buy something to wear. I bought the dress with my own money."

"I see." And he did. But he wanted to hear her admit it. "So you're running out on me."

"No." She looked at her plate instead of him. "It's just that I don't think I'm the right person to be doing your matchmaking."

"Probably not." Especially now that he had taken her to bed. And other places. He pushed the check back toward her. "I want you to keep this. You earned it."

Shock then hurt flickered over Whitney's face.

He reached for her hand but she put it in her lap. "I didn't mean it like that. I just meant that you had matched me and you helped me out this weekend. Nothing more."

"I don't want it." She acted as if he had offended her. Treated her as a woman for hire. Maybe in her mind he had. After all, he had promised he wouldn't turn the weekend into something physical and he'd broken that promise. His actions had put her in a vulnerable position both where her business was concerned and emotionally. He couldn't blame her for calling it quits between them. He didn't have to like it but he did understand.

Tanner reached for the check and shoved it in his pocket. "That's not all, is it?"

She didn't immediately answer. "Just that I don't expect anything from you. What happened between us was only because we were pretending to be a couple. I understand you're still looking for a wife."

When Whitney ran she did it in grand style.

He put his fork down and looked at her. "What if I want more to happen?"

"I don't think that's wise for either one of us. I'm not the affair type and that would only get in the way of you looking for the right wife." She refused to meet his look.

Tanner hated to admit it but she was right. He was already far too attached to her. "Then we part as friends?"

She glanced up at him. "Yes, of course." Her voice was a touch high. Was this more difficult for her than she was letting on?

"Well, then I guess I should be going. Thank you for the nap and the meal." He scooted the chair back and stood.

She did as well. "I'll call you with a name of a matchmaker after I have spoken to her. She'll be in touch."

Whitney made it sound like a business deal was being concluded. He didn't like that at all. It was far too civilized a conversation for what they had shared. A business contract was what it had been but Tanner had started thinking of their relationship as more. He walked down the hall toward the front door. Unhappy with the arrangement, he still couldn't disagree with Whitney.

It troubled him how much he disliked the idea of not seeing her again. What really got to him was that she was nothing like what he was looking for in a woman. He'd even had a difficult time making her understand what type of marriage he wanted. If they continued, he would only be using her. He admired her too much for that.

He stopped at the door. Whitney had followed him. He turned to look at her. "I've enjoyed getting to know you. You're a special woman." Tanner kissed her on the cheek and forced himself to open the door and walk out.

CHAPTER SEVEN

IT HAD BEEN a week since Whitney had let Tanner walk out of her house. What she'd wanted to do was beg him to stay. Telling herself not to listen to her practical side, even though she'd made the right decision. But there was still a gnawing pain in her chest. He could be a difficult and demanding man, but she loved it when he let loose and laughed. They'd had fun together. In more ways than one.

Without question she had done what needed to be done. But that didn't mean she didn't miss him. The day after their meal together, she'd called a woman in town who was also a matchmaker. As a professional courtesy Whitney had asked her to take Tanner on. When the other woman found out who Tanner was she had been more than willing to have him as a client. Now indirectly Whitney would be setting him up on dates. She didn't want him dating anyone. What she wished for was for Tanner to want only her. Open his heart to her.

She was relieved and disappointed in equal measure when Tanner didn't answer his phone. She left the new matchmaker's number and told him that the woman would be in touch soon. Her heart felt a stab of pain when she thought of Tanner meeting matches. Touching another woman. Kissing her. Maybe even taking her to bed. After disconnecting the line, she sat looking out the window at nothing. It would have been nice to hear his voice. This was much more difficult than she'd thought it would be.

As the days passed it wasn't easy but she managed to live through them. Had she made the correct decision? Could there be another way?

She was a grown woman who knew what she'd been getting into when she'd agreed to spend the weekend with him. He hadn't coerced her into bed. She'd gone willingly. Even now, when she missed him with every fiber of her being, she didn't regret it.

Almost daily she called the hospital to check on Mr. Wilcox. All reports were positive. He was now out of the ICU and in a room. Whitney couldn't put off going to visit him any longer. She wouldn't hide just because she was afraid that she might run into Tanner. She'd learned long ago that if she wanted to be emotionally healthy she had to face her fears. She'd done that a number of times when she had been heavy. This situation was no different. The sad thing was that she was desperate to see Tanner, yet she was also dodging him.

At the hospital she made it to Mr. Wilcox's floor without any sign of Tanner. She asked directions at the nursing station to Mr. Wilcox's room. As she walked away one of the nurses said to another, "That's the woman Dr. Locke was with."

The other responded, "Not his usual type at all."

"You're right about that."

Whitney didn't like being talked about. Most of her life had been spent worrying about what others had been saying about her. Old habits died hard.

After her knock, she was surprised to hear a strong voice invite her in. She certainly didn't expect Mr. Wilcox to be sitting up in bed, watching TV and eating a meal. This didn't look like the same man she'd seen before the heart transplant. "Hey, Mr. Wilcox."

"Hello, young lady. It's so nice of you to come by."

Whitney stepped farther into the room. "Well, you look wonderful."

"I'm feeling grand except for a few aches and pains, but Doc Locke says those will go away soon."

Even the mention of Tanner's name made Whitney's heart beat faster. "I'm glad to see it. I've been calling every day to check up on you. If I had known you would be doing so well I would have been here sooner."

"New ticker is doing the job. This day is my best day so far. So come in and tell me all the news."

Whitney had a moment of panic. Had Tanner told him about them? No, he wouldn't have done that. Mr. Wilcox must be using it as a figure of speech. She came to stand beside the bed. "What news would you like to know?"

"I'd like to know what you have done to put such a sour look on my doctor's face."

There it was. Could Tanner really have been so upset over them not seeing each other? "I don't know what you're talking about."

Mr. Wilcox studied her a moment. "I think you do but that isn't a nosy old man's business. If you won't talk about that then tell me about yourself. I know you went to Berkeley but tell me what else you do."

Mr. Wilcox had a way of getting her to talk that few people had managed. But Tanner had as well. She even told Mr. Wilcox she was a matchmaker.

"You think you could find someone for me?"

"I'll be glad to see what I can do."

There was a quick knock and the door opened. Tanner came to an abrupt stop. Whitney's heart slammed against her chest wall. She'd stayed too long. She was unable to do anything more than sit in her chair and stare at him. Tanner was just as handsome and commanding as she remembered. Every fiber of her being ached to touch him. She'd missed him so.

"Whitney."

The sound of her name was so sweet coming off his lips. "Hi, Tanner." She pulled her gaze away from him and looked at Mr. Wilcox. "It's time for me to go."

Mr. Wilcox glanced from her to Tanner and back. Those old eyes missed nothing. "You will come back soon?"

Whitney put a hand on his arm. "You can count on it. I'm glad you're doing so well."

"I have to give part of that credit to Dr. Locke here. He's a great doctor."

"I know he is." She did. How could Tanner be anything but that? "Bye, now."

When she passed Tanner he reached out and caught her arm. His touch sent an electric shock though her. The simplest touch from him had her trembling. "Would you please wait for me in the hall until I'm done here? I won't be but a few minutes."

Whitney glanced at Mr. Wilcox. He was still watching them closely. She nodded to Tanner.

Minutes later Tanner joined her. He looked at her carefully. "How have you been?"

"Fine. And yourself?"

"Let's not talk here." He took her arm and led her around the corner to a small consulting room. Opening the door, he let her step in before he entered. The door closed.

"Tanner, I don't really have time—"

His hands cupped her face as his mouth captured the rest of her words. There was an edge of desperation to the kiss as his lips moved across hers. Yet he was holding back. His mouth left hers to run kisses over her cheek. "I've missed you."

Heaven help her, she craved him still. But they must

be sensible. She gently pushed him away. "Tanner, we can't do this."

He let her go and moved away, giving her space, but still breathed deeply as if he was holding himself in check. "Forgive me. I couldn't help myself. Look, what I brought you in here for was to ask you if you would go out with me? I have two tickets to Jazz in the Park tomorrow night."

"Shouldn't you be taking one of your matches?"

"None of those have worked out. Besides, I enjoy your company. What do you say, Whitney? Go with me."

This time he was asking, not demanding, she do something with him. She knew better but she couldn't bring herself to turn him down. It didn't matter what the best thing to do was, she wanted to go. Wanted to spend time with Tanner. "What time should I expect you?"

A smile came to his lips. One that reached his eyes. He'd been worried she wouldn't go. "Seven. Don't eat dinner. I'll bring it." His phone buzzed. "I have to get this. I'll see you tomorrow night."

Whitney thought he might kiss her before he left and was disappointed when he didn't.

She had a date with Tanner. A real date.

Tanner had been out with a number of women but for some reason he was nervous about this date. Everything must be right. He enjoyed Whitney's company more than anyone's he'd ever known and he was going to do whatever it took to continue to see her, to have her in his life, permanently.

It had occurred to him that she was his match. The one he'd been looking for. She met all his criteria. Whitney enjoyed his company. She'd proven that over and over while they'd been in Napa. They were extremely compatible in bed. Which made her almost perfect. She wanted children, was a great cook, did well in social situations. What was not right about her? Their life together would be satisfying. He just needed to convince her of that.

He'd been planning to give her a little more time before he asked her out but, seeing her in Mr. Wilcox's room, he hadn't been able to wait. He'd missed her, longed for her. Before she'd been his matchmaker and now she wasn't. There was nothing stopping them from dating.

Now all he had to do was woo her, show her that they belonged together. Surely he could do that? Had that been what his mother had tried to do? But Tanner wasn't going to make the mistake his mother had. He wasn't going to fall in love. Somehow he and Whitney would make it work without that emotion.

The next afternoon after half an hour of indecision, Tanner settled on a light blue collared shirt and jeans with a navy jacket as his outfit for the evening. Dressy, yet casual. Before he left the hospital he made sure that he had two doctors taking his calls in case something came up. He didn't want any interruptions tonight.

He was at Whitney's promptly at seven in his freshly washed car. Why was he acting as if he were going to the prom? Because he wanted Whitney to see the possibilities between them.

Adjusting his collar for the third time and checking his hair in the mirror, Tanner climbed the steps to her front door carrying a small flowerpot. The lady at the flower shop had said she would love this one.

He rang the bell. No one came. Had Whitney forgotten? He pushed the button again. Waited. Relief washed over him when the knob turned and the door opened. Whitney looked amazing. She was dressed in a light pink sweater set and darker pink pants that skimmed her hips, and wore her hair down around her shoulders, and he'd never seen her look more beautiful.

"Wow."

She smiled. "Thanks. You look nice yourself."

He offered the potted plant in his hand. "I brought you a flower."

Whitney took it and gently touched one of the purple blooms. "It's beautiful. You remembered how much I like violets."

"I did." He'd won points.

"Come in while I find a home for this and get my purse."

Tanner would follow her anywhere. He'd never felt like this about a woman. Right now all he wanted to do was carry her upstairs to her bed. Hell, he'd settle for her sofa. But he wasn't going to do that. She deserved better than a rutting buck.

Instead of following her farther down the hall, he chose to remain near the door so he wouldn't be further tempted. She soon returned with purse in hand.

"I'm ready."

"Great. Let's go." He went out the door and waited on the steps as she locked up. Taking Whitney's elbow, he helped her down the steps. When she went to the passenger side of his car he redirected her to the driver's. "I promised you could drive. I thought you might like to tonight."

She grinned. "Really?"

He held the door open for her. "Really."

Whitney dropped her purse into the space behind her seat and climb in. She already had the car started before he was in his seat and buckled up. He groaned when she revved the motor.

She smiled. "This is going to be fun."

"You break it, you buy it, that's all I'm going to say."

"Oh, you're no fun." She pulled away from the curb.

Over the next few minutes Tanner sat back and enjoyed watching Whitney's facial expressions as she negotiated the narrow hilly streets of San Francisco in the powerful car. She was having fun. The evening was off to a good start.

When they were closer to the park he gave her directions about where to pull in and stop. He helped her out of the car and then went to the trunk and removed the picnic basket and blanket he had stored there.

"Nice. Fix that yourself?" Whitney asked.

He gave her a bashful look. "No, but I did call and order it."

She gave a bark of laughter. "If nothing else, you're honest."

"Yeah, about this, but I wasn't straight up with Malcolm and Marie. I plan to come clean the next time I see Malcolm."

They started toward the stage already set up in an open grassy area in the middle of the park. "Good. I felt bad about deceiving them."

They wouldn't be upset if he could tell them that he and Whitney really were a couple.

Finding a place where no one else would be sitting too close to them, he spread the blanket out. They took a seat on it. Opening the basket, Tanner unloaded the food. Tanner had requested raw vegetables with dip, ham and cheese rolls, fruit and wine.

"This is nice," Whitney said. "Who decided on the menu?"

"I did."

"Good choices." She bit into a carrot that she had pulled through vegetable dip.

More points.

They were just finishing their meal when the jazz band took the stage. After a couple of numbers Whitney shifted as if she couldn't get comfortable. Tanner moved so she could lean against him. He liked having her close.

"The music is wonderful. Thanks for inviting me," she said between songs.

"You're welcome."

She smelled of something fresh and natural. The temptation to kiss her neck was almost impossible to resist but he did.

For Tanner the concert was over too soon. He had to let go of Whitney.

He repacked the basket and she held it while he folded the blanket. When he was done he put it under one arm and took Whitney's hand. They followed the rest of the crowd toward the parking lot.

"Do you want to drive home?" Tanner asked as he stored the basket and blanket in the trunk of the car.

"No, I think I'll just enjoy the ride. You always seem to make it interesting." She settled into the passenger seat and laid her head back on the rest. Closing her eyes, she hummed a piece the band had played.

It was a sound he could get used to hearing all the time. Forty-five minutes later he said, "Whitney, you're home."

She rolled her head and looked at him. "I'm sorry. I went to sleep on you."

"No problem. I deal with people who are asleep all the time."

It took her a minute but she burst out laughing. "You know, there was a time I thought you were so uptight that you had no idea what a joke was."

"I could say the same about you."

She sat up and gave him an indulgent look. "I've never been uptight in my life."

"If you say so."

Whitney laid her head back again. Speaking more to the night sky than him, she said, "You know, I had such a crush on you in college."

"You did?" It couldn't be anything like the one he had on her right now.

"I don't think you ever noticed me. You never even spoke to me but, man, I was crazy about you."

Tanner liked the softness of her voice in the night. "I'm flattered. I'm sorry that I didn't notice."

"Hey, don't feel bad. I don't think we would have liked each other then."

"Why is that?" He turned in the seat to see her clearer in the dim light from her porch.

Whitney shrugged. "I just think we both needed to grow up. I sure did. A few more life experiences make us see things differently."

"So what do you think of me now?" he asked quietly. His future depended on her answer.

"I…uh… I…like you. Far more than I would have in college. You're a good guy."

More points. This was going from a good night to a great one. Was now the time to ask? With his chest tight with building hope, he said, "I've been thinking about this matchmaking stuff. You know, we're pretty good together. Great, in fact, I think. You're a good match for me. I don't want to look anymore. I'd like us to see where this will go."

She didn't say anything for so long Tanner was afraid he wasn't going to want to hear what she had to say when she did speak.

"Tanner, would you like to come in?"

Whitney knew what she was agreeing to. But she also knew what it was like not to have Tanner in her life. Just a week of it had been enough for her. She loved him. Maybe she could show him how to love. She wasn't going to let go of this opportunity. It might not come her way again.

Tanner was a good man. She'd seen that in his actions more than once. He had the ability to open his heart, she knew that with all of her own. She would find the key. There was no doubt that he was her perfect match as well.

They made it as far as her hallway where a small lamp burned before Tanner grabbed her. She let her purse fall as he nudged her back against the front door. "I've waited as long as I can." His mouth took hers in a kiss that said he wanted her here and now. Flexing his hips, he asked, "See what you do to me?"

Whitney's stomach fluttered in anticipation. She liked having that kind of power over him. She brought a leg up high along his as she kissed him deeply. This was where she belonged. The love would come.

Tanner stepped back and fumbled with the button of her slacks. When he couldn't release it she brushed his hand away. "Let me."

"I want you so badly I can't think." He nipped at her neck. Touching her everywhere.

This self-assured man was trembling with desire for her. It was a heady feeling. She flipped the button open and pushed her pants and panties to her feet, stepped out of them and kicked them away. Seconds later Tanner's jeans and underwear joined hers on the throw rug on the floor.

His hands skimmed up her thighs to grip her hips and lift her. "Put your legs around me."

Wrapping her arms around his neck, Whitney obeyed. His gaze held hers as he slowly lowered her until he filled her. Heat, raw and sharp, pooled at her center. Bracing her against the door, Tanner thrust and withdrew.

Whitney wiggled as the sensation rose, turning the heat into a burning flame. Her fingers bit into his shoulder muscles through the fabric of his shirt. She might die with pleasure. Tanner plunged again as his mouth plundered hers. The need grew, built on itself until she could stand it no longer. She threw her head back and screamed her ecstasy.

Tanner held her in place and drove into her until he groaned his own release against her neck.

He steadied her as her feet reached the floor then swept her into his arms. "Bedroom."

"Upstairs, room on the right."

The morning sun woke Whitney. She stretched. Her hand touched the space where Tanner had slept. She smiled. He would return. So this was how a woman well loved and in love felt.

Tanner did love her. He just didn't recognize it for what it was. He would one day soon. He must. She would show him what giving love instead of demanding love was all about. With time he would come to recognize the difference between what his parents had had and what they had. She couldn't believe any different.

At daylight he'd woken her and kissed her thoroughly. "I have an early case. I'll see you this evening."

Then he was gone. She was well aware that she had to share him with his job but she would have liked to wake up with him next to her. Maybe tomorrow. Those were the type of demands she couldn't make. He would balk at them immediately. Too clingy.

Whitney went through the day with a smile on her face. She forced herself to review some client information but her thoughts kept returning to Tanner.

That evening she was in the kitchen when the doorbell rang. Hurrying down the hall, she opened the door. Tanner waited there with a smile on his face and a bag in his hand. He stepped inside and closed the door before swooping her up into his arms. His lips found hers for a hungry kiss.

When he pulled away he said, "I've been looking forward to that all day."

"You get an A+ for greetings. You hungry?"

"Yeah. For you." He took her hand and led her upstairs.

Sometime later they came down again and went to the kitchen for dinner. Whitney could get used to this. While she placed the food on the table Tanner poured their drinks.

"How's Mr. Wilcox doing?" Whitney asked as they ate.

"I think I'll be able to send him home in a few days." Tanner cut his pork chop.

"That's great. I'm so happy for him. Did you know that he asked me to find him a match?"

Tanner looked at her. "Really?"

"He did."

"I hope he finds one as good as I have." Tanner grinned at her.

She liked being his match.

After cleaning the kitchen, they spent the rest of the evening watching TV, with Whitney curled up in Tanner's arms.

"I missed you," he said softy. "Please don't push me away again."

"And I missed you." She gave him a kiss.

The rest of the week continued much as the way that evening had gone. Tanner had to work late a couple of nights but Whitney was waiting on him with a smile and a warm meal when he came *home*.

The first night he'd been late she'd been wearing a long comfortable gown. When they'd made it upstairs to her bedroom, Tanner had pulled it off over her head and dropped it in the trash can.

"No more granny gowns. I'm going to buy you something that flatters that sexy body of yours."

Tanner's attention always made her feel sexy and appealing. For once in her life she was going to buy some skimpy lingerie.

After their first night back together Tanner had brought

over a bag of his clothes. A few days later she'd cleaned out a drawer for him and given him space in the closet. Their relationship was moving fast but she hadn't been happier. Still, there was the nagging voice that whispered when she wasn't busy, *Will he ever say he loves you?* She pushed it away with, "I haven't said it either, but that doesn't mean it isn't true."

Friday evening they were eating Chinese takeout when Whitney said, "My grandfather has a birthday party Sunday afternoon. Would you like to come with me?"

"Sure. Why haven't you said something about it before now?"

She fiddled with her chopsticks. "I wasn't sure how you would feel about meeting my family so soon."

Tanner took her hand. "You and I are a team. I'd love to meet your family."

Team? She wanted him to see them as a couple but she'd settle for team right now. "Mom and Dad will be there. My sister and her family. Some cousins."

"I'm game," he said, and went back to eating.

Sunday morning he had to go to the hospital for an emergency. "I'll meet you at your grandparents'. Text me the address," Tanner said before he gave her a quick kiss goodbye.

She didn't like showing up at her grandparents' without Tanner, but he had said he would make it if he could. Even though they had only been together a week she felt lost without him. Her heart swelled just knowing he came home to her every day.

They were just singing "Happy Birthday" when there was a knock on the door. One of her cousins answered and called her name.

"Yes."

"Your Tanner is here."

Her Tanner. Whitney liked the sound of that. She met

him at the door. He put his arm around her waist and gave it a squeeze. "Sorry, I'm so late. Case was worse than I thought."

She smiled. "I understand."

"That's one of the many things I like about you, you always do." He gave her a quick kiss.

Why couldn't that *like* have been *love*? "Come meet my parents and grandparents."

"Lead the way."

CHAPTER EIGHT

TANNER WASN'T USED to all the noise and excitement, the laughter, of a big family get-together. He decided he liked it. What he remembered about family parties growing up was that they were elaborate and his mother had often ended up breaking down in tears because his father hadn't shown up. They had not been happy affairs.

Whitney took his hand and led him into a dining room where everyone was standing around a table. He stood behind her in the crowded space. Sitting at the end was a balding, white-haired man. Next to him was a woman of about the same age who was cutting cake and placing it on plates then handing them to a younger woman who added scoops of ice cream.

"Harold, how much ice cream do you want?" the woman asked.

"Six scoops," Whitney's grandfather said.

"Harold! Even on your birthday that is too much," the woman cutting the cake scolded.

Whitney's grandfather reached for her hand and kissed the back of it. "It's my birthday, sweetheart."

She turned and looked at the woman with the ice-cream scoop. "Make it three."

"That's what I wanted anyway." Whitney's grandfather grinned.

"They're my grandparents." Whitney pointed to the older couple. "That's my mom helping with the ice cream. I'll introduce you in a minute." The love Whitney had for them was evident in her voice.

Didn't she use that same note when she spoke to him? He would have to think about that later.

"Okay, now that the birthday boy has had his share, pass the cake and ice cream around," Whitney's grandmother instructed.

Everyone did as they were told except for a few of the young kids, who grabbed theirs and disappeared into another room or outside. Soon Whitney and he had their share. Most of the others left to sit elsewhere, leaving room at the table for them. Whitney headed toward her grandfather and took a seat near him. Tanner slid into the one beside her.

"Paps and Memaw, I'd like for you to meet Tanner Locke."

"Hello, sir. It's nice to meet you. And happy birthday," Tanner said to her grandfather.

The older man gave him a long look then said in a teasing tone, "You must be the guy who has put the smile on Whitney's face."

Tanner glanced at Whitney to find her blushing. "I hope so."

"And this is my mom, Delores. Where's Daddy?"

"He's outside, getting some more chairs," Delores answered.

As if he knew they were talking about him, a man with the same coloring as Whitney entered the room. "I gave the chairs to those out on the lawn."

Delores smiled at him. "Thanks, honey. What would I do without you? Have you met Whitney's friend?"

Tanner had every intention of being more than her

friend but he would accept that title for now. He stood and offered his hand. "Hello, Mr. Thomason. Tanner Locke."

Her father accepted his hand. "Hi, Tanner. Joe Thomason. Nice to meet you."

"You too, sir."

"Joe, I saved you some cake and ice cream." Delores placed a plate in front of an empty chair across from Tanner.

Joe took the chair and smiled at his wife. "Thanks." He then turned to Tanner again. "Whitney says you're a heart surgeon. Interesting profession."

"I am. And most of the time it is." Tanner took a forkful of cake.

"It would be nice to have a doctor in the family." Joe grinned at his daughter.

"Daddy!" Whitney's voice went up an octave.

What would it be like to be a member of this family? Whitney must have really cast a spell over him. There was something rare in the air around these people, in the way they looked at one another and interacted. Rare at least in his experience. It made him want to be included. He couldn't remember that ever happening before.

When Whitney touched him he knew the feeling. Like on the balloon. Her smile alone made his life better. What was that element? Some would call it a connection. Others compatibility. Knowing Whitney, she would say it was love. Was it something he knew how to give? But if he did it would make him too vulnerable, weak like his mother.

His family, his mother and father's relationship had been so dysfunctional that he never thought of himself as wanting, or capable of being in, a loving unit. Whitney's family made him feel a little uncomfortable as well. As if he was looking in on something he had no knowledge of.

Over the next hour he met the rest of her relations, discussed baseball with her brother-in-law and listened to a conversation between her father and uncle about the best way to grill a chicken. When Whitney put her hand on his shoulder and said it was time to go, he had to admit he was ready. He wasn't sure he really fit in here.

They were inside saying their goodbyes when one of Whitney's nephews came running into the house. "There's something wrong with Papa Joe."

Whitney was ahead of Tanner as they rushed out of the house. Family members surrounded her father. She pushed through two of them to where he sat in one of the folding chairs. He was clutching his left arm.

"Michelle, get the baby aspirin." Whitney glanced at him. "He had some arrhythmia a few years back."

Tanner said to the man standing beside him, "Go to the convertible down there." He pointed down the street. "And bring me the black bag behind the seat." Tanner handed him his keys. "Everyone, please move back a step or two. Whitney, call 911. Even if this is arrhythmia he still needs to be checked out at the hospital."

Whitney pulled out her phone.

The man returned with the bag and Tanner located his stethoscope. "Mr. Thomason, I'm going to give you a listen. Just remain still. Everything is going to be fine. Whitney, I'm going to give you some information and I want you to tell the operator to relay it to the ambulance EMTs."

"I'm ready."

"Give them my name and tell them that I am on-site." She did as he requested while he listened to Mr. Thomason's heart. There was no question it was an arrhythmia issue. The man might require a procedure this time. "Tell them to patch you through to the EMTs."

Whitney relayed the message. Her voice didn't waver. She was a tough cookie even in an emergency.

Michelle returned with the aspirin in her hand and Mrs. Thomason on her heels.

Whitney said to Michelle, "Give three to Tanner."

She was even knowledgeable enough about her father's care to know what he needed in case of an emergency. Whitney took care of those she loved.

Tanner took the tablets from Michelle. "Mr. Thomason, I need you to chew these and swallow them. Make sure they go down."

"I'll get some water," someone said.

"No water. It could cause him to choke." Or if he required emergency surgery, he shouldn't have anything in his stomach.

"Joe, Joe, are you all right?" Mrs. Thomason sobbed as she pushed through the group and rushed to Mr. Thomason.

"Michelle, take care of Mother," Whitney clipped.

Her sister did as Whitney said, putting her arm around her mother and pulling her away a few steps. "Mom, back up and let Tanner see about Daddy."

Tanner knew the answer to the question before he asked but he had to anyway. "Mr. Thomason, are you on any medication?"

"He is. The information is in my purse. I'll get it," Mrs. Thomason said. She pulled away from Michelle's arm and headed for the house.

"Tanner, the EMTs are on the line," Whitney said from close beside him.

"Good. Tell them the patient is responsive. Three eighty-one-milligram aspirin given." He waited until Whitney had repeated his words. "Heart rate one hundred and sixty-seven. BP one-eight-four over ninety. Respirations forty-five." He pressed Mr. Thomason's index fingernail while she spoke. "Little discoloration of nail."

Whitney repeated the information.

Her mother returned with the medication list and handed it to him. He reviewed it then passed it along to

Whitney. "Let the EMTs know. If you can't pronounce it, spell it out."

Tanner did another round of vitals as Whitney read out the medicine names and dosages to the EMTs. Mr. Thomason appeared stable but Tanner still wouldn't be comfortable until he was at the hospital and some tests were run.

The sound of the siren from the approaching ambulance soon filled the air. Tanner looked up and scanned the concerned family group around him. "I need everyone to move way back. Give the EMTs room to work." Thankfully everyone did as he asked.

Minutes later he spoke to one of the EMTs then let them do what they were well trained to do. After they had Mr. Thomason in the ambulance, Tanner conferred with the ER doctor who would be accepting his patient at the hospital. Soon Mr. Thomason was on his way. Tanner put his supplies back in his bag and found Whitney with her mother.

"I'm going to drive Mother to the hospital," Whitney said.

She really had been cool during an emergency. Many people would have fallen apart if a family member had been in trouble. Whitney had followed his directions to the letter without any questions. She was someone he could depend on during a crisis.

"Why don't I drive you both? We can come back to get my car later," Tanner offered.

Whitney gave him a grateful look that included something he wasn't sure he was willing to put a name to.

"Thank you."

Three hours later, Whitney was standing in the hospital at the foot of her father's bed. He had an oxygen cannula under his nose and had an IV in his arm but otherwise looked no worse for the scare he had put his family through. A monitor on a pole nearby continually checked his heart rate.

"I knew you bringing home a doctor was going to be a benefit," her father said with a wink.

Whitney was just glad Tanner had stepped out to speak to her father's cardiologist and hadn't heard that statement.

"I don't like Tanner because he's a doctor, Dad. He's fun to be around, nice, caring and good to me."

Her father looked at her for a moment. "Sounds like a woman in love to me."

She was. Deeply. "There's a lot to love about him."

Her father grinned as he looked over her shoulder.

Whitney turned to find Tanner standing there. Had he heard what she had said? Would he run now, knowing how she felt? She tried to read Tanner's face but there was no indication he had heard her. If she did tell him how she felt, would he even give them a chance?

She'd had no doubt that he was a thorough doctor and a compassionate one. With Mr. Wilcox she had seen some of those attributes but today with her father she'd seen firsthand how he could command a difficult situation. He had been magnificent. Someone she could lean on in a time of trouble.

Tanner came to stand beside her. "You're all set, Mr. Thomason. I'll be in to check on you in the morning. If you need anything, just ask."

"Thanks for your help today. I don't usually make such a scene when my daughter brings home a man for the first time."

Tanner grinned. "I'm glad to know I'm special." He looked at Whitney's mother. "Delores, are you sure you're going to be okay here tonight? Have everything you need?"

"I'll be just fine. I wouldn't sleep if I went home anyway," her mother assured him, placing a hand on her husband's arm and looking at him adoringly.

Tanner seemed unnaturally focused on her parents, as if he was watching every detail of their interaction. Did their obvious affection make him feel nervous?

"Then Whitney and I will see you first thing in the morning," Tanner said.

He really was great. Tanner didn't have to go with her. She kissed both of her parents. "Call if you need anything."

As she and Tanner drove through the early evening toward her grandparents' house Whitney reached over and rested her hand on his thigh. "Thank you for saving my father's life today."

"I don't know that I did that but you're welcome. I was pretty impressed by the cool head you kept. I've had nurses who showed less control in an emergency. If you ever want to give up matchmaking, I recommend you consider nursing or med school."

Whitney chuckled. "I think you're giving me too much credit but it's nice to hear praise."

Tanner pulled her parents' car into her grandparents' drive. He turned to look at her. "You should hear praise all the time. You're wonderful."

"You're pretty wonderful yourself." Her hand cupped his cheek and she gave him a kiss that held all the love she felt.

When they broke apart he wore a strange expression. Had Tanner sensed what she was offering him? They continued to look at each other. Had something subtly changed between them? Did she dare to hope he felt the love she did?

Tanner broke the spell of the moment with, "I guess we'd better go in and give your grandparents a report."

An hour later, she was driving her parents' car back to their house while Tanner followed her. She pulled it in the garage. Whitney had promised to pack her mother some clothes and her father a pair of pajamas and a few personal items. Tanner came inside to wait while she gathered things.

"So how long have your parents been married?" he asked from the living room.

"Thirty-one—no, thirty-two years." She stuck her head out of her parents' bedroom. "Why?"

"They just seem so happy together."

"They are," Whitney said from inside the bedroom.

"My parents fought all the time. I don't remember them being able to stay in the same room together over half an hour. They certainly couldn't stay in a hospital room together. Your parents must really love each other."

Whitney's heart filled with optimism. Tanner did recognize love. She stepped out of the room. "Yeah, they do."

Tanner was standing in front of a picture of her entire family. "No wonder you didn't understand why I didn't list that as necessary in my match."

"It was hard for me to understand at the time. Now that you have told me about your parents I sort of understand. But that doesn't mean that you can't have love in your life." She looked directly at him. "I want what my parents have."

It took a moment before he said, "I can't promise that. I'm not even sure I know how to love like that."

Whitney stepped closer. "Maybe I can help you learn."

That night they walked hand and hand up the stairs to what was now their bedroom. When Whitney started to undress Tanner pushed her hands away. "Let me." He slowly removed her clothes, kissing each piece of flesh he exposed. With all her clothes on the floor, he quickly removed his. Tanner took her hand and led her to the bed.

"You are so amazing." He gently caressed her lips.

Whitney cupped his face with both her hands and kissed him with all the love she felt.

Tanner lifted her to the bed and joined her without breaking the contact. When they broke apart, he lay on his side and looked down at her. As his eyes raked her body, Whitney trembled. Tanner's look found hers, held.

"I don't know what you're doing to me, but I like who I am around you."

Whitney smiled. She knew what it was. Love.

Tanner kissed her again. When it went deeper Whitney nudged him to his back. She brought her lips to his chest over his heart. He inhaled sharply. Whitney captured his hands and held them at his sides. She kissed the curve of his neck and slowly slid over him. He moaned his pleasure. She continued to work her way up him, enjoying her skin touching his. She placed a kiss on his ear, eyebrow and finally his lips. She released his hands. He brought them to her hips, caressing her. He gently lifted her then slowly lowered her, joining them.

Their movements were deliberate and calm, yet there was an intensity between them they'd not had before. There was nothing of the frenzied coupling Tanner normally preferred. This time it was as if he was marking her as his.

Afterward, they lay in each other's arms for a long time without either of them speaking. Hope blossomed in Whitney.

The next few weeks passed much as the others had. For Tanner life was better than it had ever been yet there was something off he couldn't name.

After their lovemaking the night Whitney's father had gone into the hospital something had changed between them. The smiles Whitney gave him had an extra brightness to them. She touched him for no reason when she was walking by. She was waiting when he came home no matter what the time. The pleasure he found in bed was pure bliss and went beyond anything he'd ever experienced. Yet something nagged at him. As if he was missing something.

Whitney's father was home and doing well. He'd only visited with him once since he'd been released but Whitney gave Tanner a report each evening of his progress. When was the last time he had spoken to his father? Five years? Even his mother he only talked to a couple of times a year. The closeness, real caring, he saw in Whitney's family was a foreign concept for him.

All the attributes he appreciated most in Whitney he could see in some form in her parents. It made him uneasy on a level he didn't understand. Would Whitney continue to be happy with him? Would she demand more? Start treating him as his mother had his father?

Mr. Wilcox had been discharged the day after Mr. Thomason had been admitted. Mr. Wilcox's new heart was doing well. A friend had come to pick him up and had promised to see that he made it to his appointments.

"That young lady of ours came by to see me earlier this morning." Mr. Wilcox climbed into the wheelchair the orderly held for him.

Of course Whitney had.

Even with her father sick she wouldn't forget about someone else.

"She's a keeper. She has a big heart. To be loved by someone like that is a special thing. I know. I had it and miss it every day."

"Whitney is special." Tanner meant that. The more he was with her the more he found another facet of her personality he liked. It disturbed him that his emotional attachment was growing. He didn't want to think about that. Emotional attachment was something that he'd never wanted or planned to have.

They had been together almost two months when Tanner said at dinner one night, "We've been invited to a cocktail party on Friday evening at Malcolm and Marie's."

"We have?" Whitney sounded unsure.

"Will you go?"

"Do you really need me to?"

Hadn't she gotten past her fear of social situations after their weekend in Napa? "There'll be questions if you don't."

"Those events are just not my thing."

"But you were great in Napa. You don't give yourself enough credit. What's the problem?"

She left the table and walked to the kitchen sink, then confronted him. "The problem is that for over half my life I was made fun of or looked down on for my weight. I wasn't invited to or included in parties. Now I just plain don't care to be around those kinds of people. Up until a few years ago no one in that group would have given me the time of day."

"Why, Whitney Thomason, I had no idea you were such a snob."

"I am not! What I don't do is put myself in situations where I know I'll be made to feel inadequate."

Tanner turned in his chair to face her. "Did Malcolm and Marie make you feel that way in Napa?"

"Well, no." She crossed her arms over her chest.

"Do I make you feel that way?"

She backed up to the counter. "No-o-o… But not all the people are like you and the Jarvises."

"So you're going to let others control what you do in life?" Whitney winced. Tanner could tell that shot had hit its mark.

"No, but I don't have to be around them."

"I'll be there with you. Don't you trust me to support you?"

She came toward him. "I do, but I just think you'd be better off at those events without some insecure woman to worry about."

He faced her. "Has it occurred to you that I might need your support at the party? That social situations might not be my 'thing' either?"

"Why would you need my support? You're a successful heart surgeon, you're gorgeous and intelligent—who wouldn't enjoy your company?"

"Apparently you." Tanner sounded hurt, which he was. "I'm still trying to get that promotion. Making small talk is a little nerve-racking for me as well."

Whitney studied him for a minute. "I had no idea you felt that way. You seem to have so much confidence wherever you go."

"Now you know another one of my secrets."

She came back to the table and just before she sat he grabbed her and pulled her onto his lap. "So will you go with me?"

"I guess we're in it together."

Tanner kissed her. "About that gorgeous and intelligent remark, you really think so?"

She slapped his shoulder. "Now you're just fishing for compliments."

He chuckled. "That's because I like hearing you say them. They sound extra good coming out of your pretty mouth."

"Maybe for another kiss I could say more."

"For a kiss you don't have to say anything." His mouth found hers.

Whitney didn't make a habit of buying new clothes often but she had found that her wardrobe had almost completely changed since she and Tanner had started seeing each other. He liked to see her in clothes that fit her form and she'd taken to wearing less baggy clothes. Even her nightclothes, if she wore any, were flimsy gowns with lace and bows that had little substance. Tanner had slowly seen to it that all her granny gowns went out with the trash. She didn't mind. In fact, she rather liked the person she was becoming with Tanner.

On her own initiative, she went shopping for a dress for the cocktail party. She found a simply cut black A-line that she felt confident wearing. At home that evening, Tanner only added to her self-assurance when he saw her enter the living room where he was waiting.

He stood and came toward her. Taking her hand, he turned her around and whistled. "If I didn't need to show up for this party I'd say forget it and spend the rest of the night taking that dress off you."

"You do have a way of making a girl feel good." She kissed him. "You look superb yourself."

He did, dressed in his dark suit with a light blue tie. The man was almost too handsome to look at. It gave her a boost of confidence just being seen with him. But what she liked most about him couldn't be seen. Tanner was such a fine person.

An hour later they arrived at the Jarvises'. They were greeted warmly and Whitney was truly glad to see them both. She and Tanner had agreed on the way over that as soon as possible they would own up to their deception in Napa.

"Malcolm, Marie, Whitney and I owe you both an apology. Really me more than Whitney. I convinced her to pretend that she was my girlfriend in Napa when she was actually working as my matchmaker."

"But you're both here together now so it must have worked." Marie smiled broadly.

Tanner put his arm around Whitney's waist and brought her close. "Yes, it did."

"Then no harm was done." Malcolm patted him on the back.

"Did I hear someone say something about a match-maker?"

Whitney cringed at the sound of Charlotte's voice. Squaring her shoulders, she turned and faced the woman. "I'm a matchmaker."

"Who needs a matchmaker?" Charlotte's voice held disgust.

Malcolm said, "Apparently Marie and I did. We met though a matchmaking service."

The look on Charlotte's face was almost comical. "If you'll excuse me, I think Max is looking for me."

Charlotte left to the sound of two couples' laughter. Whitney couldn't help feeling both vindicated and sorry for her.

Tanner remained close throughout the rest of the evening and Whitney found she was enjoying herself. She liked the new person she was becoming. The one who felt good about her life.

She had excused herself and was in the hallway on the way to the restroom when she overheard some women talking in an alcove.

"I can't believe that woman Mark is with. She has an unbelievable body."

"Yeah. He went out and got him a thin one," another woman said.

"He divorced Mildred after she became so large," the first woman said. "I heard he said he needed someone who could help his career, not someone he wanted to hide."

Heat flooded Whitney. At one time that could have been her they were talking about.

A third voice said, "You're just saying that because he won't give you a second look."

Whitney shuddered. These were part of Tanner's social circle. Were these the type of people she would be forced into being around for the rest of her life?

"And that woman Tanner is with." Her tone held a note of disgust. "I know her name from somewhere. I just can't figure out where."

"Charlotte said she's a matchmaker. Can you imagine?"

"I know where I've seen her before. She went to college with me. She was President of the Literary Society. I knew I recognized her name. She used to be huge."

"A fat matchmaker," one of them cackled.

Whitney had heard that kind of talk before. She didn't like it any better now.

"She's not fat now."

"No, she isn't, but I wonder how she managed to snag that gorgeous Tanner. I wonder if he knows she was once so heavy."

Whitney had heard enough. She felt sick. Moisture filled her eyes. She wanted to get out of there. Turning, she headed down the hall again in search of Tanner.

As she reached him, he took one look at her and demanded, "What's wrong?"

"I'd like to go now." She worked not to have a quiver in her voice.

Tanner touched her arm. "Are you not feeling well?"

She pulled away. "You could say that."

A perplexed look came over his face. "Let's say our goodbyes to Malcolm and Marie then we can go."

"Why don't you do that for me? I'll wait for you in the car."

Tanner looked at her closely. "What's going on? You feeling ill?"

"I'll tell you when we get home." Whitney made her way toward the front door.

She had already called for the car by the time Tanner joined her. The valet pulled up in front of them before Tanner could start asking questions.

He helped her in then went around and slid into the driver's seat. They were out on the road when he asked, "Do you want to tell me what happened back there?"

CHAPTER NINE

TANNER'S TONE REMINDED Whitney too much of how he had sounded when he'd demanded that she go with him to Napa. He wasn't going to leave her any choice but to answer. "Can we please just talk about it when we get home?"

He glanced at her. "Okay, but I'll accept nothing short of a full explanation."

For the next three-quarters of an hour they said nothing. Tanner glanced at her a couple of times with concern. Which only made what she was going to have to say worse. Whitney searched for a way out of what she knew was coming. She was going to give up everything she had ever dreamed of or hoped for. A burning sensation rolled in her middle. Whitney crossed her arms over her stomach. She might truly be sick.

What could she do to stop herself from destroying her life? How could she not? She couldn't live thinking she was inadequate every time she and Tanner went out. That Tanner might one day be disappointed in her. Leave her. Those old insecurities she'd thought she'd put away when she had lost weight hadn't been far below the surface.

Anyway, Tanner had made it clear weeks ago when they had met to start looking for a mate for him that he was only interested in a mutually beneficial relationship. Not love. She wanted love or nothing. There had not been one word about loving her in the weeks they had been together. There might never be. How was she supposed to gain his love if she couldn't even handle herself at one of his social gatherings without falling apart?

They weren't going to work. It was best to call it quits now before either one of them got in any deeper. Only it was too late for her. She loved him beyond measure.

At her house Tanner helped her out of the car. He followed her into the living room. She went to stand near the fireplace behind a chair. She needed it to provide her support.

Tanner stood in the middle of the room, waiting.

That nauseated feeling intensified. Only with a determination she would have sworn she didn't possess did Whitney meet his look. What she had to say must be said.

"Whitney, what happened?" There was alarm in his voice. "Are you okay?"

She sadly shook her head. "Tanner, we're not going to work."

"What?" He started toward her.

She put out a hand to stop him. "Us as a couple isn't going to work."

He came to an abrupt halt. "I thought we were working just fine until an hour ago. Now I'm just confused. Could you tell me what the problem is?"

What she wouldn't give to have him quit glaring at her. Hurt had seeped into his eyes. She said as clearly as she could, "I overheard some women talking about one of the ladies being fat. They even had something to say about me being with you. I can't tolerate that backbiting. I know that social events are important to your career but I can't do it. I spent too much of my life being treated as a second-class citizen. I won't go there again."

His look turned incredulous. "You've got to be kidding! All of this is about a few women being bitchy?"

She gripped the chair. How could she make him understand? A lifetime of people thinking you're less of a person because your body hung over a chair, your plate was piled full, your clothes baggy. Being judged and found wanting. Those emotions weren't easily pushed aside.

"It's more than that. I'm not who you need. I'll end up disappointing you. What if I gain weight? I can so easily. I have to watch it all the time."

He put out his hands as if pleading. "Hell, you're old enough and smart enough to know that people are the same everywhere. They're going to talk. What they say doesn't matter."

"I wish that was true. But it's hard for me to push away those old feelings of not being good enough. Your friends and associates are the type who used to put me down or, worse, not include me. I don't want to embarrass you. Be an embarrassment to you."

Tanner's hands had fallen to his sides and he all but shouted, "That's not going to happen."

"You don't know that." Whitney worked to keep her voice even and calm while her heart raced in her chest. "We're deluding ourselves. You hired me to find you the 'right match.' I'm not it."

"There has to be more to this than women talking. You couldn't possibly be that insecure. Or think so little of me. I've never said anything but positive things about your looks. I think you are beautiful." His disbelief circled around them like an angry animal.

"That's because you've never known what it's like, being an outsider," she said, unable to meet his blazing eyes.

"The hell I haven't." He stepped toward her. "What do you think it was like to live with my parents? I never knew if my father was coming home or how crazy my mother would be when he did. My brother and I never had any idea what to expect. At least you had functional parents. A place to live where all the focus wasn't on what your parents wanted. You felt loved."

She gripped the chair, glad for its support. Maybe he did understand what it was like to have apprehensions but she wasn't going to keep putting herself into the kind of situation she'd been in tonight. "I don't know what you want from me."

"I was going to ask you to marry me."

Her look zeroed in on his. "What? As a business merger or a declaration of love?"

Tanner didn't come any closer. "You knew from our first meeting that love wasn't part of the deal."

And she had. But she had hoped he would change his mind. Would slowly come to know love through her actions toward him. "That's what you said."

He dipped his chin and cocked a brow. "You didn't believe me?"

"Yes, but I thought you'd change when you found the right woman."

His chuckle had no real humor to it. "Whitney, I know I've made it perfectly clear what I am looking for in a wife. I'm sure I've not misled you even once."

"That's just it. I want something you can't or won't give." She moved to stand beside the chair. "I love you and I want you to love me in return. You refuse. I won't settle for less. I've seen what a loving relationship can be with my grandparents and parents. I deserve the same.

"You do as well but you're so sure that it doesn't exist or that you'll be so dependent on another person for happiness that you push that happiness away. I've shown you love in every way I know how in the last few months. Mind, body and soul. Yet you won't accept it. I need someone in my life who wants me for more than laughs and companionship or good sex."

"I'll have you know that sex between us is better than good. And I want you to have my children. You would be a wonderful mother."

Whitney slowly shook her head, sadness overtaking her. "You just don't get it. The sex is so great because I'm making love to you. But I still won't bring a child into a loveless marriage. You're so fearful that you're going to end up acting like your mother that you can't let anyone in. The thing is that you act more like your father. Taking the love and life you could have and throwing it back in my face."

Tanner looked as if she'd socked him on the chin, dazed him. She had hit a nerve. A very exposed one. Whitney stepped back a pace. "I'm sorry. I shouldn't have said that."

As if performing a magic trick, Tanner made a transformation. Straightening his shoulders and with all the fire leaving his eyes, he smiled tightly at her. He shoved his hands in his pockets. His demeanor became as cold as the night air coming off the San Francisco Bay in winter. "You may be right about that. But this just proves that love isn't worth the hurt.

"Since we're being so open here, let me tell you a few things. Not everyone wants a pie-in-the-sky, everything-is-rosy marriage. Some people just want peace in their life. A haven to come home to where people coexist, have common interests and mutual respect. Maybe some people, you included, think that a loving marriage is the goal in life. Me, I don't know how to do that. And I've never said or implied that I did.

"Another thing. You can't punish me for what people did to you in your past. You can't live worried about what people might do and say now. You're not the person you were when you were heavy. It's rather vain for you to think everyone is judging you. People like your ex-fiancé disappoint others. I'm not your ex. I don't have to love you to be supportive and stand beside you. I think I have proved that more than once."

Whitney shrank back. He had proved his loyalty. Still, she wanted his heart.

"One more thing." He raised a finger in the air. "Not once have I ever said I give a damn about your weight. Even when I gave you a list of what I was looking for in a mate, I didn't once say anything about the woman being thin. All of that is in—" he pointed his finger at her "—your head.

"Don't bother asking me to leave. I'm gone. Throw my stuff in a bag. Put it on the front stoop. Text me and I'll come and get it. That way I won't ever bother you again."

Seconds later her front door closed with a shudder of the stained glass that coincided with her howl of agony.

It had been three weeks since Tanner had left Whitney's and he still didn't feel any better. He'd never been so blind-sided in his life. Whitney's announcement that their relationship wasn't working had been news to him. She'd completely overreacted to what amounted to gossip. Those women didn't matter. People talked all the time. What mattered was what was best for Whitney and him. They enjoyed the same things, were great together in bed. Wanted the same things out of life. Maybe that wasn't exactly right. She wanted love, needed it from him. Did he even understand the emotion? Was he capable of giving it if he did?

He wanted to put his hand through a wall or shake Whitney until he shook some sense into her.

When he'd left her place he'd driven to his apartment, which he'd been thinking of selling because things between him and Whitney had been going so well. That was over. Entering the cold, sterile-looking place after staying in Whitney's warm and inviting home made him more depressed. She'd added vitality to his life.

More times than he could count he'd been hurt by his parents' actions but he had never felt this gnawing, snarling anger and frustration eating away at him that he had now. It affected every part of his life. Including his work. His staff was starting to give him looks and make hushed comments under their breath after he had given an order. He was trying to get a promotion and his staff was tip-toeing around him.

The nights were the worst. Especially when he did doze off and woke reaching for her on the other side of the bed. Most of the time he just paced the floor or stayed at the hospital. Eyedrops had become a staple because he never seemed to close his eyes. If he did, Whitney's smiling face invaded his mind. Her swishing her butt as she sang to a song while cooking dinner. Whitney's look of bliss as she found her release.

He slammed his hand down on his desk, making the pen beside it jump. This had to stop.

Punching the button on the desk phone, he ran back through the messages until he found hers, leaving him the name of the other matchmaker. It was time to move on.

The sound of Whitney's clear voice almost dissolved his resolve. He missed her with every fiber of his being. Even his clothes smelled of her.

He'd gone by her place. A bag had sat on the stoop, just as he'd requested. When he'd got it home and opened it, the smell of her had wafted around him. He'd felt sucker punched. Inside the bag had been his clothes, neatly folded and arranged with care. She'd still been taking care of him. The smell had lingered to the point where he'd stuffed all the clothing back into the bag and taken them to the cleaners.

Tanner picked up the pen and quickly jotted the number down that Whitney had left in the message. He didn't want to have to listen twice. With a punch of his finger he deleted the communication. That ended any temptation to hear it again.

He was tied in knots and it was time to get undone. The first step was to call this new matchmaker and start the process of finding someone who fit his requirements. Someone who didn't see love as the main ingredient. He would make the call as soon as he saw his afternoon clinic patients. The first on the list was Mr. Wilcox. Whitney had even managed to take some of the pleasure out of seeing the older man. Why had he let her permeate his working life? He was paying for it dearly. And was afraid he'd be doing so for a long time to come.

Tanner opened the door to the small but functional examination room. Mr. Wilcox sat on the exam table with his shirt off. "Hello. How're you feeling?" Tanner asked.

"I'm fine except for the fact that I'm freezing to death. You ask us to strip down then leave us in a cold room."

That was one of many things he liked about Mr. Wilcox. The man said what he thought. Not unlike Whitney. "Sorry about that. Let me give you a listen then you can get dressed."

Tanner pulled his stethoscope from around his neck. Mr. Wilcox was doing well. His heart was working as expected and so far there was no major rejection. Tanner fully believed he would live many more years. Minutes later he said, "You sound good. You can put your shirt on now." He gave Mr. Wilcox a steady hand to hold as he climbed down from the table.

Mr. Wilcox slid an arm into a sleeve of his shirt and said, "So how's your lady doing?"

The one subject Tanner didn't what to talk about. His lady. Whitney had been. He'd been happy then.

"She's fine."

Mr. Wilcox looked up from buttoning his shirt. "That doesn't sound so fine."

Tanner acted as if he was writing on the chart. "It's not. We broke up."

"I'm sorry to hear that. But you know the old saying, 'If it's worth having it's worth fighting for.' I would say that one is worth fighting for."

"I don't think it matters. We want two different things out of life."

Mr. Wilcox nodded with his lips pursed as if in thought. "That so? I think I'd be changing what I want to keep her."

Could he do that? Tell her that he loved her? Did he?

"It's good to see you, Mr. Wilcox. Call if you need us, otherwise I'll see you in two months."

"Sounds good. Hey, you know love isn't always easy but it's always worth it."

There was that word again. Love. That wasn't the kind of relationship he wanted. Yet there was an ache where his heart was that was saying differently.

His fourth patient for the afternoon was a middle-aged woman who had progressively gotten sicker and sicker. He would soon have to place her on the transplant list.

Tanner plastered on a congenial smile and entered the room. "Hello, Mrs. Culpepper."

"Hi, Dr. Locke. I'd like you to meet my husband, Henry."

The man with graying hair at his temples stood. He and Tanner shook hands.

"Do you mind if I give you a listen, Mrs. Culpepper?" Tanner said as he removed his stethoscope.

"That's what I'm here for." She smiled and sat straighter on the exam table.

Tanner listened carefully to the slow and sluggish organ in her chest. Even her breathing was taking on a more labored sound. "Give me a sec. I need to have a look at your X-rays." Tanner typed his security code into the computer and pulled up Mrs. Culpepper's chart. With another click the picture she had just taken in the X-ray department came up on the screen. There it was, the oversize heart of the thin woman sitting before him.

He looked at Mrs. Culpepper. "I'm going to let you get dressed and have you meet me down the hall in the conference room where we can talk more comfortably. Lisa, my nurse, will be in to show you the way."

A distressed look came over her face but she nodded and slid off the table to stand. Her husband hurried to help her.

A few minutes later Tanner entered a room furnished with a serviceable table and six chairs. His nurse assistant, Lisa, and the Culpeppers were already waiting for him. Tanner took a chair facing them. Mrs. Culpepper looked close to tears. She must fear what was coming. This was the least enjoyable part of Tanner's job. Mr. Culpepper placed a hand on hers resting on the table. He too must sense what Tanner was planning to say.

"It's time, isn't it?" Mrs. Culpepper said.

Tanner nodded. "It is."

Her husband gently squeezed her hand. "We'll get through this together. That's what we do."

She looked at him. The bond between them was obvious. "I know I can count on you."

Why had Tanner never noticed that in couples before? Since Whitney had come into his life he seemed to see loving couples everywhere where he'd seen none before. For the first time in his life he'd begun to want that. But he'd thrown it back in Whitney's face when she'd offered it.

"We'll start the process of getting you listed on the United Network for Organ Sharing today. There'll be further tests in the days ahead. Lisa will help you with those."

The couple's eyes glistened with moisture as they clung together.

Could the day get any worse? He'd bet everything he

owned that Whitney would show that same loving concern if her husband was ill. Because she would love him. Their souls would be united. Would a wife based on his list care about him in the same way?

"So what do we need to do?" Mr. Culpepper asked.

The man saw his wife's health as a partnership. Why hadn't Tanner noticed that in his patients before? The Culpeppers couldn't be the only ones who felt that way. Had he just been choosing to ignore how people who loved each other acted? Was he so scared of loving or being loved that he was running from it? Wasn't that what Whitney had accused him of?

Could he live with someone who loved him without becoming emotionally invested himself? Not if he wanted Whitney. She would demand it of him. Could he give it? What he needed to understand was why his father had refused to accept it.

Half an hour later he left the Culpeppers with Lisa and returned to his office. He found the piece of paper he'd written the matchmaker's name on and crumbled it into a ball then tossed it into the trash. He already knew who his match was. Now all he had to do was be worthy of her. Find some way of meeting her halfway. That could only come from understanding why his parents had had such a dysfunctional relationship.

He picked up his phone. When a man answered Tanner said, "Dad. It's Tanner. Can I come down to see you this weekend?"

Tanner had driven faster than the speed limit, so he'd made good time on his way south on the coast road to Santa Barbara. He'd not seen his father in over five years and even then it had been brief and tense. There was no common ground for a relationship between them. That wouldn't change but Tanner needed to try to get some answers, a little understanding. There was no doubt he would be digging up painful memories but if he wanted to have the life he was dreaming of, finding that peace, he had to try to come to grips with his childhood.

Whitney had said he was like his father. The more he thought about it the more he tended to agree. So why was he like the man he disliked so much? Because he'd been so afraid of being hurt, like his mother had been?

His father had been surprised to hear from him. Rightfully so. There was a long pause when Tanner had asked if he could visit.

"Why?" had been his father's response.

"I have some questions I need answered."

Again there was a long pause. "Come on. I can't promise you'll like what you hear."

At least his father was willing to listen to the questions.

Tanner turned into his father's drive just before lunchtime. He had a simple one-story home that was well kept in a subdivision about five miles from the beach.

He and his father had agreed to go out to eat. Tanner felt they needed a neutral zone for the possibly tense discussion they were to have. His father had remarried while Tanner had been in med school but he had never met his new wife. Tanner had hardly stepped out of the car before his father exited the house and walked toward him. He was an older version of what Tanner saw in the mirror. He was like his father in more ways than one.

"Hello, Tanner."

"Hi, Dad. It's nice to see you." To his amazement Tanner actually meant it.

"Good to see you as well. The restaurant is just half a mile from here."

Was he protecting his wife from what might be said between them by not inviting Tanner in? "Okay. Would you like to ride with me?"

For a second Tanner thought his father might say no. "That'll work."

His father had picked a local place with plenty of room between the tables. Tanner was glad. They wouldn't easily be overheard. It wasn't until they were settled at their table, drinks served and orders taken, that Tanner said, "I have some questions about you and Mom."

Seeing his father's expression, Tanner was glad he'd requested a quiet spot off to the side. This discussion might be more difficult than he'd expected.

"Just what do you want to know?" His father fiddled with his napkin.

"Why you even married? Why were you never around? Did you even love her? Us?"

His father sighed deeply. "I should have had this discussion with you and Mark a long time ago but it was easier not to. I ought to have known it would happen one day. Yes, I loved your mother. Married her because I did. I've always loved you and Mark."

"So why did you and Mother always act like you were so unhappy?"

"Because we were. Your mother was so jealous. She smothered me. It wasn't that way so much at first. But as time went on she became obsessed. She'd accuse me of seeing other women. I wasn't but there was no convincing her. I tried to keep it all from you and your brother. We went to counseling but nothing worked. So when I had a chance to take a job traveling, I did, hoping that things would be better if I wasn't around so much. But that only made the situation worse when I came home. Her jealousy killed my love and then our marriage. I would have taken you and Mark with me but you were all she had. I feared she might take her life if I did that."

"You know that I hated you for how you treated her."

Tanner couldn't keep his bitterness out of his voice. He'd lived with it too long.

"I know. But I thought it better for you to hate me than her."

His father had loved him enough to make that sacrifice. Was that the type of love Whitney had been showing him? She understood sacrificial love over possessive love. He'd still been the kid that couldn't see the difference.

"Dad, why have you never said anything? Mark and I have been adults for a long time."

He shrugged. "It wouldn't have changed anything."

"Yeah, it would have. I've had a wonderful woman in my life who I wasn't willing to love because I didn't think it was possible to have a marriage based on emotion."

There was a sheen of moisture in his father's eyes. "Tanner, I never meant for you to feel that way. I'm sorry. Will you tell me about her?"

Over the next few minutes Tanner shared how he and Whitney had met. Why they had broken up.

"Life is too short to spend it without love," his father said.

"Another man told me the same thing recently."

His father met his look. "So what're you going to do?"

"Beg her to forgive me for being an idiot and shout from the Golden Gate Bridge that I love her."

His father's smile was genuine for the first time. "That sounds like a good start. Then tell her that every day for the rest of your life."

"I will."

During the meal they caught up on what they had missed in each other's lives. When they returned to his father's house he invited Tanner in to meet his wife. Tanner hesitated but then agreed.

"Julie, I'm home," his father called as they came in the front door.

The living room looked comfortable. Lived in, much like Whitney's. A place that made you feel welcome.

His father kissed the petite brown-haired woman on the cheek and put his arm around her waist when she joined them. That was something Tanner had never seen him do with his mother.

"Tanner, I'd like you to meet my wife, Julie. Julie, this is Tanner."

Julie surprised him by hugging him. Her smile was warm and inviting. "It's so nice to meet you. Your father brags about you all the time."

Tanner looked at his father, who shrugged and smiled affectionately at Julie. "Honey, don't tell all my secrets."

"Well, it's true. Why don't we sit down and I can find out if your father has been telling me the truth?"

Tanner couldn't help but smile. The warmth Julie exuded made him feel at ease. He liked her. She sat close to his father on the sofa and every so often she touched him when she was making a point. Julie obviously cared for his father. There was a happiness about him Tanner had never seen before. To his amazement Tanner was glad for him.

As Tanner was leaving his father called out, "Let me know how it goes with Whitney."

"I will." The relationship between his father and himself wasn't what it should be but they had made a step forward.

Now Tanner had to face Whitney. Could he possibly let go enough to admit how he felt about her? If he wanted Whitney, he'd have to. What sickened him was that he hadn't recognized her love when she'd given it. He'd had it right there in front of him and he hadn't grabbed it. After all, he did love her. Had for a long time.

Whitney had cried to the point of being sick. In the past there had been days when people had hurt her feelings and she'd been upset but nothing matched the agony she felt over the loss of Tanner. His absence was a void she couldn't fill.

She had managed to place Tanner's clothes in a bag and text him but it had almost torn her heart out. Against her better judgment she'd kept one of his T-shirts. It was an unhealthy thing to do but she'd become so accustomed to having him next to her in bed that she put the shirt under the spare pillow and pulled it out to smell it before she went to sleep. When she could sleep.

So much time had passed since she had spoken to her parents they'd become concerned enough to check on her. When they did she gave them a blurry-eyed, tearful and painfully short version of what had happened. They were supportive and worried but in the end there wasn't anything they could do to help. As they were leaving her mother said, "We never know what life will give us. Never give up."

Whitney knew life sent you experiences and people that you never expected. Tanner had proved that. The problem was this time she was the one who had told Tanner to go. It had been the right decision but it still hurt.

In the middle of the second week she'd been in mourning for Tanner a new client called. That was the catalyst that started bringing her out of the darkness. She needed to keep herself busy for sanity's sake. To do that she was going to have to start clawing her way back to being a functioning adult again. She took a bath and washed her hair before sitting down at the computer. To her horror Tanner's profile was the first one to appear in her business file.

She looked at his smiling face for too long before she deleted it. She wouldn't need his profile any longer. Was he already dating other matches? The idea was crushing. But she had pushed him away. He was free to do as he pleased.

She kept repeating like a mantra that she had done it

for their own good. Love was important to her. Necessary and nonnegotiable. For Tanner it was unimportant. He had issues that he needed to resolve. He'd stated clearly that he believed she did as well.

Hadn't she dealt with those long ago?

Whitney looked around the kitchen where bags of chips and dessert snack covers cluttered the table and counter. She'd turned to food again to sooth her stress and fear. Jumping up, she gathered the litter and uneaten junk food, cramming it in the garbage can. That too had to stop. Returning to her desk, she picked up her phone and punched in the number to speed dial the overeating support group she'd once attended. It was time to get her life back on track without Tanner.

Over the next two days she set up two socials and made an appointment to meet a new client. She didn't feel alive yet but at least she was making an effort.

Her client was a woman of about her own age. In fact, she looked familiar. Extremely attractive, she still seemed a little unsure of herself. She kept looking around as if she were expecting someone to catch her doing something she shouldn't. Her name was familiar too. Lauren Phillips.

High school. That was it! She'd been one of the popular girls. The one who'd got all the boys. Now she needed Whitney to help her make a match.

"I believe we went to high school together," Whitney said at their meeting.

Lauren studied her but there was no recognition in her eyes. "I'm sorry, I don't remember you. High school was a tough time for me. My parents were getting a divorce. I didn't pay much attention to anyone but myself."

"It's okay. We can't remember everyone." Whitney meant it. Before Tanner she would have been resentful of Lauren but now she understood too clearly that no matter how someone might act on the outside, they could still have problems. "So how can I help you?"

"I am looking for companionship. Someone who enjoys the same things I do," Lauren answered. "I want someone who's looking to get serious and settle down. All the guys I meet are just interested in my looks. I want someone who sees past that."

Whitney had had that with Tanner. What if she had waited longer? Maybe Tanner would have come around to loving her. He had certainly accepted her for who she was. Instead of giving him any real chance, she'd let her insecurities control her. How was she supposed to match other people when she couldn't handle her own? Her self-doubt had left her with nothing.

How he must hate her.

Whitney pushed through the glass door of the community center for the first time in years. It would be tough to join the Happier You support group again but these were her people and here she would be accepted without question. It had taken her years to admit she needed support when she'd lost weight. She'd started managing her eating again but what she had really been looking for had been the emotional care. The help for what had been behind her overeating. The Happier You group had given her that.

She walked down the hall to the classroom. Inside she found the circle of chairs she expected and a few people already in them. She smiled in their direction and took a seat. Another couple of people entered before Margaret, the facilitator, showed up.

"Whitney Thomason, is that you?"

"It is." Whitney stood and hugged the woman.

"So what brings you here tonight?"

"I guess just for a reminder of how far I've come," Whitney said.

"So it's like that?"

Whitney nodded.

An hour and a half later Whitney was feeling strong enough to face the world and Tanner as well. While others had been talking she had been formulating a plan. She would write Tanner a letter. Tell him that she was sorry for treating him the way she had.

She was on her way out of the room when Margaret called after her. Whitney turned.

"Hold on a minute. I want to ask you something."

Whitney waited until Margaret finished speaking to the last person and came to her. "What's up?"

"I was wondering if you would consider something," Margaret said.

"What's that?"

Margaret moved a chair back into place. "Taking over this group for me. I have a chance to start one over near my house but can't leave this one high and dry. I think you would be great at it."

Her lead a group? "Can I think about it? Get back to you?"

"Sure. Just don't take too long."

Whitney didn't know if she could. She had always been in the background. "I'll let you know something by next week."

"Perfect."

Whitney made it to the door before Margaret said, "You know, you've changed, Whitney. There is more confidence about you. And you look great. Whatever is causing it, keep doing it."

That was because of Tanner. He'd made her feel supported, confident. Even though she'd pushed him away, he had left her that gift.

"Thanks, Margaret."

At home that evening Whitney pulled out a piece of stationery. She was going to write that letter. After careful thought she decided that a text or email message was too impersonal. She had to show that she meant what she wrote, was making a true effort.

Dear Tanner...

She marked that out.

Tanner,
I want you to know that I'm sorry for the way I treated you. You did not deserve it. I should not have assumed the worst of you, your friends or colleagues. I should have accepted your support for what it was, just that.
Please know that in many ways you've helped me grow as a person, and for that I will always be grateful.
I wish you well always.
Whitney

She rubbed the moisture under her eyes as she reread the note. To the point with no emotion. Folding it perfectly, she slipped it into an envelope and addressed it to his hospital office. Not allowing herself to rethink it, she put it in the mailbox beside the front door for pickup the next day.

Now it was time to move on. The door with Tanner's name on it was closed.

CHAPTER TEN

TANNER ONLY HAD a few minutes before he was due in surgery to read the mail his secretary had left in a stack on his desk. He picked up a letter that looked out of place. His chest tightened. Whitney's handwriting. Why would she be writing to him? Tearing it open, he scanned the brief but sincere note.

His heart filled with hope. Maybe there was a chance with her after all. She was at least opening a door for him to approach. Now if he just knocked loud enough she'd have no choice but to let him in. He was going to start working on making that happen right away.

Tanner picked up the phone. When the man on the other end answered Tanner said, "Hey, Charlie, I need a favor."

"What's that?"

Tanner wasted no time in saying, "I need you to hire a matchmaker."

"I don't think my wife would like that." Charlie chuckled.

"No, I need you to pretend you need a matchmaker. I'll go in your place." Tanner couldn't afford for this to go wrong.

"You're not making any sense. Why can't you just do it?"

Tanner explained he wasn't sure that Whitney would

meet him if he didn't surprise her. That he needed to get her to a public place so she was more likely to hear him out. "You do this for me and I'll take your calls for a month."

"Wow, you want this pretty bad."

"I do."

"Then it's a deal. What's the number?"

A few days later Charlie called back with a date and time at Café Lombard. "Good luck, man. She must be pretty special to go to this kind of trouble."

"She is. Thanks."

Three days later Malcolm stopped him in the hallway outside the CICU. "Tanner, can I have a word with you?"

"I've only got a second." He was due to meet Whitney in two hours and he wouldn't be late. Tanner was anxious and hoped Malcolm wouldn't be long-winded.

Malcolm smiled. "I wanted to give you a heads-up on this. The board met last night. You got the directorship."

Tanner should have been super excited but all he could think about was meeting Whitney. The directorship paled in comparison to winning Whitney back. He took a few steps backward, anxious to leave. "Thanks for letting me know."

Malcolm gave him a quizzical look. "Maybe you and Whitney would like to have dinner with us to celebrate."

"I'll let you know," Tanner called over his shoulder as he headed down the hall.

Two hours later Tanner sat at a table in the patio area of the café where he and Whitney had met his prospective matches. What would her reaction be when she saw him? Would she turn and walk away? Would she listen to him?

His pulse jumped. There she was. His heart swelled. She looked beautiful. He'd missed her so much that it had almost become a tangible thing he carried.

Wearing a sky blue dress that fit her torso then flared

gently around her legs, Whitney looked nothing like the dowdy shopkeeper of old. There was a spring in her step that was new. A sick feeling came over him. What had put that there? Had she found someone new? Maybe she wasn't missing him as much as he was her.

Tanner saw the second her step faltered as she crossed the street. She'd seen him. Their gazes met. He held his apprehension in check by sheer will. Standing, he never took his eyes off her. She continued toward him at a slower pace.

When she reached him he said, "Will you join me?"

"I have—" she cleared her throat "—to meet a client."

"I'm the client."

"What?" She looked as if she might run.

He quickly said, "I wasn't sure you'd meet me so I asked a friend to pretend to need a match."

She sighed and her shoulders slumped. "Tanner, I don't have time to waste with games."

"I'm not playing a game." It was his life they were talking about here. He pulled out a chair. "Please, join me for just a minute."

For a second he feared she was going to say no but she reluctantly sat, her hands clutching her purse. "What's this all about?"

"I was wondering if you could help me find someone to love and who will love me?"

Me. Me. Me. Whitney wanted to shout.

Did he mean it? Could she trust that she had heard him right? He had said love. Something he'd said he wouldn't give. Did she dare hope? She watched him closely. "What're you talking about? I thought we settled this weeks ago. I'm not the right matchmaker for you."

"You're usually not this slow to catch on," Tanner said with a smile.

"To what?" Now he was starting to irritate her.

"*You're* my perfect match. I'm telling you I *love* you. I hope you still feel the same about me."

Whitney's hands trembled. She could hardly breathe. She'd never thought she'd hear him say that. Could her dreams be coming true?

Tanner was looking at her with anticipation and a touch of uncertainty. Was he afraid she might turn him away? With his experience with love he might think it was something that came and went easily. Hers lasted forever.

She jumped to her feet and flung herself into his arms. His hands went to her waist, giving her a furious hug. Her arms circled his neck and her mouth found his. His kiss was all about acceptance and pleasure. But more than that—love.

As Tanner began deepening the kiss someone behind them said, "Excuse me."

They broke apart. Heat ran into Whitney's face. She looked at Tanner and he had a bashful look on his as well. They had both forgotten they were in a public place. Whitney eased back into her chair.

"Sorry," Tanner said to the young waitress. "She can't keep her hands off me."

"Tanner!"

He smiled and gave her an innocent look. "It's true. Would you like something?"

Whitney glanced at the waitress then said to Tanner, "What I'd really like to do is go home."

He asked, "I'm invited?"

Whitney smiled brightly. "You are. We need to talk."

"I agree." Tanner stood and dug in his pocket, pulling out a bill. After giving it to the surprised waitress, he offered a hand to Whitney.

Grinning and feeling like the sun was shining just for her, Whitney slipped her hand into Tanner's larger secure one. They made their way around a few tables and out to the sidewalk. Tanner led her down the street toward where his car was parked.

"Where's your car?"

"I took a streetcar and walked," she said.

They continued down the hill and Tanner said, "Thank you for your letter."

"It was the least I could do. I was pretty ugly to you." She'd spend the rest of her life making that up to him.

Opening the car door for her, Tanner said, "That you were."

She gave him a teasing swat on the arm. "But you deserved it."

"We'll discuss that more when we get to your house." He pulled out of his parking space and headed up the street. When he had moved into the rhythm of the traffic he took her hand and placed it on his thigh under his. She'd come home. It felt so good to have his touch again. But they still had things to discuss.

It didn't take long until Tanner slid the car to a stop in front of her house. She climbed out as he did and met him on the sidewalk. "Would you rather walk awhile or go inside to talk?"

"I think we'd better walk." Tanner took her hand again. "If I get you behind a closed door my mind is going to be on other things besides talking."

Tanner's raspy voice sent a shiver down her spine. "Walk it is."

They started up the sidewalk along the grassy knoll across the street from her home.

"Whitney, I'm sorry I've been such an idiot. The truth is I've been in love with you since you came to my rescue in the balloon. I just didn't want to admit it. My parents and what I saw in their marriage screwed me up."

"No more than the insecurities I carry around with me because I was once fat."

"Yeah, but my issues weren't even based on facts. It turns out that my father loved my mother. She was just so jealous that she killed it."

Whitney stopped and looked at him. "How did you find that out?"

"I went to see my father the other weekend. We had lunch together. He didn't much want to answer my questions but he did. Turns out he's been protecting my mother all along."

"Really?"

"Yeah. He let my brother and me believe he was the bad guy so that we wouldn't blame my mother. He wanted us to love her." There was acceptance in his voice she'd not heard when he'd spoken of his parents before.

"It takes a special person to sacrifice themselves for another." She started up the sidewalk again.

"I hadn't thought about it like that. It figures a woman with a big heart herself would see it that way." Tanner squeezed her hand.

Whitney gave him a sympathetic look. "But she wasn't all that bighearted when she sent you out the door, blaming you for all the things she didn't like about herself."

He smiled at her. "I don't remember you doing that."

Could she ever say sorry enough? "Well, I do. That's what it boiled down to. I was finding a way out so I wouldn't have to face situations I wasn't comfortable in."

"We all dodge those."

"I know. But not everyone judges others with such broad strokes." She hated to admit that she had done that.

"You have good reason."

"Maybe but it's time to grow up and face my past and not automatically think the worst of people." It would still be hard for her in some social situations but now she was aware of her shortcomings so maybe she could make some changes.

"What brought on this reevaluation?" He sounded as if he really wanted to know.

"Would you believe that the most popular girl in my high school class came to me for help? It turns out the beautiful people of the world all have problems too. I realized after she left that I was the lucky one."

"Why?" Tanner turned and they headed back toward her house.

"Because my issues were ones that I could control. I just had to be willing to do it. I went back to my eating disorder class. I'm even going to become a facilitator. I want to help others through my experiences."

"That's great. I know you'll be good at that. You've certainly taught me a thing or two."

She looked at the handsome face she'd missed so much. "Have I, now? I can't imagine me teaching you anything."

Tanner stopped and brought her into his arms. "You've done something no one else could do."

"What's that?"

"Shown me how to love and be loved." He kissed her gently.

"Do you really love me?"

Tanner grinned. "Did you hear me say it?"

"I did, but I'd like to hear it again."

"I love you, Whitney." She had no doubt he meant it. "And I love you with all my heart."

Tanner pulled her close. "That's more than I've ever deserved. Now, if you don't mind I'd like to go back to your house and show you just how much I love you."

Whitney rested her head against his chest. "I can't think of anything that I would like more."

EPILOGUE

It HAD BEEN nothing but blue sky and sunshine at the Garonne Winery and Château. Whitney couldn't have asked for a more perfect wedding day. She had walked between two rows of grapevines to where Tanner stood on the exact spot where they had shared their first real kiss.

They had chosen to share their own vows. Tanner's were so full of love that Whitney hurt with the poignancy of them. For a man who'd said he knew nothing about love, he was a quick study. Once he'd learned to feel and say the words, he never stopped.

She was surrounded by her family and friends, all smiling and enjoying a good time in the cellar of the winery where the reception was being held. Marie and Malcolm had insisted on taking care of the wedding details when she and Tanner had told them they wished to marry at the winery. Marie had tastefully taken Whitney's wishes and created a day to remember.

To both her surprise and Tanner's as well, his parents attended. There was a tenseness to their meeting but otherwise there was nothing but blessings for the bride and groom. Tanner had asked his brother, Mark, to be best man and he had accepted. They had grown closer during the weeks before the wedding. For that, Whitney was grateful.

"What's the bride doing over here by herself?" Mr. Wilcox asked.

"Just thinking about how happy I am."

The band started up a new tune.

"May I have this dance, Mrs. Locke?" Mr. Wilcox made a slight bow her direction.

She liked the sound of her new name. "I'd be honored."

He led her in a box step around the open area surrounded by tables. "I told you I would be dancing at your wedding."

Whitney smiled. "You did but I didn't believe it."

They made one more turn before Tanner tapped Mr. Wilcox on the shoulder. "Mind if I break in? I'd like to dance with my beautiful wife."

Mr. Wilcox gave her hand to Tanner and kissed her on the cheek. "Life and love are fragile things. Treasure them. Not all of us get a second chance."

"So I have learned." Tanner looked into her eyes. "Now that I recognize it, and have it, I'm never going to let it go."

* * * * *

REUNION WITH HIS SURGEON PRINCESS

KARIN BAINE

For Tammy and Kieran xx

CHAPTER ONE

'I NEED YOU.' Apparently, that was all Kaja had to say after five years apart to get Seth Davenport back in her life.

Now here he was striding through the airport in his short-sleeved, blue cotton shirt and linen trousers, wrinkled from the flight. Time and distance melted away as she watched him walk towards her, her heart beating that little bit faster the way it always had when he was around. He hadn't seen her yet, distracted by his travel companion. It gave her time to study this older version of the man she'd loved when they were both very different people. A world away from where she truly belonged.

His hair was longer than she remembered but remained as unruly as ever. His sun-kissed brown locks refused to be tamed, curling behind his ears and framing his tanned face. The dark scruff of his beard roughened the smooth jaw line hiding in the bristles and when those unfathomable brown eyes met hers she had to swallow down the sudden thirst she'd worked up. The physical changes were minimal but there was one huge difference in his life that would take some getting used to.

'Seth, Amy, welcome to Belle Crepuscolo.' She advanced towards them the way she would when meeting any foreign dignitaries or people of importance arriving in her country. With her arms raised in welcome, she kissed him on both cheeks, telling herself this was nothing out of the ordinary. She knew she was lying to herself when his beard rasped against her skin and the mere touch of him caused a total blood rush to her head.

'Thank you for the VIP treatment, Kaja. It is Kaja, isn't it? Or should I address you as Your Majesty?' There was a twinkle in his eye as he said it but also an underlying tang of bitterness in his tone. Understandable in the circumstances.

'Kaja's fine.' She kept the smile painted on her face as the small hint at her betrayal hit its mark on her conscience. There was so much she had to apologise for, to explain, but nothing would take away the hurt she'd undeniably caused him five years ago. The best she could do was make this stay as comfortable as possible for her visitors.

'Well, Kaja, we've had a lovely trip so far. Haven't we, Amy?' Seth turned his attention to the munchkin clinging onto his hand.

'I'm glad they took good care of you. Now, if you're ready, you'll be escorted to the palace. Would you like that, Amy?' Kaja hunched down to talk to the little girl, trying to make a friend but understanding that this must be overwhelming for her. She'd been dragged away from the only place she'd ever known and flown halfway across the world. It was natural the child should be wary.

Amy looked to her father for guidance on the matter and when he nodded his head, she copied him, her brown curls bobbing in agreement.

When Kaja extended her hand, the child accepted it, her little fingers curling around the stranger she was being urged to trust. Amy smiled up at her with eyes so much like Seth's, Kaja's heart felt as though it were being torn into tiny pieces. The four-year-old was a walking reminder that Seth had moved on from their relationship all too quickly.

Within a couple of months of her leaving he'd married and started a family. A life he'd offered to Kaja first, so it was her own fault he'd found someone else. When he'd proposed, he'd been offering her a commitment she'd realised too late she couldn't give in return. It had been the wake-up call she'd needed to snap out of the dream she'd been living in England with him. She wasn't anything like the woman she'd pretended to be to Seth or their work colleagues. Princess in her own country, she had responsibilities and duties she'd been avoiding in her quest for a normal life. As much as she'd wanted it, it was beyond her grasp. None of it real when she hadn't even confided her true identity to Seth. A betrayal so great she couldn't bring herself to tell him she'd lied to him from the moment they'd met.

She had no right to be jealous now when she'd fled England without giving him an explanation. She was lucky he'd been willing to even speak to her again. Never mind come all this way to do her a favour.

'I'm sorry to hear about your father…and your mother, of course.' It was Seth who addressed the reason for this reunion first. Although, it wasn't a conversation she particularly wanted to have in front of her security team, who were shadowing their journey to the exit.

Her mother's death from a heart attack soon after Kaja's return to her homeland was one more layer of guilt heaped upon her shoulders. She'd been so intent on living a 'normal' life she'd distanced herself from her family and lost precious time she could have spent with her mother. A regret she'd thought she could make up for by falling into line with the rest of the family and throwing herself into what was expected of her as a princess. Including marrying someone out of duty rather than love.

Kaja was sure it hadn't taken Seth too long to work out her true heritage from the ensuing press coverage of her mother's death, though she'd kept it from him and everyone else while living in Cambridge.

The unspoken *Why?* and the hurt she'd caused were blazing so brightly in his gaze she was forced to turn away.

'Thank you. I wasn't able to help my mother but I'm hoping you can do something to save my father.' After years of being on dialysis, her father's kidneys had failed. They were lucky that he hadn't had to go on a waiting list for a new organ when her brother had turned out to be a match and was willing to donate one of his kidneys. With Seth one of the UK's most esteemed transplant surgeons, he was the first person she'd thought of when the nephrologist had told them dialysis was no longer working.

She reminded herself that was why she had brought Seth here. Not to resolve old personal issues or pick up where they'd left off—if that were even a possibility. Which it wasn't.

'We can discuss the details later.' The tensing in Seth's jaw gave her chills. It would seem he hadn't forgiven or forgotten after all and why should he? In the intervening years she'd yet to come to terms with her actions at that time and the consequential events.

She nodded, knowing it was a conversation she couldn't avoid. Seth had come all this way to help her family and an explanation for running out on him was the least she could give him in return.

'Are you really a princess?' A tiny voice broke through the adult tension.

'I really am.' She was second in line to the throne of

this principality after her father and brother but a four-year-old wouldn't be interested in the politics or boring small print of her position. In a little girl's eyes, at least, she had all the trappings of a fairy-tale princess. Of course, the reality was much different and less enchanting than the bedtime stories.

'Do you have a glass coach and a fairy godmother?' Clearly, Seth had no problem in letting his daughter believe in the fantasy, regardless of his own experience and knowledge that happy-ever-afters didn't exist.

'I'm afraid not. I wish I did but this is it.' They stepped out onto the pavement, the sun warming Kaja's skin again after the chill of the air-conditioned airport.

The white limousine with her chauffeur at the helm was a privilege she didn't take for granted after her years using public transport in England. Although it likely wouldn't impress this Cinderella-loving youngster as much as an enchanted pumpkin and mouse coachman.

'I suppose this will have to do.' Seth let out a long whistle.

Kaja was aware this wasn't the norm for most people and only served to highlight the differences in their worlds.

Isak, her cheery chauffeur, got out, tipped his cap, and opened the door for them to get into the car.

'If you can bear it… Alderisi Palace is a short distance from here.' She stood back to let her guests climb onto the back seat first, seeing Amy's eyes light up when she heard their destination. If she had been disappointed by meeting Kaja, hopefully her home for the next few weeks would better live up to expectation. At least trying to keep a small child entertained should distract her from the prospect of her brother and father's operations. Along with the man who'd be performing them.

Her personal security guard, Gunnar, was riding up front and Amy had chosen to sit on one of the long side seats in the rear, leaving her and Seth on the back seat. Despite the vast car interior she found the amount of secrets and ghosts wedged in around them suffocating.

Amy was humming to herself and dancing one of the dolls she'd pulled out from her backpack along the leather upholstery, completely oblivious to the rest of the world around her.

'I hope having Amy with me isn't causing you any inconvenience.' Seth leaned across to speak to her privately, his warm breath brushing her cheek the way his fingers used to right before he kissed her…

'No. Not at all,' she said much too loudly, and sprang back from further thoughts of his touch upon her.

'I don't have anyone else to take care of her. Gran passed away last month. Although she hadn't been able to watch her for some time. Alzheimer's,' he confided, letting that one word fill in all the details he failed to give her.

Finding out he had a daughter when she'd contacted him had come as a shock. She hadn't expected him to be frozen in time in their semi-detached house, waiting for her call, but having it confirmed he'd led another life after her still hurt. Especially when he had the one thing she could never have. A child.

Kaja hadn't had time to mope around after her lost love due to her mother's passing. Then she'd been determined to atone for the neglect of her family by throwing herself into the royal duties she'd avoided until then. She'd met Benedikt at a fundraiser for the public hospital where she worked in the emergency department once a week; a position she'd had to fight to keep hold of as some measure of independence. Although her brief working week meant she'd never really fitted into the hospital team as well as the one she'd worked with in England.

Benedikt had been older than her and from one of Belle Crepuscolo's wealthiest families. She'd believed marriage to him, becoming a power couple on the world's stage, would please her father, to whom family and tradition meant everything. That somehow a prestigious match would fill the void left by her mother and make up for the years she'd abandoned her post in her home country. Having a baby was part of that duty, to secure the family line and make her husband and father happy. Her failure to get pregnant and her spouse's philandering shattered that dream. Benedikt's affair and subsequent filing for divorce to marry his pregnant mistress had played out for the world to see and gossip about. Whereas Seth's life was a closed book to her. One she suddenly wanted to binge-read.

'I'm sorry to hear about your grandmother. I know you were close.'

'Yeah. Her and Gramps raised me as their own. Now they've both gone I'm a bit lost, to be honest. I think the trip out here will do Amy some good to get away from my moping around.' His sad smile was one she could relate to, having lost her own mother and still having to function for other people's sake.

At a time when a person simply wanted to wallow and wail over the loss of someone important in their life, one had to plaster on a happy face for appearances' sake and pray it would stop everyone else falling apart too.

'I assume your wife couldn't get away to join you here?' She didn't imagine the child's mother would let her come out here unless she had other serious commitments preventing her from being with her daughter.

'Paula and I…er…aren't together any more. Haven't been for some time.'

'Sorry. I didn't know.' Once she'd heard he'd married so quickly after their separation she hadn't wanted to know any more. She'd simply accepted he'd moved on without her and taken steps to do the same. Something she'd later come to regret.

'Yes, well, Amy was the best thing to come out of that relationship.' His steely set jaw and change in his tone conveyed there were bad feelings lingering about the situation.

'You share custody?'

'No. Her mother left and never looked back. It's just the two of us now. That's the way we like it, isn't it, Ames?' The little girl nodded, though she couldn't have heard the nature of their conversation.

Kaja got the impression this was a mantra he repeated often so they'd both believe it.

'You certainly seem as though fatherhood is agreeing with you and she's gorgeous. A real credit to you.' She could see Seth as a single dad, braiding his daughter's hair and organising playdates. He'd always wanted children even though they'd both been busy with their careers. It was a topic she'd tried to avoid. She could see now that it was because she knew they would never have been able to settle down as a family. Not when she hadn't been honest with him about her background.

Ironic, when she probably couldn't have given him a baby anyway. Irregular periods and her failure to get pregnant with Benedikt had led to a diagnosis of polycystic ovaries and the end of her marriage. Not even the invasive laser treatment she'd undertaken to try and fix the problem could prevent her husband from straying.

Now Seth was a father she was certain Amy was top

priority in his life. Despite his dedication to his profession and his patients, Seth always put his loved ones first. Unlike her. In looking out for her own interests Kaja had managed to hurt the man she'd loved and her family.

He'd looked after his grandparents in their old age and he'd been committed to her during their relationship. To the point of proposing marriage.

Now she'd invited Seth back into her life she was reminded of everything she'd lost when she came home.

'Thanks. It's not exactly how I saw my life panning out but I wouldn't be without her for the world.' The proud father confirmed what Kaja had already seen for herself in the short time since their arrival.

'You're lucky to have each other.' Seth was currently having a dolls' tea party in Amy's honour on the back seat of the limousine. Anyone could see they had a special bond. One she was quite envious of when she'd never get to have that close relationship with her own child. Even if continued treatment meant she could conceive some day, it was a lot to go through without a guarantee of success. To her, love, marriage and children were all inextricably linked and Benedikt had proved that without one of those links everything else fell apart.

'You never thought of having kids yourself?' It was the sort of question adults asked each other all the time, catching up on each other's news after losing touch. Yet it touched a still exposed and very raw nerve.

'I thought about it. It just didn't work out for me.' Even saying that, reducing what she'd gone through to a vague disappointment brought forth a swell of sadness from the pit of her stomach threatening to swamp her. It was the ensuing anger that had accompanied that period that had prevented her from drowning in her sorrow altogether.

'I know you've had a rough time too.'

There. Her humiliation was complete to find Seth hadn't missed the spotlight shone on her own disastrous marriage, even if he wasn't party to the devastating details of her infertility problems.

'I never was very good at making those big life decisions.' She'd wondered how differently her life would've turned out if she'd accepted his proposal and settled in England for good. Although, it wouldn't have solved the problem that had caused the end of her marriage. She'd loved him too much to ever force him into a future without the family he was born to have.

'We all make mistakes. What's important is that we learn to forgive ourselves, as well as each other.' He fixed her under his gaze, warm like melted chocolate. She hoped it was his way of telling her he'd forgiven her for her past mistakes. If they'd been somewhere more private, perhaps in better circumstances, she would've asked him for clarification and taken that as a cue to apologise. There'd be plenty of opportunity to do so over the course of the next few days when they'd be living under the same roof.

'That can be hard to do when you know you're the facilitator of your own downfall.' No one had forced her to leave Seth, marry someone she hardly knew or to stay in a country where she no longer garnered any respect. She'd managed that all by herself. It was no wonder she'd been given the dubious nickname of 'The Unlovable Princess' when it was such an accurate description.

'I don't think you have it as bad as you make out, Princess. You might take all this for granted but look around you. This is priceless.' Seth wasn't telling her anything she didn't know or showing her things she hadn't seen before. Although, as he leaned across her to direct her gaze out of the window, she wasn't inclined to tell him so. It was an age since she'd been this close to a man, *this* man, and she revelled in the warmth of his body and the masculine scent of sweat and cologne clinging to his skin.

Belle Crepuscolo, as the name suggested, was a beautiful country. Landlocked by Switzerland, Italy and Austria, it had an enviable climate and a culture influenced by all the surrounding countries.

While Seth watched the blur of blue skies and sprawling whitewashed villas flash by the window, Kaja was more interested in the view she had. Seth was more a sense of home to her than the vista outside and she realised everything she'd truly left behind in England that fateful day.

'There's more to life than money and sunshine. That old adage holds true. None of it can buy you happiness.' To her, privilege had become a prison. It kept her trapped in a life she was desperate to break free from.

Her happiest time had been during those rain-drenched, barely-time-to-sit-down working days in Cambridge. At least then she'd had Seth to come home to. They'd cooked dinner, curled up together in front of the telly and made love in their own bed. Nothing out of the ordinary and yet it had been everything. Being so close to him now reminded her of those cosy nights in when she'd been pretending she could lead a normal life. Before reality crashed in and reminded her it wasn't possible.

'That's easy to say when you have this on your doorstep. What else could you possibly want?' He turned his brilliant smile on her and she was powerless to hold her tongue or tell him anything but the truth.

'Love.'

She saw that spike of pain on his face before he composed himself and returned to his own side of the car. They both knew she'd had that once in her life and thrown it away. The Unlovable Princess deserved everything that had come to her since then.

Seth hadn't been as prepared to face Kaja as he'd thought. For some reason he'd thought he'd fly out here, do the job he was required to do and, once he'd seen her, all that past hurt and betrayal would melt away. He'd got it into his head that facing her would make him realise everything had turned out for the best. After all, if Kaja hadn't run out on him he wouldn't have slept with someone else on the rebound or had Amy as a consequence. While he regretted the hasty marriage, he'd never be sorry for his daughter's existence. She was his everything.

He'd known the minute he'd set eyes on Kaja again closure wasn't going to be achieved so easily. It didn't matter that five years had passed, that they'd both married, and divorced, since, or that he'd become a father. In that moment, seeing her again had transported him back to the day he'd proposed. When she'd rejected him, packed her bags in the middle of the night and disappeared without a trace. All the confusion and fear of that time was tied up in the memory. Along with the anger and sense of betrayal he'd felt when he'd seen her on the news as word of her mother's death had spread. A princess. He'd had no inkling of her heritage, couldn't imagine Kaja as anything other than his busy surgeon girlfriend. Until now.

She'd swapped her green scrubs and sneakers for pink silk and diamonds but she was as beautiful as ever. As though her fairy godmother had waved a magic wand and enhanced her natural beauty for the oblivious prince who'd needed it spelled out to him what an amazing woman she was. It was unfortunate her real Prince Charming had turned out to be anything but, according to the papers. Seth took no pleasure in reading about her heartache but perhaps there was something to be said for the commoner she'd snubbed after all. Seth had loved her for who she was, or, at least, who he'd believed she was, with no need for a substitute.

He knew what it was to be hurt and to think you were inadequate. After all, he'd been abandoned by a teenage mother who'd thought having a baby would ruin her life and a wife who'd pretty much thought the same about him and their daughter. Kaja hadn't even bothered to give him a reason why his love wasn't enough for her.

Despite their personal history, Kaja had deserved better than being cheated on. Just as he'd deserved better than being ghosted.

'I mean, when it comes down to health matters we're no better off than the average person. We can fly the best renal surgeon out here to perform the transplant but there's no guarantees my father and brother will survive. If anything happens to them I'll have no one left in my life.' Her voice broke. It was at odds with the cool composure she'd shown at the airport. He'd known in that instant she hadn't regretted her actions when she'd seemed so personally unmoved by seeing him again. Meanwhile his insides had been churning as though he'd hit turbulence even after he'd stepped off the plane.

For a split second he'd wondered if she'd missed him or what they'd had together. She'd quickly shut down that idea, letting him know it was her family she was getting emotional over. He should've known better. Kaja's family was all she'd cared about in the end. It was a pity he hadn't known about their existence until it had been too late to do anything.

'Hey, have a little faith in your transplant surgeon. Nothing's going to take them away from you. Besides, don't you have a whole country to keep you company?' Since his gran had passed he'd been more aware than ever of his limited social circle. With his time no longer eaten up talking to carers or visiting the home, outside work Amy was his whole world. While he was content with that, he knew it wasn't healthy for a four-year-old. Before that cruel disease had robbed her of cognitive thought, Gran herself had made him swear to get a life of his own after she'd gone. To take Amy to see the world and have adventures.

Kaja's call for help had been a well-timed gift, an easier way out than forging new friendships in a place where he'd happily existed on the periphery of society. His busy life as a renal transplant and general surgeon made it challenging to balance work and home life. As a result any thoughts of another romantic relationship had gone on the back burner in favour of spending time with his daughter and grandmother when he could. Now he'd packed up and fled the country with his daughter so he didn't have to face life without the woman who'd been the only constant in his life. This trip had been the cowardly way out of his grief and he knew that sense of loss would be waiting for him on his return.

Kaja might be feeling sorry for herself now but she had no idea what it truly meant to be abandoned by the ones you loved. He'd been abandoned by his own mother and wife. Whereas she was the one who did the abandoning.

Kaja disputed his take on her life with a, 'Hah!'

'Daddy, look!' Amy was straining to see out of the window. He leaned over to see what had caught her attention.

His mouth dropped open as they drove up a winding avenue lined with blush-pink cherry blossoms and crystal-clear dancing water fountains.

'Home, sweet home,' Kaja mocked as the imposing mansion at the end of the drive came into view.

Gleaming white stone pillars, marble steps and balconies on every level of the ornate building gave it the appearance of a grand, layered wedding cake. A congregation of immaculately dressed people spilled out to meet the car. Seth immediately unbuckled Amy's seat belt and took her hand so she didn't get lost in the throng.

'Baby, we're not in Cambridge any more.'

CHAPTER TWO

'I'LL GET THAT for you, sir.'

'Let me take your bag for you, sir.'

The car had barely come to a halt before there was a flurry of helping hands refusing to let Seth so much as open the door on his own. He clutched Amy closer in case she was spirited away by Kaja's staff with his luggage.

'Hold my hand so you don't get lost, sweetheart.'

'I suppose it is all rather much.' Kaja winced.

It hadn't been his intention to make her self-conscious about her life here. She must have preferred it to the one they'd had together as she'd left it behind so readily.

If they were going to spend the next few weeks under the same roof they were going to have to get along. All issues—personal or socio-economic—would have to be set aside in order for him to treat her father. His patients' backgrounds were none of his business unless it impacted on their health. From everything he'd seen so far, Kaja's father had the best of everything money could buy. Including health care. However, his status wasn't going to affect Seth's ability to do his job. He always did his best regardless of wealth or the status of his patients.

'I'm sure we'll get used to it.' He flashed her a grin. Reassurance that they could make this work. It was his duty to put the minds of his patients' family members at ease where he could. Even if these were unusual circumstances.

'Daddy? Can we have a sleepover in the princess castle?' Amy tugged on his shirt, her eyes wide as she took in the majesty, the likes of which he'd only seen in picture books.

'See?' he said to Kaja with a laugh. 'I think we'll fit in just fine.'

'Good. Why don't we go in and I'll show you to your rooms.' The worry lines marring her forehead evened out into a smile matching his daughter's.

Now that the palace staff had disappeared inside with his belongings it was slightly less intimidating. At least, until they walked through the doors.

The 'wow' escaped his lips before he could temper his reaction. It was difficult to say anything else when faced with the sheer opulence of the décor within the palace.

The rich purple and silver colour scheme combined with the draped silks and brightly coloured tapestries lining the walls was how he imagined the genie's pad inside the magic lamp looked.

When the imposing oak door swung shut, echoing through the halls, it made the situation very real. The heavyset dude who shadowed Kaja's every move without saying a word remained on the outside acting as a sentry.

'Your apartments are this way.'

Not room, he noted as Kaja led them up a flight of steps to the 'apartments'.

'There is an elevator should you wish to use it but I prefer to take the stairs otherwise I'd never get any exercise.'

The Kaja he'd known would've been bored rigid at being chauffeured everywhere, barely allowed to lift a finger. Like him, she'd been someone who'd thrived on being busy, being needed, and had enjoyed her privacy. The alone time they'd spent together had been more precious than he'd realised.

'I don't think you have anything to worry about on that score.' He could see she'd lost weight and some of her curves but none of her beauty. She had an elegant grace about her now befitting a princess. That look-don't-touch vibe was so different from the warm, tactile Kaja he'd planned to marry.

She paused on the steps with her hand resting on the mahogany bannister and slowly turned to look back at him. It was then he realised her backside had been in his eyeline when he'd made that last comment, and he attempted to backtrack.

'I mean, I'm sure you get a workout simply moving from one room to another in here. A few circuits sprinting up and down these steps every morning will help keep me in shape too.' It wasn't a total lie to cover his tracks. He'd let his gym membership lapse when he'd been busy running between Amy's childcare and Gran's nursing home. He'd have to begin a fitness regime when the hospitality thus far had been so effectively displayed. Getting fed around here didn't seem as though it was going to be a problem. Especially when there were silver dishes piled high with juicy citrus fruit and pastel-coloured almonds dotted around the palace at regular intervals.

'Uh-huh.' Kaja gave him a disbelieving look then carried on up the staircase.

Amy broke away from him, sprinting on up to reach the landing first. Not waiting for the adults to catch up, she bolted down the corridor, giddy at having so much space to go wild in after being cooped up in a plane for so long.

'Amy, keep the noise down and don't touch anything.'

He had visions of her bursting in on an unsuspecting dignitary and causing an international incident as she treated the place like her own. A child her age had no comprehension of the complex relationships going on around her. Only the scope of the place for potential fun and mischief. Seth didn't know if Kaja understood what she was in for hosting his daughter.

'Oh, don't worry. You're the only ones on this floor apart from me and the staff. She won't disturb anyone. Bruno and father are already at the private hospital where you'll be working. I'll take you to see them later. I'm sure you and Amy would appreciate some time to settle in first.'

'Thanks. That's very kind of you. I think a nap might be in order.'

'No problem. I know at your age you need all the sleep you can get.'

The jibe caught him off guard, as did the mischievous grin she was sporting. It was a glimpse back at the girl who'd teased him constantly about being a whole three years older and of the close relationship they'd once had.

'Ha, ha. I was thinking more of Amy.' He would never admit the day had taken its toll on him as well, albeit on a more emotional level than he'd anticipated. If Kaja remained unaffected by his presence after all these years as she seemed, there was no point in letting her know he still had unresolved feelings surrounding their past.

He'd only jumped into the relationship with Paula because he'd been so desolate without Kaja and he'd needed someone to provide the company, the intimacy he'd lost with her gone. In hindsight he could see that by rushing headlong into that relationship he'd opened himself up to further rejection from Paula. They hadn't known each other long enough to survive a pregnancy and a marriage so soon after meeting. Perhaps he'd been so keen for the family he'd pictured with Kaja he'd transferred those dreams unfairly onto his spouse. In some way perhaps he'd also wanted to prove his absent mother wrong, prove that it was possible to have a successful career and children. And that someone could love him and want him in their life. Though as of now, the only person who did was his daughter.

'Of course you were...' She patted him on the shoulder with the tease but he noticed the flare of panic in her eyes when she realised what she was doing and snatched her hand away again. It was too late for him to forget her touch now he had physical proof this wasn't a dream and she was real after all.

'Now, this is where you will be staying.' She snapped back into courteous hostess mode and opened the ornately carved oak door etched with leaves and flowers, leading to a suite so big Seth feared he'd lost Amy already. The gold and cream colour scheme wasn't easy on the eyes as it screamed money. Along with not being childproof.

'Just us? I'm sure we could fit in a few more single-parent families if you wanted to open this up as a holiday retreat.' He wasn't trying to be facetious but this one room would swallow up his entire house and still leave enough space to build another.

Kaja ignored the comment, picked up a porcelain bell from the glass table just inside the door and gave it a tinkle. Immediately, one of the staff he'd seen outside appeared in the doorway.

'This is Nils. If you need anything ring the bell. He's here to assist you in any way he can.'

'I really don't think that'll be necessary.' He wasn't aware how long it had taken Kaja to get used to having people running around after her but he was sure it was longer than a few weeks.

His home with Kaja in Cambridge had once been their oasis away from the outside world. A private place to be themselves away from the stresses of hospital life and people who wanted something from them. That hadn't changed for him. He was still in the same house and it remained his safe haven. No matter how luxurious Kaja's residence was, he wasn't going to trade his and Amy's privacy to take advantage of the perks offered.

He couldn't imagine Kaja slobbing around in her PJs here on a day off, eating cereal out of the box and binge-watching her favourite TV shows. Mind you, he couldn't see this perfectly polished princess knowing how to chill out at all any more.

'It's no trouble at all, sir. I'm at your disposal.' The deferential bow didn't go any way to assuaging Seth's discomfort at having someone at his personal beck and call.

'I think that will be all for now, Nils.' Kaja dismissed her employee on his behalf. It was disconcerting to find she could summon this impressive male specimen at the mere ring of a bell. Although Kaja's personal life was nothing to do with him any more. He was here in a professional capacity. To perform a life-saving operation, then get the hell out of fantasy land and back to the real world.

'Seth, I know you value your privacy but you're going to need help. With Amy, at least. It's not a comment on your character to accept some assistance. Think of it as a perk.'

'Daddy, come and see my room. It's got toys and everything.' Amy appeared and grabbed him by the hand, tugging him away from Kaja and any chance of a meaningful conversation.

'We got a few things in to make your stay more enjoyable. I'll arrange transport over to the hospital when you're ready. Amy is welcome to help herself to the toys.'

'I appreciate you going to all this trouble for us.' She'd gone to a lot of effort to make them comfortable. Some might say too much. He couldn't help but think it was due to a guilty conscience and was beginning to wish they'd booked into a hotel instead.

Kaja excused herself and left the room. With the door closed behind her, separating her from Seth and Amy, she let out a long, ragged breath. Seeing him again was never going to be a straightforward meet and greet when theirs had been much more than a professional acquaintance. She'd known that. Yet, she hadn't been prepared for the tumultuous emotions seeing him again would churn up.

Her entire adult life seemed to flash before her eyes in the short time since they'd been reacquainted. All the mistakes she'd made, the regrets, and, almost worst of all, the good times she'd had with Seth, came flooding into her brain. Cuddled up together back then, there'd been none of this awkward formality she'd adopted to protect her status in her home country and her heart.

When she'd heard he had a daughter he intended to bring with him it was undeniable evidence that Seth had been in another serious relationship. A marriage no less. Except Amy, the spitting image of her father, was completely adorable and Kaja had fallen in love with her the second she'd taken her hand.

Now it was going to be doubly hard not to get personally involved with her house guests. The sooner she got Seth settled at the hospital to oversee her father's kidney transplant, the better. Then her whole focus would be on her family's survival.

'Is everything all right, ma'am?'

'Yes, Fatima. I'm going to retire to my quarters now. Perhaps you could bring me some tea.'

'Right away.' Her faithful lady-in-waiting was more of a friend and a confidante, the only person Kaja could talk to, but when it came down to it, Fatima was paid to listen. Just as Seth was being paid to be here. It appeared the richer she was, the higher status she had, the lonelier she became. She didn't want to be alone in her ivory tower any more and would give anything to be back in England where she'd had work colleagues, friends, neighbours and a loving boyfriend. But she'd given it all up to do her duty to her country and could never go back.

Even here in her own home she couldn't simply take a duvet day for some time out of her duties. There were always people coming and going, expecting an audience with her without offering any real, personal interaction. She also had an image to maintain, if only in the presence of the palace staff. Sometimes she wondered if Seth was the only one who'd ever truly known her but she hadn't been honest with him either about who she was or where she'd come from.

Now he knew the truth, Seth would see right through her to how unhappy she was in this life she'd left him for. It was karma, she supposed, for what she'd put him through. Not only had she lied to him but she'd abandoned Seth and the life they'd had together as though it were nothing. The truth was it had been everything.

CHAPTER THREE

'FATIMA'S GOING TO mind you while Daddy's at work. I'll see you when I get back, okay?' Seth kissed his baby on the top of her head then joined Kaja at the front door.

'She'll be fine, Mr Davenport. Amy and I have this whole house to play in. We can make some cookies for everyone to enjoy later too.' Fatima separated the clingy youngster from her father's trouser leg.

'You'll enjoy that, Amy. Fatima makes the best cookies in the country.' When she had free time, Kaja helped Fatima bake too. It took her mind off matters outside the kitchen and she got to comfort eat afterwards.

While it didn't help maintain her trim waistline, whipping up a few biscuits went a long way to clearing the clutter from her mind. Worries, memories, regrets—it was better to bake them in the oven than spend another night locked away in a room with them.

'I'll see you later, sweetie.' Seth gave Amy one last hug then Fatima distracted her with one of the new toys they'd bought so she wouldn't fret after him—a bright yellow convertible car to drive her dolls around in was just the thing to draw her attention.

'If there are any problems, call me. You've got my phone number, right?'

'Yes, Mr Davenport.' Fatima was smiling but she probably just wanted them to leave so she could get on with taking care of her charge. She loved children and helped raise Kaja and Bruno. They'd preferred her company over any of the nannies their parents had ever employed and she'd become like their second mum. As someone who'd devoted her life to looking after others, the prospect of spending the day with an excitable four-year-old was undoubtedly preferable to her usual housework routine.

'Don't worry. The Royal Alderisi Hospital is only five minutes down the road.' There were some advantages to ruling such a small country and having access to the best health care money could buy was one of them.

She led Seth outside where the afternoon sunshine cast a golden glow on everything it touched, illuminating the immaculately manicured gardens and showing off her country in the very best light.

'Can't we walk? It's a beautiful day and, well, I'm finding everything a little stifling in there.'

Kaja understood. Between the staff, and their history waiting patiently to be unpicked, it was claustrophobic. There was barely room to breathe despite the size of the place. However, when you were royalty simple things such as a walk alone weren't possible. Another thing she missed about England, where people were too busy, too involved in their own lives to be concerned with hers.

'Sorry.' She shrugged, continuing to apologise for the way she ran her life here. 'It's a security issue. With the amount of preparation it would take in advance, it's quicker and easier to take the car. Perhaps we can work something out for tomorrow.'

Seth sighed and approached the limo already waiting for them with the doors open and the chauffeur readied. He'd obviously tired of the regime after only a couple of hours but seeing it might help him understand why she'd left in the first place and moved to Cambridge.

'It doesn't matter. I'm being a nuisance. It'll take a bit of time to get used to things here, that's all. You don't have to keep apologising for everything.' He gestured for her to get into the car first and once the door closed she wished that walk were a possibility. Now there was no escape from confronting their troubled history.

'Don't I?' If she said sorry every day for the entire time he was here it wouldn't be enough to cancel out the wrong she'd done him.

'It's your life. You shouldn't have to apologise for the way you live. I'm only here in a professional capacity after all.' He'd sat at the opposite end from her on the back seat. For all her worry about being enclosed in here with him, now she wanted to close some of that emotional distance that had settled between them.

'That's not strictly true, is it? I got you here to carry out my father's kidney transplant because I know you're the best, but it would be remiss of me not to address what happened five years ago.'

'I don't want to drag that up and cause any ill feeling that might impact on the job I'm here to do.' Seth's attempt to evade the subject only succeeded in making Kaja feel worse by admitting there was lingering resentment on his part. She didn't want to create a toxic environment at the hospital, or in her home, but neither did she want to keep acting as though they were strangers. In her opinion it was better to get things out and clear the air instead of tiptoeing around each other faking congeniality.

'That's why I thought it best to tackle it now and explain myself. It's the least you deserve.'

He didn't argue any further, proving her right. She

took a deep breath and settled her hands in her lap in the hope they would stop shaking.

'I should have told you about my family from the start. I am sorry about that.' Along with everything else, but apologies couldn't alter history.

'Why didn't you, Kaja? We had a life together. I thought I knew who you were.' When he did look at her the pain shining so brightly in his eyes took her breath away. All this time she'd convinced herself he'd got over her was rendered a convenient lie when he was clearly still so affected by her actions.

'You've got to understand, Seth, I went to England to escape my life here. I never envisaged anything beyond that. After graduating high school I was expected to take on my own royal duties and projects. A scary prospect for an eighteen-year-old who wanted to be like everyone else. I persuaded my parents that getting a medical degree would be useful to my position when I returned. That I could put it to good use in the community. I told them England was the best place to study. Where no one knew me. Selfishly, I chose it because it was so far away I reckoned I was beyond their reach. They couldn't make me go back. As time went on I created a life there and I met you. I lived, studied and worked there so long I didn't think my heritage mattered any more. I didn't tell you the truth about who I was because I was in denial myself. I had no intention of coming back.'

'Until I asked you to marry me. Then you disappeared without a trace.'

She hung her head, not knowing how she could begin to make amends for her cowardice. 'That was my wake-up call. My reminder that I was living in a bubble with you. You weren't asking a lot except for a normal, family life. Something you would've found with anyone other than me. There's nothing normal about my family or my life, as you can see, but you're right, I shouldn't have gone like that. You deserved better.'

'Yes, I did.' He clearly wasn't going to make this easy for her.

'Your proposal made me realise I was fooling myself in living out this fantasy I could marry you and simply be Mrs Davenport. I had obligations at home that would have caught up with me eventually and I thought it best to end things before I entered into a marriage based on lies.' The right thing to do, evidently, when she couldn't have helped him realise his dream of becoming a father either.

'You could have told me that. I'd rather have talked things over than wake up to find you'd gone.'

'I panicked, didn't know where to begin explaining myself and thought I could do it better from a distance. I intended to get in contact but then my mother died and I was swept away in a tidal wave of grief.'

'You could have at least got a message to me.'

Even with the air conditioning on Kaja was feeling the heat, shame burning her from the inside out. 'I was a mess, Seth. I was grieving for my mother, and feeling guilty for everything I'd put everyone through. Believe it or not I thought by leaving I was somehow saving you from getting hurt too instead of stringing you along pretending to be someone I wasn't.'

Seth's soulless laugh disputed her warped sense of logic. 'How did you work that one out when you didn't explain any of that to me? Didn't you think I'd be worried that something had happened to you when you vanished without a trace? For all I knew you could've been abducted or had some sort of accident. I called everyone we knew and the hospitals and police. Of course, when they heard you'd rejected my marriage proposal they decided it was your way of dumping me. It took me a little longer to work things out.'

'I'm sorry.' Her voice came out as small as she felt right now. She'd never meant to humiliate him but she was guilty of thinking only about herself. In her attempt to avoid a confrontation or get talked into staying, she'd jumped on the next flight without thinking about the impact her disappearance would have on him.

He didn't need to know that her fertility issues had helped her to maintain that distance since. There hadn't seemed a need to reach out to him when there was no chance of a happy-ever-after and so she had only done so when her father's survival was at stake. It was a private matter she didn't have to share with anyone because she had no plans on repeating past mistakes. Getting involved with anyone would only bring heartache and pain when she could never live up to expectation. She had reconciled herself to never having children, perhaps never being in another relationship, because experience had shown her it wasn't feasible. That didn't mean she didn't yearn for both of those things. More so now that Seth was here, representing everything she wanted and couldn't have.

'When I saw you on the news at your mother's funeral I thought I was hallucinating. Never mind that you'd told me both your parents had died a long time ago, there you were walking behind your mother's coffin with your father, the grand duke.' He shook his head as though he was still trying to come to terms with it all.

'What can I do to fix things between us, Seth? I don't want you to hate me.'

'I could never hate you, Kaja, that's half of the problem. What's done is done, I suppose. We can't change what's happened so there's no point in dwelling on it. I don't think I'll ever forget but I can learn to forgive.' The smile he gave her was devastating on so many levels it made her want to weep. The fact that this man she'd obviously wounded deeply had been willing to fly halfway around the world to help her family and forgive her showed the strength of his character compared to hers.

There were other questions she had about his life but this was more than she could ever have asked of him. Anything else she needed to say to him could wait. It was more important that they started out on this journey on amicable terms when these next few days were going to be tough. A kidney transplant was no small operation. It came with risks to everyone involved. She was putting her faith in Seth to get them all through this and that would be easier to do with the knowledge he didn't hold a grudge against her.

'Thanks.' It seemed inadequate to express how grateful she was for everything he was doing for her when he would've been within his rights to refuse to even take her call. For now, it was the best she could give him. It probably wouldn't improve relations between them if she burst into tears and told him leaving him was the biggest mistake she'd ever made in her life.

They were going to have plenty of time together as her family members went through this huge procedure and, hopefully, she'd be able to show him just how sorry she was about ending their relationship. Maybe then they'd both find some closure.

Seth was glad the journey wasn't too long between the palace and the hospital. Kaja's attempt to call a truce so they could move on had actually caused them to lapse into an even more uncomfortable silence. One only broken when they reached their destination and she advised him on the proper protocol for meeting her father. He found it disconcerting being in this alien situation when she'd been a huge part of his life for so long. A woman he'd been so comfortable around once upon a time.

With their conversation slipping back onto more familiar, albeit rockier, ground he'd almost forgotten he was dealing with royalty. He suspected etiquette would be more scrutinised by her father.

As it was, he was glad he hadn't tried to gain access to the hospital, or his patients, alone. A stranger's face didn't seem welcome as they were met with imposing guards at every corner.

'Isn't this a tad OTT? As far as I'm aware your country doesn't have a high crime rate, never mind a history of assassination attempts. I thought your family was more of a figurehead than a political party?' He'd done his homework. Not only did the country have a ban on personally held firearms, with the exception of the military and police, they had one of the lowest crime rates in the world. From everything he'd read the population was pretty content here since most residents had their own wealth and status. It was a tax haven for the rich and famous after all, as well as those born into a booming economy.

The royal family appeared popular even if the articles he'd skimmed concerning Kaja's love life were less than complimentary. He knew she'd abhor the constant attention and the patronising, cruel nickname the press had awarded her.

She spoke in her own language to another of the guards who'd attempted to block their access down the corridor. Another reminder he no longer knew the woman beside him when he'd been unaware English wasn't her mother tongue. He could only assume the gist of the conversation was something along the lines of, 'Don't you know who I am?', given Kaja's stern body language and the chided guard stepping back to let them pass. He continued to glare at Seth as they passed, perhaps unconvinced about his credentials rather than his companion's.

'We can't afford to take any chances. The whole world knows where my brother and father are. You can't expect us to let people swan in and out as they choose.'

Apart from the extra staff, it looked like any other private hospital Seth had worked in. It was clean and airy, with the extra touches of artwork on the walls and aquariums lit up with brightly coloured marine life setting it apart from the facilities attended by lesser mortals.

In his experience the added luxury of comfortable beds in private rooms or in-house chefs serving up specially tailored meals didn't mean a lot in the grand scheme of things. It wouldn't matter if the walls were made of pure gold or the floors were encrusted with diamonds. At the end of the day he was employed to do the same job he did everywhere else. Money couldn't buy a clean bill of health.

Kaja knew that. Perhaps that was why she was so on edge. She could fly someone out with the best surgical reputation in the world to perform this transplant but the rest of the recovery was down to fate. There was a possibility her father could reject the new organ. As always, Seth would do everything he could to prevent that happening but there were no guarantees in this life. He'd found that out for himself the hard way.

Another guard outside her father's private room greeted their arrival with a curt nod of the head, followed by a conversation on his walkie-talkie before they gained admittance. Seth assumed his face was on an all points bulletin by now, his whole background undergoing a thorough check if it hadn't already. He prayed his recent site visits to research the country—the ones about their princess in particular—wouldn't come back to haunt him if they looked into his online search history.

'Father, this is Seth Davenport. The surgeon who's carrying out your transplant.' Kaja stood in the centre of the large private room announcing him to the frail gentleman swamped in his bed by pristine white cotton sheets and plump pillows.

'Ah, come forward, young man. My eyes aren't what they used to be. Along with the rest of me.' The grand duke sat up, immediately adopting an air of authority, which forced Seth to advance from the doorway towards the bed.

'I'm honoured to meet you, Your Royal Highness.' Seth dipped at the waist into a bow as prompted by Kaja, secretly hoping he wasn't expected to do this every time he walked into the room. It would become tiresome when he had a job to do.

The grand duke waved a dismissive hand. 'We can dispense with all of that nonsense. Call me Olov. I fear it is I who should be bowing to you. I can't thank you enough for coming to our little corner of the world to help me. My daughter tells me you once worked together and that you're the best there is.'

His excellent English was heavily accented compared to Kaja's. Seth assumed it was the time she'd spent in Cambridge studying that had made her sound more like a local.

It was clear she hadn't shared their personal history with her family. The grand duke might not have been so humble and welcoming if he'd known Seth had lived in sin with his only daughter for years, or that he'd had the audacity to propose marriage to her. Now he'd seen her life out here and the people she was surrounded by it was becoming clearer why she wouldn't entertain the idea of marrying a commoner like him. What more could he have possibly offered her that she didn't have already? Nothing except his love. Which hadn't been enough for her to even stay in the same country.

'That's correct, sir.' He wasn't going to be modest about his credentials when that was the reason he was here. Kaja's father would expect confidence from the man who would have his life in his hands.

'Good. At least something positive came out of Kaja's time away.' The focus of both men's attention lowered her head. Seth didn't know if it was in deference to her father or because she couldn't look at him.

Goodness only knew what she'd told her father about her career or her personal life during that time. It was a punch in the gut to think that their life together was nothing for her to be proud of when they'd been some of the best days of his life. Along with some of the worst after she'd gone.

'I've read up on your medical history and your nephrologist's recommendations. As far as I can see the procedure should be relatively straightforward.' Seth adopted his professional persona, determined not to linger on anything liable to distract him from the upcoming surgery.

'Glad to hear it. The last thing I want is to find out there could be more complications or setbacks. Time's running out for me.'

Seth didn't argue with him. He'd read the files and agreed that the transplant was the last option available given his condition. If he'd been any older or less fit than he was, a transplant might've been deemed too risky.

'This kind of operation comes with its own risks. We can't predict how your body will react to the transplanted organ. Obviously, we'll be monitoring you very closely and will do everything we can to prevent rejection. I'll need to meet with the rest of the team to discuss contingency plans to cover every eventuality.' Although he was the medical lead he wouldn't be able to do this without a team of other professionals with the same goal of making this operation a success.

'I can organise that for you.'

He'd forgotten Kaja was in the room until she voiced her intention to help.

'I'd appreciate that.'

'Is there anything else you need me to do?'

Seth knew only too well how it felt to be powerless as your world continued to spin out of control and there was nothing you could do to halt it. Yet, her suggestion to contribute fell flat when it had been made clear to him it was only the present that interested her. With no real consideration towards him or their history.

'Not at the moment. If that changes I'll let you know.' He turned his back on her, doing his best to block her out of his head so he could think straight.

'What do you require from me, Doctor? Apart from my kidney?' Another male voice entered the fray. Followed, of course, by another shadow figure who was quietly dismissed at the door.

Even if the new arrival hadn't been wearing an identical hospital gown to the one Kaja's father was sporting, the family likeness was uncanny. All three Alderisis had the same sea-green eyes, aquiline nose and height befitting royalty.

He held out a hand towards Seth. 'Bruno. Pleased to meet you.'

'Seth Davenport,' he countered as strong fingers gripped his in a handshake.

'This is my big brother. Bruno, this is the surgeon

who'll be carrying out the transplant.' Kaja introduced them in case there was any doubt about their identities.

'Ah. So you're the man who'll be cutting me open and rummaging about in my insides?' The dark humour he employed wasn't unheard of in these situations. A lot of patients joked to cover their fears. Bruno did seem relaxed about the impending operation considering the sacrifice he was about to undertake to save his father.

'Bruno, I wish you would take this seriously.' Kaja chastised him with a clip around the ear.

'Don't tease your sister. You know how she worries,' the elder Alderisi scolded.

It was clear this was a family who cared deeply for one another. He had no idea why Kaja had found it necessary to keep them hidden from him during the course of their relationship. Yes, her heritage had come as a shock but he would've got over it given time.

'I am taking this seriously. Trust me, giving away one of my kidneys isn't something I would do on a whim.'

'If it's any comfort, donors have the same life expectancy, general health and kidney function as anyone else.' He said it as much for Kaja and Olov's benefit as Bruno's.

'See, Kaja? I trust my new best friend here not to botch this when he comes so highly recommended. I'm going to be under anaesthetic so I'm not the one who'll be doing the worrying.' A meaty hand slapped Seth on the back. He liked this guy. His whole attitude and demeanour was a refreshing change from the earlier heavy-hitting conversation he'd had with his sister.

'We will need you to fill in the consent forms and other necessary paperwork before we proceed.' If anything did go wrong, it was necessary to have everything down in writing to protect all those involved. They all

knew the risks but Seth would be the one primarily shoul-
dering responsibility or blame if necessary.

'No problem. It's not as though we have much else
to do while we're waiting. We've exhausted the whole
board-game collection and I don't think Father is up to
a game of table tennis just yet. Maybe in a week or two
when he's fully recovered with a new lease of life, thanks
to my young, highly sought-after vital organs.'

Kaja rolled her eyes and groaned. 'I give up.'

'I'll arrange everything once I've had a meeting with
the team. The paperwork, that is, not the table tennis.'
Seth exchanged grins with the handsome prince, satisfied
they were both on the same wavelength. It was a serious
procedure but a positive one if everything went to plan.

'Good stuff. I can jot kidney transplant into my diary
for this week, then?'

'I don't see why not once we have everything in place.
I'll go back and check on my daughter and return later
to go over any questions you think of in the interim.' He
was keen to find out how Amy was getting on. He'd be
spending a lot of these next few days at the hospital and
wanted to spend as much time with Amy as he could now.

'I'll call for the car and get Isak to take us back to the
palace.' Kaja motioned for the attention of the guards at
the window.

'If you don't mind, I'd rather walk. I'm sure I don't
need an entourage to keep me safe and I'd much rather
get some fresh air.' Along with some distance from
Kaja and the memories he couldn't quite manage to
shut out altogether.

CHAPTER FOUR

'I LOVE YOU, BRU. I love you too, Papa.' Kaja struggled to say goodbye and leave them in the hands of the surgical team even though she knew it was for the best. They were the only family she was ever going to have.

She couldn't bear the thought of losing either of them but her father's age and health were against him. Despite that, she managed to stem the emotions welling up inside her. The last thing they needed to see was her crying before they went under the anaesthetic.

'You'd think we weren't coming back to hear you, sis.' Trust Bruno to be making jokes even at a time like this. Her father simply raised his hand to give a wave as though he were simply popping to one of his lengthy state dinners.

'Don't worry. They'll be back on the ward before you know it.' Seth met her at the door, already prepped in his surgical scrubs. It was the most he'd spoken to her in days, his time split between his patients and his apartments. He hadn't sought her out at all.

Of course, he had a lot of meetings with the rest of the transplant team to occupy him, but she thought he'd gone out of his way to avoid her since his introduction at the hospital to her family. Perhaps it was being faced with the reality of life here and the patients he'd agree to take on or down to her completely disregarding their life together in England as purely work-related. Although she didn't think either of them would have wanted to bring up their painful romantic history right before Seth performed the transplant. There didn't seem any need.

The truth was she'd never spoken to her father about her life in England. She didn't think it was necessary to rehash it all and detract from the work she'd come back to do. He didn't need to know about her disastrous love life now she was back in her rightful place at the palace. Except of course it wasn't that easy for her to forget.

It might have been different had her mother still been alive. She would've had someone to confide in, a female shoulder to cry on. As it was, she only had Fatima and she'd had to draw a line somewhere between friend and employee.

'This is going to be a very long day. As the donor, Bruno will go into Theatre first for the laparoscopic donor nephrectomy.'

'It's a less invasive procedure than the old method so that means a quicker recovery period, right?' Despite her own medical knowledge, she needed Seth's reassurance that they weren't taking unnecessary risks by going ahead with this surgery. He was the expert and could be more objective on the matter when it wasn't his own family he was dealing with.

'Yes. There'll be a few tiny incisions and we'll remove the kidney with the scope camera and miniaturised surgical instruments. It's a straightforward procedure I've been involved in on many occasions.'

'I know this is the best thing for my father but I can't help worrying about them both and what this means for the future.'

'A kidney from a living donor does give better long-term results and from a family member there are lower risks of complications or rejection. We hope for a better early function this way. You know all this, Kaja.'

She could detect his frustration with her, perhaps taking it personally that she had doubts about this transplant being a success. It wasn't Seth's abilities she was wary of but that possibility of losing another family member.

'I'm just trying to get things clear in my head. Perhaps I could watch you carry out the transplant?' She needed to do something to feel part of what was happening. If anything did go wrong then she would know she'd done her best too. She couldn't live with the extra guilt if she failed anyone else she loved.

'Honestly, I don't think that's a good idea. My advice would be to leave the hospital grounds for a while and find a distraction.'

'I couldn't do that. They need me here. I could just stay here—' She tried to go back into the room where her brother and father were keeping each other company before they went for surgery. Seth caught her none-too-gently by the elbow and pulled her back.

'Kaja, will you please just leave and let me get on with my job?'

Her mouth flopped open and closed at the audacity of Seth basically calling her a nuisance. Telling her she could be no help to her family and only a hindrance to him. It illustrated how far apart they'd drifted in the space of a couple of days. There was no way he spoke like this to any other anxious family members he encountered at work or she would've heard about it a long time ago. Colleagues had only ever said good things about him. It seemed this level of brusqueness had been reserved solely for her and it wasn't an honour she was enjoying.

As if she weren't tense enough already, Seth's sudden bout of control-freakery set her teeth on edge and her blood pressure rising.

'I'd prefer you kept our personal issues out of this, Seth. This isn't about you, or us, for that matter. You have no right to deny me access to my own family.'

'I don't want to call security to have you removed from the premises for being disruptive but I will if I have to.' Seth didn't acknowledge the accusation that he was exercising his authority in a vendetta against her. Which riled her even more.

'Disruptive to whom?' As if she didn't know.

'We'll phone you to let you know when they're out of surgery so you can visit. Okay?' He seemed to soften a little towards her even if he wasn't backing down.

Kaja nodded. There seemed little point in arguing further and causing a scene. Especially when this was the man carrying out the transplant. She didn't want him going in to surgery distracted. They could hash this out at another time.

She hurried back to her waiting car giving no thought to Gunnar running to keep up with her, or Isak, who'd been snacking in the front seat. It didn't matter a jot she had to open her own door when she simply wanted somewhere to hide her tears, emotions catching up with her all at once.

'Take me home,' she commanded shakily and pushed the button to raise the privacy screen between her and her staff.

Only then was she safe to demonstrate her fragility. The tears didn't take time to fall once they started, streaking down her face as though someone had released a pressure valve and years of upset and turmoil had finally been allowed to be expressed. It was grief for her mother and the relationship with Seth she'd lost. Worry over her father and brother. Most of all it was sorrow for the life she'd been denied with Seth. If circumstances hadn't conspired against her she could've had a lifetime of being his wife instead of the half-life she had here as The Unlovable Princess no one wanted.

Seth wasn't proud of the way he'd spoken to Kaja but he needed her to be away from him while he operated on her father. He had to concentrate on what he was doing rather than worrying about what she was going through waiting for him to finish. As her anxiety had increased so too had his want to comfort her. That would have undone his efforts to put some distance between them these past few days and only brought them closer.

He'd succeeded in alienating her now and would be lucky if she forgave him for his behaviour at all. Regardless that he'd thought sending her home would be best for both of them. Kaja sitting here watching, worrying and waiting wasn't going to help anyone. Seth was the one who had the success of this procedure resting heavily on his shoulders.

As a living donor Bruno had to have routine checks to ensure he was suitable—health screening, physical exam, X-rays to check for signs of any kidney disease. His father also had to have pre-transplant tests to check for any signs of infection. The transplant couldn't go ahead if there was any problem with either the new organ or the patient.

Bruno's operation had already been completed, with the kidney safely removed, and by all accounts he was recovering well with no sign of infection or unusual blood loss. Although the kidney was able to survive out of the body for up to forty-eight hours, the optimal time from removal to transplant was four hours. A factor always on Seth's mind when the operation itself could take anywhere from ninety minutes to six hours depending on the complexity of the situation.

With the duke's bloods and urine tests satisfactory, Seth scrubbed into Theatre along with the anaesthetists and other attending medics. He'd carried out this operation countless times over the course of his career but there was even more pressure on him today to be the best at what he did. This was Kaja's father and the leader of an entire country.

Watching his progress on the monitor, Seth made several small surgical cuts under Olov's ribs. Each one a reminder that he had the responsibility of this man's life in his hands.

This keyhole technique, while delicate, aided speed of recovery when there were smaller incisions to heal. While there was no need to remove the damaged organs, he would have to hitchhike the blood into the new kidney.

He wished he could apply a similar procedure to his relationship with Kaja so they could live with the damage from their past and use the good parts to jump-start a new working relationship. He couldn't continue banishing her from the hospital to avoid their personal issues. Once this surgery was over he needed to hold out an olive branch and hope she didn't use it to whip him.

Now he'd consigned himself to making reparations with Kaja, he focused on his patient, whose body was lying open to him.

'Clamp, please.'

He isolated the renal vein, and iliac artery and the new kidney was retrieved from cold storage ready to be transplanted.

It was a demanding, technical operation but there was

satisfaction seeing the kidney turn pink and come back to life as it was warmed up with a warm saline solution.

Seth wondered if his relationship with Kaja could ever be resurrected in a similarly healthy fashion.

Once he was certain everything was working as it should, they began closing. Only then was he able to relax a bit, content he'd done his job to the best of his abilities. Equally important, he could tell Kaja the transplant had been a success.

'Miss Kaja! I don't know what to do. I know you are very busy with your poor brother and father...' Fatima crossed herself as she ran into Kaja's room.

'Fatima, what's wrong?' She didn't have the time or energy for any more dramatics. She was exhausted. Drained by the emotions and intensity of the day so far. Not only because of her worry about her family members but she was trying to fathom the reasons behind Seth's sudden personality change. He'd never spoken to her so abruptly before and she wasn't sure what she'd done to deserve it other than be concerned for her family's welfare. Whatever his reason, it was clear he'd wanted her out of the way.

Unfortunately, with all of that running through her mind she hadn't been able to shut her brain down even for a few hours' sleep. Despite Seth's insistence, being at home hadn't made her any less anxious.

'I had a phone call...my sister needs me. She's had a fall and been taken to hospital. I must go and see her but what about you and Miss Amy? I can't leave you alone.' Poor Fatima sounded as though she was about to have some sort of breakdown as she wrung her apron with her hands.

'Yes, you can. Take as much time as you need to look after your sister. Now, where's Amy?'

'She is sleeping. Are you so very sure you can manage without me?' Seeing Fatima's distressed face, Kaja was tempted to say no to assure her she was indispensable. She had managed alone for the longest time but Fatima was a comfort to her when she needed it. A mother figure providing some sense of belonging where she no longer felt she had any.

'We will do our best to cope while you are away. Don't worry about us. Go, be with your sister. Family must take priority.'

'Thank you.' Fatima kissed her on both cheeks and the gratitude expressed for a few days' leave humbled Kaja. She'd become so engrossed in her own world and problems she'd selfishly forgotten Fatima had a life outside the palace. The woman she took for granted was needed and loved by her own family too. It would do them both good to be reminded of that.

'Take as much time as you need and let us know how your sister is keeping.' Although it might have sounded like an afterthought she was genuinely concerned and decided taking an interest in Fatima's personal affairs was long overdue. It might stop some of this continuous self-pity she'd been indulging in for too long.

It was only when she waved her devoted companion off that Kaja realised what she'd agreed to. She was taking charge of Seth's daughter in Fatima's absence. Without his knowledge or permission.

Kaja couldn't relax. She couldn't focus on the book she was attempting to read, the words blurring every time she looked at the page as her mind wandered. There was too much going on for her to sit on her plush plum velvet banquette surrounded by plump cushions pretending she didn't have a care in the world.

Despite any appearance of her as a princess lounging around waiting for her prince to come and rescue her, her nerves were shredded to ribbons. She was on high alert, ears straining for the sound of the telephone call from the hospital, or a sign of Amy stirring in her bedroom. The afternoon was a fraught one as she waited for it to be disturbed. Even more so now she had to come up with some idea of how to entertain a four-year-old. She had little experience of children, save for those she'd treated in a medical capacity. It was important to get this right for Amy because if she was upset, Seth would be too. More so than he apparently already was with her.

Not only did she want to prevent Amy from becoming bored and starting to miss her father, but she had to prove to Seth she was capable of taking care of his daughter. If she let him down again he'd never forgive her.

Kaja didn't know how long she'd been sitting here in Seth's apartment waiting to be useful to someone. Every tick of the brass clock on the mantelpiece seemed longer and louder than ever, echoing around the empty lounge. With only Seth's personal effects for company.

His jacket, clearly redundant in these current temperatures, was slung over the back of a chair. A pair of trainers sat by the door ready for his early morning jog around the palace gardens. The one she watched from behind her bedroom curtain and which had steadily become the highlight of her days. There was a stack of crime thrillers sitting perilously on the side table by her seat and a trail of Amy's toys stretched across the carpeted floor. It already looked like a family home. Lived in. She was sure he'd dismissed any member of staff who'd offered to tidy and clean the rooms, regardless that he was too busy to do it himself.

These were signs of a man content with who he was, without a need to impress anyone else. She envied him that freedom along with that one huge responsibility who demanded his time and attention.

Kaja lifted one of Amy's pink plastic teacups from the floor. Father and daughter had obviously been having a tea party together before he'd gone out to do his other job as a life-saving surgeon. It was such a simple indulgence of his daughter but the image it conjured up brought a smile to her lips and a pang in her heart. That was the kind-hearted, warm man she remembered. Someone who'd never be too busy to play with his child because he understood the gift he'd been given. Not everyone was lucky enough to be a parent.

Seth might have appeared a distant stranger to her in comparison but there was one thing that continued to niggle her. If he remained resentful about their past relationship, or as indifferent to her as he'd have her believe, why on earth had he come here? He had plenty of work at home and clearly no desire to tread old ground on a romantic level so what had prompted him into helping her? Seth didn't owe her a thing. It was the other way around. She couldn't help but think that the only reason he had for coming out was the unfinished business between them.

A shiver of excitement tickled the back of her neck. He must have forgiven her to some extent to have considered her request to help her father. Perhaps his love for her hadn't simply died the way she'd believed after hearing about his subsequent nuptials. He'd practically told her he'd done that on the rebound.

Kaja tried her best not to get carried away by the idea. Given recent events, she had a long way to go to get him to even talk civilly to her again. Besides, even if their feelings for one another hadn't evaporated completely, their circumstances wouldn't be any more compatible now. They were still worlds apart and he had his daughter's feelings to consider along with his own. She stared into the plastic receptacle wishing it could tell her fortune, map out her future for her when she couldn't do it herself. As much as she had wanted Seth to look at her the way he used to, she was afraid awakening old feelings was a wasted exercise.

Kaja was plagued by the confusion over what it meant to have him back in her life. She still couldn't be the woman Seth needed her to be.

It was exhausting being in her head. When she heard Amy's little feet patter across the floor it was a relief to have something else to focus on.

'Hello, sleepyhead. Fatima had to go home to her family for a little while. Her sister's very poorly.'

The four-year-old was still rubbing her eyes when she wandered in, her clothes and hair in disarray. 'Like your daddy?'

Kaja's heart lurched, surprised that the child had picked up on what was going on in the adult world around her.

'Not quite, but she's in hospital and Fatima has gone to visit.'

Amy thought for a moment. 'Can Daddy fix her too?'

'Your daddy is very busy but Fatima's sister will have a doctor like him to take care of her.' That seemed to be enough to satisfy her curiosity as Amy climbed up onto the settee and tucked her legs beneath her.

'I'm hungry. Fatima said we were going to make cookies and play hide and seek.'

'I guess that's what we're doing, then. Let me get

changed and I'll take you down to the kitchen.' That took care of how she was going to keep Amy occupied for the afternoon. Only time would tell if Seth would be appeased so easily on discovering Fatima's replacement.

CHAPTER FIVE

'LET ME KNOW when they're ready for visitors,' Seth instructed the staff in the intensive care unit before exiting the hospital.

At this moment he was regretting telling Kaja to send away her chauffeur and stretch limo. His job might not involve heavy manual labour but it was exhausting just the same. The intense concentration, knowing the fatal consequences if he messed up, along with the hours spent on his feet took their toll mentally and physically. He was sorry he didn't have someone to pick him up outside and deliver him to Kaja's door.

The short stroll he undertook suddenly became a marathon when his whole body was crying out for rest.

It wasn't only shunning a bit of luxury he was kicking himself for either. He'd been short with Kaja today. Not at all supportive at a time when she needed it because he was too wrapped up in his own issues. If he'd been dealing with the family of any other transplant patient he would've been more sympathetic. He hadn't been fair treating her differently at such an emotive time. If this had been either of his grandparents, or, heaven forbid, Amy, he would've been beside himself with worry too. Sending her away hadn't been his call to make.

He had no right to be rude to her simply because he

was afraid of getting too close again. Behind all the glamour and privilege, he could see she was still the same woman he'd wanted to marry. The problem with that was she'd already rejected him once before. After a divorce, losing his gran and with all of the baggage his mother had left him with, those shutters around his heart should've been on lock down. Yet he kept thinking of the good times he and Kaja had once shared, scuppering any chance of remaining impervious to her charms.

Since Kaja wasn't party to the complicated web of thoughts causing him to act so unreasonably, he wanted to deliver the news about the surgery in person rather than let her hear it in a two-second phone call where he was desperate to get off the line. It was an effort of reparation on his part and would give her a chance to voice any question she might have. This wasn't about him and Kaja, it was about her and her family. That was why he was here. If she tore strips off him for the way he'd spoken to her today he'd have to stand and take it. It was the least he deserved in the circumstances.

'Seth Davenport.' He waved his ID at security as he'd become accustomed. Regardless that they knew him by sight now he had to wait until they waved him through and some unknown entity opened the gates.

As after every other tense shift, he was looking forward to some downtime with his daughter. He needed some normality more than ever. An uncomplicated period where nothing was asked of him other than loving his daughter. Something he didn't need to work at when she was the only person he could guarantee wouldn't want him out of her life.

'Hello?' His voice echoed around the hall, eliciting no response. It was so different from the usual homecoming he received when Amy launched herself at him, pleased to have him to herself again. Here, everything seemed flat, lifeless, lonely. It was impossible not to pity Kaja if this was what she came back to on a regular basis.

Despite his weariness Seth jogged up the stairs to his apartments, eager to get to his daughter and that familiar sense of home, family and being loved.

There was no sign of Nils, which wasn't surprising since he'd told him in no uncertain terms he didn't need assistance. Fatima was a different story. Seth wouldn't have been able to work without her looking after Amy and the two had already forged a bond, which he took as confirmation his daughter was content. That was all that mattered.

He was surprised the two of them hadn't come haring straight at him the second he'd come through the door. Along with Amy's demand for his attention he'd become used to the older woman constantly trying to feed him up.

'I'm home!' The sound of an excited squeal reverberated around the entire floor of the building but his daughter remained elusive.

He frowned, a tad put out but also too tired to go child-hunting just yet. Instead, he gave into exhaustion, kicked off his shoes and sank into an armchair, which was surprisingly comfy for something that resembled a golden throne. It was something he suspected had been chosen only for the aesthetics. Amy was clearly enjoying herself wherever she was and as long as she was happy he could afford to close his eyes for a moment.

He was about to nod off when the sound of bare feet slapping on the tiled floor and a familiar voice called him back from oblivion.

'I didn't realise you were home.'

He opened his eyes to see Kaja skidding to a halt in front of him and was momentarily lost for words. Like his daughter standing beside her, Kaja's face was splattered with either mud or chocolate, or both. The elegant princess had been replaced with a ragamuffin. Her sleek, perfectly coiffured glossy hair had been tied up into a messy ponytail. Loose tendrils, which had escaped during her obvious exertions with his daughter, clung damply to her rosy cheeks. However, it was her choice of outfit that made him do a double take. She'd swapped the chic trouser suit he'd seen her in this morning for something more practical.

With one swipe she transferred most of the chocolatey mud onto the sleeve of her—his—oversized grey sweatshirt.

'I think I recognise that.' He nodded towards the hoodie she'd teamed with a pair of loose tracksuit bottoms.

Kaja's cheeks pinked a little more. 'Um…yeah, I think this one's yours. It was the only comfy thing I could find. My wardrobe isn't exactly conducive to childminding.'

Seth could only imagine the carnage if her expensive silks had been plastered in the same way as his old university sweater. She looked like the old Kaja standing there wearing her favourite item of his clothes. He wondered if it had accidentally found its way into her suitcase when she'd fled or if she'd packed it as a reminder of him. His bruised ego and wounded heart hoped it was the latter and that she'd thought of him, might have even missed him over the years. As he had her.

He decided not to reference her clothing any further or attach any significance to it aloud. Not when she'd essentially told him she'd only worn it because it was dispensable and it didn't matter if it got dirty or torn.

'Why are you minding Amy? Where's Fatima?' He didn't know if it was more surprising that the officious older woman had abandoned her post or that the previously stand-offish Kaja had enthusiastically stepped up in her place.

'Fatima had a family emergency. I'm afraid she's had to return home for a while. I hope you don't mind but I've been looking after Amy in her absence.'

'Not at all. Thank you. I hope everything's okay with Fatima.' How could he object to her stepping in when she was doing everyone a favour? It had simply come as a surprise to see Kaja like this, playing with his daughter and looking more carefree than he'd seen her since he arrived.

'On the subject of family…' Kaja was toying with the elasticated cuffs of her sweatshirt. Fidgeting was always an indicator of how anxious she was about something and there were no prizes for guessing what that was today. It wasn't fair to keep her in the dark any longer.

'Amy, why don't you go and wash your face while I have a talk with Kaja?'

'Will you play hide and seek with us after?'

'Sure. Now go. Shoo.' He clapped his hands and Amy scuttled off with a giggle.

'You sure have a way of getting people to do what you want.' Kaja's sardonic tone was to be expected after their last encounter.

'I'm sorry for the way I spoke to you earlier. I was out of line.'

'You think?' She folded her arms across her chest, fending off his attempt to apologise.

'It wasn't my place to tell you to leave the hospital but I promise I was doing it with the best of intentions. I didn't want to think of you sitting in the corridors all day fretting about something you had no power to control.' That was the main problem. He was worried he'd be distracted by thoughts of her so close by while he was busy saving her father's life.

She waved away his explanation with the hand she'd now untucked from her defensive position. 'All that aside, you didn't call. Does that mean something went wrong? Are Papa and Bruno okay?'

'Everything's fine. I just wanted to tell you in person. The transplant went as planned and they're both recovering now. Someone will page me when they're ready for visitors and we can go and see them together.' He waited for Kaja's exclamation of relief, braced himself for her enthused gratitude, certain she'd forgive him now, but she remained stock-still and wide-eyed.

'Kaja? Did you hear me? They're going to be all right.' He wished she would say something, even if it was to swear at him. Instead she'd gone into some sort of shock. Seth was contemplating shaking her out of her stupor when she suddenly burst into tears. Her whole body appeared to collapse into itself as she finally took in what he was saying. A tsunami of all that emotion she'd apparently been holding back.

'Oh, sweetheart.' Any resentment he might have subconsciously harboured over their break-up dissipated along with the notion that theirs should remain a strictly professional relationship when she was so clearly in need of a hug.

It was pure instinct that drove him to catch her in his arms and provide that comfort and support she must've been lacking to fall apart in front of him. She didn't rail against his compassion, instead, crumpling against him in emotional exhaustion. He dreaded to think what it would have done to her if she'd had bad news.

'Let it all out.' Seth held her close, his arms wrapped tightly around her to keep her upright and let her tears soak through his shirt. That protective need to take care of her hadn't left him. Even though these were tears of happiness he knew she needed someone to lean on who understood her. Someone who knew she hated showing any weakness and would hold her until it passed without thinking less of her. She needed him. That superseded his, probably futile, endeavours to emotionally detach himself from the only woman he'd ever truly loved.

'All clean, Daddy.' Amy burst in again reminding them that time and their relationship had moved on and comforting Kaja was no longer in his job description.

'Good girl.' He praised his daughter and ruffled her hair, giving Kaja time to wipe her eyes and take a step away from him.

'What's wrong with Kaja?' Quick to notice all wasn't well, Amy frowned at him as though he'd obviously done something to upset her. Seeing the thunderous look on her face, he had a hunch she'd take her new friend's side if she had to choose.

'I'm fine, honey. Your daddy just gave me some really good news.' Kaja's eyes and smile shone a bit too brightly as she faced Amy, making Seth inclined to hug her a little longer.

'Is your daddy all better?' Amy's frown evened out into a smile and, though it would be easier to let her think everything was all rainbows and unicorns, he preferred to be honest with his daughter.

'We hope so. He needs to stay in hospital for a while to make sure.'

Amy digested that new information before asking her next question cautiously. 'Does that mean we can keep playing hide and seek?'

'I don't see why not.' Kaja pulled her into an embrace, making Seth proud of the child he'd raised who'd consider someone else's feelings before thinking of herself. Unlike her father this morning.

The squealing and running about that had woken him made more sense now. Hide and seek always made Amy excitable, though her hiding places required a high level of acting on his behalf to pretend he couldn't see her feet sticking out from beneath the curtains.

'Good. I'm it this time. You and Daddy go and hide.'

Seth and Kaja looked at each other with the same expression of horror before stumbling over each other's excuses to avoid being paired for the game. Regardless that he'd lent her his shoulder to cry on, there were several layers of unresolved tension between them, which weren't conducive to playing happily together.

'I'm sure your daddy needs a rest after working all day—'

'You and Kaja were having plenty of fun without me—'

Amy ignored their protests, putting her hands over her eyes as she began to count. 'One, two, three...'

His daughter had a habit of getting him into all kinds of predicaments but this one topped the lot. Playing hide and seek with an ex-girlfriend who probably despised him more now than when she'd dumped him wasn't awkward at all.

He looked at Kaja but she shrugged her shoulders, apparently unwilling to help him find a way out of this. When she took off running his competitive nature rose to the fore with his pride at stake if he couldn't outwit a four-year-old.

At the adorable sound of Amy trying to count, sometimes stumbling over her numbers, missing a few, and repeating others, he did his best to find a suitable hiding place. It wasn't easy at his size but Kaja hadn't had a problem since she'd disappeared completely from view.

He dived under his bed only to be met with a painful roadblock, forgetting he'd stashed his suitcase there.

'Ready or not, here I come!' Amy sing-songed with glee.

Crawling back out from his failed hiding place, Seth searched frantically around his room for a last-minute alternative. He yanked open the wardrobe door and jumped inside as Amy's footsteps echoed down the hall.

It was only when he closed the door it became apparent he wasn't alone. Before his eyes managed to adjust to the dark he heard the distinct sound of someone breathing next to him. He batted his way through the row of hanging shirts seeking the source.

'Kaja?' he whispered. 'I hope to goodness it's you in here and not some creepy stalker hiding in my closet.' It was disorienting in the cramped dark space. Not to mention unnerving knowing he wasn't alone.

'Do you get many of those?'

'You'd be surprised.' He didn't care that she was making fun of him if it took her mind off everything else that had gone on today.

'Where are you? It's disconcerting hearing a disembodied voice in the dark.'

'Tell me about it.'

He heard her shift position, then felt hands patting across his chest and up to cup his face. 'Ah, there you are.'

She inched closer until he could see the twinkle of her eyes shining in the shadows as she toyed with him. The soft touch of her hands on his skin made him temporarily forget to breathe. All he could do was stare at her beautiful smile and remember how it used to be to wake up next to it in the morning.

'Kaja… I really am sorry about the way I behaved at the hospital today. I didn't mean to upset you.' When they were here, so close to one another, it was impossible to maintain that detachment he'd been striving for. He wasn't fooling anyone, least of all himself.

'I was too full on, fussing around Bruno and my father when you were just trying to get on with your work.'

He reached out and brushed his fingers along the side of her cheek. 'It wasn't your fault. This is on me.'

'Well, you've apologised, more than once, and held me while I cried like a baby.'

Seth saw the sheen of tears in her eyes again and he had no choice but to reach out to her so she knew she had some support. 'That's nothing to be ashamed of when you've been dealing with so much. I'm always available for hugs should you need them.'

'I'm going to hold you to that.' She sniffed as she leaned her head against his chest and wound her arms around his waist with a sigh.

His attempts at being emotionally closed off from Kaja were short-lived when her every tear was a hit to his solar plexus. He couldn't bear to see her hurting and when she was clinging on to him like this, trusting him to provide her with some comfort, he could almost forget they'd ever parted. A treacherous path to venture down with someone who'd almost destroyed him once before.

'Come out, come out, wherever you are…' Amy's Child-Catcher-like song encouraged Kaja to giggle. A sweet, welcome sound in the aftermath of today's stresses.

When she looked up at him he placed a finger on her smiling lips. 'Shh!'

They locked eyes in the darkness, their bodies still entwined with only the sound of their synchronised breathing to be heard. Although, he was sure it had become more ragged over the course of the past few minutes. This wardrobe had suddenly become their whole world. Population two.

Kaja's mouth parted beneath his touch, her breath hot against his skin. He remembered the honeyed taste of those lips and the way they moulded perfectly to his even though it seemed so long ago now. Tentatively, he drew his finger down, slowly uncovering her delectable mouth. He wanted, needed to kiss her when she was looking up at him with equal longing, drawing him down towards her, encouraging him to act on his urge.

'Found you!' Bright light infiltrated their cosy cocoon once Amy discovered them, flinging both doors open wide. Kaja's arms fell away from the embrace, leaving him bereft. It had been so long since he'd felt that intimate interaction it came as a shock to be reminded he wanted it. That beneath his roles as a father and a doctor he was simply a man with needs of his own. Her touch had reawakened feelings he'd put on hold in the pursuit of being the best parent he could be for his daughter. Only Kaja had the ability to do that.

Since she was an ex who'd rejected his marriage proposal and he was currently treating her family members, he knew exploring that route would only lead to trouble. Especially when they were living under the same roof and now sharing his daughter's care. Renewing their relationship would be a bad move for all manner of reasons, primarily that she'd already broken his heart and he couldn't go through that again. Nor would he inflict that pain on his daughter when she was growing closer to Kaja by the minute. As far as Amy was concerned, once his patients had recovered they'd be flying home. He wanted to keep it that way rather than let her think

Kaja was going to be part of their lives only to have her run out when it all got too real.

Seth stepped out into the real world leaving Kaja in the land of make believe where a kiss was possible and wouldn't cause a multitude of problems.

'You are too good, Amy Davenport. I think you deserve a prize for finding us so quickly. Why don't I take you out for a special treat?' He put his hand on his daughter's back and ushered her out of the door. Thankfully, she was so jubilant at having found them she hadn't picked up on the tension between the adults. He wished it were going to be so easy for him to put the incident out of his mind and dismiss what could have ended up as their second first kiss.

Kaja was tempted to close the closet doors and slink back into the shadows. Seth was making it clear he didn't want to spend any more time with her. He couldn't even look at her. She knew why. A moment together, unguarded and isolated from their responsibilities outside this room, and old feelings had been given space to breathe. Another second alone and she knew they would have given into temptation to kiss, to touch and taste one another again.

She'd been on her own for too long. Well, she'd been living with her family and the entourage of staff her father insisted upon, but she'd been short of actual company. Why else would she have turned to an ex in her hour of need? Clearly, she was confusing her gratitude for the surgeon who'd saved her father's life with desire.

She'd known from the start having Seth here was going to be difficult, but she'd thought putting her father's health above her failed romance should take precedence. That was until she'd become aware that the physical attraction between them hadn't lessened over the years.

She'd wanted him to kiss her and if Amy hadn't busted them she was pretty sure he would have.

'Can Kaja come too?' Amy's plea for her to be included put a stop to any thoughts of slinking away unnoticed. It also prevented Seth from leaving the room as quickly as he'd intended.

Realising it would look strange if she continued to hide in the wardrobe, she had no choice but to step back out into the spotlight.

Gone was the passion burning in Seth's eyes for her, replaced with a look of frustration. He didn't want her hanging around with him and his daughter. Whatever that moment had been between them, it was over.

'I'm sure Kaja would rather wait here until the hospital rings with news.'

'I'm not really dressed for going out, Amy.'

'Right, and it would take ages to organise cars and security.' Seth was quick to add to the list of excuses why she couldn't go with them but they both knew the real reason he didn't want her tagging along. They'd almost kissed in there and he wanted to put some distance between them so they'd forget it had ever happened. It stung to have him reject her so casually when the moment had literally made her go weak at the knees. There hadn't been anyone since Benedikt. She hadn't even been tempted. Until now. Probably because she knew the passion of Seth's kisses, wanted them and was surprised he still looked at her with that same burning desire. After everything she'd done to him, she knew he would never hurt her and for a lonely divorcee that was the greatest aphrodisiac of all.

'We don't have to go out, Daddy. Me and Kaja made cookies. Can't I have some of those for my treat?'

Amy always had an answer for any obstacles preventing her from getting what she wanted. It was a credit to Seth how smart she was, and determined. He'd raised a strong daughter and Kaja bet there was never a dull moment in the Davenport household.

'I...er...'

'I did promise Amy we could sample some once they'd cooled.' She watched with increasing amusement as Seth tried desperately to come up with another counter argument and failed. They were only going down to the kitchen to scoff a few biscuits. It wasn't as if they were on their own and about to act out some erotic scene from the contents of the fridge. Not unless he asked her to...

CHAPTER SIX

'THEN I SUPPOSE we have no choice...'

Amy was Seth's conscience as well as his get-out clause. He had tried to use her to run away from his re-surging feelings for Kaja. He'd wanted to kiss her and he'd come close to it. When they'd been fooling around, the only thought in his head had been that need to be with her again. The time he'd spent worrying where she'd gone, what he'd done wrong and how he was going to live without her dismissed all too easily. Worrying when she had the power to make him feel as rejected and unwanted as his mother had by her absence in his life.

What he didn't understand more than his own reaction was why Kaja had been leaning in for that kiss in the first place. Not only because he'd been abrupt with her today, but she was the one who'd ended their relationship. While he might have unresolved emotions and issues, Kaja had made her feelings pretty clear five years ago. She didn't want him. What had changed in their time apart? Nothing as far as he knew. It was possible she was simply lonely out here and had been confused by his company and their romantic history.

He wasn't going to mistake his feelings towards Kaja for anything other than a want for her, which apparently hadn't died simply because she'd left him. More than that, left him open to be hurt all over again.

They were different people now but the problems that had taken Kaja away from him in the first place remained. He didn't belong as a permanent feature in her life any more than she did in his. She lived in a different country, moved in higher social circles, was born royal. Their backgrounds couldn't be more different or incompatible. Rejection had been an all too common feature in his life and he'd sworn not to put himself in a position to let it happen again. If this trip had been the ultimate test of that vow, he was failing miserably.

Thankfully, Amy's appearance snapped him back to his senses and made him willing to forget the incident ever happened and redouble his efforts to protect his battered heart. Except Kaja apparently had bewitched his daughter too, preventing total escape. There was no way he could forbid contact between them simply to prevent himself from making any further potentially disastrous decisions. It wouldn't be fair to either Amy or Kaja and would give them both cause to despise him.

Tensions were already running high around here without doing anything to upset either princess in his presence.

Despite his resolve to remain unmoved by his reacquaintance with Kaja, he was persuaded into the kitchen by two aspiring, giggling chefs to taste their goods.

'What about this one?' Amy, sitting on a high stool, was force-feeding him the misshapen biscuits she'd made. The crunchy brown lumps weren't appetising in either appearance or taste but she was so proud of them he couldn't refuse.

'Delicious,' he managed to utter through a mouthful of crumbs.

'I thought you preferred these?' Kaja popped a delicate shell-shaped cookie into his mouth with a mischievous grin.

'No, he likes mine better.' A laughing Amy wedged another lump into his full mouth and Seth realised he'd become the butt of their joke. They weren't competing for his praise, they'd joined forces until his cheeks were bulging like a hamster storing sunflower seeds, and he was in danger of going into a sugar coma.

It had just been the two of them as a family for so long it was a new experience to have someone else join their fun. Paula had never been part of Amy's life so the only mother figure she'd known was his gran and he doubted she remembered much of that time, being so little. Watching her with Kaja was a bittersweet experience. In different circumstances perhaps this could have been a real family scene between them. Something he'd always wanted and, judging by the delight on his daughter's face, something she would like too.

He was a good father but that couldn't make up for the lack of a mother in her life. Someone she could confide secrets to that she didn't want to share with her father and someone to gang up with and play pranks on him. He'd pictured this life with Kaja. It was a shame she hadn't wanted it. She'd given up their future to return to her duties as a princess. He hadn't been enough incentive for her to stay when she'd made her choice five years ago. That was something he'd do well to remember instead of believing it could still be possible.

'Stop! I'll be sick if I eat any more, you rascal.' He tickled Amy, incapacitating her with laughter so she couldn't do any more damage to his waistline.

'Nonsense. I know you, Seth. I'm sure you haven't eaten anything all day.' Kaja dipped one of her golden-brown morsels into a bowl of melted chocolate sitting on the worktop.

She knew him too well. With a day of surgery ahead of him he hadn't stopped to refuel since the breakfast Fatima had provided this morning.

Kaja made sure hunger raised its head again as she bit down, the chocolate coating her lips, keeping Seth mesmerised as she licked it off with her pink tongue. Somehow, he'd turned another playful moment into an erotic display in his lustful mind. It didn't help matters when she dipped another cookie into the chocolate and offered it to him. He couldn't resist, even though he knew it was bad for him.

The confection was sweet on his tongue but nothing compared to the taste of Kaja as he sucked the remaining chocolate from her fingers. His eyes didn't leave hers, watching until they darkened and a small gasp sounded from her lips.

'Where's my chocolate?' Once again Amy saved him from himself, demanding to be included in this new game.

'Last one before dinner.' He half coated another and gave it to the appreciative audience before washing away the chocolate on his fingers at the sink. Anything to get away from temptation and a woman with whom he seemed determined to tread old ground.

'I'll put the rest away for later.' At the other end of the kitchen Kaja busied herself parcelling up the remainder of the treats, but he could see her sneaking glimpses at him when she thought he wasn't looking.

This push and pull between them was torture. Especially when he already knew how good they were together on a physical level. It was geography, class divide and a lack of honesty that had been their downfall. If her reason for leaving him had been not loving him, or that they'd no longer been attracted to one another, living under the same roof wouldn't have caused the same intense level of tension simmering between them. It might have been better for his peace of mind if she'd stayed mad at him.

'Your Highness, I'm so sorry I was gone for so long. Please forgive me.'

'Fatima?'

Kaja's faithful aide bustled into the kitchen as if from nowhere. She untied the headscarf keeping her curly brown hair in place and struggled out of her heavy coat, which made Seth sweat simply looking at it. He supposed she was accustomed to the climate but, as a visitor more used to inclement British weather, he found the temperature and humidity stifling.

Kaja seemed more stunned by her arrival than her outdoor wear. 'I wasn't expecting you back so soon. How is your sister?'

'She hurt her back but it's nothing serious. I telephoned her daughter and she's driving over to be with her. Now, let me get back to work and clean up this mess you've left in my kitchen.' After hanging up her coat she pulled a floral apron from a drawer and tied it around her waist, then herded them out of her territory.

Seth's phone vibrated in his pocket with a text message.

'That's the hospital. You can go and see your dad and Bruno whenever you're ready.' He halted their procession down the hallway to tell her immediately. Now there was no doubt about where, or with whom, he'd be spending the rest of the day.

Kaja dithered when he'd half expected her to race off at once. 'I need to change but, er, would you come with me?'

'To get changed?' She made it too easy for him to tease her but joking around was safer ground than those hot, loaded looks they kept exchanging.

She rolled her eyes. 'To the hospital.'

'Can I stay with Fatima?' Amy had already turned on her heel and was running back towards the kitchen before he could answer. Clearly, she hadn't been spoiled enough today. He couldn't begrudge her some attention from an alternative female role model than an ex they were both growing dangerously close to, however.

'Yes, Kaja, I'll accompany you to the hospital. I have to check on my patients anyway. Yes, Amy, you can stay with Fatima, if that's all right with her.' Seth addressed each of them in turn telling himself it was the right thing to do for all concerned.

'Okay, I'm ready to go. Sorry for the wait.' While Kaja wanted to sprint immediately to the hospital to see for herself that her family was safe, it wasn't as simple as that.

'No problem.' Seth rose from the armchair he'd been sitting in waiting for her to make herself presentable for the outside world.

It was easy for him. A quick shower and a change of shirt and he was ready. As handsome as ever. She needed a bit more assistance to be camera-ready in case she was snapped on the way. The chances of that happening were high with the press camped outside the front of the hospital waiting for news.

Her car was out front, engine running. Seth graciously helped her into the back seat before climbing in next to her. The photographers were there at the gates too, wanting to catch her reaction, some sign of what had happened to her father during surgery. It was draining having to keep up a façade when any display of emotion was deemed unbecoming for a member of the royal family. That was why she'd wanted Seth to accompany her. At least when she was with him she no longer had to keep that stiff upper lip. She'd already broken down in front of him, clung to him for support, and the world hadn't ended because she'd let someone in. Although it still could if she got too used to having him around.

'Thank goodness for tinted windows. They give some illusion of privacy even if the press always manage to sneak a picture somewhere along the way.'

'Don't you get sick of all this? Wish you could just run away from it all and live a normal life?' There was pity in Seth's eyes and she found it worse than the pain she'd seen there most of the time when he'd looked at her.

She didn't really deserve anyone's sympathy when she led such a privileged life. Regardless that she found it trying at times. People had been hurt worse than her in her pursuit of normality. Seth for one.

'I tried that, remember? I made my escape to England but running away doesn't solve problems. Everything catches up with you in the end. I'll never regret our time together, Seth, but I was living a lie. I'm sorry you got caught in the crossfire while I figured that out.' Her love for Seth had been genuine but coming back here only proved it could never have worked out. Protocol impinged on basic things most people took for granted, such as privacy. Something she knew Seth was struggling with in his short stay here so far.

Neither of them would want that kind of intrusion for Amy either. Playing together today, having fun like any other normal family, only served to increase her sense of loss. Being a mother was never going to be possible for her. The more time she spent with Amy, the more she realised what she was missing out on. Despite appearances, Seth was the one who had everything.

Perhaps she should've stayed single rather than ever getting involved with anyone. Then no one would have been hurt. Including her.

'I wish you'd told me that before I flew all the way out here.' There was that sad smile again, which wouldn't have been noticeable to someone who didn't know him as well as she did.

'Why?' There had been a couple of unguarded moments between them but Seth had been quick to stamp out any flames when heat sparked between them. She doubted rekindling their romance was the reason he'd agreed to help her father in the first place.

He sighed and leaned back into the leather. 'I think that's what I was doing by accepting your request to treat your father. After Gran died I was lost. Coming here has been a distraction from the reality of her no longer being around. If what you're saying is true, the grief will be waiting for me on my return.'

She fought back the sudden and surprising disappointment as he confirmed his motive had nothing to do with her and reached out to squeeze his hand. Seth glanced down at the fingers clasped around his, then up at her, his eyes misted with unshed tears.

There were similarities that had brought them to where they were now. She was apparently mourning their relationship and her chance to be mother to someone as wonderful as Amy as much as he was grieving the loss of his grandmother.

'It's not easy facing up to the things that keep you awake at night. I don't know how many times I rehearsed that call, dialled your number and hung up before I asked you for help. I know it's not the same but you'll feel better when you deal with your fears once and for all.' She'd thought of Seth often over the years, wanting to make amends but convincing herself to shove it all to the back of her mind and pretend to move on. When, in truth, she'd never got over him. Her heart hadn't let go of him simply because she'd thought it the right thing to do.

'Did it work? Do you think you've exorcised some demons by seeing me again?' He was searching her face for answers, making it difficult for her to lie to him.

Her blush would give her away anyway. She had no business dishing out advice when her life had been such a car crash up until now. Plus, if she was going to be honest with him it meant confessing she still had feelings for him. News that might not be welcome after everything she'd done.

'I'm glad I called. For my father's sake and I, um, I'm pleased I got to see you again. It gave me the chance to explain why I did what I did.'

'But… I get the sense this hasn't played out the way you imagined?' He was able to read her way too easily. Perhaps after being burnt so badly already he watched her more carefully these days.

She glanced out of the window trying to get her bearings. Why did this journey seem to take longer when she was in the car with him?

'I, uh…' she cleared her throat '… I didn't expect that we'd, uh, still have that spark.' Or that she'd be faced with the reality of her infertility issues again. Babysitting Amy reminded her what she was missing out on and even if circumstances made a relationship possible with Seth, she couldn't give him everything that should come with that.

The ensuing silence was interminable as she waited for him to confirm or deny her observation.

Then Seth said quietly, 'Nor me.'

There wasn't time to analyse what that meant for them other than it hadn't been all in her head as the car pulled up outside the hospital.

'Before we go in, I need you to be prepared. Remember, they've just come out of surgery. You know they're going to be weak and groggy.'

She nodded, not concerned about anything behind those doors other than seeing her family again. Despite her fears her father might not get through this, she'd always had faith in Seth's abilities. There was a long way to go until they could say her father was in good health but at least the transplant had gone to plan so far.

'I'm here for you,' he said, resting his hand gently on her arm.

She bit her lip to stop from begging him to hold her again as he'd done earlier. That connection with someone who expected nothing from her in return was invaluable. Something she hadn't appreciated as much as she should have when she'd had it.

Then there was that rush of arousal he still managed to incite with a mere look. Her heart, and body, were crying out for his touch but they couldn't do anything in public without causing an uproar.

Instead, they exited the car separately, ignoring the cameras and the microphones being thrust in their direction as security hurried them inside.

'Oh, Papa.' Kaja rushed to her father's bedside battling for space amongst the attachments and machines assisting his recovery. He had drips going into his body, drains coming out and a morphine driver for pain relief, but he was here.

'Kaja…my daughter,' he rasped through dry, cracked lips under his oxygen mask. The effort of opening his eyes to look at her proved too much and they fluttered shut again. He was obviously still tired. She'd never seen him so frail. He'd refused to let them accompany him when he'd been having dialysis and had always put on a brave face afterwards, even though he'd spent the rest of those days in bed. One to always defy his age and keep himself busy with the running of the country, now he was in his hospital gown without his tailored suits there was no hiding the truth. He was as vulnerable and mortal as everyone else.

His paper-thin skin was almost translucent, except for the lurid red and purple marks where his body had been through the wars. It was clear there would be a long recovery period.

Seth, who'd been talking to the other doctors about his meds to prevent rejection of the new organ, came over when she kissed her father's forehead.

'We should let you get some sleep, sir. I hate to drag you away again so soon but he needs as much rest as possible, Kaja.'

'I know. I just wanted to see him for myself. Can I look in on Bruno quickly too?'

'Sure. He's still next door.'

'I'll come back and see you again tomorrow, Papa,' she whispered before following Seth into the adjoining room.

'Hello, sis!'

'Bruno!' Seeing him sitting up in bed looking so well considering what he'd been through, she wanted to hug him so tightly. She saw the fleeting panic cross his face as she ran to him and reined herself in before she caused him any further pain.

'How are you feeling?' She settled for giving him a peck on the cheek instead.

'Sore,' he said with a grimace. 'How's Dad?'

Seth stepped forwards then to put his mind at ease.

'Everything went to plan. He's understandably tired but doing well.'

'He's awake?'

'Only briefly. He knew I was there at least.' Kaja would've hated for him to have woken up and found himself alone in a strange room.

'That's good. Maybe I'll get to see him tomorrow when I'm back on my feet?' Bruno looked hopefully at Seth to authorise the visit.

'We'll see how you both do overnight.' Seth apparently wasn't going to be swayed by sympathy when it came to his patients' recovery times. He was the kind of doctor who'd do whatever he could to buoy his patients' spirits. It went a long way to aiding recovery. She'd seen for herself how much having beloved family members around helped people get better quicker compared to those left languishing alone with no visitors to boost their mood.

'Is there anything I can bring you from home, Bruno?' She wanted to do something, anything, to make her brother more comfortable when he'd sacrificed so much to save their father. The fact she hadn't been a match had put paid to any idea of her being a donor even if either of them would've let her do it. As a result, her conscience insisted she needed to pay some sort of penance because she wasn't the one lying in a hospital bed recovering from an operation.

He shook his head. 'I think I'm all set. I have books, magazines, puzzles and a phone somewhere.'

'Has Missy been in?'

'Where do you think I got the supplies from? I'm sure she'll be back later. I asked the staff to let her know when I was awake too.'

'In that case, I'll let you recharge your batteries. You've got to look your best for your sweetheart.' Her brother was still head over heels about his long-term girl-friend and vice versa. They made an adorable couple but she couldn't help but envy them their future together.

'Thanks for calling in, Kaja. Hopefully, next time I see you I'll be on my feet.' He flicked another glance at Seth.

'We'll see.' Her visiting companion refused to be drawn any further on the subject despite Bruno's plea. She knew her brother well enough to predict him ignoring all medical advice to try and get on his feet before he was ready. When they were out of earshot, where she couldn't be accused of being a tattle-tale, she'd tell Seth to keep an eye on him for that very reason.

'Get some sleep. I just wanted to call in and say hello.' She kissed her brother on the cheek for a second time, content to leave now she'd been assured he was his back to his mischievous self.

'In that case, hello and goodbye. I'll see you tomorrow and don't forget to bring my running shoes with you,' he teased one last time before lying back down and closing his eyes.

'He seems in good spirits.' Seth echoed her thoughts aloud as he closed the door behind them.

'It would appear so. Although my brother wouldn't be inclined to tell me if he was in any pain.' She couldn't resist another peek through the window, finding him already fast asleep.

'All the reports so far are positive so I don't think there's any real cause to worry.'

'Not that that will stop me,' she said with a self-deprecating grin.

'It must be nice having a sibling. Even if it is one more person to fret over on a daily basis.'

'We weren't always this close but, yes, I'd be lost with-out him now. Do you think you've missed out on something by being an only child?' Bruno had been another casualty of her selfishness during those years she'd spent incommunicado in England but he hadn't held a grudge. He'd welcomed her back with open arms and told her how much he'd missed his little sister. Kaja hated herself for the estrangement but it was in her brother's good nature to forgive and forget. She had a much harder job forgiving herself.

Perhaps if she'd been honest with Seth, he and Bruno would have been friends from the start.

'I was never lonely when Gran and Gramps were alive but now… It would be nice to have someone to lean on. You know, someone who understands what I'm going through.' He let out a sigh and Kaja knew how truly lucky she was to have the family she did. At least when her mother had passed away she hadn't grieved alone. Her father and brother had lifted her up when she'd been at her lowest. Seth had no one except his young daughter.

'I know it's not the same but you can talk to me, if it helps?'

'Thanks, but, um, this is only short term, remember?'

How could she forget when he was always so desperate to get away from her?

'I know Amy's a comfort to you but you know where I am if you need a listening ear.'

'She is, but it's made me realise I want more for her. Given the chance I'd like to settle down with someone again and give her a stable family life. Perhaps even give her a brother and sister. Although, I suppose you need a partner before there's any chance of that happening.'

Kaja faked a laugh to accompany his, ignoring the lead weight that had dropped into the pit of her stomach. The family he wanted wasn't something he'd find with her. A quiet, ordinary life was something she'd sacrificed long ago because it had never truly been her destiny. Seth, on the other hand, could still have it all. Without her.

'Where is my driver?' she demanded from the nearest security officer, the effort of hiding her heartache becoming too much to sustain on top of an already emotional day.

'I'll check for you now, ma'am.' The burly shadow clone began issuing orders over his walkie-talkie.

'Are you in a hurry to get back?'

She momentarily stopped pacing the corridor like a caged animal.

'Yes. No. Well, there's no point in hanging around here getting in the way.' As she was wont to do when reminded of her inadequacies, she wanted to lock herself away from the outside world and hold herself a pity party.

'I think Amy and Fatima were expecting a bit more time together. We could do with a timeout too. Between the stress of the op and, I'm sorry to say this, but the oppressiveness of that house, I think we need a break.'

'What are you suggesting? I'm all for a change of scenery but you know I have to run it past a lot of other people first.' He'd intrigued her but protocol spoiled any notion of spontaneity.

'That's my point. You need some breathing space and a distraction from all this stress. It's not good for your mental health to be cooped up all the time like a trapped bird. You need to spread your wings once in a while. Come on, while he's not looking. Let's bust out of this joint.'

Kaja glanced at the guard walking down the corridor in the opposite direction with his back to them, then at Seth's hand, which was wrapped around hers.

'I can't just disappear. All hell would break loose.

They'll think I've been kidnapped, for goodness' sake.' She resisted as he tried to pull her away.

Seth narrowed his eyes and she could almost see his brain working overtime to come up with a solution. Then he turned back towards the door to Bruno's room. 'This should do the trick.'

He lifted the marker pen tied to the whiteboard, where someone had scribbled *Bruno Alderisi—No Food*, and added his own message in bold letters.

Taking a mental health day on doctor's orders. No need to look for us. Back soon.

He handed her the pen. 'Well, they're not going to take my word for it.'

She let out a titter in disbelief he was serious about this. They weren't merely ditching class like a couple of naughty schoolkids, he was asking her to go against all the rules in place to keep her safe.

'You're a grown woman and one who has worried herself sick all day. Surely, an afternoon off isn't too much to ask for?'

It wasn't, unless you were part of a royal family being constantly scrutinised under a microscope. She thought about what Seth was offering, what he represented. A freedom she hadn't had since she'd left England, and him.

She took the pen off him, ignoring his triumphant grin, and signed her name to their sick note.

'I guess not. What's the worst that could happen?'

CHAPTER SEVEN

'WHAT ARE WE waiting for, then?' Seth tugged her by the hand again and this time Kaja let herself be led astray.

This naughty side of Seth's made him appear years younger than the serious surgeon dealing with her brother only moments ago. It was impossible for her not to get caught up in the moment. For a little while at least it would be nice to pretend they were the two young, care-free people they used to be. Except it wasn't as straight-forward as giving her security the slip.

'Wait. I'm going to be recognised the second I set foot outside. We're not going to get very far with me look-ing like this.' She could hide her jewellery in her pocket and tie up her hair but the expensive, brightly coloured clothes were going to draw attention.

'We'll figure something out. For now we need to put some distance between us and your human shield there.'

Kaja chuckled as they hurried down the corridor hop-ing their escapade wouldn't be suddenly cut short or that they would cause too many problems for the staff. She simply wanted to have some fun for a change.

'This reminds of that time on night shift together. Remember?'

'How could I forget?' The husky tone of Seth's voice and the memory itself warmed Kaja from the inside out.

She didn't know why she'd chosen that particular intimate snapshot from their history together to share when it was a million miles away from who and where they were today. Even in her thin layers of silk she was burning up thanks to the images she'd conjured up in her head.

That night had been during their first flush of love when they'd wanted to spend every second together. Preferably in bed. Work and conflicting schedules had made it difficult to get that quality time. So, when they'd found themselves working together on an unusually quiet night shift they'd made the most of it.

'In here, quick!' He opened a door halfway down the corridor and pulled her inside.

'What are you doing? I didn't mean for us to recreate that night together. I have to be more discreet about these things now, Seth,' she spluttered as he shut them into the tiny store room.

He tried to stifle a laugh, then reached out and cupped her face in his hands. Kaja held her breath, convinced he was about to kiss her. The adrenaline spiking through her body indicated how much she wanted him to.

'As much as I would love to, that's not why I came in here. I thought you might want to get changed.' He directed her gaze to the rows of freshly laundered scrubs hanging on the rails above them. She'd been so concentrated on Seth and the thought of his mouth on hers she hadn't noticed their surroundings.

'Oh. Yes. Of course.' She turned away, breaking physical contact so he couldn't see her turn scarlet with mortification. Now he knew exactly where her thoughts had gone to he might change his mind about spending the rest of the day with her.

'I'll grab one of the lab coats.'

With her back still to him Kaja lifted down a plastic-wrapped set of scrubs, swearing to launder and return them as soon as possible. She slipped out of her purple jumpsuit and shimmied into the less flattering, baggy outfit. The thin gold rope belted around the waist of her discarded clothes doubled up as a makeshift hair tie as she caught her tresses up in a ponytail and she used a fresh towel to wipe away her make-up. Now she was no one remarkable at all. If only she could disguise her true self from Seth too, she might be able to stay out of trouble.

Seth slipped his arms into the sleeves of the crisp white coat despite the sweat already clinging to his back. He was all too aware of Kaja standing behind him stripped to her underwear. It had been a spur-of-the-moment decision to duck in here when she'd been looking for excuses not to take some time off. As had the notion of running away in the first place.

He wanted to make up for his behaviour this morning along with easing some of the sadness Kaja had been cloaked in since the day he arrived. Five years was a long time to hold a grudge when he had a successful career and a daughter he doted on. She was the one in pain now, a wild exotic bird trapped in a gilded cage here, and he wanted to do something to set her free again.

It had come at a cost. The reminder of their passionate encounter on that nightshift was something he couldn't get out of his head. Especially now she was so close, half naked, with her familiar perfume filling the air.

The sensual memory of the last time they'd been locked in a storage room, clothes in disarray, getting hot and heavy up against the wall, blazed brightly in his head. Even though they'd tried to be quiet Kaja had made those little moans that drove him crazy.

Damn, they had to get out of here fast.

'I'm ready when you are.' Kaja's quick change came not a moment too soon.

'Great. Once I'm sure we're all clear out there we'll head for the fire exit.' Seth's relief was short-lived when he spun round only for her disguise to steal his breath away. The fresh-faced, beautiful surgeon he'd fallen in love with at work was standing right before him.

'I'm not sure these go with the outfit but beggars can't be choosers.' She lifted her trouser leg to show off the purple, open-toed sparkly heels she was wearing.

Seth reminded himself he wasn't a Regency hero who should be bowled over by a well-turned ankle. 'As long as you can walk in them I think we should be fine.'

They were going to have to stop cosying up in tight spaces if he was to resist temptation for the duration of his stay. The way Kaja continued to look at him with that reflected longing was severely testing his restraint and rendering his broken heart a distant memory.

He cracked the door open a fraction and peered out. 'Corridor's clear. Let's go.'

Kaja followed him out and the few staff they passed didn't bat an eyelid.

'So far, so good,' she whispered with a hint of excitement in her voice. She really had been locked away in her princess tower for too long.

'Don't speak too soon.' He grabbed hold of her and pretended to study the chart pinned to the wall as another guard charged past them.

His heart was thumping so hard he swore their pursuer would hear it. It was crazy to have suggested this. More so to have acted upon it. Kaja was royalty and for all these guys knew he could've abducted her. If he wasn't careful he'd find himself locked up for kidnapping their precious princess. She was no longer a mere work colleague he could blow off some steam with when the mood struck.

It was only the sound of heavy work boots continuing on past that let him breathe again and stop him imagining the rest of his days doing hard labour.

'It's amazing what a change of clothes and a make-under can do,' Kaja tutted.

'Indeed.' He withdrew his arm from around her shoulder, aware he'd broken all sorts of etiquette today. Both royal and personal. However, he had more serious matters to deal with. If he wasn't careful he'd find himself taken out by a SWAT team.

Moving swiftly away from the commotion building elsewhere, Seth led her towards a side exit next to the ambulance bay. Heads down, they walked past the paramedics unloading a gentleman in a wheelchair, doing their best not to raise suspicion.

'Where are we going? Kaja was tottering along in her spiked heels struggling to keep up as they tried to get as far from here as quickly as possible.

'I have no idea. The only parts of this country I've seen are the airport and the palace. Both of which I'm guessing will be on lockdown by now.'

'This is your great plan? To bust me out of the hospital and what? Take me on a day trip around the car park? I'd have been better off at home.' It was no wonder Kaja was ticked off at him. He really hadn't thought this through. This level of risk should've had a reward at the end to be worth all the trouble. If he'd planned this properly there would've been chilled champagne and a gourmet picnic waiting for them on a secluded beach somewhere. He wasn't good at spontaneity when the unknown presented a threat to his well-being.

'Hey. It was a spur-of-the-moment decision. Give me some credit for trying to shake things up around here.'

'In case you missed it, we've had enough drama recently to last a lifetime.' She hopped along on one foot while trying to dislodge her shoe from the other. Once completely barefoot she stomped silently towards the patch of grass at the back of the car park.

'Look, we've managed to get some time away from rent-a-hunk. We can spend it discussing my inadequacies as a member of the resistance or we can make the most of it.' He cocked his head to one side and fluttered his dark eyelashes.

It had been a long time since he'd had to employ that move to win her over but he was pleased to see it had the same desired effect as she failed to hide her grin.

'Okay, okay. I'm glad you took the initiative. I've forgotten what it was like to play hooky every now and again. You're a bad influence, Mr Davenport.' The faux scolding only confirmed the decision had been the right one. For both of them. How long had it been since he'd had a break from being Mr Responsible too? They needed to cut loose for a while. If only to remember the people they used to be before life got in the way.

'Now we've established this is entirely my fault if anyone asks, perhaps you'd like to have some input? This is your country after all. I would've thought you'd have some idea where to hide out for a couple of hours?' Back in England they could've disappeared easily with open fields, forests or seaside towns a mere train stop away. He knew nothing about the hiding potential here and with their history they needed somewhere with plenty of space around them.

Kaja knew she was taking out her bad mood on the wrong person. It was herself she was mad at for agreeing to this when after a couple of minutes alone in a locked room she was back to having lustful thoughts about Seth. Now, to all intents and purposes, they were on the run. As if they needed this romanticised any more when he was the man who believed he was giving her some freedom back.

In a way he was, when every moment she spent with him made her feel like the Kaja who'd spent those years in England living a normal life.

Something she shouldn't be reliving when she was doing her best to live up to her family name.

'There is a place not too far from here where Bruno and I used to sneak off to when we were kids.' It was her time to take the lead, carefully picking her way barefoot down the grassy incline away from civilisation.

'Won't Bruno rat us out? Surely that'll be the first place he'll think of if he hears you've gone AWOL?' The more cautious Seth began to re-emerge as he jogged down the slope to join her. His fancy, dress shoes weren't coping on the wet grass any better than her bare feet. Despite today's warm weather it must've rained some time during the night, ensuring Seth's every other step was more of a slide. Adding even more of an element of danger to their outing when there was the extra risk of him falling onto his backside at any given moment.

'First off, Bruno is probably asleep and the chances are no one is going to wake him up after donating a kidney to tell him his kid sister has gone for a walk. Secondly, he'll have forgotten about this place by now. If it even exists any more. Besides, he knows how exhausting this whole royalty deal is, better than anyone. Who do you think found this place and planned our escape days in the old days?' Before Seth, her brother was the only person who'd understood her need to get away. That was before duty had called him away from their childhood games and she'd realised the reality of the responsibilities of royal life when he'd no longer had time for her or anything else.

The unmistakable squeak of smooth leather losing its grip on wet grass sounded nearby, followed by muffled curses.

'Take your shoes off, Seth. Your socks too. There's something very liberating and earthy about being barefoot in the countryside.'

He leaned against a nearby tree to do as she'd suggested and rolled up the bottoms of his trousers so they didn't get wet.

'If this is what getting back to nature feels like, it's slimier than I imagined.' Any Austen-esque notions about romantic walks in the country were obliterated thanks to Seth's unpoetic observations.

'Man up. For someone who spends his days elbows deep in other people's innards you shouldn't be this squeamish.'

'I tend not to walk barefoot through the operating theatre,' he said with a heavy dose of sarcasm. 'So, where does this slimy green road lead to anyway? A technicolour world with flying monkeys and grass-resistant ruby slippers for all?'

'Tobel. It's a derelict medieval village. If there's anything left of it by now. It's far enough from the usual tourist routes to hopefully avoid detection.' To be honest she'd forgotten all about the place until now. It had been relegated to the back of her mind as merely a childhood fantasy. A mythical land she'd imagined exploring in the mists of time.

Now, treading familiar ground, there was a bloom of excitement coming to life at the prospect of seeing the place again and reliving those carefree days.

'Forgive me but it doesn't sound like the ultimate escape. What's the fascination with some old ruins and how far away are they?'

'It was a place for us to hang out without being studied like lab rats. We just played hide and seek, had a moan to each other about how unfair life was, drew chalk pictures on the walls... You know, the usual kid stuff.'

'You're breaking my heart here, Princess. Some of us only had a back yard to play in. Not a whole abandoned village.'

She stuck her tongue out and teased him right back. 'I know, I know, and all you had to play with was a stick and a hoop...'

'You cheeky—'

For a second she thought she might have actually offended him as he halted their woodland walk. When he started after her, tossing his shoes aside, she let out a squeal before taking off at high speed. It was exhilarating running through the forest, branches whipping past, her heels discarded in her desire to escape Seth's false indignation. His deep laugh was sweeter than the sounds of the chirping birds watching them from high up in the treetops and she began to wonder why she was running at all.

Fate stepped in and plonked an exposed tree root in her path, causing her to trip.

'Are you okay?' Seth caught up with her in time to see the inelegant display as she landed face down on the ground.

She rolled over and sat up, dusting the dirt and leaves from her hands. 'I'm fine. It's only my pride that's taken a knock.'

'Let me give you a hand up and I swear I'll say nothing about karma.' He held out his hand to help her back onto her feet but the smug grin on his face demanded payback.

She slapped her palm against his but instead of letting him pull her up, she yanked his hand, unbalancing him so he too fell victim to the trip hazard.

Seth stumbled over the root and landed on top of her.

'S-sorry. Clearly I don't know my own strength.' She swallowed as his chest pressed so hard against hers she could feel his every rapid breath. His hands were either side of her head, braced on the ground giving him every opportunity to lever himself off her if he chose to. He didn't.

Instead, he dipped his head lower, his eyes not leaving hers, waiting for her to stop him. She couldn't find the words, or the inclination, to do so. He hesitated for a heartbeat, lips hovering so close to hers she could almost taste him. That need to kiss him suddenly consumed her body and soul. The soft pressure of his mouth on hers immediately gave way to something more passionate, more intense, more than a mere kiss.

Kaja closed her eyes and surrendered to the thrill of having Seth all to herself again. She wound her hands in his hair, revelling in the silky curls beneath her fingers, pulling him towards her to deepen their connection. Mouths and tongues entangled, breath hot and ragged, it was clear they'd both giving up fighting this powerful attraction defying their separation. For once, she didn't think about anyone else. Seth was everything. They could've been locked back in that stock room on the night shift again or tangled up in the sheets of their old double bed when the need for one another was just as great.

She shifted position, parting her thighs so Seth's body was hard against her right where she needed him most. He groaned.

'Kaja...what are you doing to me?'

The second he spoke she knew the spell had been broken.

He stopped kissing her and pulled away. She lifted her head and tried to coax him back into that blissful abyss of blood-rushing lust with kiss after kiss. Pride and dignity took a back seat in her desire to fall back into that fantasy world where only the two of them existed. Seth's touch made her forget everything bad in her life to focus on the way he made her feel. Damn good.

'We can't do this.' This time he did push himself up off her, leaving her hands empty and her body cold.

'It was only a kiss,' she said, trying to claw back some dignity as she hugged her knees to her chest to find some comfort. Aware she had been the one trying to turn it into something more.

He fixed her with his heavy-lidded eyes and gave a coy half-smile. 'Kaja, you know with us it's never going to be only a kiss.'

Seth didn't appear ashamed of succumbing to his desire, only afraid of where it would lead. Kaja understood that fear when it was exactly the same reason she should be resisting. Their circumstances might be different now but they still faced the same obstacles. Only now with added complications.

Less defensive now she knew it wasn't her he was rejecting, but the implications if they took things any further, Kaja got back on her feet. It was only then she realised she'd hurt her ankle as it buckled under her.

'Ow!' She grabbed for Seth, afraid she was about to fall over again.

'What's wrong?' He moved quickly, wrapping his arm around her waist to support her.

'I must have twisted my ankle. I can't put any weight on it.' She tried to take a step forward, which resulted in a sharp pain shooting up her leg. The adrenaline rush Seth had caused with his mouth-to-mouth technique must have temporarily blocked out the pain. She would've asked for a repeat prescription if she'd thought he'd oblige.

'You can't hobble around on that all day. We probably need to get it strapped up. Maybe we should head back?'

As well as wanting to spend more time with Seth, Kaja wasn't in a hurry to go back with her tail between her legs, or, in this case, her ankle in a plaster cast.

'We're closer to the site now than the hospital. I'll be fine.' She brushed off his concern and tried to walk on, grimacing through the pain but not yet ready to let go of her human crutch.

Seth huffed out a sigh. 'Sit down.'

He manoeuvred her over to an upturned tree trunk and made her sit while he wandered off. After a few minutes of sitting there on her own Kaja began to panic that he might have gone to get help. Visions of search teams swarming the woods looking for her made her regret this outing even if she had finally been able to kiss Seth again. She could only hope he wouldn't find himself in trouble when he reported back.

The sound she expected to hear next was helicopters or blaring sirens, not the rustle of leaves as Seth trudged back towards her swinging her heels in one hand.

'I'm not sure they'd suit you,' she said, trying to hide how inexplicably teary she was to see him, grateful he was going to help her find a way out of this mess she'd got herself into. He could easily have handed over responsibility to any one of the entourage paid to look after her.

'I'm not sure they go with a twisted ankle either but I brought them back for you.' He whacked them against the edge of the tree until the heels came off, making them into a pair of flats and leaving her wincing at the sacrifice.

It took everything she had not to squirm when he knelt down to take her foot in his hand. She was ticklish at the best of times but Seth touching her bare foot was too much to take. How often had he taken advantage of that weakness until she was screaming with laughter and they'd fallen into bed in a tangle of limbs? Except this time he was deadly serious as he examined her, showing no memory of those fun times that had always led to something more passionate.

'Can you move it? Good. It's a bit red but not too swollen. You probably need to rest it.'

'How am I going to do that? Hover?' Okay, her ego was as bruised as her ankle if he'd forgotten her little quirk so readily.

He turned around and crouched down. While he was giving her a good look at his tight backside, she wasn't sure what he was expecting her to do.

'Right, jump on.'

'Excuse me?' It was true she wanted to climb him like a tree but he'd made it abundantly clear that wasn't an option.

'You can't walk and taxis are scarce out here. Think of me as your trusty steed.' He whinnied and pawed the ground with his foot. Boy, she missed his silly sense of humour. It hadn't died after all. He must have buried it along with his feelings for her but the more time they spent together, the more she got to see flashes of the old Seth.

'You're kidding, right?' He couldn't possibly expect her to climb on his back and let him carry her not inconsiderable weight to their destination.

'Not at all.' He slapped his backside and crouched down a little more until his trousers were stretched tight around his peachy behind. 'Now climb on before I can't get up again.'

'Only if you're sure. I don't want us both lying crocked out here waiting for a rescue team to come and find us. Think of the scandal!' She shook her head, wondering how she'd found herself in such a ludicrous position. Kaja climbing onto the back of her father's transplant surgeon, barefoot and covered in grass stains, was a million-dollar photo op. Seth Davenport was making her reckless and she'd be lying if she said that wasn't the biggest thrill she'd had in years.

CHAPTER EIGHT

SETH'S PLAN TO break out of Kaja's claustrophobic existence with her in the hope it would provide some space
had backfired spectacularly now she was clinging onto
his back like a baby monkey.

'Are you comfy back there?'

'I wouldn't say "comfy", exactly, but you're saving
my ankle. I'm not so sure about your back though.' She
shifted her position to sit higher and strengthened her
hold around him.

With the soft mounds of her breasts rubbing against
him, legs wrapped territorially around his waist and
cheek brushing against his, his back wasn't the part of
his body he was worried about.

'Don't you worry about me. You're light as a feather.'

'Liar!' She slapped him playfully on the shoulder but
made no attempt to disengage herself. Seth was simply
glad he could do something to help. This whole sorry
debacle had been his idea and now, not only were they
probably causing mass panic back at the hospital, but
she was hurt. Something he'd never seen coming. Along
with that kiss.

He didn't know where he'd found the strength to end
it but it had saved them both from making any further
mistakes. Getting together again could only end in a mess

and more heartache when he inevitably returned home to England. Perhaps that was part of the reason he'd agreed to come to her country when he knew he'd be the one leaving this time. Ensuring his departure meant there was no way she could hurt him. He hadn't counted on causing his own self-destruction by kissing her.

Now they'd crossed that boundary and let passion take over it was going to be difficult not to let it happen again.

The pilgrimage to her childhood hangout wasn't an easy one without a well-worn path to follow. There were dips and hills, rocky outcrops and streams to navigate along the way. As a reasonably fit adult man he would've struggled even without his Kaja backpack. It would've been even more of a trek for two young kids from the palace. He could only imagine the pressure of their heritage, which had driven them all the way out here on their own. It showed the strain she was currently under when this was the first place she thought of to escape to for a while.

'Oh, no. It looks like we're not the only ones visiting today.' Kaja pointed up ahead. Right beside the site of the crumbling grey ruins of a once bustling village was the juxtaposition of a bright red, super modern hatchback.

'Best case—they don't know who you are and we can hitch a lift back with them. Worst case—you let them take a few selfies and they give us a lift.' They'd had their adventure en route, rolling around in the grass together.

'I suppose so… In that case I should probably walk the rest of the way. We wouldn't want to draw any more attention than necessary.'

She had a point. Regardless if these other visitors knew they were in the presence of royalty or not, the sight of two people in medical attire piggybacking in from the woods was going to seem a little strange.

He crouched down to allow her to step away.

'Do I have to book a time slot for the tour or can we do it now?' As keen as he was to get Kaja back for medical attention and prevent any further concern as to her whereabouts, he was curious about the place. From the day she'd left him it had struck him that he'd never known her at all. He'd learned something of her background having lived it himself these past few days, but hearing more about her childhood might provide him with better insight into what had made her who she was today.

'There's not much call for my services. I can't tell you a lot about the history of Tobel. I'm sorry to say that wasn't important to an impetuous nine-year-old. However, if you'd like to see the very spot where I first beat my big brother in an obstacle race, or hear about the time I befriended a stray dog and kept him as my secret pet, then I'm your girl.' She limped ahead of him, apparently eager to revisit this place that held such treasured memories for her.

'Sounds perfect.' This was what he'd wanted for her all along. A chance to forget everything going on at the hospital and simply enjoy herself.

Thankfully the occupants of the car were more interested in the picnic they'd spread out on the outer wall of the old village and didn't see them approach. Seth made a note to do the same with Amy when he got the chance. Perhaps not here, but he was sure she'd love a picnic out in the countryside.

Seth's stomach growled with hunger as they made their way along the cobbled street towards the tumbledown houses of yesteryear. He could see Kaja's foot already beginning to swell. Stumbling over this uneven ground with her foot wedged into broken shoes wasn't going to help. She'd be lucky if she could walk on it at all by the end of the day. Although, as she hovered in the doorway of one higgledy-piggledy building it was obvious she wanted to do some exploring before they thought about making their way home again.

'Is it the same as you remember?' There was a certain kind of beauty about a place where wild flowers were springing out of the glassless windows, the pale lemon and blues providing some colour against the grey stone. Nature had taken over from the last inhabitants and decorated accordingly. Even the weeds and moss that had set up home in every crack and groove of the crumbling structure had a certain aesthetic charm.

'A little more overgrown perhaps, but basically the same.' She ducked her head under the arched doorway and ventured inside with Seth following close behind.

'Smaller than I remember.' They walked through the remains of someone's house with only partial walls separating each of the rooms. 'I think the elements have taken their toll too.'

Seth could hear the tinge of sadness in her voice as she traced her hand over the faded mural barely there on what remained of the plaster. There were some flourishes and cornices left from what must have been a decorative abode at one time. Definitely a place where one could let their imagination run wild.

'Sometimes we look back on things with rose-tinted glasses. Reality doesn't always match up with the memories we might have embellished over the years.' Though, if this had been abandoned centuries ago he couldn't see it was in much better condition when Kaja and Bruno were here as children.

The look she gave him made him feel as though he'd taken her favourite childhood toy and set fire to it.

'I'm sorry if meeting me again has been such a disappointment to you, Seth. Speaking for myself, I have no regrets about anything we've done. You met all the expectations I had based on my memories.' With that, she flounced out, leaving Seth scratching his head about what had caused the outburst. It took a minute too long for him to realise the misunderstanding.

'Wait… Kaja… I wasn't talking about us. I don't regret what happened between us back there either. If anything, being with you, kissing you, is even better than I remember.' He followed her into the next almost-room, her upset at believing he was unaffected by their tryst totally understandable.

She had her back to him, arms wrapped around her waist in a gesture of self-comfort that caused him physical pain on her behalf. He placed his hand on her elbow and gently turned her to face him.

'Hey, I was talking about the village, not us.' He gave her a soft smile, trying to coax one back in response. 'I didn't want to stop kissing you. That was the problem.'

Her mouth formed a perfect 'O'. 'Honestly?'

'Honestly.' He knew he shouldn't do it, yet Seth couldn't seem to stop himself from reaching out and tipping her chin up to make her look at him. The beautiful sad eyes and the pouting pink lips were too much for him to ignore.

He rested his lips on hers. Only for a second. Enough to comfort her and satisfy his need to feel her mouth against his one more time. He closed his eyes and blocked out the forsaken terrain around them, the soft touch of Kaja's lips transporting him to paradise instead.

It wasn't supposed to be a replay of their time on the forest floor, yet when Kaja sighed and let her arms fall away from their defensive position he wanted her closer. He pulled her body flush with his and that comforting kiss developed into a passionate display of his feelings for her.

It was pointless denying it any more when he'd known from the second he'd set eyes on Kaja again he'd never stopped loving her. With Amy to take care of he'd been able to deny that fact and convince himself his heart only had room for his daughter. Now he was confronted with the person he'd so desperately wanted to share his life with and slowly rediscovering the woman he loved, those feelings refused to remain hidden.

They might not have a future together but he was willing to fully embrace the present.

Kaja was a fool. Why did she ever think she could live without this man and how had she managed it until now? It was only having him here in her world she understood what she was missing when his kisses were giving her life. She didn't care how stupid she'd been mistaking his comments about the ruins as a narrative on their relationship when it had prompted him into confessing his feelings for her. At least he still had some even if they weren't as strong as before. With her hands she reacquainted herself with the contours of his body while reuniting her tongue, her lips and her heart with his.

Seth held her, warming her back yet still managing to make her shiver. He was here, he was real, and, for now, all that mattered. When he slid a hand up inside her scrubs she held her breath, his palm grazing her ribs and reaching further to cup her breast. She let out a shaky breath as he brushed his thumb lightly across the silky material of her bra, bringing the sensitive peak of flesh to attention.

She wanted his touch, to feel skin on skin so badly she was practically begging him with her body. Grinding against him, she could feel his arousal standing proud and ready through the thin layer of clothing between them.

Seth groaned and in one swift move lifted her off her feet, hitched her legs up around his waist and carried her over to the recess at the window.

'Seth…we can't do this here.' Somewhere at the back of her mind beyond the rushing blood and carnal thoughts she remembered they had company outside.

'I know,' he said before claiming her again in another frantic coupling of mouths and tongues. Confirming he knew they couldn't get carried away any further than they already had but was as powerless as Kaja was in fighting this tidal wave of desire. Now it had broken free she didn't know how they were going to stem it again.

A loud rumble reverberated through the room, so strong it seemed to shake the very ground beneath them.

'I didn't know trains ran this far out.' Seth broke off the kiss, apparently as startled as she was by the loud sound suddenly approaching.

'They don't. There aren't any tracks out this way.' Come to think of it, the dirt roads out here wouldn't usually be travelled by any vehicles larger than the car parked outside.

It was only when the very walls of the building seemed to move with them that it dawned on her what could be causing the noise.

'Earthquake,' she shouted over the grinding noise coming from the earth below.

The warning came too late to get out of the seriously precarious structure as the underground monster roared its arrival. The ground undulated and warped as though they were on a roller-coaster ride they couldn't get off. Where once Kaja and Seth had been in the midst of a passionate embrace, now they were clinging to one another in an attempt to stay upright.

'Aren't we supposed to go and stand in the doorway?' he shouted, trying to pull her in that direction.

She resisted, shaking her head. 'It's not stable enough.'

With that, the world seemed to cave in around them. Walls were collapsing, including the arched doorway, their only means of escape. Plaster began to fall in chunks around them. Seth covered her head with his hands and pulled her down onto the ground with him, using his body as a shield to protect her from the falling debris.

Kaja had never been in an actual earthquake as there hadn't been one here in living history but she had a vague recollection of what to do should one ever occur. She thanked the heavens she had Seth with her providing comfort in a terrifying situation. He was the only stable thing she had to hold onto at a time when she couldn't even rely on the *terra*-not-so-*firma*.

She scrunched her eyes shut, her head against Seth's chest. Unfortunately, she couldn't turn off the sound, every dull crack and thud as debris rained down reminding her how very small and fragile they were. There was every chance that neither of them would come out of this when there seemed no end in sight to the destruction happening right on top of them.

'We are going to get out of this, Kaja.' He kissed her forehead, providing a moment of calm tenderness in the midst of such overwhelming chaos. Then he added, 'We have to,' with such a determined look on his face she believed him.

Amy. He was thinking about his daughter, of course he was. With that came the horror of what was happening to all of their loved ones: her father, Bruno, Fatima. There was no time to descend into hysterics and what ifs as another crash of rubble sounded. Along with a sharp curse from Seth.

'Are you all right?' She'd felt him tense at the same time as the new fall of debris and poked her head out of her Seth cocoon to make sure he was all right when he was bearing the brunt of the blows to save her.

'I'm fine.' He was much too abrupt to convince her.

Sure enough as she reached up to brush the dusty swoop of hair from his face, her fingers encountered a sticky patch of blood at his temple.

'You're bleeding.'

'I'll live.' He kept turning his head and trying to put her off but she could see the cut and wasn't going to rest until she examined it. A head injury wasn't something to simply brush off. Thankfully there was only a trickle of blood so it likely didn't need stitches.

'You'd better.'

As quickly as the world seemed to erupt around them, the upheaval subsided again, the roar fading along with that sensation of being at sea. It couldn't have lasted for any more than a minute but it had been an eternity waiting to find out if they'd live through it all.

'Quick, let's get out of here in case there are any aftershocks.' Paying no heed to his injury Seth grabbed her hands and pulled her to her feet.

Her legs wobbled as though she'd spent months on the ocean and had just set foot on land again. It was difficult to see, darkness having descended along with a curtain of dust, but when it cleared the state of the devastation was obvious.

'The door's gone.' The archway, along with most of the walls that had been holding up what was left of the building, were a mound of slate and brick. Looking around, she could see how lucky they'd been in the grand scheme of things.

They could have been buried alive. She shuddered

when she recalled how Seth had cradled her with his body. She would never have forgiven herself if he'd died sacrificing himself to save her.

Unfortunately, they discovered none of the original exits had survived. They'd literally been entombed in her favourite childhood playground. The angle one of the beams had fallen and thankfully created a pocket of air around them so they had space to move.

Seth began shifting the biggest obstacles, kicking and pushing until there was a large enough gap for them to break out of their stone igloo.

'C'mon!' There was an understandable urgency in him as he reached back for her. They had to get out into an open space before any further ructions erased any chance of them escaping.

Kaja followed through the tunnel he was burrowing through the rubble, incapable of speech until they saw daylight and Seth pulled her through to safety. They collapsed in a heap on the grass outside, breathing heavily from a combination of physical exertion and fear.

'I don't even know where we are.' It was disorienting when nothing looked the same as when they'd first arrived. Most of the old buildings were now reduced to little more than a pile of rubble amidst a cloud of dirt and debris. She didn't know why she wasn't a hysterical mess screaming and crying after the trauma of what they'd been through. What they might still go through. She was clearly in some sort of shock, trying to process what had just happened.

Seth stood up and paced around. Even he didn't look quite as steady on his feet as usual. Kaja wasn't sure she could even stand again.

'Come over here and let me look at that head injury.'

'It's nothing.'

'Let me be the judge of that,' she insisted, unwilling to take any chances in the circumstances.

He reluctantly came back to her, not wanting a fuss but bending down so she could make a closer inspection of the wound. Using the hem of her top, she gently dabbed at the blood, cleaning the site enough so she could see the extent of the cut. 'It's not too deep. I think it'll heal itself. No need for improvised stitching.'

'Good. Can we focus on something more important now?'

'There's no need to be tetchy. I just want to make sure you're safe.'

'I know. Sorry. I think we came out the back of the house. We should be safe out here away from any more falling wreckage.'

Kaja glanced back at the way they'd come. From this vantage point on the hill she could see plumes of smoke in the city and now the thundering sound had stopped she could hear sirens going off everywhere. They were isolated with no idea what had gone on in the rest of the country or who was hurt. It was part luck, part Seth that had saved them, but there was no way of knowing what was happening elsewhere to everyone else or how bad the devastation.

Seth had the same thought as he pulled his phone from his pocket. They both waited as the call rang out until they eventually heard Fatima's voice.

'Are you and Amy okay?'

'Yes, Mr Davenport. We hid under the dining table. No one got hurt. How are you and Miss Kaja?'

The line went dead and Seth tried again and again to reconnect without success. 'I don't have any signal. At a guess I'd say all lines are down and the power's probably out.'

'At least we know they're all right. Fatima will keep Amy safe. What about Papa and Bruno...? Seth, what'll happen to them?' Her heart was in an ever-tightening vice as she thought back to all the machinery monitoring them. Her father especially, who was so vulnerable after the transplant.

Seth walked back to her and took a seat on the grass again. 'Hey, they'll be fine. Surely the hospital will have emergency power for a situation like this?'

She knew they would, yet it wasn't any consolation. Logic wasn't getting a look-in when emotions and her imagination were running wild. 'We have to get back.'

'Don't you think I know that?' he snapped. 'My daughter is miles away, frightened, without her daddy but we can't go anywhere. We'd be taking a risk going back through the trees if there are further aftershocks. The same if we take the road. We could get hit by all sorts of debris and there's always a chance the roads themselves could open up. That's if you hadn't hurt your ankle and were capable of walking back. We're going to have to wait this out. No matter how hard it is not knowing what's happening to our loved ones.'

He was trying so hard to be strong for her but Kaja could hear how choked up he was about Amy. The way he'd protected her and dug them out of that house with his bare hands...she knew he'd have done the same for his daughter. This separation had to be so much worse for him.

She reached across and squeezed his hand. 'Fatima will take care of her and the palace is one of the safest places to be. When it was remodelled for our family it was extensively renovated to withstand any eventuality.'

'It's just...there's so much in that house which could fall on her. The heavy furniture, the chandeliers...she's only a little thing.' The catch in his voice threatened to undo them both. Kaja needed him to stay strong or she'd lose it altogether too.

'Fatima knew to take cover as soon as the earthquake hit and they're fine. I'm sure the rest of the staff will be taking care of them too.'

'You're right. If we start thinking the worst we'll go around the bend. We need to focus on us for now. Until we can get back and do something to help.'

Good. Seth was taking back control. That made it easier for her to hold it together too.

'That siren sounds awfully close.' She couldn't help but hope someone knew where they were and had sent the emergency services to their rescue.

Seth scrambled to his feet. 'It's a car alarm.'

'The tourists. Maybe we can get a ride back with them.' The notion that they had a solution right here galvanised her back into action too. She tried not to think about the pain in her ankle returning now that the adrenaline had worn off. With any luck she wouldn't have to walk much further.

They followed the blaring noise and the flashing lights back to where the car was parked. The windows were smashed, glass everywhere, but it was still standing.

'Where did they go?' She looked around but there was no sign of the family who'd been sitting nearby. It felt as though the roller coaster went into free fall again, leaving her stomach somewhere on the ground.

'What if they're in there?' Seth voiced her fear as he looked back towards the empty skyline where the village had once stood.

Neither of them wanted to venture back there for their own sake but they were both medics and knew it had to be done.

CHAPTER NINE

'YOU STAY HERE. I'll go and look for them.'

'Like hell. I'm coming with you.' There was no way she was going to let him go back in there alone. If the past few minutes had shown her anything it was that they needed each other to survive and she wasn't going to stand back and let him put himself in danger.

Seth opened his mouth to protest and she folded her arms across her chest and pursed her lips. He wisely closed his mouth again and headed back towards the devastated village they'd literally just crawled out from.

'Hello? Is there anybody here?' he called as they walked into the courtyard that had once been the centre of the village. Now it was simply the epicentre of the destruction.

Any bright colour nature had once displayed had been obliterated by layers of grey as far as the eye could see. Glancing at what little was left of the buildings, Kaja realised how incredibly lucky they'd been. The house they'd wandered into was unrecognisable as a structure at all, her beloved mural now nothing but a few painted bricks scattered here and there.

'Maybe they ran off when it started?' Optimistic, perhaps, but she really didn't want Seth putting himself in jeopardy again for anyone.

'They wouldn't have had time to get very far and there's no one to be seen for miles out here.' Undeterred by the resounding silence, he kept walking further into the danger zone.

Kaja took a deep breath, refusing to let him go it alone but not without some trepidation. The next time the earth shook they mightn't be so fortunate.

'Hello? Can anyone hear us?' He put his hands to his mouth to amplify his plea for signs of life. With the car alarm still blaring in the background it was difficult to hear anything else. The place had a distinct Pompeii vibe. How Kaja imagined it after everything had been wiped out by Vesuvius.

They climbed up what felt like two storeys of wreckage listening for anything to indicate there was someone here who needed their help.

Kaja thought she heard movement where the row of houses opposite the one they'd been inside had once stood.

'Seth! Over here.' She moved closer to investigate and beckoned him over. They began excavating the site on their hands and knees, certain there was someone beneath the remains.

'We're going to get you out,' Kaja called out, trying to provide some reassurance to whoever was trapped.

They heard whimpering far below and Seth became a man possessed, tearing away boulders with his bare hands, sweat trickling down his face. Both of them were covered in dirt, skin and nails torn to shreds before they made any progress. The small gap they managed to open up provided a peephole where Kaja could see the tear-streaked face of the little girl who'd been picnicking with her family staring back at her.

She sat back on her heels, stunned at the sight of the

frightened child buried alive. It took Seth a heartbeat too before he resumed scrabbling at the rocks in desperation and she knew he was thinking this could easily have been his daughter.

'We'll get you out, honey. Is there anyone else with you?' Kaja kept talking, getting the child to focus on her as the rocky world around her shifted once more.

The little girl nodded her head. Not a good sign. There had been a family, parents and a child enjoying the afternoon sunshine, and now only silence.

Kaja had to look away so the little girl wouldn't see her welling up. She was bound to be terrified enough without having an adult making things worse.

All of a sudden Seth stopped digging and sat up.

'What is it? What's wrong?'

'Shh! I thought I heard something over there.' He pointed to a spot close to him and they took a breather, listening until they heard a faint cry for help.

Seth glanced at the place where the little girl was waiting to be rescued, then back to where they'd located a new survivor.

'Go. I'll get her.' He'd already done most of the heavy lifting and the little girl was okay as far as they could tell. If there was someone else buried here Seth could rescue her and Kaja would concentrate on the child.

He didn't waste any time debating the subject, having the same confidence in her capabilities as she had in his.

Kaja cleared the obstacles as quickly and as deftly as she could. Hearing Seth murmur to the woman who was stuck down there was comforting and she believed every word he said about getting everyone out safely.

She was lying across the rubble now, stones and bricks jabbing into her ribs and every other part of her body in contact with the jagged floor beneath her.

'Here's my hand, honey. Can you grab it? Good girl.' Her cheek was practically embedded with part of the village landscape as she reached down through the gap. Even if she couldn't get the girl out right away she could assure her she wouldn't let go of her until someone did.

'Okay, sweetie, hold on with both hands and I'll pull you out of there.'

Although she was only a little thing, Kaja was sure she was going to dislocate both shoulders with the strain of wrenching her up through the hole alone.

'If you could put your foot on that rock…good girl.' With one last heave she pulled the child free and collapsed on the uneven ground, panting for breath.

Once she managed to control her breathing Kaja turned to check on the little girl. 'Are you hurt anywhere?'

She shook her head. Eyes wide with fear, face stained with dirt and clothes torn, she resembled a Victorian street urchin. Not someone who only a short time ago had been having the time of her life with her family. Kaja's heart went out to her, hoping she'd be reunited with them soon.

She remembered the child had indicated someone else was down there with her but Kaja hadn't seen or heard anything other than the debris continuing to fall.

'Is there someone else down there?'

She nodded.

'Are they awake?'

She shook her head. Kaja understood she was in shock but she could really use some help to establish who was down there and in what condition. With Seth still bulldozing his way through the adjacent site it was down to her to locate any further survivors and get to them as soon as possible.

If there was someone else stuck down there she wasn't going to be able to get them out herself. Then again, she couldn't call Seth away from his task until she knew what they were up against.

'I'm going to go down and see if I can help. I need you to run over to that man there and he'll keep you safe until I come back up. Okay?'

Another nod. If anything happened while she was down there she knew Seth would get this little one to safety. There was a slight hesitation but Kaja assured her she'd join her soon. She took a deep breath to steel herself before she climbed into the gap they'd made in the rubble. It was a tight squeeze but the discomfort as she shimmied down was bearable. Whoever was down here had surely endured worse.

She dropped onto the ledge accessible through the new skylight they'd installed. From there she had to pick her way carefully down the loose stones and step down onto the ground. 'Hello? Is there someone down here? I got your daughter out. She's safe. Can you make a noise so I can find you?' The only sound she could hear was Seth's nearby excavation work.

It was dark and ominous in the depths of the devastated building. There was every chance the whole lot could come down on her at any time as she moved from room to room, climbing over mounds of rock. Her ankle screamed every time she jarred it on an uneven surface but she persevered.

When she came to the area of the building that seemed to have suffered the brunt of the damage, making it largely inaccessible, she was ready to give up the quest. Except as Kaja went to leave she spotted a flash of colour breaking through the grey. She bent down to take a closer look and there, buried in the landslide, was the very definite shape of an adult male whose bright Hawaiian shirt might have just saved his life.

'Can you hear me?' Kaja began to move the rocks around the rest of his body, careful not to knock anything more on top of him. His face was turned away from her but when she checked his wrist she could feel a rapid pulse beating against her fingers. It was a relief to know he was still alive but a fast heartbeat could also be an indication of serious injury. She needed a better look but he was unconscious and there was no way she could move him on her own when he was pinned under several large boulders.

'What the hell do you think you're doing coming down here on your own and scaring me half to death?' Seth's disapproval boomed around the enclosed space and gave Kaja such a fright her heart nearly popped out of her chest. Any more surprises today and she'd find herself in a hospital bed along with the rest of her family.

'There's a man trapped under the rocks.' She ignored his irritation at her to concentrate on the important matter at hand.

He came over to help but not without muttering about how stupid she was for putting herself in danger. As though he wouldn't have done exactly the same thing.

'He hasn't gained consciousness since I found him and his pulse is too fast for my liking.'

'We're going to have to get him out of here.'

'What about the woman you were helping?' She was almost afraid to ask in case the latest rescue attempt hadn't been successful.

'She's fine. A few cuts and bruises but she's with her daughter now. It was her who directed me over here. When I couldn't find you...' His face was dark. He was angry with her and it was only now she could see what it would've looked like when she disappeared. The last time he'd seen her she'd been digging in the rubble. A few minutes later she'd vanished, with only a hole remaining where she'd once stood.

'Sorry. I wasn't thinking about anything other than helping.'

'Right, well, no more disappearing acts. I don't think my heart can take it.'

It was a throwaway comment but the sentiment behind it meant the world. He was worried about her. As he'd so gallantly displayed during the earthquake, he cared. She wasn't going to let that slip through her hands again but they could talk about that when this crisis was over.

'First things first, we need to move him.' This guy was twice her size and she had been foolish to think she could do that on her own. It remained to be seen if they could do it now.

It would've been preferable for them to stabilise him with a neck brace and a back board until he had his injuries assessed properly in hospital. There was a danger of paralysis but life came before injury and getting him out of here was crucial to his survival. They couldn't risk another rock slide in here in case it injured him further. Crush injuries could prove lethal unless promptly treated.

Kaja pulled her ponytail loose and used the hair tie to apply a tourniquet above the injury site prior to moving the rock. 'Hopefully that will prevent the release of toxins into his bloodstream.'

Once she had limited the blood flow to the injured leg, Seth jumped over to try and shift the weight hampering their progress. Working together like this was reminiscent of those busy nights in A & E when their paths had occasionally crossed during an emergency. It was the same rush of adrenaline and understanding of each other's roles that made them such a good team. That didn't always happen with fellow surgeons and was probably more to do with their genuine affection and respect for one another.

'I'm…not…sure…I…can…lift…it.' Regardless that Seth was bound to be exhausted she could hear the effort he was putting in attempting to dislodge the obstacle.

'If you can shift it a fraction, maybe I could drag him out from under it.' Kaja grabbed the shoulders of the gawdy shirt and got ready to pull him free.

Seth manoeuvred himself between the man and the boulder and with a huff of breath braced his back against the rock to lever it off. His legs were shaking and his face was a violent shade of red with the strain he was putting on his body.

'I've got him.' Kaja hauled him out while Seth took the weight of the rock. Once he was free Seth let out a grunt and dropped the boulder as gently as he could without dislodging any more stones.

'His pallor is a little blue. A direct trauma to his chest during the rock fall could have fractured his ribs and punctured his lung.' Kaja had done her best not to jolt the man too much as she'd wiggled him free but there was no way of telling how much internal damage might have been caused during his ordeal. If air had collected in the space between the layers of tissue lining his lungs it would prevent them from expanding properly.

She put her ear down to the man's chest to listen to his breathing and the short, gurgling breaths did nothing to relieve her anxiety. 'We could be dealing with a traumatic pneumothorax. If we don't release that pressure he could suffocate.'

'We don't have the luxury of medical facilities to help him or even access to a chest tube to help drain the air.'

'We'll have to improvise. I don't suppose you've got a pen on you?' She was only half joking, having seen this scene dramatised in a number of TV programmes. In real life it was a risky move with too much room for error. However, in these circumstances they were out of options.

Seth emptied the contents of his trouser pockets into his hands. While there wasn't a pen, he did have a mini pocket knife. Literally, a lifesaver.

'What's in this?' Kaja pointed to a small metal tin he held.

'It's a reusable metal straw. Amy's very insistent on using it instead of the plastic ones, which could find their way into the ocean and choke a turtle or something.'

'Good girl. That has to be an improvement on an empty pen barrel. Although, I think you might have to buy a new one after this.'

'No worries. I keep it scrupulously clean so it should be sterile enough to use.' The tin contained the tiniest brushes Kaja had ever seen so she didn't doubt him.

'Okay. I'm going to make a small incision with the knife for access and insert the straw to let the air out. That should let the lungs expand again and help him breathe.' These weren't the ideal conditions to work in with so much dust and dirt but they were far from help and if they did nothing, this man wouldn't make it. Neither she nor Seth would stand and watch him die without trying their best to save him.

Seth opened up the man's shirt, exposing the torso so Kaja could work. 'You can do this.' Seth urged her on as the butterflies in her stomach threatened to fight their way up and out.

In England she'd thrived with every emergency that came through the hospital doors. Although she did her best to keep her hand in at the hospital here, this felt as though it was the first time she'd really been tested on her home turf.

She could do this, she knew that deep down, but she was thankful for his encouragement. Any other capable surgeon might have tried to muscle their way in and take over. It was reassuring that he believed in her as much as he always had where her job was concerned. They worked as easily together as ever, happy to let the other take the lead when necessary. Much like their relationship. Seth had never put any pressure on her to do anything, letting her do everything at her own pace so she was comfortable. Including moving in with him, which had taken her some time to agree to as it had seemed such a huge step at the time. Seth had always believed in her and, despite everything since, that had never changed.

Kaja felt her way along the patient's torso until she was sure she'd located a gap between the lower ribs. A deep breath to steady herself and she plunged the tip of the small knife in, allowing the trapped air to escape. Seth passed her the metal straw to insert in order to keep the airway open.

'Ideally, we'd have some surgical tape to keep that in place.'

'Sorry. I don't keep that on me but it's a foldaway straw. Perhaps if you retract it as much as possible there's less chance of it falling out.' He held the base of the straw steady in the site, letting her push it down as far as it would go.

Kaja tried to be as gentle as possible when there was no pain relief available but their patient remained unconscious throughout.

It was vital they got him to hospital as soon as possible so surgeons could use the appropriate equipment to repair the injuries but how? They were both running on empty, he was a big guy and there was no way they could carry him back up the way they'd come in.

'We need to find a way to keep him lying flat and stretcher him out.'

'Easier said than done, Seth.' If they'd had access to the emergency services that wouldn't have been too much of a problem. However, this emergency rescue rested solely on their shoulders.

'We should be able to tunnel our way back out to the main courtyard.

Kaja didn't know if he was trying to convince her or himself. Even if they managed to get him out there were still risks of him suffering from infection, inflammation or fluid developing in the lung. At worst, cardiac arrest. For everyone's safety they needed to get out of here before they were hit by any further complications.

'Should we enlist some extra help from outside?' The only other available pairs of hands belonged to the two they'd just dug out but they had run out of options.

'Good idea. I'll go back out, try and pinpoint where we need to go and get his family to start working from the other side. At least that way we might cut down on the time.' Along with the effort required.

She waited for Seth to climb back out of the hole above and listened for him on the other side. Eventually, she heard him shouting. 'Kaja, let me know when we're close.'

'Kaja?' Seth shouted again, closer this time.

She moved as close to the outer wall as she could. 'I'm here, Seth.'

That all too familiar sound of scraping and tumbling rocks began again and she waited for those on the outside to clear a path to them. It was hard manual labour in the heat as well as stressful. She was beginning to wonder if the nightmare would ever end. It seemed as though they'd been living on the edge of hell for hours now when in reality it was probably only a matter of minutes.

After a while she could see a chink of light through the gap made in the outer wall. It grew steadily bigger until Seth was visible on the other side working alongside the woman he'd rescued from nearby. Even the little girl was helping to move the rocks aside.

Once there was enough room for Seth to pass through he joined her inside and between them they lifted the incapacitated man. Seth grabbed him under the armpits and Kaja grabbed his legs. He was heavy but they were careful not to knock out the straw chest tube, carrying their patient until he was free from the danger of being hit by any more falling debris.

'Do you have the keys to the car?' Seth asked the woman crying over her husband's battered body, stroking his face and begging him to wake up.

'My husband had them.' She sniffed and searched his pockets. There was a collective sigh of relief when she produced them. They would never have found them if they'd fallen out along the way.

'We need to get him to the hospital for X-rays. He might have a punctured lung so we've put this tube in to help him breathe better. Can you drive?' Kaja asked the woman, aware that this car was the only available means to get back and they didn't even know if it was drivable.

She nodded, pulling her little girl close.

'Go and get the car and bring it back here. We're going to have to put the back seat down and lay him flat in the back to prevent as much movement as we can. You'll have to keep an eye on that straw to make sure it's not dislodged on the journey.' Seth issued the orders with so much authority no one questioned him.

It was a blessed relief when the car alarm was turned off. Once the car was reversed in as close as they could get it, Seth cleared the glass from the interior.

They lifted their patient again, Seth backing up inside the car so they could fit him comfortably on the passenger side lengthways.

Kaja gave the terrified wife directions to the hospital as she clutched the steering wheel. 'Try to avoid driving close to any trees or any other large structures in case there are any aftershocks.'

'I think you should squeeze in there too, Kaja.' Seth's last-minute suggestion threw her so much she nearly lost her professional composure.

'No!'

'You're hurt. It makes sense for one of us to try and get help. I'll be fine here. There's nothing to stop me walking back along the road.' He was being sincere but that only strengthened her resolve to stay with him.

'There's no way I'm leaving you behind.' She'd done that once too often.

'Kaja—'

She ignored his plea and put her own to the woman in the car. 'If you could let someone know we're out here and need transport back, we'd be very grateful.'

'I'll do my best. Thank you so much for everything.'

They said their goodbyes and wished each other luck before Kaja and Seth waved the family off.

'You didn't have to stay with me.'

'Yes, I did.'

He sighed, apparently getting the message she wasn't going to back down over that. She was done being selfish.

'You were amazing back there,' he told her, downplaying the lives he'd rescued too.

'All part of the day job. It felt good to be back in the thick of things. Although, I'd have preferred to have been working in a more traditional setting.'

'That makes two of us. Still, if we hadn't been here that family wouldn't have got out alive.'

The thought made her shiver but it also gave her a boost knowing she'd made a difference today. Her work as a surgeon was more important than anything she did in a royal capacity and infinitely more fulfilling. A matter she couldn't ignore now their close call with death was making her reassess the choices she'd made and the unhappy life she'd been living as a result.

CHAPTER TEN

'YOU KNOW, YOU could've increased our chances of getting rescued if you'd told her who you were,' Seth said with a bemused grin.

Kaja wrinkled her nose at the suggestion. 'I wouldn't do that. In this situation we're all in the same boat. It wouldn't be fair to divert emergency services when they're needed much more elsewhere. We're not hurt, we're safe. If she passes the message on someone will get to us eventually.'

She didn't count her ankle as a serious injury when it was neither life-threatening nor caused by the earthquake. Even if it was throbbing like hell.

'My Kaja. Always putting other people first.' Seth put an arm around her shoulders and kissed her forehead.

She wanted to fall into his arms and pick up where they'd left off before nature had roared its disapproval but so much had happened since then. Seth's worry for his daughter, for all those caught in the quake, had overridden any discussion about their relationship. Even if there was some way of sustaining a long-distance romance the issue over her divided loyalties remained. They were both going to have to make big life changes to make it work. In her case there was one huge problem that couldn't be overcome with desire alone.

He led her outside the perimeter of the village back onto safer ground out in the open.

Kaja spotted some objects lying in the field behind the ruins of the wall where the family had been having their lunch earlier. They walked over to find a rolled-up blanket and the remains of their picnic in a cooler box.

'Okay, we've got a bottle of water, an orange and some breadsticks.' Seth discarded the half-eaten sandwich and the dubious-looking yoghurt back in the cooler. Hopefully they'd get picked up before they had to resort to eating any of that.

He spread the tartan rug out on the grass for them to sit on. The light was beginning to fade as the evening drew in but thankfully it was still warm. If help didn't arrive soon there was every chance they'd be spending the night under the stars.

'Do we need to ration the food or can we feast?' Kaja teased as she held up the meagre provisions they'd scavenged.

'I'm willing to take the chance we're going to get rescued before we resort to divvying out crumbs. We haven't eaten since breakfast and I think we deserve a little treat. Now, would madam prefer an orange segment or the bread course first?'

'Mmm, I think I'd like to start with some orange, thank you.'

It was ridiculous sitting out here in the aftermath of an earthquake joking and pretending that things were all right but Seth wanted to make Kaja laugh rather than have her dwell on things beyond their control.

He didn't want to think about what could have happened to her back there either, when he'd come close to losing her. For ever this time. Her stubborn refusal to go with the others and stay with him had been touching. If she'd been more concerned with her own welfare she would've gone to the hospital. It proved, along with their earlier kisses, that he was more to her than a house guest or simply here for her father's benefit. He didn't know what that meant for them but, for now, he was happy they were together.

He peeled the orange for her, the sweet, refreshing scent of citrus preferable to the earthiness and dust they'd been breathing in since the quake hit.

Kaja popped a piece in her mouth and closed her eyes. 'Mmm. That tastes so good.'

He had to agree. On a day like today one small piece of fruit had suddenly become the best thing he'd ever eaten.

'Could I also recommend our house water to accompany the dish?' He opened the bottled water and offered her the first sip.

Kaja waved the bottle under her nose, took a drink and swilled the water around her mouth before swallowing. They were being silly. A kind of hysterical reaction to the trauma they'd just been through. It didn't last and they fell silent as they devoured the rest of the orange. His body was becoming weary now and his muscles were aching after all the heavy lifting he'd been doing. He lay down on the blanket leaving Kaja sitting up, nursing what was left of the bottle of water.

Only moments after closing his eyes there was that ominous rumbling below the earth. He felt Kaja tense beside him, as the ground shook and forced them back onto that unwanted fairground ride. It was impossible to remain flat when every tremor was reverberating through his body. He sat up and hugged Kaja until the world stopped trembling. It was all he could do to protect her out here.

'I think that's it over for now.' It was little reassurance to her, he was sure, as they could still hear the sound of loose rocks tumbling nearby and see the new fissures opening up in the road ahead. 'Hopefully the family got to the hospital before the aftershock. Although I'm sure it won't be the last.'

Kaja was quiet. Too quiet. Then it seemed as though a mini earthquake of emotions began inside her. The shaking came first, her shoulders heaving beneath his arm, but it was the sobbing that took him most by surprise.

'Hey, we're gonna be okay. That one was quick.'

He cursed himself for being the voice of doom predicting more nerve-shattering aftershocks even though it was the truth. Usually Kaja preferred that kind of straight talking but perhaps under the circumstances she was a bit more fragile. From now on he'd be careful not to upset her. Not when he'd been drawing from her strength to keep going throughout this ordeal.

She leaned back into his chest, content to let him hold her. A cry for help in itself for someone who'd single-handedly waded into a collapsed building to rescue a man twice her size. Kaja was a strong woman who didn't accept help easily, as he'd discovered in those early days of working together when he'd tried to get closer to her. It took her a long time to trust anyone but he'd been persistent, willing to put in the time getting to know her when he'd been so entranced by the newest medic on the block. There'd been something so endearingly naive about her beyond the efficient, focused surgeon. Of course, now he knew why she wasn't as worldly wise as some of her counterparts and the reasons she liked her privacy so much.

He let her cry it out until they were both soaked with her tears and she was ready to talk.

'It's just too much to take in. We could've been killed. We still could.' Her face crumpled again as she contemplated their fate.

Seth didn't want to upset her but neither would he lie to her. There was no way of knowing how this would end for anyone. It was probably the shock setting in that was making them both so emotional. Without the drama and distraction of saving others they had time to replay events and think about their loved ones. If he let himself go down that rabbit hole and start catastrophising what was going on with Amy back at the palace he'd be sobbing too.

'We're still here,' he reminded her. 'Mother Nature has tried twice to take us out and failed. Hopefully she'll take the hint and leave us alone for a bit, yeah?'

She managed a half-hearted smile. 'Thanks for today. I know this wasn't what you had in mind when you suggested an adventure but I'm glad I'm with you.'

'Me too.' He snuggled in closer to Kaja, nuzzling his nose into the curtain of her hair. In the short space of time since they'd got to know each other again she'd quickly become an important element of his life once more. As if those intervening years had never happened and their life together had carried on where it had left off. Easy to do out here where there were no reminders of how different her world was or the relationships they'd had after their separation.

He breathed her in, her hair smelling of dust and earth but also the sweet floral perfume that was unmistakably Kaja. If he closed his eyes he could almost believe they were back in their house in Cambridge.

She turned her head so he was almost nose to nose with her now. Eyes open, lips parted, their breath mingling as they mirrored each other. Seth didn't know who made the first move, they were so in tune with each other, gravitating towards that kiss they both knew was coming.

Here, now, she was all that mattered to him. She was everything reminding him he was still alive. He kissed her as though it might be for the last time. Hard and passionate enough that he forgot to breathe. They fell down onto the rug still wrapped up in one another, hands tugging at one another's clothes, impatience erasing all logical thought. Seth wanted Kaja as he'd never wanted any woman before. He needed that reaffirmation that she was back in his life, that she hadn't fallen out of love with him after all and that she wanted him too. She was telling him that with her words and every stroke of her tongue against his.

He slid her top over her head but his shirt buttons proved more time-consuming. After fumbling with the first two she gave a frustrated groan and yanked the shirt open. The night air cooled Seth's fevered skin but not for long when Kaja trailed first her fingers then her tongue down his chest and lower. Now his breaths were coming in excited pants as she snapped open the buttons on his fly and left him in no doubt what it was she was expecting from him. Seth flipped her over onto her back to slow things down. He hadn't been with anyone since Paula and he needed to regain some control over his body as well as savour every moment with Kaja while he could.

Not that she was doing anything to help that vow as she wriggled out of her scrub trousers so she was lying beneath him clad only in skimpy black silk lingerie.

'You're beautiful.' The sentiment slipped from his lips. She didn't need the expensive clothes or the royal title to be anyone special when to him she was the most beautiful woman on the planet.

'And you're still dressed,' she purred as she grabbed

him by the collar and pulled him back down into another brain-melting kiss. If this was all she wanted from him for now he wasn't going to turn her down. This memory would be a more pleasant one than the last night they'd spent together. Only this time he'd be the one leaving and hopefully on better terms.

This was madness. Kaja knew it yet she didn't want her sanity to return any time soon. She'd never felt more alive than she did right now getting naked with Seth in the open air. They had all the reasons in the world not to pursue a relationship further but none that could convince her that sleeping with him here and now was the wrong thing to do. They'd been through a lot together and in the scheme of things it seemed silly not to act on these feelings they had for one another. Life was too short to deny themselves some pleasure. She didn't want to wait any longer.

Seth was taking his sweet time kissing the skin along her neck and across her clavicle, until Kaja was aching with need. She undid her bra and tossed it aside, revelling in the hungry look he gave her as she exposed her breasts to his gaze. He cupped her soft mounds in the palms of his large hands, kneading and kissing the sensitive flesh until her nipples were throbbing in anticipation of his touch. When he pinched them between his fingers and thumbs she bucked off the ground, that painful ecstasy only furthering her desire. He flicked his tongue over the taut tips, teasing her, the glint in his eye promising her so much more. When he took her in his mouth and sucked, he delivered on that promise.

Arousal swept away the very last of her inhibitions and patience. She pushed down his briefs and pressed her body against his engorged erection. It was the final straw for Seth too. He let out a primal grunt, pulled the last of her underwear away and plunged inside her.

Kaja's gasp was one of surprise and satisfaction that she'd finally got what she wanted. They paused for a second, their bodies both adjusting as they joined together.

His eyes searching hers. 'Are you okay?'

'Uh-huh.' She nodded, though she doubted she'd ever be okay again after this. It was such a wanton display of need and raw passion she knew nothing or no one else could ever surpass it. He kissed her softly on the lips then began moving rhythmically inside her, reminding her how good they could be together. She rocked her hips against his, losing herself in that full feeling every time he rammed her to the hilt.

'I've missed you so much,' he whispered in her ear, sending tiny shivers of delight up the back of her neck both from what he was saying and doing to her.

She was incapable of talking right now. Even if she hadn't been in the throes of ecstasy the sincerity of his words would've rendered her speechless. He should hate her for the way she'd lied to him, the manner in which she'd left him, but most of all for denying them a future together. Hearing him say those words, knowing he would've forgiven her and taken her back, made those bad-decision years all the more painful. At least she had him in this moment and she intended to make the most of their time together.

Kaja clung to him, never wanting to let go as he took her higher and higher on that wave of pure bliss. Why had she ever given up on this? On them? Especially when…

Oh.

All regrets and tears, any thoughts at all, were now simply background noise as Seth set off a fireworks display inside her. Lights flashed behind her eyelids as a succession of delicious explosions detonated in her body, all triggered by what Seth was doing to her. Her orgasm was prolonged and repeated over and over again as he continued working his magic, not letting up on his now frantic pace until she was limp and sated beneath him. Totally exhausted and completely satisfied. Only then did he give into his own fierce need, his climax seeming as overwhelming as hers when he cried out into the night.

When she was able to see straight and breathe again—albeit hindered by the gorgeous hunk currently sprawled across her body—she fully appreciated the beauty of the moment. '*Belle Crepuscolo*—it means beautiful twilight.'

A dazed Seth looked down at her, his hair flopping over his face and his eyelids heavy with exhaustion. He kissed her again and though she knew she was getting carried away by the romance of the moment she couldn't help it.

'This is madness,' she reminded them both.

'What, sleeping with me?' He genuinely looked hurt but her comment had absolutely nothing to do with sex.

'Of course not. You know that was amazing.' Despite everything they'd just done she felt her skin flush at acknowledging the mere memory. She wrapped her arms around his neck, pressing her chest to his and nibbling his earlobe. 'I mean the fact we're lying naked in the middle of a field.'

But she didn't care. Being with Seth was her happy place.

'It's certainly a night to remember,' he said with a grin.

'I wish it could be like this all the time. Only without the whole earthquake and danger-to-life thing.'

'I know what you mean.' He lifted her hand to his mouth and kissed it. A contented moment that should have been played out in the privacy of a bedroom but out here under the stars somehow seemed equally intimate. They knew they were alone and today's events had taught them to live in the moment in case it was their last; a feeling Kaja wished she'd be able to hold onto and carry back to real life.

She let out a wistful sigh and laid her head on his bare shoulder. Right now a simple life seemed very appealing. One where all she needed was a naked Seth and somewhere to rest their heads. 'How long do you think we'll be out here before someone comes to find us?'

'Hopefully a while longer.' One suggestive look was all it took for Kaja's body to wake again in anticipation of more mind-blowing, bone-melting sex with him.

He tangled his fingers in her hair and pulled her in for a long, sensual kiss reaching every nerve-ending in her body. She put up no resistance when he lowered her back onto the ground and showed her what it was he intended to do with the extra alone time.

There were some aftershocks through the night but they gradually decreased in intensity. Kaja was certain they weren't the only ones sleeping outside when most residents would be afraid of staying indoors tonight in case of further structural damage. Although she was sure she was the only one waking up with a smile on her face. She knew there would be a fallout back in the city. Not only would they have to deal with repairs and casualties and generally getting the country back on its feet, but their loved ones would take precedence over examining what was happening between her and Seth. For now she was content to remain where she was.

As the sun rose, the sky around them changed from the inky black they'd fallen asleep under, to a warming *ombre* of pinks and golds, the beauty only eclipsed by the sight of the man she woke up to. His dark stubble combined with his mop of unruly hair gave him a wild look in keeping with the animal passion he'd unleashed.

She shivered with memories of what had kept them awake most of the night.

'Are you cold?' he mumbled, still half asleep, misunderstanding the trembling in her limbs. He pulled her closer to his chest and threw his leg over hers to share his body heat.

The movement brought them into contact in the most intimate of places so she could feel his body waking to start the new day. His burgeoning erection pressing against her was the early morning wake-up call she missed. Making love with Seth was something she'd never tire of or take for granted when she'd been without him in her bed for so long.

Kaja shifted position until he was sheathed inside her and hooked her legs around him as he drove deep into her core. This was the only place she wanted to be right now. The only place she wanted Seth. Worrying about everything else could wait until they could do something about it.

Once the sun had fully risen and the morning had well and truly begun it felt too indulgent, as well as risky, to continue lying au naturel in the open countryside. With the last of the water drained and every breadcrumb consumed they hadn't enough sustenance to keep on with their energetic sensual reunion. Well, her mind was willing but her body needed a rest before they resumed relations again. Something she was looking forward to after a proper meal and, preferably, in a comfortable bed.

They got dressed in yesterday's dirty, torn clothes. Going home in these was the ultimate walk of shame although she hoped no one would guess what she had actually been doing all night. If the clothes didn't give her away the great big smile on her face might. Then she looked at the scene of utter devastation on top of the hill and quickly quashed the smug feeling. Residents had a lot more to worry about than her love life today. What was more, there would be a lot of people concerned about what had happened to her during the earthquake.

'Everything okay?' Seth glanced over at her as he pulled on his shoes and began tying his laces. 'You're very quiet.'

'I'm just wondering what we'll be going back to.' She was surprised to find her lip beginning to wobble as she spoke, the enormity of yesterday's events in full force now they would have to face the aftermath.

He shifted over beside her and helped her put her scrub top on, scooping her hair from inside the neckline to let it fall onto her shoulders. She leaned against him, gaining strength from simply having him taking care of her in such a small way. 'Whatever it is we'll face it together.'

'Will we, or are we just fooling ourselves, Seth? As much as I want a relationship to be possible, sleeping together won't magically make our problems disappear.'

'No, but it's a starting point. If we decide that's what we both want, surely we can work to make it happen?'

'It'll mean big changes for all of us.'

'Something I would be prepared to make as long as I know you're in it for the long haul this time.' He wasn't making a jibe at her; she could see he was being totally serious and with good reason. The last time he'd been planning a future with her she'd taken off and left him to pick up the pieces. Kaja knew she'd made the wrong decision at the time but there was one thing she was still holding back from Seth that could affect them as a couple.

She was hesitant to make that promise to him now without being completely honest with him. In doing that there was a chance he wouldn't want to be with her at all and she wasn't ready to end things before they'd really begun.

'It's a big decision for me to make. Not because I don't want to be with you but there's a lot of stuff I would have to sort out before that could happen.' She knew it wasn't the answer he wanted but it was all she could give him for now.

He studied her quietly for a moment then said, 'I'll wait.'

It was such a comfort knowing he intended to stay by her side until she dealt with the issue that could end their relationship once and for all. She hadn't had that level of understanding for a long time, not since the day she'd left England. Now it was down to her to decide the next move.

In the distance she thought she heard the sound of a car out on the road. 'Seth, is that—'

He was already on his feet and running towards the first sign that they weren't out here alone. Kaja should've been elated but a heavy cloak of sadness settled around her shoulders, preventing her from getting up to follow. Once they left this place the fantasy was over and a selfish part of her wanted it to last for ever. The part of her who'd had this happy life with him once and thrown it all away. Only now did she truly realise how stupid she'd been.

'It's a police car,' he yelled back, jumping up and down trying to attract its attention.

'Great.' Kaja had to psych herself up to go and join him rather than lying down and praying she'd remain undiscovered.

If this was someone come to rescue them it was time to put her game face on. They were no longer two lovers stranded together enjoying some quality time, but a princess and her father's transplant surgeon, who'd been displaced during the country's worst earthquake in living history.

She could see the flashing lights on the car roof as it pulled into the car park and her stomach rolled at the prospect of being recognised in her current state or, worse, having to explain it. Without a mirror she didn't even know how bad she looked but she was guessing a day rescuing people trapped in the rubble of an earthquake and a night sleeping rough weren't going to make a pretty picture.

When she attempted to put her shoes on again it became apparent the swelling around her ankle would make that impossible. She had to limp barefoot towards the approaching police vehicle but held her head high, attempting to maintain some modicum of decorum.

Seth was leaning in through the open window of the car when she got there, shaking hands with the officer in the driver's seat.

'Kaja, this is Constable Bailey, the white knight riding to our rescue.'

She winced at the casual use of her name, which suggested an intimacy between them that, while true, was no business of this complete stranger or those he would later retell his tale to.

'Good morning. Thank you for coming.' She was always self-conscious meeting new people but she had more reason than usual to worry about being judged. Especially when the young officer was openly gawping at her. Too late, she wondered if she had any grass stuck in her hair after rolling about in a field with Seth for most of last night.

'Oh, my goodness... I didn't realise...we were so busy

with calls last night…they just said there were people stuck out at Tobel. No one said it was you!' He got out of the car and opened the door to the back seat, giving a little bow as he did so.

He hadn't known who he was coming to rescue. Whether he'd recognised her immediately or only when Seth had tossed her name into the conversation wasn't clear, but he knew who she was now and that was what mattered. It was important for her to try and claw back some respectability when she was at her most vulnerable.

'I'm sure you had more pressing matters to deal with last night. If you'd be kind enough to take us to the Royal Alderisi hospital we'd be very grateful. Mr Davenport, perhaps you'd like to ride up front with Constable Bailey here.' She wanted to reduce the chance of further impropriety to gossip about by separating them but if Seth's glower was anything to go by he wasn't impressed by the idea.

'Of course, Your Highness. I know my place.'

Kaja had hoped he'd understand her need to keep up a front even in these circumstances, but as he gave her a mock bow and jumped in the passenger seat she realised she was asking too much. Even more so when they were all settled in the car and he put in a request to their driver.

'If you don't mind, could you drop me off at the palace first? My daughter is there. She's all I have in the world and I want to make sure she's safe.' Seth's words cut deep. She understood his need to see his daughter as she also wanted to check on the welfare of her own family, but he was making it clear to her that things said or implied last night had simply happened in the heat of the moment. She was no more a priority in his world than she had been yesterday.

'Sure.'

'Do you know how the hospital and the palace fared in the earthquake?' Kaja kept her voice measured although her heart was cracking open, those old wounds she believed healed now ripping apart the old scar tissue.

The police officer spoke to her in the rear-view mirror. 'Yes, ma'am. The palace, as far as I know, wasn't too badly affected. All hospitals, as you'd imagine, are busy with the casualties, although no fatalities reported so far.'

'Thank goodness.' Despite all the reassurances she'd given herself and Seth, she exhaled all her fears for her loved ones in a long breath with the confirmation. She could see some of the tension released in Seth's shoulders in the passenger seat though he remained facing away from her.

'What about the people who reported our location? There was a man with serious crush injuries. Do you know anything about his condition?' Seth kept the questions coming and while Kaja genuinely wanted a progress report on the family she was glad it was keeping the focus off what they had been doing all the way out here in the first place.

'Sorry, I don't know. I just got the call to do a welfare check. I'm sure if they'd known it was you they would've had someone out here sooner.' He was twisting in his seat to apologise face to face but Kaja didn't want to risk an accident on her behalf.

'It's fine. We can make some enquiries when we get to the hospital. I'm sure Mr Davenport can use his influence to get that sort of information.'

'Oh, I don't know. I think Princess Kaja is pretty good at getting what she wants out of people.'

Officer Bailey glanced at each of them in turn. Seth wasn't exactly being discreet and neither was the heat steadily rising in her face. The atmosphere in the car was almost more unbearable than the one in the aftermath of the earthquake. She and Seth needed to talk, clear the air and lay down some ground rules. He couldn't play around with her reputation like this. That was, if they were going to have any relationship at all. At the moment the vibe he was giving her certainly wasn't all hearts and flowers.

'We're nearly at the palace. Perhaps I should get out here with you, Mr Davenport, and check things are all right at home?'

He met her gaze in the mirror with a steely glare of his own. 'No, I don't think that's a good idea. You should go on to the hospital. After all, you've sustained an injury and I don't think I'd be very popular if I prevented the country's princess from getting the necessary treatment.'

She couldn't swear to it but she thought the young constable put his foot down on the accelerator when he heard that. Kaja knew there was no point in arguing that it was not likely to be anything more than a sprained ankle when Seth would come back with some other smart answer. He wanted to be with his family and that didn't include her. She got the message loud and clear.

Kaja slumped back into the seat. There was no point arguing. It wasn't going to make her feel any better, only push Seth further away. If that were possible.

As they drove through the city, the car bumping around craters in the road, the sight of now derelict buildings spouting pillars of smoke and fire made her chest ache for all those affected. The desolate wasteland replacing the once vibrant country was an accurate depiction of her emotions over the past twenty-four hours.

Last night she'd been on top of the world thinking this was the beginning of a new life together for her and Seth. Now they were back to the real world where she didn't have him by her side.

She watched as the residents of the worst-affected houses set to work outside, banding together to clear away debris and salvage what was left of their lives here. If there was one thing she and the inhabitants had in common it was that survivor spirit. That ability to pick oneself up and get on with things though you'd lost everything dear to you was something she'd mastered. At least, she was good at pretending she had.

When Seth got out of the car and slammed the door she knew what they'd had was over before it really began again. So why did it hurt so much more this time around?

CHAPTER ELEVEN

SETH STORMED UP to the house gates. If he'd been thinking clearly he would've let Kaja come on up as she'd
suggested so he wouldn't have to go through the security rigmarole.

'I need some ID,' today's sentry demanded.

He flashed his hospital pass. 'You know who I am.
You've seen me often enough. Now can you please let
me in so I can see my daughter?'

The guard waved him through and Seth uttered a be-
grudging thanks.

This was typical of the nonsense in Kaja's world and
he was sick of being reminded he wasn't part of it. Even
in emergency situations they couldn't give him a break.
Regardless of the fact that he'd probably saved the grand
duke's life, he was never going to be accepted as Kaja's
equal. She'd made that very point herself when she'd
segregated herself in the back seat of the police car from
the lesser mortals.

He hadn't come out here with the intention of getting
back together with Kaja but it had happened last night
and it had been glorious. What he hadn't been prepared
for was the fallout of being rejected again.

There had been no class distinction lying out there
naked entwined in one another's arms. They had just

been two people who'd needed each other. That had changed the second they'd been in the public domain and she'd acted embarrassed to be seen with him, reminding him once again that their lives weren't compatible and she could turn her back on him at any given moment.

The only person he should be concentrating on spending time with was his daughter. Especially as he hadn't been there at a time when she'd needed him most.

The interior of the palace remained relatively the same. It did look a tad more minimalist than he recalled, devoid of a few of the ornate—and perhaps fragile—furnishings. It wasn't immediately obvious if they'd been broken during the earthquake or hurriedly stored away but the place had been cleaned and tidied back to its original state. He could only guess by the absence of the huge chandelier in the hallway that they hadn't got away totally unscathed. Things could be replaced, loved ones couldn't. So when Amy came running at him he had to stifle a tear or two of relief.

'Am I glad to see you.' He crouched down so she ran straight into his arms and hugged her as tight as he could.

'Daddy, you're squishing me.' She pushed him off, then came back for a second, less squishy hug.

'Are you okay? Were you hurt?' He brushed her curls away from her face, checking for any signs of injury.

'It was scary, Daddy. The noise made me cry.' Her bottom lip trembled and Seth could feel his going too. He'd been afraid so he could only imagine what had gone on in her head in a strange place, so far from home without her father.

'I know, sweetheart. I'm so sorry I couldn't make it back to you.'

'She is fine. This was the safest place for her. A little noise, some shaking, but no one hurt. What about the princess? She is not with you?' Fatima was frowning at him as she wiped her hands on the apron tied at her waist. The thought that they might have been baking again made his stomach growl and remind him he hadn't had anything to eat other than the picnic leftovers last night.

'Thank you for taking care of Amy. I took Kaja out for a walk to clear her head after seeing her father at the hospital. I didn't know we'd get stuck out there all night. She's gone back to the hospital to check in with him.' Something he'd be sure to do too once he'd spent some time with Amy. As well as whatever upheaval had been caused by the earthquake at the hospital, they'd need a progress report on the grand duke's recovery post-surgery. There was a good chance of Bruno getting released today too if he hadn't had any complications overnight.

'I hear on the news the hospital is very busy. A lot of people hurt yesterday. We were all very lucky.' Fatima crossed herself and thanked the heavens they had all survived the experience.

'I should probably head down there too and see if I can be of any assistance.' It would be all hands on deck in the emergency department to get through the wave of casualties coming in. They probably didn't have the staff numbers available with this kind of nationwide incident.

'You can do that after you have a shower and I make you something to eat.' Fatima steered him towards the staircase but it seemed selfish to be thinking only of himself during a crisis.

'I don't really have time—'

'Nonsense. You will be no use to anyone if you die of hunger first. Go, get washed and changed. I'll cook.' Fatima wasn't going to take no for an answer.

'Yeah, Daddy, you stink.'

'Charming,' he mumbled as he trudged up the stairs, dejected and rejected all at once.

'If you are going to be seen with the princess you really need to look the part. You don't want to shame her.' Fatima wasn't to know Kaja was equally grimy and unkempt but he supposed that would only earn her some fans to be seen mucking in with the rest of the community.

'No, Fatima, I would never want to shame her.' He would never do anything intentional to hurt her. That was why it was so galling when she could be so cruel to him without seeming to give it a second thought.

As expected, the hospital was a hub of activity. There were people, staff and beds everywhere as Seth walked in—unimpeded this time, although he was sure there were still guards posted outside the royal hospital rooms.

'Seth Davenport. I'm a surgeon. Can I do anything to help?' He'd been directed towards the co-ordinator in Reception, which was now serving as a triage area.

'We need all the help we can get. It's mostly stitches and broken limbs in here. The seriously injured were seen to first. You should have been here last night.' She snorted a humourless laugh as she handed him a stack of files before calling her next patient.

Seth could tell from her stained uniform and the bags under her eyes that she'd been here long past the end of her usual shift. 'Sorry, I was…stuck out at Tobel.'

She stopped shuffling files long enough to stare at him. 'You weren't the one who saved that family out there, were you?'

He wasn't sure he deserved praise next to someone who'd probably been on her feet since yesterday. 'I didn't do it alone and I'm sure the staff here did more than we did at the scene.'

'I was here when they came in. That straw trick was a stroke of genius for the punctured lung. The father's on the ward now if you want to go and see him?' It was a magnanimous offer when she was clearly under a lot of pressure to attend to the waiting patients but Seth was keen to see for himself how the man was doing.

'Would you mind? I swear I won't be long, then I'll come back here and get stuck into these.'

She held out her arms for him to offload the patient files. 'Don't worry, they'll still be here when you get back.'

Seth thought he'd take a quick look at the man's notes, maybe have a word with whoever was treating him, then he'd come back and set to work on that waiting list in the emergency department.

He hadn't counted on running into Kaja visiting at the same time.

'Hello. I wasn't expecting to see you here.' He should have been. She was always going to check up on a patient as well as setting to work to help everyone else who needed it. It was a foregone conclusion they were going to meet up at some point in the same building.

He hovered at the doorway, uncertain if he was going to stick around now when relations between them had turned sour.

'I just ducked in to see how he was doing while I was in between patients. He had emergency surgery when he came in but he's sleeping it off now. The surgeon said he'll recover. In time.'

'Good. What about the others?'

'Mum and daughter were a bit shaken up but they're okay.'

'And you? How's the ankle?' They were acting like strangers or, at most, colleagues with a patient in common, but it was safer than tackling what was really on his mind when it would only bring more pain.

Kaja lifted the bottom of her trouser leg up to show off a fresh bandage and an unattractive white clog. 'I think being seen in these shoes is more painful than the sprain. They could probably do with a little bling and more of a heel to fit in with the rest of my wardrobe.'

'They're not very you,' he agreed with a smirk. She was definitely more at home here in the midst of this organised chaos with barely enough time to breathe never mind care what she looked like, than swanning about in a palace.

'I shouldn't complain. The staff were very kind to lend me a change of clothes and patch me up. This is nothing compared to some of the injuries that have come in through the doors.'

'Speaking of which, I said I wouldn't be long. I promised to help out with the walking wounded.'

'Me too. I'll walk down with you.'

They left their sleeping patient and tiptoed out of the door. Well, Seth tiptoed. Kaja kind of squeaked across the floor.

'Did you manage to get anything to eat? Fatima wouldn't let me leave until my stomach was fit to burst.'

'Some of the locals have been fuelling us with coffee and cake. I'm glad Fatima made you take a break. You worked so hard yesterday; you deserve a rest.'

He didn't miss the coy look and guessed her mind had wandered to their energetic relations last night, and this morning, as well as the physical labour they'd put into rescuing the family. The way his had.

She cleared her throat. 'I see you had a chance to clean up as well. You look good.'

In trying to avoid using the elevator in case of any

further power outages, they'd taken the stairs. It was the one relatively quiet area in the hospital but it also seemed to amplify their awkwardness around each other, along with their voices. Seth decided to address what had happened this morning rather than ignore it and let it fester. There was nothing worse than drifting apart from someone without having a chance to understand what had gone wrong.

He waited until they were halfway down, pausing on a landing to broach the subject. 'Kaja, are you ashamed of me?'

'What? No. Whatever gave you that idea?' Her frown gave the impression she was being honest with him but with evidence to the contrary he couldn't be certain.

'After last night I was willing to give things a shot. To the point of setting my ego aside until you decide if I'm enough for you. Then the policeman turned up and you went cold on me, making sure I sat up front with the other "civilian".'

'Seth, it wasn't like that at all. I don't know, I panicked when he recognised me and I was worried he'd guess what had happened between us. I don't want people gossiping and speculating before we even figure out what's going on between us. Last night was special. I'm certainly not ashamed about what happened.' She rested her hand lightly on his arm, imploring him with those big eyes to believe her.

'Nor me, but I need to know where I stand. I'm not going to set myself up for another fall, Kaja. Not when I've got Amy to consider in all of this too. If we're going to make a go of things we both have to be on board one hundred per cent. I'm not convinced you're ever going to be.'

'That's not fair, Seth.'

'I'm being honest. Something I think you need to be with yourself too.' He was no longer willing to leave room for confusion. It was all or nothing; he wasn't going to risk his heart again.

The silence as Kaja contemplated what he was saying went on for an eternity before she broke it. 'I've been thinking about that and I would like to go back to medicine.'

'So what are you going to do about it, Kaja?'

'Pardon?'

'There's nothing to be gained by simply thinking how you could improve your life here. You have to actually do something to make it happen and fight for what's important to you. What is it you want, Kaja?' It had to come from the heart if she was going to be honest with herself and him.

'I want... I want...'

'What?'

'I want the life I had in England.' She blurted it out, surprising them both, judging by the shocked look on her face. Seth had no intention of leaving it there.

'Why, when you gave it up to come back here?'

'Because I was leading my own life. I had a job I loved and...and... I had you, Seth.' When her voice cracked he had to swallow down the urge to hold her and comfort her. This was make or break for him.

'Five years ago you didn't want any of that.'

'I did, I swear, but I thought I had to give it all up because none of it was real.'

'What's changed now?'

'I'm miserable here, Seth,' she sobbed. 'I came back to do the right thing by my family but it cost me everything. Being with you last night was the first time in a long time that I was actually happy. I want that to last.'

'So, I'll ask you again. What are you going to do about it?' He rested his hands on her shoulders, resisting the full-on embrace he wanted to give her.

'I'm going to speak to my father about stepping down from my royal duties. I'll tell him I want to go back to medicine full time. I don't know how we're going to do it yet but I also want a life with you, Seth. If that's what you'd like too?' She looked up at him, so full of hope, his heart soared. Everything was out in the open now. No more secrets preventing them from forging ahead. She wouldn't have the conversation with her father if she wasn't serious about making the changes it would take for him to risk his heart on her again. It was his turn to take a leap of faith and prove his commitment to their relationship by forgiving her for her earlier slight.

'It's all I could ever ask for.' They could work out the logistics later. For now it was all the confirmation he needed to go with his heart.

He leaned in and laid his mouth gently upon hers just to experience that connection once more until they had a chance to get some quality time alone again.

'So, we're good?' Kaja broke away to check but Seth didn't want to stop kissing her now that the obstacles to true love had apparently been removed.

'We're good.' He smiled against her lips. Just one more kiss and he'd get back to work.

They heard the squeak of a door being opened at the top of the stairs and he remembered to cool it. Kaja was right, they didn't need to have their every move analysed or have bystanders commenting on what they thought of their relationship. They had to figure things out for themselves.

'Can we pick this up again later?'

'Just give me the word and I'll come a-calling.'

That demure, lowered-lashes look she was giving him, unaware of how completely under her thrall he was, would ensure he came back time and time again.

'You are such a dork.' She slapped him on the arm, her laughter every bit as intoxicating as her kisses.

'You're such a princess,' he teased back, and to the female visitor coming down the stairs behind them they probably looked like two friends engaging in a bit of banter, which was exactly what they wanted people to think.

Now he understood her need to protect their relationship he wasn't going to take it personally. This way it kept Amy out of the spotlight too. It would be such a change in their family dynamic for him to have a partner it was something he'd have to lead into gradually with her. She didn't need to see their faces splashed all over the newspapers with the gossip columns listing all the reasons this single, divorced dad wasn't a good match for the country's princess. He didn't need reminding when he felt it so acutely every time he looked at her.

He bounded down the remainder of the steps, much lighter for having set the record straight with Kaja and with something to look forward to at the end of his shift.

They worked on into the night assisting where they could, patching people up so they were able to go home as soon as possible. Occasionally Kaja caught sight of Seth behind a cubicle curtain or walking by with his next patient as she treated hers.

After their talk on the stairs she hoped this was the start of a new life together for them. But there was still something she'd kept from him and if they were going into this with a clean slate she knew she'd have to tell him about her infertility issues. Her stomach tied itself in knots every time she thought about the last time she'd told a man she couldn't have his child, but Seth was nothing like Benedikt. Hurting anyone on purpose simply wasn't in his nature.

She could hear him now, his deep voice soothing the screams of a small child obviously in pain.

'I know it hurts, Lottie, but I need you to keep still so I can take a good look at that eye. Mrs Gallo, perhaps you could help hold your daughter still for me.'

Kaja had a few minutes to spare and small children were never the easiest patients to wrangle. Perhaps she could provide a suitable distraction for the little girl to enable Seth to do what he had to.

'Hey. Sorry for disturbing you, Mr Davenport. I'm in between patients at the minute and wondered if there was anything I could do to help?' There was a fine line between offering assistance and being seen as interfering.

If anything, he seemed relieved to see her.

'Thank you. I think Lottie here might need a little more persuading to sit still for me.'

Her mother was trying to stop her from rubbing her already red eyes with her bunched-up fists.

'Did you get something in your eye, Lottie? They must be very sore.' Kaja took a seat at the side of the bed as the little girl nodded and sniffed.

'I think she might have some grit irritating her. We need to get some fluorescein stain in to check.' He was as reassuring to an infant with a sore eye as he was to a fully grown woman trapped under rubble. It didn't matter what background he came from, Seth's caring and understanding nature was the mark of a true gentleman. He was pure class as far as she was concerned. A prince amongst men.

'The doctor needs to see what's hurting you, Lottie. We need you to keep your eye wide open so he can do that. Do you think you could be a big girl and tilt your head back for me?' There was no more reason to trust her than the handsome man trying to help her, but Kaja was hoping that by teaming up they would manage to persuade her.

If there was something stuck to the cornea it would explain the red, watery reaction. It could also be something more serious, such as a piece of metal. That could require surgery.

Kaja gently eased the girl's hands away from her eyes. Although Lottie let her, she did let out a pitiful whine and tensed her whole body.

'I couldn't see anything in there but I did try to give her an eye bath with some hot water. It didn't help.' The mother fretted from the other side of the bed as she brushed her daughter's hair away from her forehead.

'That's fine. We advise people not to try and remove any foreign bodies from the eye themselves in case they do further damage. You were right to bring her to us.' Seth's assurance she'd done her best eased the anxious look on the woman's face.

Kaja stood up alongside Seth so the child was looking up at her, keeping her hands tightly in hers so she wouldn't suddenly lash out. 'You just keep watching me, Lottie, while Mr Davenport takes a look in your eye.'

Seth held her eyelids open so he could have a look and the little girl squeezed Kaja's hand.

'I can't see anything in there so we're going to have to use the dye.' He clearly didn't want to distress her any more than necessary but if there was something irritating her it could cause conjunctivitis or lead to scarring.

'Lottie, the doctor is going to touch your eye with a small piece of paper. You just keep looking up at me, okay?' Another hand squeeze and whimper in response.

'I need you to blink on this for me, Lottie,' Seth coaxed, then addressed her mother to explain the process. 'The blotting paper contains an orange dye, which, when used in conjunction with a blue light, detects any foreign bodies or damage to the cornea. Blinking helps spreads the dye.'

He did the test as quickly as his patient would allow then whisked the paper away again.

'You're so good, Lottie. Now I'm going to shine a torch on you. There's nothing to be afraid of. It's a very special torch.' Seth turned the torch on so she could see the light for herself, shining it on her hand then on the ceiling so she could see it wasn't harmful.

'Is it magic?' Lottie was captivated now, the tears giving way to childish curiosity.

'Well, hopefully this will help us make you feel better again. Just keep your eye open for us, Lottie.' It was down to Kaja again to reassure her while Seth inspected the site. Any problems on the cornea would show up green under the blue light.

He had to look under the eyelid first, causing Lottie to tense up again. 'Okay... I think I can see something on the surface. I'm going to put some special eye drops in to stop it hurting, Lottie.'

It was difficult to make sure she didn't blink out the local anaesthetic drops but Seth persevered.

'I'm sure we'll have people of all ages coming in with the same problem given the air quality after the earthquake. It will be full of dust.' Kaja kept talking as Seth used a cotton swab to remove the grit.

Every adult in the room breathed a sigh of relief and when no one else was looking, he gave Kaja a wink. Confirmation if it was needed that they made a good team.

'All done. I'll put a dressing over that eye just to make

it more comfortable for a day or two. Try not to rub your eye if you can help it, Lottie. It shouldn't give you any more trouble but if it does Mum should make an appointment with your GP to get it checked out.'

'Thank you, Doctor.' Mrs Gallo waited until he'd taped a dressing over the eye before enthusiastically shaking his hand. Then she bent down and gave her daughter a kiss on the top of the head before they disappeared out of the cubicle, leaving Seth and Kaja alone.

'I'm glad we didn't have to refer her to the surgical team to cause any more trauma. Thanks for the moral support too. I'm sure it would've taken me twice as long if you hadn't been here.'

'It's never easy with the young ones and nearly always a two-person job. It's not the easiest task to perform either. I presume you've done that a few times to take on the job yourself?'

'Once or twice during hospital placements. You weren't so bad yourself, with the kiddie-whispering. She was putty in your hands once you gave her some attention, much like Amy. It seems no one is immune to the princess's charms. At least, no one under the age of six.' Beyond the complimenting was that teasing that made her blush and bluster at the same time.

'Then your daughter is a good judge of character, even if her father's opinion of me wavers from time to time.' She wasn't going to let him completely off the hook about earlier. Although she hoped she'd put his mind at rest by telling him about her plans. It wasn't going to be an easy conversation with her father, but one that was overdue.

'My opinion on you is rock solid.' He wrapped his arms around her waist before gently fitting his lips expertly around hers. Seth was the tonic she needed for her increasing tiredness but it couldn't last when there were more patients piling in by the moment.

'The next shift is here to take over.' Seth poked his head into the cubicle to notify her that it was the end of their working day.

'I'm just finishing up in here and I'll be with you in a minute.' She'd been so busy she hadn't had time to think about taking a break but every part of her poor body was aching.

Resisting the urge to leave with him there and then, she turned back to the young man sitting on the bed with his hand in a cast. 'If you make an appointment out at Reception for the fracture clinic, we'll see how your fingers are healing in a few weeks' time.'

'Okay, thank you, Doctor.'

Even though most of the people through the door had recognised her at some stage, or had been made aware of her identity, once they were in their doctor/patient roles it didn't seem to matter. She preferred it that way, being accepted and respected for her medical expertise rather than her family background. It gave her a sense of purpose and, if she was honest, more self-respect to be of some use to her country rather than merely tabloid fodder.

The earthquake had put life into perspective for a lot of people and most of those affected were only too glad to have an extra pair of doctor hands available to care about who she was outside the hospital doors.

With her last patient discharged she went straight to find Seth. 'I could get used to this freedom, you know.'

He looked at the people still waiting to be seen in the reception area. 'I'm not sure your colleagues would be keen to be so "free" every day.'

'You know what I mean. Haven't you noticed?' She

leaned in to whisper in case saying it aloud would somehow jinx it all. 'No bodyguards shadowing my every move.'

It brought Seth up short and she could see him checking for any ninja-like security hiding in the shadows, waiting to pounce. 'What happened to them?'

'I told them they weren't needed. They weren't around yesterday when my personal security was threatened and I survived. I couldn't very well work efficiently in the midst of the emergency here with them getting in the way or vetting every single person I came into contact with.' That conversation with Gunnar had been the first step in reasserting herself. She had a long way to go, decisions to make and conversations to have, but Seth had shown her she should be enjoying her life, not simply existing.

'Good for you. If I'm not careful your father will have me thrown out of the country for being a bad influence on you.' He laughed but Kaja suspected there was a smidgen of real concern mixed in there too.

'Don't worry, Papa is well aware I know my own mind.' She knew he was still groggy when he'd agreed to get security to back off but he was the same man who'd given into her desire to leave the country and study in England all those years ago. That hadn't been down to anyone's influence other than her own, even if Seth had been the main reason for her extended stay.

'I think you've proved your medical worth here today, if that was ever in doubt. You are so much more than a pretty princess, Kaja, and it's time the rest of the world knew that too.'

Kaja could virtually feel her skin smouldering under his intense gaze. They had to get out of here if they intended to keep their love life under wraps. Eye-sexing each other in the middle of a busy hospital wasn't being discreet.

'I…er…mightn't have given up all of my royal privileges. I hope you won't think any less of me but I've texted for the chauffeur to come and pick me up.'

One step at a time. Perhaps some day she'd start driving herself but not all changes were going to happen overnight.

He didn't say anything as they left the reception area and she braced herself for criticism about her sense of entitlement or, at the very least, a look of disapproval. Instead, he turned to her once they were outside and simply said, 'Thank goodness. I don't think I could walk after the past twenty-four hours and I'm not the one with a dodgy ankle.'

She wanted to kiss this man and, in keeping with her new vow to be true to herself, she did just that. Albeit at the side of the entrance where there was no lighting or prying eyes. Small steps. Big smooches.

When she saw the headlights approaching the front of the hospital instead of parking around the back with the normal visitors she had to let go of him again. At least he knew now it wasn't a rejection of him but of those around them knowing their business. When they were ensconced in the back seat of the car, Seth reached for her hand and she took it gladly. With him in her corner she knew she could make it through whatever challenges were thrown at her. In her uncertain world she was sure of one thing. Her love for Seth Davenport.

CHAPTER TWELVE

'NEXT TIME YOU go walkabout in the middle of an earthquake give me a heads up, will you?' Bruno lit in on Kaja as soon as she walked in through the door, but his tentative hug said he was more pleased to see her than angry at her.

'I can't promise you anything but I am sorry I didn't get to see you before you were discharged.' He looked so good considering he'd just had surgery the day before, better than she did after a long day on the front line of emergency medicine.

He shook hands with Seth. 'No worries. I think you had more important things to deal with. Good to see you again, too. Thanks for keeping an eye on my little sis yesterday. I knew we didn't have to worry too much if she was with you and since you both disappeared at the same time...'

Her brother wasn't stupid. There was no way he could know exactly what they'd got up to but the wink he gave them implied he was aware something was going on between them. Thankfully he was too polite to ask them outright.

'Daddy!' Amy made a flying leap at her father, confident he would catch her. Which he did, holding onto her legs as she wrapped them around his waist and hung her arms around his neck. She was always so overjoyed to see him Kaja was almost moved to tears. The way Seth hugged and made such a fuss of Amy his love for her was unquestionable. She tried to ignore that tug on her heart telling her she would never have that bond with a child of her own so it wouldn't spoil the moment.

'Oh, Miss Kaja, you're so filthy.' Fatima scuttled over, hands up in horror as she took in the spectacle of her working clothes. An unknown concept in the Alderisi family wardrobe.

'I did get stuck out there during an earthquake.' She laughed to cover her embarrassment when everyone else was so clean and tidy in comparison. Thank goodness she'd had at least one change of clothes since yesterday.

'I know, I know, Mr Davenport told me. You're so brave and compassionate to go and help those people without thinking about yourself.'

'I don't know about that.' Kaja shied away from the praise. It was circumstance and a desire to be useful that had driven her to act.

'What other princess would do that? Tell me. Who?' Fatima demanded from Bruno and Seth and they were stumped to come up with an answer. Which, it turned out, was the correct response. 'See? Only Miss Kaja.'

'Seth was there too—'

'Yes, and when he came home I made him shower and eat too.' She took Kaja's hand and tugged her towards the staircase.

'I wouldn't try arguing if I was you.' Seth was openly laughing at her as he swung Amy around so she was hoisted on his hip.

Not even her brother was in her corner. 'We've all had the same treatment. It's your turn.'

She stuck her tongue out at him when Fatima wasn't

looking, just as she had when they were kids. Like then, Bruno simply laughed it off.

'You need a nice relaxing bath. I could arrange a massage if you want?'

'That won't be necessary, thanks.' For a moment she truly believed Fatima was going to accompany her upstairs to bathe her. As much as she appreciated the concern Kaja drew the line at that.

'Well, you need to take it easy. And eat. I will make you something. Yes, I will make dinner for everyone.' Hands on hips, Fatima decreed that was what was going to happen. A sit-down, home-cooked meal.

'Thank you, Fatima. That would be lovely.' Kaja was exhausted, usually this sort of thing would prove even more draining, but as she looked around she realised there was no one else she'd rather be with tonight than the people around her right now. They weren't all blood relations but they certainly felt like family to her.

The bath had gone some way to helping her relax. She'd used some perfumed oils and lit some candles and the stresses of the day had begun to melt away. It was only her still-throbbing ankle, now an attractive purple and yellow hue, reminding her of yesterday's trauma.

She threw on Seth's old sweatshirt—freshly laundered—and her tracksuit bottoms so she could properly relax for the rest of the evening.

The sound of chatter and the smell of freshly baked bread led her down to the dining room. Amy darted out in front of her just outside the door, almost causing her to trip.

'Be careful, Amy, that floor can be slippery.'

'Okay, Kaja. I'm helping Fatima.'

'Good girl. Remember to walk, don't run. We don't

want any accidents or you'll end up like me.' Kaja showed off her freshly bandaged ankle and watched as the excited child skipped off so full of self-importance at whatever task Fatima had assigned to keep her out of mischief.

She hadn't intended to eavesdrop but when she heard the men talking she couldn't bring herself to interrupt the conversation. It would be good for them to get to know each other better if Seth and Amy were going to prove a more permanent feature in her life.

'Amy's a real whirlwind. You're very lucky, Seth.' Bruno's voice rendered her immobile.

'I know. I couldn't imagine life without her.'

'And her mother? I haven't heard anybody mention her. Sorry if that's insensitive of me to ask.'

She could imagine Seth shaking his head to ease her brother's conscience that he might have inadvertently offended him in some way. 'Paula left not long after Amy was born. We're divorced now.'

'Sorry to hear that. I'm looking forward to marrying Missy and having a family of my own one day. What about you? Do you think you'll ever do it again?'

'Absolutely. I'll make sure to pick the right woman next time. Joking aside though, I can't wait to settle down again and have more children. I adore being a dad.'

It took a while for the reality of Seth's words to sink in, Kaja's heart plummeting when she realised his plans for the future included an extended family she couldn't provide him. Her heart couldn't take disappointing him month after month.

Seth was a fantastic dad. It was clear in every second he spent with his daughter and even today when he'd treated that young girl so compassionately. It wouldn't be fair to deny him the chance of settling down with someone who could give him everything he wanted. More children and the chance to experience it all again. Amy would make a great big sister too. It was Kaja who didn't fit into that picture-perfect happy family.

Just because she was forced to suffer a childless future it didn't mean he had to.

Seth was a good man who deserved better than a barren princess who would bring him nothing but pain. Perhaps they should stick to the original plan and let him go back home without her. She shouldn't expect him to disrupt the life he had with Amy for her sake. Not when she still couldn't be the woman he needed. Even if she gave up her royal title, her loyalties no longer divided, she was failing him in the most basic fashion. She'd been selfish in not telling him before now simply so she could have him in her life a little longer.

Ending things now had to be better than waiting until he resented her for not giving him a baby. She'd been there before with Benedikt and knew how this panned out: disappointment, accusing fingers and crying herself to sleep every time she didn't meet expectations.

'What are you doing out here? Food is on the table going cold. Go, join the others.' Fatima, closely followed by her little shadow, Amy, both carrying baskets of bread rolls, harried her into the dining room.

Seth and Bruno were pleased to see her and she didn't think it was merely so they could finally tuck into their dinner. It was unfortunate she was going to have to spoil the evening for one of them.

'Much better.' Seth approved of Kaja's new attire. It was funny how he found an old baggy sweatshirt on her just as attractive as the expensive couture she wore in public. Probably because it reminded him of the previous life they'd had. One he hoped they'd have again. This time with an alternative ending.

She flashed him a subtle smile and took a seat beside her brother on the opposite side of the table. Amy jumped up on the seat beside Seth, on the cushion they were using as a booster seat so she could see over the table. It was how he imagined a medieval banqueting table would look in terms of the amount of food and the length of the actual table, although the assortment of shining cutlery and obviously expensive china created an altogether more regal experience. He wasn't used to all this pomp and ceremony for dinner. Usually, if Amy had already been fed by the childminder, he settled for dinner on a tray in front of the TV.

'I was just telling Seth the hospital rumour mill was working overtime today.' Bruno poured Kaja a glass of wine so she could catch up with the one they'd already downed waiting for her.

'Oh?' Seth noticed the wary look in her eyes. She probably assumed the worst, the way he had when Bruno had mentioned it to him too, but she didn't need to worry. Their al fresco tryst remained a secret as far as he knew.

'Yes, you impressed quite a few with your dedication, pitching in with everybody else. I mean, I know you were there too, Seth, but people don't expect to see anyone from the royal family getting their hands dirty in the midst of a crisis.' Bruno was very matter-of-fact about the way his family was viewed by the public. Unlike his sister, he didn't seem to care a jot what other people thought of him.

It was always different for men, of course; they weren't judged as much as their female counterparts on their looks or their relationships. However, Seth got the impression Bruno wouldn't compromise his sense of self for anyone.

'It wasn't anything I hadn't done before. Just because you haven't been down at the coalface, big bro, doesn't mean I haven't.'

'Well, I heard you had to staple a man's scalp back together.'

'True.'

'And the kid impaled on the handlebars?'

'Also true.'

'What about the baby you single-handedly delivered in the back of the ambulance.'

'Not true. There were three of us.'

Seth scooped some of the pasta dish Fatima had made for them onto Amy's plate before serving himself while the siblings discussed some of the patient stories that had circulated about Kaja's time at the hospital. He devoured the cheesy, creamy comfort food as though he hadn't eaten all day. If he stayed here much longer letting Fatima fatten him up he might have to invest in some trousers with an elastic waist. Goodness knew how Kaja kept her svelte figure. Stress, he supposed. It was impossible to enjoy a hearty meal properly if your stomach was constantly in knots with worry.

Even now he noticed her picking at her dinner, not eating more than a forkful or two. He'd have a chat with her later to put her mind at ease that no one had mentioned the possibility of a romance between them in his presence. After Amy and the others went to bed he was looking forward to having some alone time again with Kaja. Libido aside, they needed to figure out how they were going to make this work between them. If she was as unhappy as she appeared here and so keen to get back to work, he hoped it wouldn't take too much to persuade her to return to England with him once her father was fully recovered.

'No more hospital talk, please. People are trying to eat.' After hearing one too many surgical procedures Fatima held her hands up to her ears, although she was the only one who seemed bothered. Amy was more concerned with getting a second helping of pasta than any hospital drama.

'Sorry, Fatima,' Kaja and Bruno chorused, sounding nothing of the sort. He could imagine the two of them as mischievous children running rings around her when she was the only one giving them any attention without their parents around.

'I told Dad what you'd been doing. He was very impressed.'

'I don't know why. I am a qualified surgeon. I worked in England for a long time in the emergency department and I do the same here once a week, as he very well knows.' Kaja stabbed her pasta.

'He's very old-fashioned when it comes to our roles. Perhaps it's different now he knows it's not some vanity project you're running. It could be that he's going through some sort of epiphany. After all, he's received a second chance at life.'

'Thanks to you.'

'Thanks to all of us. If it weren't for you, we wouldn't have got Seth here involved, and Fatima has been the one keeping us all going. Not to forget Amy, who is a ray of sunshine here and I'm sure will play a part in Dad's recovery.' Bruno held up his glass of wine. 'To us.'

'To us,' the rest of them toasted along with him. Including Amy with her beaker of milk.

Kaja set down her glass and her cutlery, abandoning

any pretence she was eating. 'I've decided to go back to medicine full time.'

'That's a big deal, sis. There will be a lot of logistics to consider. People to consult.'

'I'm aware of that but I can serve the country better that way.' For the first time since bringing up the subject she looked at Seth.

'You're staying here?' He didn't care that no one else was aware there was a different option available to her if she chose. She did. He'd really believed this was going to be their second chance. If she was expecting him to fall into line with her decision and relocate here permanently, uprooting Amy from everything she knew, she really should've consulted him on the matter first.

'Yes.'

'Oh, Miss Kaja, you are a very honourable woman. Your mother would be so proud.' Fatima, close to tears at the news, rose from her seat and threw her arms around Kaja's neck in a hug. Bruno remained seated, his gaze travelling between her and Seth.

Seth couldn't move even if he wanted to.

'You're really going to give everything up here for the stress and drama of an emergency department?'

'Give up what, Bruno? I don't have anything I'm not willing to drop to give my life some meaning.' She didn't look at Seth but every word was a thousand daggers plunging into his flesh. There were so many reasons for him to take offence in that one simple sentence. Apparently he was nothing.

That wasn't what she'd told him hours earlier when they were planning a future together. She'd told him she was giving up her position to do what she wanted in life. Now, suddenly he wasn't a part of that? If she'd changed her mind and decided he wasn't worth giving up her position for after all, there were kinder ways to do it. She could've broken it to him in private, for a start. There was no way she wouldn't have known how hurtful those words would be and she had to have a reason why she'd wanted to wound him so deeply. By doing this to him in company she was denying him the chance to call her out on those empty promises she'd made. Not that it mattered now, when the damage had already been done.

He was mad at himself for falling for her all over again and believing her vow to speak to her father. She'd probably only said it to stop him hounding her when he'd been pushing her so hard to give him the answer he wanted to hear. Now she'd had time to think it through, a life with him wasn't any more attractive to her than it was five years ago.

'I think we should leave you to discuss family matters in private. Amy, it's bedtime.' Seth tossed his linen napkin on the table and pushed back his chair, desperate to escape the room and this conversation.

'I'm not tired, Daddy.' Amy folded her arms across her chest and pouted in an uncharacteristic bout of petulance at the worst possible time.

'It's getting late and I've had a very trying day. Let's go, Amy.' He was pleading with her in his head not to cause an even greater scene when he was already at breaking point. It wasn't his temper he was worried about losing, rather control of his fragile emotions. In the space of a few minutes his dreams of becoming a family with Kaja had been shattered, only to be faced with returning to his lonely life back in England. And he had no idea why.

Thankfully his daughter gave up on her sit-in and climbed down off her chair. 'Night, night, everybody.'

'Night, sweetheart.' Seth had to wait not so patiently while Kaja came to give her a hug, closely followed by Fatima.

He managed an abrupt, 'Goodnight,' before taking his daughter by the hand and leading her away from the family they'd both begun to feel a part of. Returning home was going to break both of their hearts.

There was no way he was sleeping until he confronted Kaja about her comments tonight. Once Amy had brushed her teeth and settled into bed he crept out onto the landing separating their apartments from Kaja's. He made sure to leave the doors open in case she stirred while he was waiting for answers.

When Kaja appeared he was sure he saw her take a deep breath as she met him at the top of the stairs.

'Do you mind telling me what that was all about down there?' He practically spat the words at her.

'I told you I'm going back into medicine permanently.'

'But you're staying here?'

'Where else would I work? This is my country. My family are here.'

'What about Amy and me? I thought we meant something to you.'

'You'll always have a special place in my heart, Seth. Amy too. But I've had some time to think and I want to focus on me and my career. I can't do that if I'm playing house with you and your daughter.' She was so calm and cool as she devastated him Seth thought it was worse than having her simply disappear from his life, seeing first-hand of how little significance he was to her.

'What's changed in the space of a few hours? Earlier we were making plans to get together again, then you dump me halfway through dinner. It doesn't make any sense.'

'We want different things. I heard you talking to Bruno, telling him your plans to get married and have more children. That's not going to happen with me.'

'That's what all of this is about? A snatched bit of small talk between me and your brother?' He wanted to laugh at the absurdity of it. 'In an ideal world, yes, I'd like to settle down again. That's not so bad, is it?'

He moved towards her, wanted to hold her again so she could remember how it felt to be wrapped up in each other's arms and forget everything else.

Kaja stepped back, reluctant to let him touch her. 'What if I told you I can't have children, Seth? I can't give you that family you want. Would you still want to be with me?'

That bombshell rendered him speechless. It was such a huge thing for her to have kept from him all this time and he was trying to process what that meant for them. He'd pictured building on their family but now he had to adjust to the idea of a future without further children.

Unfortunately, Kaja took his pause as he processed this news as the rejection she'd been expecting.

'I'll take that as a no. Just as I thought.'

'That's not what—'

She rejected his attempt to placate her with a wave of her hand. 'Forget it, Seth. I've made up my mind.'

'And what? That's the end of it? No discussion?'

'Exactly. What's the point of pretending there's a future for us? My career is all I'm interested in now. It's the only thing I have going for me.'

'What am I supposed to do? Forget anything ever happened between us and carry on living here and treating your father?' It had been hard enough to do that first time around but now, with such new and erotic memories of their time together, it would be impossible. Not to mention painful, with the knowledge she wasn't going to fight for them this time either. It seemed Kaja was ready to walk away every time they faced an obstacle and that wasn't a stable foundation for any relationship. Perhaps she was right after all. This was never going to work between them.

'I wouldn't expect you to do that. That's why I think you and Amy should go home. You were flown in to do the transplant and you managed that successfully. We have a team of surgeons and consultants who can oversee the rest of his recovery. If there are any complications they can't handle I'm sure they'll be in touch.'

'You have it all figured out, don't you?' He wondered if this was the royal equivalent of ordering a taxi for a regrettable one-night stand the morning after. She couldn't wait to get rid of all traces of him.

'I don't see the point in dragging things out.'

'Thanks for being so honest with me. It makes a change.' He was lashing out now, wishing to cause her some of the pain she was currently causing him, but she didn't flinch. Only one day returned to her world and that cool princess was well and truly back in charge. When she offered no defence against his jibe he knew the battle was lost. She didn't even feel strongly enough to argue with him any more. He walked away defeated, knowing he wasn't wanted enough for anyone to fight to have him in their lives.

Kaja opened her bedroom curtains, the morning sunshine unreflective of her current disposition. She'd slept later than she'd intended. Mainly because it had taken her so long to get to sleep, her guilty conscience replaying her harsh words and the image of Seth's crestfallen face on a loop in her head. She knew she'd hurt him. Again. This time, she told herself, it was for his benefit, not hers. It was completely different.

Five years ago she'd run from their relationship, realising she couldn't make a lifelong commitment to him when she wasn't being true to herself. Now, she was saving him from doing the same. It didn't make her feel any better. He wanted to be with someone who could give him a family and he could pretend otherwise to be with her but they both knew it was the truth. Her body had failed her and the man she loved.

Unwilling to face anyone this morning, she made the decision to go straight to the hospital and assist where she could once she washed and dressed. There'd be time later for her to deal with her brother's questions, Fatima mourning the inevitable loss of her young companion and, worst of all, being faced with Seth's look of betrayal. Unfortunately, the pain in her own heart couldn't be avoided so easily. The best she could do was try and work through it.

CHAPTER THIRTEEN

'I'M GOING TO take a break and go and check on my father.'

'No problem. It's quietened down a bit for now. Thanks for your help. You've really gone above and beyond over these past few days.' Cecilia, the woman who'd been co-ordinating all available staff in the emergency department, threw her arms around Kaja and hugged her. It was unexpected on a number of different levels. Kaja hadn't been working here to garner praise of any kind, but she had enjoyed being seen as part of the team rather than simply for novelty value. Cecilia was hugging her as a colleague, perhaps even a friend, without thought to her royal status.

The simple gift of a hug had her too choked up to bat away the compliment or offer any response. Instead she gave her a squeeze back and walked away before she made a fool of herself bawling in the middle of the corridor. Of course, when she came to her father's hospital room she had to erase all traces of that vulnerability. If she was asserting her right to work and step back from her royal duties it was necessary to show confidence in what she was doing.

'Kaja.' Her father struggled to sit up when she came in through the door.

'There's no need to strain yourself, Papa. I just wanted

to see how you were today.' She walked over and kissed him before helping him into a more comfortable position. He had more colour in his cheeks today and appeared brighter than he had in months.

'Sore, but I'll live and that's the main thing.'

'Yes, it is.' It seemed he'd inherited her brother's dark sense of humour along with his kidney, but that wasn't altogether a bad thing. If he'd stopped taking everything so seriously it might make it easier for her to discuss her plans for the future without the dramatics she'd been expecting.

She pulled a chair over so she could sit by the side of his bed and took his hand in hers.

'Papa, I've been thinking a lot about my life and I'm not happy with where I am right now. Some things have happened while you've been in here, which have made me reassess what I'm doing and what sort of legacy I'm leaving behind.' She mightn't be able to secure the royal line with children of her own, but she could make a difference by saving lives.

'It's about time.'

It certainly wasn't the response she'd anticipated. 'Pardon me?'

Her father rested his other hand on top of hers. 'Kaja, you haven't been happy since you came home from England. I had hoped marriage would give you something to focus on rather than whatever it was you'd left behind. I wanted you to have the love and happiness your mother and I shared. I'm sorry that didn't happen with Benedikt. What he did to you was unforgivable. I've been waiting so very long for you to find something to make you smile again.'

If she didn't have so many questions Kaja might have been stunned into silence. 'You don't mind if I go back into medicine full time? What about all your talk about family traditions and keeping up appearances?'

'All I ever wanted was for you to be happy, my darling. Without your royal duties these past five years I was worried you wouldn't leave the house at all, you were so miserable.'

'You never said any of this before. I thought I was a disappointment.'

'Never. I know I may not have been the best father over the years, consumed by my responsibilities elsewhere, but I was always proud of you.'

'Why didn't you reach out to me when I was in England?'

'Your mother thought we should give you space and you'd come back to us when you were ready. You did. We both just wanted the best for you. Then you met Benedikt and I thought you were focusing on the future.'

'I tried, but apparently I never did get over my past,' she muttered more to herself than for her father's ears. She'd never loved anyone but Seth and in hindsight it must've been obvious to her ex that she was on the rebound and not fully committed to their marriage. Looking back now, she couldn't completely blame him for seeking affection elsewhere. He could've discussed it with her, of course, rather than humiliating her with his affair, but they'd been doomed from the start when she was still in love with another man.

'You seemed to over these past few days.'

She wasn't entirely sure what he meant by that when he didn't know a fraction of what had been going on outside this room, but he was right. With Seth back in her life she had been able to put a lot of their bad history behind her. Mainly because he'd forgiven her, but also because she was happier simply having him around. Both of which were moot points now that she'd hurt him all over again and told him she didn't want him in her life.

'Are you telling me that all the decisions I've made have been based on my own paranoia?'

'I can't say that. I don't know what goes on in your head but please understand I don't want anything to stop you living your best life. Do what makes you happy, not what you think other people want you to do.'

She thought back to last night's painful conversation with Seth. He'd been quiet when she'd told him she couldn't have children but, instead of letting him digest the news, she'd jumped to the conclusion he wouldn't want to be with her. The same way she'd assumed her father would prefer to have her as some kind of waving automaton rather than a contributing member of society without ever talking it over. She hadn't let Seth answer or discussed any option other than splitting up. She really was her own worst enemy. It was Seth who made her happy and she was only punishing herself by pushing him away.

'I've been so stupid. I told Seth we didn't need him here any more.'

'I know; he told me when he visited with Amy.'

'When?' An overwhelming sense of dread crept through her. The house had been awfully quiet this morning and Seth would never have brought Amy to work with him.

'On his way to the airport. He said there was no point in him staying any longer when I was doing so well and I'm in the hands of the best team. I don't think he wanted to disrupt his daughter's life any more than was necessary.'

Kaja barely heard what he was saying beyond that first revelation. 'He's gone?'

She might have said the words prompting that departure, told everyone including herself it was for the best, but being faced with the possibility that she would never see him again was too much. To her horror she burst into a flood of tears. That careful composure that had weathered all storms until recently slipped again. She wasn't wearing her heart on her sleeve, it was tripping down her face and splashing onto the floor.

'I thought that was what you wanted?' Her father arched an eyebrow at her, questioning her tears but with a hint that he knew the answer already.

'No. I want him to stay.'

'I could see it in his eyes that's what he wanted as well. If you're quick you might be able to catch him at the airport. If that's what you want?'

That was the million-dollar question. This was her decision and if she made the wrong choice she couldn't blame anyone else this time. She'd have to live with the consequences of what she did next for the rest of her life.

'Thanks for being our chauffeur, Fatima.' Seth hugged her before opening the boot of the car to retrieve the bags. He hadn't wanted the hassle of getting the limo and he had a hunch Fatima's offer to take them in her jalopy was so she could spend as much time as possible with Amy before they left.

'It was my pleasure. I wish you were staying.' Tears welled in her eyes and he prayed she wouldn't start crying in earnest or she'd set Amy off, and him. Neither of them really wanted to leave but Kaja wanted him gone and there wasn't anything he could do to change her mind.

He shouldn't have to. If she felt the same way about him as he did about her she would never have said the things she did. He wasn't going to hang around and prolong the agony. Leaving this way, without any fuss or dramatic showdown, left him a smidgen of dignity. He was even beginning to see why she'd walked out on him without a word five years ago. It wasn't payback, he just didn't think he could face her without giving her a good shake or breaking down in front of her.

'We have to get home.' He went to open the car door to help Amy out but Fatima grabbed his arm.

'Miss Kaja has always been afraid to do what's in her heart in case it's the wrong thing. As a little girl she had a lot of pressure put upon her. Don't give up on her.'

'She's a grown woman now and for my sake, and Amy's, I can't do this any more. How did you know about us anyway?' They thought they'd been so careful not to let anyone know they'd ever been romantically involved, never mind that they'd rekindled their affair. It was part of the reason he was leaving so soon after being rejected. If he stayed it would become obvious to everyone how much his heart was breaking at not being able to be with her.

Fatima shrugged. 'I have known her for a very long time. She can tell me so much without saying a word. I saw the same look on her face when she came back from England as I did last night before she went to bed. I may be old but I'm not stupid, or blind. If you didn't love each other it wouldn't hurt you both so much.'

'There's nothing I can do about it now. We've made our minds up.' He opened the door and unstrapped Amy from the car seat, knowing they wouldn't carry on this conversation with her around. Fatima could call him a coward if she wished but he had more than just himself to protect this time around.

'Can't we stay a little longer, Daddy? Please?' Amy's quivering lip and big, pleading brown eyes almost made him agree to anything rather than hurt her, but he knew she'd be fine once they got home and she was back in her old routine.

'You can phone Fatima any time you want to hear her voice.'

Fatima nodded through her watery smile.

'You have my number and you're welcome to visit us in Cambridge any time.' It was unlikely this loyal mother figure would ever desert her post at the palace but he thought he should at least offer, as she and Amy had grown so close. In other circumstances he would've cultivated that bond, when they seemed to draw so much comfort from each other's company, but as things stood it was impossible.

'I won't come in with you. I'll say my goodbyes here.' She leaned down and hugged Amy as though she never wanted to let go. When she finally did, Seth saw her wipe away the tears before Amy noticed. 'Now, you be a good girl for your papa and I'll talk to you soon.'

'Thank you for everything, Fatima.' He kissed her on both cheeks, then led Amy towards the airport building, dragging their suitcase, and his heart, behind them.

'Stop the car!' Kaja's heart was hammering as she grabbed for the door handle. She'd recognised Fatima's car on the road from the airport and put two and two together. That was why the house had been unusually quiet when she'd got up. Even Fatima had gone AWOL. It was clear whose side she was taking if she'd personally driven Seth and Amy away without telling Kaja.

Fatima pulled over and wound down her window. 'I did my best to get him to stay.'

Her face crumpled and Kaja could feel her pain as acutely as her own at the loss. What had she done?

'Is it too late?' Her voice was a mere whisper, caught in her throat at the thought that she'd lost Seth and Amy for ever.

'I left them at the airport. I couldn't bear to go in and watch them fly away.'

'There might still be time. They still have to check in and go through security.' She was clutching at straws but without hope she might as well lie down on this road and weep. The talk with her father had made her realise it was up to her to take action and fight for what she wanted in life. That was Seth and Amy. She was the only one who could get them to stay and even that wasn't guaranteed.

'I tried telling him it was fear which had made you reject him. I think we both know you still love him.'

'Apparently everybody—except us—does,' she said as she got back into the limo intent on giving chase. All she needed was for Seth to believe it and be willing to give her a third chance.

They drove to the airport, lights flashing, horn blaring at any traffic so they'd let them pass. She made as many phone calls and asked for as many favours as she could en route in order to slow Seth's departure. It might make for a frustrating wait on his part but it would buy time for her to get there.

Security met her at the airport entrance after she'd called ahead and asked for their help to jump any queues. She'd purchased a flight ticket online in case she had to get on that flight to convince him she loved him. At this moment she was prepared to do whatever it took to win him back.

'Excuse us.'

'Make way, please.'

The human cordon around her moved as many travellers out of her path as they could. Kaja didn't usually take advantage of her position for her own benefit but on this occasion she was willing to use all available resources to get her man. When she got to the departure gate and saw it was empty save for the attendants at the desk, a cold sweat broke out over her skin. If she was too late she might never see him again.

'Do you have your boarding pass? The plane's sitting on the tarmac. You might just make it if you're quick.'

One last ember of hope burned a little brighter. It only took the woman a moment to scan her ticket but it might as well have been days when every second was so crucial. There was no time for niceties and Kaja snatched the boarding pass back once she was finished with it. Security hovered, uncertain of the protocol.

'I can take it from here,' she told them, then started running.

She didn't care if anyone caught a picture of her racing across the runway like a lunatic; Seth was more important than anything. It was the thought of him flying back to England and the life she'd have to endure without him that kept her legs pumping even when her lungs were fit to burst. They'd been happy together. Not just for that brief time when they'd shut out the rest of the world, but for years living together when she hadn't worried about anything except being in the moment. She wasn't going to let that simply go to waste when they might have a chance of being happy. Together.

'Wait!' she shouted at the member of the cabin crew who was getting ready to shut the door.

In her years of attending photo ops, ceremonial openings and giving public speeches she didn't remember having so many faces staring at her as she did once she stumbled on board. The whispering and gasps started off as a low rumbling, but by the time she'd made it halfway down the plane it was building up to a roar. People were turning their heads and leaning over the backs of their seats to get a better view.

'Kaja!' It was Amy who grabbed her attention first, standing up on her seat to wave while Seth gawped at her, mouth hanging open.

She rushed to his seat and knelt in the aisle. 'Seth, I'm so sorry about what I said. I didn't mean any of it.'

'Kaja, what on earth are you doing? Everyone can see you. This is going to be all over the news by the end of the day.' He was looking at all the heads peering around to see what she was doing, camera phones at the ready, not taking in what she was saying.

'I don't care. I want you to stay. I love you and I want to be with you.' It was on record now. For ever. She just didn't know if it was enough to counter all the mistakes she'd made along the way.

'You love me?' He frowned and leaned in closer for some degree of privacy. 'Only last night you told me to go. You keep blowing hot and cold, Kaja, and I'm sorry but I need stability for Amy. For my heart.'

'I'll move to England with you if that's what it takes to prove to you that I'm serious.'

'You did that once before. It didn't work out too well, remember?'

'This is different. I'm different. I thought you'd be better off with someone who could give you the family you want and I'm sorry that I can't. All I can offer you is me.' She grabbed him with both hands and kissed him full on the lips to a plane full of whoops and cheers. This was her way of showing him she meant every word and he was all that mattered. When he kissed her back and the cheers faded into the background she knew she'd finally made the right decision.

At least Seth remembered where they were before things got too heated. 'How on earth did you manage to get here on time? I thought you were at the hospital.'

'I was. I went to see my father about going back to work and I realised I've been the one holding myself back from being happy. No more. You and Amy are my happy place. In case you didn't hear it the first time, I love you. Nothing else matters to me.'

'Then we'd better get off this plane because all I need is you. I love you too. I always have and I don't care where we live as long as we're together. Besides, I've never seen Amy so happy as I have out here. It already feels like home.' Seth took Amy by the hand and followed Kaja back down the aisle. She held her head high as the cheers rang out from the other passengers, uncaring about what they thought. All that mattered was that she was being honest with Seth and true to herself. It was all that was needed to make her happy.

This princess had never needed a prince to save her. She simply had to do it herself.

EPILOGUE

One year later

'WELL? WHAT DOES it say?' Seth was waiting for her the second she came out of the bathroom.

'We have to wait a couple of minutes.' Kaja understood his urgency when she'd been wishing away the time all through her shift in the emergency department to get to this moment. She loved her job almost as much as her husband and her stepdaughter of six months, but the anticipation had been killing her.

She'd kept the test until she got home so they could see the result together. Although that hadn't stopped Seth texting and phoning her all day once she'd told him her period was late.

Do you feel pregnant?

When do you think it happened?

Can't you take a quick break and come home?

She hoped they weren't getting their hopes up for something that might not ever happen. It seemed too good to be true after all those years she'd failed to get pregnant. Perhaps her baby had been waiting for Seth too.

'Is it time now?' Seth leaned over her shoulder, watching the window on the pregnancy test with rapt attention.

'You're worse than Fatima,' she said with a laugh. Although Fatima hadn't said anything to Kaja directly, according to Amy she'd taken to knitting lots of dolly clothes recently, 'And she doesn't even have a dolly, Kaja!' Perhaps there was something to her claims of having 'the gift' after all if she'd known something before Mother Nature.

Seth was beaming now as much as he had on their wedding day at the palace. One good thing about having such a huge family estate was they'd been able to get married in private. The ceremony had been held in the gardens with only family and friends from the hospital where they both worked in attendance. They'd only made the announcement public after their honeymoon in England, where she and Seth had been able to reminisce about the old days and tie up loose ends before he and Amy moved over for good.

'Sorry. I'm just excited.'

'I know. Neither of us thought it was going to happen.' She'd been honest with Seth that another child might not be a possibility but he'd been insistent that he still wanted a future with her. Now it seemed those impossible dreams might be about to come true.

PREGNANT

The word filling the tiny LED screen made them both gasp and stare at each other like loons.

'It's true? We're going to have a baby?' He was practically vibrating with excitement as he grabbed her into a hug.

'Yes. I'm pregnant. You're going to be a daddy again

and Amy's going to be a big sister.' It was the icing on her perfect year after marrying Seth and becoming stepmother to Amy.

'You're amazing.' He held her tight and the feel of his strong arms around her was reassuring at a time where she was a little out of her depth.

'I didn't do it all on my own, you know.' The passion for one another hadn't ebbed since they'd married or moved into their own place away from the palace. Especially now they had some privacy. After the initial furore when they'd got together, the press had lost interest in a busy working mum. A happily married medic wasn't very glamorous but it was exactly the life she wanted.

'I'm going to have to book in with a midwife and organise antenatal classes. Then there's all the things we're going to need for the nursery.' A to-do list getting longer by the second popped into her head as the reality of the situation began to sink in.

'Hey. We're in this together, Mrs Davenport. I can handle all of that. I don't want you worrying about anything.' He tilted her chin up with his finger and the sheer love she saw reflected in his eyes, felt in every pore in her body, was everything she'd ever needed. Their marriage was a shared partnership and, good or bad, they would go through everything together.

'Love you, Mr Davenport.'

'And I love you. You'll always be my princess.' He kissed her on the lips, sealing the promise, and she knew when the baby came they'd be the happiest little family in Belle Crepuscolo.

* * * * *

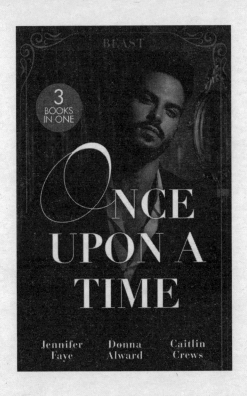

OUT NOW!

**Available at
millsandboon.co.uk**

MILLS & BOON

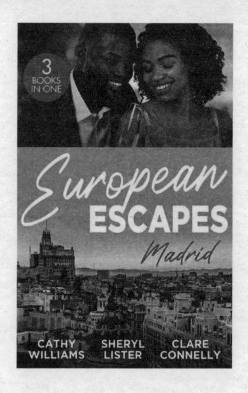

LET'S TALK

Romance

For exclusive extracts, competitions and special offers, find us online:

- **MillsandBoon**
- **@MillsandBoon**
- **@MillsandBoonUK**
- **@MillsandBoonUK**

Get in touch on 01413 063 232